WINTER MAGIC

CURATED BY
ABI ELPHINSTONE

FEATURING
STORIES BY

MICHELLE HARRISON

PIERS TORDAY

LAUREN ST JOHN

AMY ALWARD

KATHERINE WOODFINE

GERALDINE McCAUGHREAN

BERLIE DOHERTY

JAMILA GAVIN

MICHELLE MAGORIAN

EMMA CARROLL

ABI ELPHINSTONE

First published in Great Britain in 2016 by Simon & Schuster UK Ltd
A CBS COMPANY

This paperback edition published 2017

3 5 7 9 10 8 6 4 2

Simon & Schuster UK Ltd
1st Floor, 222 Gray's Inn Road
London WC1X 8HB

www.simonandschuster.co.uk
www.simonandschuster.com.au
www.simonandschuster.co.in

Simon & Schuster Australia, Sydney
Simon & Schuster India, New Delhi

A CIP catalogue record for this book is available from the British Library.

PB ISBN 978-1-4711-5982-4
eBook ISBN 978-1-4711-5981-7

Typeset in Caslon by M Rules
Printed and bound by CPI Group (UK) Ltd, Croydon, CR0 4YY

Introduction
ABI ELPHINSTONE

Winter is a season that sparkles with magic and transforms our ordinary world into a glittering kingdom: rooftops covered in snow, lakes glazed with ice and windows frosted white. It is a time of year that invites exploration and whispers of adventure. And at the heart of it all there is a sense of longing – for snowflakes, stockings and sledging, of course – but also, for stories.

My childhood winters were filled with snowball fights and wintry walks, but it is perhaps the evenings cuddled up by the fire with a book that I remember most. Because it was there that I discovered a wardrobe leading to a land locked in an eternal winter, a pack of wolves prowling through the snow around Willoughby Chase and a young girl riding an armoured polar bear across the Arctic ice plains. There are few things as enchanting as reading a snowy story during the depths of winter, and it is my absolute pleasure to introduce this collection of *Winter Magic* stories, written by some of the most talented and acclaimed writers in the country.

Let frost fairs enthral you, husky dogs whisk you away on fur-lined sleds and wishing books answer your heart's desires. Here, fairytales are reimagined, lost legends are remembered and folk tales are re-told as you've never heard them before. There are snow dragons, elf tunnels, winter ballets and frozen rivers, but there are also pied pipers, unlikely time travellers, witches and renegade French teachers. This is winter magic at its best. So, take a seat, wrap up warm and don't forget to send your Christmas list to the Svenland elves – because eleven shiveringly magical stories await you . . .

Contents

A Night at the Frost Fair
EMMA CARROLL

1

Leaving Gran was the hardest part. Harder, Maya thought, than seeing her in weeks-old clothes or finding a hairdryer instead of milk inside her fridge. They'd done the right thing, Dad said, as they left the care home today. He said it again on the way to the station. And again when buying takeout coffee as they waited for their train. It sounded less convincing each time.

And now they faced the long journey home. Maya never enjoyed it, even on better days. It meant two different trains and a taxi ride across London, all of which made her travel-sick. It also meant four hours with Jasmine, her older sister, who hogged the armrest and talked endlessly about people Maya didn't know. Today, she didn't even pretend to listen.

There isn't a word for how I'm feeling, Maya thought as she stared through the taxi window. *Sad* didn't cover it.

Or *angry* – though she felt both. She'd always had a special connection with her gran. It was a fierce, unspoken thing that didn't always make sense to her because they weren't the slightest bit similar: Gran loved travel and exploring; Maya got queasy just from going to the supermarket in the car.

Yet sitting in London traffic she felt a different kind of awful. The care home with its wipe-clean chairs and shepherd's pie smell was a million miles from her gran's own house. That was full of strange carvings and bright-coloured rugs that hung on the walls – souvenirs from the many adventures Gran had been on in her life.

And now it had come to this.

It would've been easier if Mum was here to talk to. She didn't jump in, telling you what to do, she listened to what you said. But she was in India visiting her sister who'd just had a baby. Everyone and everything important seemed a long way away.

Beyond the taxi window, darkness had turned the city into a sea of lights. It was raining. As the traffic crawled across London Bridge, Maya pictured the River Thames, black and glistening, beneath them. Cars stopped. Started. Stopped again. The windscreen wipers were the only fast-moving thing.

Dad leaned forward to speak to the driver. 'We've got another train to catch in half an hour. Reckon we'll make it?'

Maya didn't hear the answer. She glanced at Jasmine,

who'd given up talking and was listening to music on her phone. Jasmine who did perfect flicky-eye make-up and wore amazing vintage clothes.

'I'm not jealous,' Maya would say, though today she'd definitely felt it. Just before they left the care home, Gran had given them both presents.

'These things are very precious to me,' Gran said, as she'd pressed packages into their hands.

Jasmine opened hers first. It was a gorgeous little star-shaped brooch that came in its own red leather box. She made gushing noises and straightaway pinned it to her coat.

Maya began unwrapping her own present. Something brown and ugly emerged from the paper. Her heart sank. She'd no idea what it was, but it certainly wasn't a pretty brooch. She glanced at Gran, confused.

'It was Edmund's,' Gran whispered. 'No one believed him, either.'

'Oh,' said Maya, eyebrows raised. 'Right.'

She sensed Gran wanted to say more, but Dad was tutting irritably. 'Oh, Mum, not this *Edmund* again?'

The name had come up a lot recently – ever since Dad suggested that the carers who came every day weren't enough, and it was time for Gran to consider moving into a home.

'You're mollycoddling me,' Gran had said. 'It was just the same for poor Edmund, and it didn't do him any favours, did it?'

5

No one knew who this 'Edmund' was. When they'd asked Gran, she said she'd met him on her travels, but beyond that she was pretty vague. They'd searched for clues in her old photographs and the other stuff she kept – the ribbons and bus tickets, coat buttons, birthday cards and wrappers from old chocolate bars. With so much heaped in her bedroom, it had been hard to even open the door.

None of it led to Edmund, so in the end they'd supposed he was another of Gran's fixations. And she did have a few – like keeping her bath full of water in case the pipes froze.

Despite Dad's irritation this afternoon, Gran had soon started on again about Edmund.

'You might not know Edmund,' she'd said to Dad. 'But that doesn't mean he didn't exist.'

'Mum, I really think—'

Gran interrupted. 'That's just it, James, you *don't* think. The world is full of things you've never seen or heard of, but they *are* there, you know – and sometimes you have to go looking for them.'

To Maya this was probably the most sensible thing her gran had said all day. But Dad, thoroughly fed up, stormed off to speak to the nurses.

'I thought you might be interested in Edmund, my dear,' Gran said, patting Maya's arm. 'You're like your mother – you listen to people. And believe it or not, you're also rather like me.'

'Am I?' said Maya, surprised.

Gran nodded. 'You've got an explorer's mind inside that head of yours. Now please go and use it.'

Maya stared at the brown lump in her hand. She felt she should understand what Gran was trying to tell her. It seemed important – more important than the pretty brooch that Jasmine had already stopped gushing over.

'Thanks for the present,' she muttered, stuffing it in her pocket.

Now, in the quiet of the taxi, Maya took it out. The package, messily wrapped in pale blue paper, was about the size of a phone, though heavier. She'd no idea what it was, and she definitely didn't see how it linked to this person called Edmund. She wasn't quite sure what an explorer's mind was, either. But if it meant that your thoughts often came out as questions, then she supposed Gran had a point.

Maya slumped back in her seat. The traffic still hadn't moved very far; they were stuck about halfway across the bridge. It was raining heavily now, the wipers swishing faster over the taxi's windscreen. What fell against the glass looked grainy. Icy. In the headlights of other cars, Maya saw flecks of white. The rain was turning rapidly to snow.

A bit *too* rapidly.

She sat up, alert.

'What's going on with the weather?' she asked, but no one else seemed to have noticed.

The wipers went faster and faster. Watching them made her dizzy, but she couldn't tear her eyes away. Something very strange was happening. Beyond the windscreen, London had changed.

The road was now completely white. All the rooftops along the riverbank were coated in snow, and the traffic ... well ... there was no traffic any more, at least not of the car-kind. And Maya was no longer sitting inside a taxi.

She was standing in a busy street, shivering.

2

'Out of the way, numbskull!'

Bewildered, Maya spun round. She stumbled into the gutter just in time, as a cart pulled by horses thundered past. From the opposite direction came a man on horseback and plenty more people on foot. It was too dark to see much, but from the pushing and jostling she sensed she was somewhere very busy. The taxi was nowhere to be seen.

I'm dreaming, Maya decided. *I've fallen asleep and in a minute I'll wake up.* At least she hoped she would, for though she'd kept her coat on, it really was *freezing* – the sort of cold that seeped under her scarf and through her jeans. Maya shivered miserably. She started walking; it was the only way to get warm. The taxi must be here somewhere; she just hoped she was heading in the right direction to find it.

Quickly, the road became even busier, till it was a heaving

mass of people. She couldn't stop or turn or even see much above the heads and shoulders that swarmed around her. Every now and then, a cart would trundle through the middle of the crowd, parting it like a ship on the water. Then the crowds would close in again. It almost felt like drowning. Or being stuck waist-deep in mud that you couldn't get out of.

'Don't panic,' Maya told herself, though her heart was thumping hard. 'Just go with it. It's only a dream. It'll be over soon.'

The road led under a huge stone arch and out onto a bridge. Not the same London Bridge as before – this one had even more people crossing it, and tall buildings on either side of the road. Most seemed to be heading north across the river. She began to notice the men, women and children pressing in around her. They had an air of excitement about them, like people on their way to a football match. She wondered where they were going.

There weren't any street lights. The only light came from fires in metal baskets that burned on the street. As Maya's eyes adjusted, she realized how oddly dressed everyone was. The women wore skirts to the ground and the men had triangular-shaped hats and trousers that stopped at the knee.

She was beginning to wonder if this really *was* a dream. Somehow, she felt a bit too wide awake. *Perhaps I'm on a film set*, she thought, *or there's a fancy-dress party going on*. But her mind slid back to what Gran had said earlier, about things existing even if you'd never seen them.

You have to go looking.

Whatever strange stuff was happening, Maya was very definitely *here*. In the moment. She could feel every cobblestone beneath her feet, every little icy snowflake that fell against her face.

Yet how could that be possible?

Maya grew steadily more confused. But better that than feeling panicky or cold – and actually, she no longer felt either. She'd stopped thinking about where the taxi was, too. By now, she was halfway across the bridge. On both sides buildings towered above her – old, wonky-looking places that stood so close together they almost touched. Some, with crumbling stonework and half-collapsed roofs, stood empty. Others hummed with life. She passed pubs. A chapel, a steakhouse, pie shops and shoe shops, and a house advertising quiet rooms for ladies to rest and drink tea. It was mad to think so much happened *on* a bridge.

Stuffing her hands into her coat, Maya walked as fast as the crowds allowed. Her pockets, as usual, were full of old tissues and sweet wrappers. Back in the taxi, Gran's present had been in there, too. Yet it wasn't now. It must've fallen out on the seat, and she felt guilty for being careless. Though there was no way she could go back for it, not through these crowds.

Then, through a narrow gap between the buildings, Maya glimpsed the river. Except it wasn't black and shiny any more. It didn't even look like water. Out of the gloom, the

Thames glowed a greyish-white. There were things on it that definitely weren't boats. Things with legs that shouted and waved.

People.

Maya stared in amazement. The river, she realized, was completely frozen over. She'd never seen the Thames like this: actually, she'd never seen a frozen river before – only in films and those ones were probably computer-generated.

This didn't look anything like a movie, though. It looked real. It *felt* real, just as the cobblestones and the snowflakes did. She kept walking, keen to get to the other side of the bridge. Passing under another archway, she found herself on the opposite bank of the river.

The second her feet touched solid ground again, she knew. No, this wasn't a dream. She had a sudden sense of purpose, as if she was here for a reason, though she still didn't know what.

At the water's edge were signs advertizing some sort of fair. Maya tried to read what they said. The writing was dreadful. Some of the letters she couldn't make out, but what she could sent excitement shooting through her:

'Once in a lifetime experience! Meet Mr Jack Frost!'

'Eat, drink and be merry at tonight's marvellous Frost Fair ...'

There were queues as far as the eye could see. So this was where the crowds had been heading; everyone was here to go out on the ice. Perhaps it was why she was, too.

Finally, she reached the front of the crowds. Men were taking money at the river's edge: people queued up to pay.

'A shilling a go on the ice, ladies and gents! The Thames is frozen two yards deep,' said the man collecting people's payments. 'More chance of me turning into King George than of that ice cracking.'

King George?

That couldn't be right. The person on the throne was a queen, not a king. But everyone was dressed so strangely, weren't they? And in return, her jeans and trainers had been getting some funny looks.

She rubbed her eyes. Blinked. Nothing changed. She was still here, queueing up on the riverbank. So if this wasn't a dream, what was it?

Something very odd had happened back there in the taxi. And now she was in olden-times London. The only explanation was a mad one. She – Maya Mulligan, who got car sick and train sick on the very shortest journeys – had somehow *time-travelled* all the way to the past.

Maya didn't know whether to be scared or over-the-moon excited. Either way, she was penniless.

'Look,' she explained, on reaching the front of the queue. 'My purse is in my bag and it's back in the taxi, but I've got a bank card and ten pounds left over from my birthday, so I *can* pay, it's just that …' Seeing the man's confused expression, Maya stopped. Gulped.

Bank cards? Taxi? Who was she kidding? If this really was olden-times London, she might as well be talking Greek.

'A shilling,' he said, holding out his hand.

'That's the problem – I haven't got a shilling.'

'No money, no ice,' said the man. 'Hop it.'

Dismayed, Maya backed away. She didn't have the foggiest idea what a shilling even looked like. But she needed to visit the frost fair – that much she *did* understand. She'd walked a few yards when someone with very cold fingers seized her wrist.

'Help me. Please, I beg of you.'

Maya's mouth fell open in surprise. As the crowd shifted sideways, a boy of about her age emerged. He looked very pale. Very scared. On instinct, she stepped backwards. The boy came, too – the fingers holding her wrist were his.

'You've got to help me. Someone's following me. I'm in terrible danger,' he said. 'If you could—'

'Let go of me. Like, NOW!' Maya yelped, trying to shake him off.

The hand didn't move. Gritting her teeth, she tried to prise off each finger. But as soon as she'd lifted one, the others clamped down again.

'I don't know who you are,' she said crossly, 'or what you think you're doing.'

'If I'm with you, it'll throw him off the scent. He won't expect me to be with . . .' The boy eyed Maya's jeans and trainers suspiciously. 'A girl.'

This boy's mad, Maya decided. His eyes were a bit too big and bright for his face. The purple coat he wore flapped about his legs like one of Gran's old dressing gowns. He certainly *looked* mad.

'You'd better let go of me, I'm warning you,' she snapped.

With a quick glance over his shoulder, the boy dropped his hand.

'So will you help me?' he asked. He seemed jumpy. Excitable. He couldn't keep his gaze on anything.

Maya scowled, rubbing her wrist. 'Why would I want to help *you?*'

'A man in a black cloak is following me,' said the boy. 'I've escaped, you see, and he wants to recapture me. He'll stop at nothing to get me back.'

'Really?' Maya folded her arms. It sounded far too much like the plot of a cheesy film.

'Really, truly,' he replied, then as if seeing Maya properly for the first time, he grinned. 'I say, you're rather feisty for a girl, aren't you?'

Maya glared at him: he certainly *was* from a different century.

'But I'm not the one asking for help,' she reminded him.

He smiled again, which made him look slightly less mad, and – in a way Maya couldn't put her finger on – almost *familiar*.

She shook her head. No, she wasn't going to smile back or encourage him. She'd walk away, that's what she'd do. Get

14

on with what she was here for and not be dragged into his problems. The trouble was, she didn't know why she *was* here, in the past. She only knew that she wanted to go to the frost fair. And that she was still standing here, rooted to the spot, not walking away from the boy at all.

3

Over the boy's shoulder, Maya glimpsed the river again. She couldn't see much beyond the bank, but heard whooping and laughing, and music from somebody's fiddle. Dogs were barking. Horses neighed. A whole world was going on out there on the frozen Thames: a strange, magical world. More than anything, she wanted to – *had to* – be part of it.

'Listen,' she said, looking the boy firmly in the eye. 'I don't know how much help I'll be to you … Oh.' The boy held up two small silver coins between his thumb and forefinger.

'Shillings,' he said. 'You need to pay to go on the ice.'

'So I found out.'

She didn't especially want to get mixed up with this boy. Being chased by a man in a black cloak didn't sound much fun, either. But that shilling glinted at her temptingly.

'You're offering to pay?' she asked.

'Of course.' The boy gave a little bow. 'These frost fairs don't happen that often, you know – once every twenty or thirty years, I've heard. So I pulled out all the stops to get here tonight.'

Me too, Maya mused. Two hundred and twenty-eight years of stop-pulling to be precise.

'I wouldn't miss tonight for the world,' the boy gushed excitedly.

'Me neither.' Maya was glad they agreed on something.

'But as soon as they know I'm missing, they'll come looking for me,' he explained, his mood darkening. 'They won't be searching for a boy with a girl, though. You'll be my cover, you see.'

Maya chewed her lip. The idea of being followed made her uneasy. But if she wanted to get onto the ice, she needed him as much as he needed her. And, she had to admit, this boy was a bit, well, intriguing, like he had too much life stuffed inside of him and it kept spilling out. To go to the frost fair with him might actually be fun.

'So if we could hurry, that would be wonderful,' said the boy. 'I've escaped—'

'What d'you mean *escaped*?' Maya interrupted. It made him sound like a mad person or a criminal, and with his edgy appearance he could easily pass as both. She had a rush of second thoughts.

'The door's always locked, but he's not so careful with the window. That's how I got out.'

She narrowed her eyes at him. 'Were you in prison, then?'

'You could say that. Not a public one, though. I'm not dangerous.' His smile returned. 'Anyhow, I've come here for the frost fair, not an interview. Let's not waste another minute.'

'All right, I'll come with you,' she said. 'But any sign of trouble I'll be off.'

The boy's grin stretched until, like his eyes, it was too big for his face.

'Here, catch!'

He flicked a shilling up into the air. She caught it squarely with her palms.

'What's your name, by the way?' the boy asked.

'Maya,' she said, pocketing the coin. 'What's yours?'

'Eddie.'

Once they'd paid their shillings and stepped down off the riverbank onto the ice, excitement took over. Maya was desperate to see everything, all at once. The ice wasn't smooth like a rink. It was ridged and rippled where the river had frozen mid-flow, which made it less slippery than she expected. Yet despite the fire baskets that burned at intervals along the ice, it was also quite dark so they had to tread carefully.

'Where first?' she asked Eddie.

He grinned. 'The terrier races. Come on!'

They followed the sound of yammering dogs to a spot right in the middle of the river. A large crowd had already gathered, standing in two long lines facing inwards. The strip of ice in the middle was the track.

'What happens now?' she asked, straining to see over people's shoulders.

'Folks bet on the dog they want to win,' said Eddie. 'It's often the stumpy-legged ones that go fastest.'

As they watched, a dozen or more manic little dogs tore down the middle. What they were chasing, Maya couldn't see, but it sent them all crazy. The race ended with a pile-up of wriggling, squirming dogs. The winner, as Eddie predicted, was a tiny white terrier that panted so much it seemed to smile. Maya laughed hard, and so did Eddie, though it set him off coughing.

'It's the cold air,' he explained.

Funny, but she wasn't even shivering. All she felt was a tingly sort of excitement, and a sense she was *right* to be here.

'Where next?' she asked, once the dogs were back with their owners and the race declared over.

Standing on tiptoes, Eddie scanned up and down the river. There was so much to choose from: skittles, card tricks, skating and dancing. His gaze finally came to rest on something to Maya's right.

'We absolutely HAVE to go on those!' he cried. 'Come on!'

Linking arms, they hurried over to a spot where a circle of torches stood upright in the ice. Inside the lights was a pair of brightly painted swingboats. Crammed full of squealing people, they swung back and forth in opposite directions. They made Maya think of old-fashioned fairgrounds – the sort with helter-skelters and candyfloss that Gran used to take them to every summer.

'Are you ready?' She turned to Eddie, but he'd already found his way to the front and was waving madly at her.

'Quick! We're next!' he cried.

Moments later, they squeezed into what looked like a rowing boat. The seats were wooden benches, the floor slushy-wet wooden planks. There wasn't a safety harness or seat belt in sight. Not that Maya could move: she was jammed in on all sides by people.

'Hold on tight!' Eddie cried, as they started to rock.

The movements were gentle at first. Then, with more force, they swung backwards. The swingboat went high into the air, so high Maya feared they'd flip right over. Her stomach bounced. The swinging stopped and for one long second they hung in mid-air. She sensed the people sitting beside her stiffen. Easy laughs became squeals as they plummeted downwards. Someone's long, smoky hair streamed against Maya's face.

Down and down they went. Then up and up and up again. At the top of the arc, the swingboat tipped backwards. She saw the inky dark sky above. Then a blur of white as they swung towards the ground once more.

When the swingboat finally slowed and stopped, Maya was one of the first to get out.

'I'm glad that's over,' she said, clutching her stomach.

Eddie swayed as he stood up. 'Me too. Crikey, that was wild, wasn't it?'

But the look they shared said neither of them had had enough.

'Come on, let's try along here,' said Maya, indicating a row of stalls that seemed to be selling everything from hot ale to roast pig to newspapers with their ink still wet.

There was so much to look at. And plenty to laugh at, like the hairy-snouted roast pig and the man serving it whose thick black nose hairs Maya couldn't stop staring at.

After the stalls, they played skittles very badly. Then, on stopping to hear a fiddler playing lively, toe-tapping tunes, they joined in by singing along. But Eddie's voice was so terrible, Maya had to plug her ears, and in the end someone in the crowd complained: 'Whoever's strangling their cat, do us a favour and take it somewhere private, will you?'

Which set them both off laughing so much, they sloped away to the next stall. There, when they'd finally stopped sniggering, they tried to guess for a penny how many buns were in the jar. Maya hadn't had so much fun in ages. Back home in the twenty-first century, her parents rarely let her out after dark. Yet here she was, with a boy she barely knew, having a great time. She was glad she'd followed that gut feeling about coming to the frost fair.

And Eddie had turned out to be pretty decent, too. She needn't have worried about him – though it did make her wonder *why* he'd been locked away, when he seemed so easy-going and good-natured. That part of things still didn't add up.

Once they'd lost another penny on the buns-in-the-jar game, Eddie fell suddenly quiet.

'What's up?' Maya asked. 'Have we spent all your money?'

He didn't answer. Swiftly, he tucked his arm through hers and hurried her away. He didn't stop at the next stall. Or the next. He ploughed on through the crowds.

'Hey! What's the rush?' she cried, tripping and sliding just trying to keep up. Reluctantly, Eddie slowed to a walk. Guessing what this was about, she felt her stomach go into knots. So much for being Eddie's cover: it hadn't fooled the man in the black cloak after all.

She swallowed. 'You're being followed, aren't you?'

'I think so. If I'm right, things could turn nasty so you'd better go.'

'*Go?*' she said, startled. 'I'm not going anywhere.'

Eddie gave a weary sigh. 'You said you wouldn't stay around if there was trouble, and there will be, I promise you.'

She didn't like the way he said it. But she was determined not to be scared. Something had changed between them in this last hour or so. They'd become, she supposed, sort of friends. And friends didn't leave each other when the trouble started.

So they kept walking. Then, just as they reached a stall selling coffee, Eddie stopped dead. He'd spotted someone nearby in the crowd.

'Maya,' Eddie said quietly. 'Don't look. Don't point. Just stick with me. And RUN LIKE MERRY HELL!'

4

Eddie charged straight for the crowds. Maya kept on his tail as best she could. But as they dodged people and darted around fire baskets, her trainers slipped on the ice. Once or twice, she went down on her knees, feet scrabbling to get a hold.

They took a sharp right between two food sellers. It brought them out at the back of the main row of stalls. Instantly, it was quieter. Darker. The ice was spread thinly with straw. Maya caught the waft of onions being fried, and another smell not as appetizing, like toilets and animals all mixed together.

Eddie didn't stop until he'd reached the opposite riverbank. There were stone steps leading up off the river, the type used by people getting on and off boats. Maya half expected Eddie to bound up them onto dry land. But a fit of coughing caught him. He stood doubled over as Maya skidded to a halt beside him.

'Have we shaken him off?' she gasped.

Eddie nodded, unable to speak. He kept spluttering till she wondered if she should get him a drink. Now, for the first time, Maya noticed how skinny he was. He looked flushed, like he had a temperature. There was definitely something more to this than he was telling her. But then he hadn't actually *told* her very much, had he? And she hadn't wanted to know, until now.

'What's this all about, Eddie?' she asked. 'Who are we running away from?'

He shook his head. His face was closed. It was a look that said very clearly he wasn't going to talk about it.

'Well, you shouldn't be out here dressed like that.' She gestured to the soaking-wet slippers on his feet. 'Or running about like a crazy person. You're ill, aren't you? So you should be in bed.'

Wearily, Eddie rubbed a hand across his face. 'That, my dear Maya, is exactly *why* I'm here.'

'But you're free now, aren't you? You can do whatever you want.'

'I can. I am. And having freedom makes me feel so much better – people need freedom to breathe.'

To Maya, though, he looked very pale. 'I still think you should go home,' she muttered.

Home.

Thoughts of Dad and Jasmine suddenly flashed into her mind. She didn't know how this time-travel business worked exactly. Often in films, no one noticed that you'd gone. But this was real life and she just hoped her family weren't two hundred-odd years away, wondering how she'd disappeared from the back of a stationary taxi. They'd be worried sick, and probably phoning Mum who – in *her* different time zone – would be just going to bed. And it made Maya feel awful.

'Eddie, perhaps we should—' She stopped.

Standing, not five feet away on the ice, was a man in a long black cloak. He was tall and thin-shouldered. Maya couldn't see his face; it was hidden under the shadow of a triangular hat. All around him, the crowd ebbed and flowed, oblivious. Yet he stood completely still, his eyes fixed on Eddie. It made Maya think of a cat stalking its prey.

'Uh-oh,' she muttered under her breath.

The man took a step towards them.

Maya didn't know what to do. *I could leg it*, she thought wildly. *I could stay and fight. I could shout MURDER at the top of my lungs.*

But her feet didn't want to move. Neither did Eddie. He swayed a little and shut his eyes, and for one desperate moment Maya thought he was giving up. 'No,' she pleaded. 'You've made it this far. We have to keep going.'

Grabbing Eddie by the arm, they dodged round the man so fast it took him by complete surprise. Then they plunged back into the crowds. The sheer number of people swallowed them up. They'd lost him for the moment, but Maya sensed he wasn't far behind. Whatever it was that he wanted Eddie for, he didn't look the type to give up easily. She could almost *feel* him, hot on their heels, snapping and snarling. Her heart boomed in her throat.

They ran past another row of stalls. More makeshift tents. A rowdy game of skittles. Then the fire baskets ended. There were no more stalls, no more crowds. Up ahead, Maya could see the outline of the bridge itself, its buildings perilously overhanging the river.

'Where now?' she asked.

Eddie was seriously short of breath. 'Back towards the swingboats. Keep moving.'

As they wove between the stalls this time, *she* was the steady one; he kept stumbling and slowing down. Finally Eddie begged her to stop. 'Just till I get my second wind.'

Another coughing fit tore through him; it pained Maya to watch. Jiggling nervously from foot to foot, she wondered how much longer they could keep running. A strange sensation grew in her chest – anger, sadness, frustration – all mixed together. *Any sign of trouble I'll be off,* she'd said to Eddie. Yet she was way past doing that now. How funny it was that though they'd only just met, she felt this connection, this bond, that she couldn't explain in words.

At last, coughing fit over, Eddie straightened up.

'Better?' Maya asked hopefully.

He smiled, though even that was fading fast. 'You can't come to the frost fair and not buy a souvenir.'

'But we need to keep moving,' Maya reminded him.

'The seller's right there,' he said, pointing to a nearby stall surrounded by customers. 'It won't take a moment, I promise.'

The stall sold gingerbread. And not just any old gingerbread, either.

'Made to a special Arctic recipe,' Maya read from the board above their heads. 'What does *that* mean?'

'It's a gimmick to make people buy it, that's all. But we have to have a piece, Maya, as proof that we've been here. A memento, if you like, of this evening.'

Maya pictured Gran's house, stuffed full of all the things she'd collected on her travels over the years. Souvenirs were important to her, too.

'It's bringing a little bit of magic home with you,' Gran once explained. 'Years later, you'll look at that object, and remember – just like that – the very day you bought it.'

Not that Maya could imagine gingerbread lasting that long. Yet plenty here tonight wanted a piece of it, for the stall was very popular. Though they had to wait their turn to be served, the crowd, four people deep, hid them from view. The closer they got, the stronger the smell of spice and sugar grew. It made Maya's stomach growl.

'The best gingerbread in the whole of London!' the woman serving it shouted. 'Get your slices here!'

Finally, it was their turn.

'How much you having, then, ducks?' the woman asked him, knife hovering over a tray of cake. The cake smelled delicious – toasty and fruity. But the look of it made Maya start. It was square-cut, dense, brown and familiar-looking.

'A brick-sized piece, if you please,' Eddie said. He gave her some coins – Maya didn't see how many. Behind them, the crowd shifted a little. Glancing round, Maya caught sight of a man in a black triangular hat. Her chest tightened in panic.

'We need to go, Eddie,' she muttered. She worried again that the fight had gone out of him, that once he'd bought his souvenir, he'd hand himself in rather than keep running.

'You want it wrapped? And there's to be writing?' the woman asked him.

Eddie nodded. Deftly, the cake was wrapped in blue paper and tied with string.

'Come on, come on,' Maya hissed. Her glances were becoming more frantic. The man was advancing towards them.

Then the woman handed the package over, with a pen.

'We haven't got time!' Maya cried. 'Hurry!'

But a sort of calmness had come over Eddie. As she hovered at his shoulder, he took the pen and wrote on the package. She glanced at the man. Then at the pen moving over paper.

The man.

The pen.

The man.

Back and forth her eyes darted till it made her dizzy. She couldn't bear it.

'Hurry up, Eddie! Please!'

He was done. She grabbed his arm. And then her feet were sliding. And not in the right direction. Someone else had hold of Eddie now, dragging him away with such force she couldn't fight back.

The crowd, like traitors, parted. And it was just the three of them.

'I've found you,' the man said. 'At last.'

5

There was a moment. A stillness. No one moved. Then Eddie turned too fast; his feet skidded underneath him. Maya caught hold of the back of his coat. But the man was pulling against her again.

'Get off him!' she cried.

The man dug his heels in. 'Come quietly, Eddie,' he said through gritted teeth. 'Let's not make a fuss.'

Eddie tried to twist free. There was still a bit of fight in him, but he was too weak to struggle hard. Blocking the man with her whole body, Maya matched his every scratch, every kick with one of her own. She had a duty to Eddie. A loyalty. And not just because of the shilling he'd given her so she could get onto the ice in the first place. It felt more than that now. She wasn't going to give up easily.

'Leave him alone! Get off him!' she yelled.

The man shoved her aside with a sweep of his arm. She staggered a little, then launched herself at him again.

'I'm warning you. Keep out of this, girl,' the man spat. 'This is a private concern.'

'You can't shut him away again. He's sick, that's all. He needs a doctor!'

All at once there was a tearing sound. The cloth of Eddie's coat gave way. It sent Maya wheeling backwards. And sent Eddie forward, straight into his captor's grasp. Before Maya could regain her balance, the man had whisked Eddie out of sight.

'Stop him! He's kidnapping Eddie! Don't let them get away!' Maya screeched. A few people stared at her oddly. But most bustled on past, too caught up in the delights of the frost fair to notice her distress.

Frantic, and on tiptoe, she tried to see where the man and Eddie had gone. It was as if they'd vanished into thin air. She asked stallholders, sellers, random passers-by, but no one had seen them. No one seemed to care much, either. People were still whooping in the swingboats, still buying gingerbread. Maya clenched her fists. How could they carry on as normal? How could they not want to help?

She didn't know what to do next.

Determined not to cry, Maya headed in the direction of the riverbank. She'd suddenly lost heart in the frost fair. Nothing would be any fun without Eddie to share it with. And just when she'd been getting to know him, too. It all felt really unfair.

But, she thought darkly, there was still plenty she *didn't know* about Eddie. Despite her first impressions, he hadn't seemed the slightest bit mad. He was just someone who wanted to have fun. So why had he been locked away? Where was it that he'd escaped from? And who was that creepy man who'd snatched him back again?

Her bottom lip trembled just thinking of the awfulness of it all. She'd tried to help Eddie, really she had. Trouble was, she wanted to do more, but how could she when he'd disappeared?

Beneath her feet, the ice had turned grainy. Water seeped into her socks so when she walked it made a squelching sound. She was tired. Wrung out. Whatever this experience was, she'd had enough of it. That great sense of purpose she'd felt walking over London Bridge had gone. Without Eddie, she didn't see the point in being here. Time travel, she decided, was even less fun than real-life travel. She was ready to go back to the present.

Yet Maya wasn't sure how this part of things worked. Everything had started on London Bridge, so she decided to head back there, hoping this time the taxi would prove easier to find. It was as good an idea as any. But what if the taxi wasn't there? What if she was stuck in the past for good?

Climbing the steps up off the river, she took a deep breath to slow her whirling brain. The air smelled different – not of cold any more, but of the city starting to warm up, like old, forgotten fruit at the bottom of her school bag. It had started to rain. Turning up her coat collar, she hurried on.

The shouting didn't register at first. It was coming from a side street somewhere to her right. As she approached, it got louder. She could just about make out the words.

'I won't go inside again! I won't!'

With a jolt, Maya recognized the voice. She also knew the

dark, spindly outline of a boy in a flapping coat, wrestling with someone on the pavement.

'Let go of me!'

'Quiet!' said the man. 'Enough of this ridiculous noise!'

Maya gasped in relief. She raced down the street towards him. 'Eddie!'

At the sound of Maya's voice, he looked round. The tiniest distraction was all it took. In one sly move, the man grabbed Eddie's arms and bundled him up the steps and inside. Just as she reached the building, the front door slammed shut. As she bounded up the steps, she heard a key grind in the lock.

'Eddie? I'll get you out of there somehow. Don't worry. I'm here.'

No answer.

She banged her fists against the door. 'Hello? Eddie? Are you all right?'

There was no reply. The door stayed smugly shut.

Eventually, she backed down the steps and gazed up at the house – for that's what it was, a *house*. She was surprised by how ordinary it looked, with two front windows on each floor and chimneys in the roof. It wasn't how she'd imagined a prison to be.

She went to the door again and thumped on it.

'I'm not going away until this door is unlocked. I'll stay here all night if I have to!' she yelled.

A little way along the street an upstairs window slid open. A lantern appeared, followed by woman's white-capped head.

'You won't be keeping up this hollering till morning, will you?'

Maya stared at the woman.

'Because we all need our sleep, my dear – your friend Eddie especially.'

'Eddie's been kidnapped! We have to do something!' How could she worry about sleep? Maya wondered. Shouldn't she be contacting the police?

But the woman actually *laughed*. 'Kidnapped? Good gracious! Why on earth would you think that?'

Maya folded her arms. This woman had no idea, did she? She lived next door and didn't have a clue what had been going on.

'He told me . . . he's being kept prisoner!'

'My dear,' the woman said patiently. 'Poor Eddie doesn't *like* being kept inside, but it's doctor's orders.'

Maya didn't understand. 'Doctor's orders? He said this place was a prison.'

'Indeed, it probably does feel like a prison to him.'

'But the man who came after him,' said Maya, shaking her head. 'Eddie said he'd stop at nothing to get him back.'

The woman sighed. 'That was Eddie's father, my dear.'

'His . . . *what*?'

Now Maya was confused. *Very* confused. That man in the black cloak hadn't looked very fatherly. He hadn't acted it, either.

'His father,' the woman repeated. 'He's at his wits' end. Eddie won't accept how ill he really is.'

'Hang on.' It was getting hard to keep up. 'So he's ill? I know he's got a bad cough, but—'

'Yes,' the woman cut in. 'He's very sick. A congestion of the lungs, so they say.'

Mixed with her relief for Eddie, Maya felt a sinking dread. Eddie hadn't been kidnapped after all – not properly. But this business with his lungs sounded pretty bad.

She had a feeling the woman wanted to keep talking. There were neighbours of Gran's like that, who sucked up bad news like vampires. But there wasn't anything left to say. Then, suddenly, Maya had an idea.

'Have you got a pen?' she asked.

The woman pulled a face. 'You'll be wanting the inkstand too, will you?'

'A pencil, then. And some paper, please?'

Moments later, both dropped from the window to land on the pavement beside her. Using her leg to rest on, Maya scribbled a note – not to Eddie, but to the man who was his dad. She thought it might be harder to ignore than a knock at the door, and it was the one thing she could think of that might help.

In the note, she tried hard to be polite and persuasive, but the best line was Eddie's own: 'People need freedom to breathe,' he'd said to her. Now it was his dad's turn to hear it.

Once the note was posted through Eddie's door, it really was time to go home.

Joining the main road again, Maya headed towards London Bridge. The rain was falling harder; her hair hung limp around her face. At least no one could tell that she was crying.

What made it sadder was the fun she'd had with Eddie. It was such a waste to spend what time he had locked away inside a house. It was as if his father's own worries were more important than Eddie's happiness. She just hoped he'd at least read her note. And this made her sad for Gran, too, stuck in her horrid care home because Dad thought she couldn't cope. The more Maya walked, she more she began to see the similarities.

Down on the river, the crowds were coming off the ice, moving almost with the same speed they'd gone on it. The frost fair was being dismantled. Tents were folded, baskets packed. The stallholders hurried to the river's edge with whatever they could carry – swingboats, terriers, trays of gingerbread.

'Quickly! The cracks are growing!' someone shouted.

Once again, Maya found herself deep in the crowd; she let herself be carried along the road. The rain, falling in great curtains, turned the cobbles from white to slushy grey. By the time she reached the stone archway that led onto London Bridge, she was soaked through.

Pushing back her wet hair, she braced herself. The bridge,

as before, was heaving with people. But this time, instead of barging into her, they seemed to melt away.

The rain – great droplets of it – started dancing before her eyes. A hush fell across the whole bridge. Everything went still. Only Maya's feet kept moving, beating out a rhythm on the cobbles as she walked. Up ahead, she saw two red lights glowing through the rain. It took her a moment to realize what they were.

The taxi sat in traffic with its engine running. It was *her* taxi – she recognized the adverts for West End shows all along its sides, and almost cried out with relief. Climbing in, she flopped down exhausted on the back seat.

'Ouch,' she muttered, as something hard dug into her hip. Her hand went to her coat pocket. Inside was the funny brown lump Gran had given her, right where she'd left it. Yet it definitely hadn't been there at the frost fair. And if it had fallen out here in the taxi, then how on earth did it get back in her pocket again?

She'd no idea – about any of it.

'A really weird thing's happened,' Maya began. Then, seeing her father and sister, she stopped. Jasmine, eyes shut, was listening to her music. She hadn't moved an inch. Nor had the taxi. The same song was playing on the radio. And Dad was still talking to the driver. Maya's hair was dry, her trainers no longer squelchy-wet.

These things definitely didn't happen in dreams.

All she had to show for her adventure was the pencil

Eddie's neighbour had lent her. It was still in her other pocket; she'd forgotten to give it back. Her family hadn't noticed she'd gone. She hadn't actually *been* gone, which made things more complicated and – strangely – easier.

6

Back home in Brighton, Maya went straight to her room, closing the door behind her. She wanted a quiet moment to think. There was a buzzing in her head, like she'd been standing too near the sound system at a party. She still didn't understand what had happened. But somehow, Gran's present had played a very big part in it.

Taking it from her pocket, Maya looked at it again. The unwrapped brown end of it was, she saw, old gingerbread. Even the shape of it was similar to the great slab Eddie had bought. The paper around it was tatty: as Maya held it up to the light for a proper look, she noticed something written on it. Immediately, she pictured Eddie at the frost fair, pen in hand, and her skin began to tingle. Though the ink was faded, she could just about make out the words:

This piece of gingerbread was bought at the Frost Fair on the Thames, 5th February 1788, by Edmund Mullig—

Edmund.

Her hunch was right. The 'Mulligan' part of his name was almost there, too.

So there really was a link.

No wonder Eddie looked a bit familiar. Thinking back on it, his eyes crinkled up just like Gran's when he smiled. And that strong bond she'd felt with him – well, that was family, wasn't it? He'd trusted her to help him when he was desperate, just as Gran was reaching out to her now. How could she ever have been jealous of Jasmine's brooch? This piece of gingerbread meant more than all the brooches in the world.

She had to speak to Gran right away.

Maya's mobile was out of credit. She raced downstairs for the landline phone. Dad was skyping Mum in India, and out in the kitchen Jasmine was banging around, making supper. The coast was clear. Once back in her room, Maya picked up Gran's present. Her skin did that tingly thing again.

Sitting on the floor, her back against the door, Maya dialled directory enquiries for the number to Gran's care home. That part was easy. Getting put through to Gran in person was a whole lot harder.

'Who?' the receptionist kept saying. 'Mrs who?' There were clicks and crackles on the line and muffled voices in the background, until finally, she got Gran herself.

'Have you asked your father if you can use the phone?' Gran barked on hearing Maya's voice.

'Gran,' said Maya, trying to stay patient. 'I'm not five

any more. Now listen, it's about that present you gave me today.'

'Edmund's gingerbread?'

'Yes, Eddie ... I mean ... Edmund.' It felt funny to call him that. 'Can you tell me some more about him?'

'I'm tired,' said Gran tartly. But Maya knew she was just testing her out, seeing how much she really wanted to hear about the person no one else believed existed.

So Maya tried again. 'That thing you said today about the world being full of stuff we don't understand – well, I took your advice and went looking for it.'

She heard the hesitation.

'You did?' Gran's voice sounded strangely small.

'I did.'

Another pause, then Gran simply said, 'Good.' And neither of them had to explain themselves. They had an understanding: that was all they needed.

'The present was wrapped in blue paper, and it's got writing on it,' Maya went on. 'It says Edmund's full name. He was a Mulligan, wasn't he?'

'He was.'

'And he was alive in 1788 because he bought this piece of gingerbread.' *And I saw it happen*, Maya thought.

Gran sighed wearily. 'Poor Edmund. He was my father's great-great-great-grandfather – too far back for anyone to remember much about him. But somehow that piece of gingerbread survived and got passed down through our family. No one really wanted it, but it fascinated me. So I did a bit of research into Edmund Mulli—'

'How?' Maya interrupted. She couldn't imagine Gran browsing the internet. Then she remembered something Gran had said earlier. It sent a shiver of excitement down her neck. 'You met him on your travels, didn't you? You said so this afternoon.'

Though Gran was pretty old, she'd not been alive in 1788. It meant one thing: Gran must've time-travelled, too. But if she had, then she wasn't about to discuss it. A prickly silence was the only answer she'd give to her granddaughter's question. And Maya, who didn't quite know how to ask more directly, had to leave it at that.

'I'll tell you this, though,' Gran said. 'He was mollycoddled terribly by his family. They never let him do anything – go outside, see friends, *anything* – especially after he got ill. Something to do with his lungs.'

Maya nodded. Gran's memory was working – this was just how the neighbour had explained things.

'Did he . . .' She cleared her throat nervously. 'Did Eddie die?'

'Of course he did – dear, dear me.' Maya heard the smile in Gran's voice. 'But not in 1788.'

Her stomach did a swoop of relief. 'So what happened?'

'Eventually, his father realized that shutting him away simply made his health worse. You see, he wasn't just going to give up and be an invalid. He kept on escaping from the house and going on wild capers across London.'

Maya grinned down the phone. She could absolutely imagine Eddie doing this, and it was so brilliant to hear it from Gran.

'The final straw was when he escaped the house to go to a frost fair on the river. It was all very public, catching him and bringing him home again, and someone wrote a letter to the family, begging that they reconsider their treatment of him.'

'Really?' Maya gulped. 'Did it work?'

'Amazingly, it did. Soon after, they stopped all the bed rest, the pandering, the weak tea and lean meat diet. And what do you know? Eddie got better. He lived to a good age in the end, made happier by living it in the way he wanted.'

A lump grew in Maya's throat. So things had all ended well for Eddie after all. 'I'm so glad,' she said, her voice thick with tears.

Maya leaned her tired head against the door. So that was Eddie's story; Gran's story, though, felt like it hadn't ended yet.

In the background, she heard another woman's voice. She was telling Gran it was too late to be on the phone.

'We have rules in here, Mrs Mulligan . . .'

Maya didn't catch the rest. Suddenly, it sounded like Gran was pressing the phone right against her mouth.

'People need their freedom, Maya. They need to breathe,' Gran whispered.

The line went dead.

Maya stared at the phone in her hand, her heart suddenly

pounding. Those words were Eddie's words. She'd borrowed them herself to write that note, and now Gran was using them, too. She glanced at the gingerbread, still there in her other hand. It had made its way through the Mulligan family in pretty good shape for a 200-year-old piece of cake. So had those words. They were, Maya realized, a sort of souvenir themselves. They meant something.

And that something was Gran.

She wasn't going to be happy in her care home. She'd hate being told when to take her phone calls, and everything else. She needed to breathe.

I'll speak to Dad in the morning, Maya decided.

In the opposite hand to the one holding the phone, the gingerbread was becoming almost hot. There was a smell coming off it, too, like Easter biscuits. It didn't go away when she wrapped it up again. Nor when she put it away in her sock drawer. If anything it, got stronger – so strong it filled the room.

In the end, she brought it out again. And took it downstairs to where Dad, still skyping Mum, was trying to sound upbeat about Gran.

'We've done the right thing,' he was saying. *Still* saying. 'She's been living in a fantasy about this Edmund person for weeks.'

On the laptop screen, Mum looked concerned. 'You don't sound very happy about it.'

Maya slid into the seat next to him.

'Hi, Mum.' She waved at the screen and held up the gingerbread.

'Hi, sweetheart.' Mum blew a kiss, then frowned. 'What on earth is *that*?'

'Gran gave it to me today,' said Maya. 'It's a very old piece of gingerbread bought by a boy called Edmund Mulligan, who needed to breathe.'

And she began to tell them all about Eddie.

The next weekend Gran moved to a different care home. This one had a library full of books and old maps on the walls; Dad insisted that Gran chose the place herself.

'A home fit for an explorer,' Gran said. 'Though I'm more the armchair variety nowadays.'

'You've still got an explorer's mind,' Maya reminded her. And she understood now that she did, too, for these things never went away.

From the care home lounge, there were views out across the Thames. It didn't freeze over, not even in winter – those days were long gone. But in summer, when all the windows were thrown open, Maya would sit with her gran and they'd stare out at the water. Often, they'd talk about Edmund. And sometimes – just sometimes – when the breeze blew off off the river, they'd smell something spicy like gingerbread.

the Magic of Midwinter
AMY ALWARD

'The Magic of Midwinter' is a short story from the world of *The Potion Diaries*, a series also written by Amy Alward.

From the Office of the Floating Palace of Nova

the Royal Advisor is commanded by

His Majesty King Ander of Nova

to invite

Samantha Kemi

to the Midwinter Gathering
at Castle Nova
on Midwinter's Eve at 7p.m.

Special note from the Palace – for the traditional
Secret Solstice gift exchange, you have been selected to
choose a gift for Princess Evelyn of Nova.
Please bring your gift to the Gathering.

MIDWINTER'S EVE

Gentle snowflakes drift onto my yellow-striped woolly hat and I squeeze my fingers together against the cold. Puffs of steam coincide with every breath, quick and erratic, like the breath of a baby dragon. I'm nervous. But then I'm about to kidnap the Princess of Nova.

Okay, so maybe kidnap is a strong word. But she's not allowed to leave the palace without the express permission of her parents (the eminent King and Queen of Nova) and a huge entourage of bodyguards and secret service agents. Today, however, she's sneaking out – all alone – just for me. But if we're caught? I'm the one who'll get the blame.

There's a crunch of snow, and I spin around. Princess Evelyn is running towards me, blonde hair streaming behind her, barely contained by a pair of pink fluffy earmuffs.

'Sam!' She raises her arm, waving wildly.

'Evie, you made it!'

When she catches up with me, her cheeks are flushed bright red from the cold and she tackles me in a giant bear hug. When we pull back, I see she's wearing a bright white down jacket and skinny jeans. 'I thought I told you to dress in a disguise?' I say.

'What? This is a disguise! These jeans are last season!'

A grin tugs at my lips. Princess Evelyn stands out even when she tries to blend in.

She brushes a blonde curl from her face. 'Ready to go?'

'Just about! How'd you manage to lose your security?' I ask.

'Oh, if a princess doesn't have a few tricks up her sleeve, what good is it having magic power?' She grins. 'Don't worry, they think I'm at a one-on-one intensive yoga session with my personal trainer, who I bribed with Midwinter mulled wine not to say anything about my absence. As long as I'm back in time to get ready for the Gathering tonight, they'll be none the wiser. Plus, this is a *very* good cause. I can't believe we're going to see the Svenland elves!' Princess Evelyn squeals in a manner that is most *un*princessy. My smile matches hers as it spreads from ear to ear.

'I know, right? It's so exciting!'

The research I've done pops into my brain before I can stop it.

Svenland elves: naturally reclusive creatures who live in a vast network of glaciers and underground ice caves in North Svenland. They only leave their dwelling one night of the year, Midwinter, when they use their elf-magic to travel around the world, delivering handmade presents to young children. They are also rumoured to have the special ability to choose the perfect gift for any child. A small village nearby, Sventown, is a popular tourist destination for all things dedicated to Midwinter.

'I've *always* wanted to go to Sventown, but it's not exactly the kind of place a princess goes. Oh, we're going to see all the beautiful lights and the trees and the huskies . . . it's going to be so cool! And at the end of it, you'll have the perfect present for Zain. How lucky are you? Even if you did leave it until the *very* last minute,' she adds, with a sly smile, her elbow digging into my ribs.

At her words, my smile slips before I can catch it. Because technically, *technically*, I'm dragging the princess all the way to North Svenland under false pretences. The present I've asked for help with isn't Zain's.

It's hers.

For a month I've known that *I'd* been chosen to find Evelyn a Secret Solstice present, and that I'd have to give it to her at the Palace's Gathering on Midwinter's Eve, in front of the royal family. And for a month I've wracked my brains, scoured all the shops in Kingstown ... and come up empty. It's the first time I've had to choose a gift for Evie since becoming her friend, and I want it to be perfect. Pretty tough, considering she can have anything she wants at the snap of her fingers. Talk. About. Pressure.

Plus, Secret Solstice presents are supposed to be unique. Personal.

And *secret*. So I can't even ask anyone for help.

Any *person* that is. No one said anything about magical creatures. Writing to the Svenland elves had been a last-chance gamble, a risk I didn't think would pay off. It was something young kids did, asking for their perfect gift, not sixteen-year-old alchemists. *Please help me find a Secret Solstice present for Princess Evelyn. I'll do anything.* I'd literally begged in my letter.

So when a reply arrived just yesterday, inviting me to visit them in North Svenland, I could hardly believe my luck. The only requirement they had was to bring the princess with me – and *only* the princess. No problem. Except for the whole ditching her security thing.

The ruse I'd come up with was for her to help me find a present for my boyfriend Zain. Of course, she'd said yes immediately. Her ability to be such a great friend to me made me feel ashamed I couldn't be a good friend to her and think of a perfect gift all on my own.

It's not as if I hadn't tried. After shopping failed, I tried the handmade route, but the only things I know how to make are potions. There are decorative potions – liquids that serve no purpose except to swirl prettily from silver to gold and back again – but no matter what I mixed, nothing seemed special enough.

And it has to be something special.

The Svenland elves are my last hope.

'Come on, we're close to the car,' I say, making my smile wide again.

Thanks to a few connections I have with an amazing potions-ingredient Finder named Kirsty, I've managed to get all the equipment we need for a winter outing and a car to drive us there. In true Finder-style, the equipment covers every eventuality – like a disguise for Evelyn, crampons for walking on ice and extra sets of warm clothing. The backpack she's given me is so heavy,

I haven't even looked through it all. North Svenland is supposed to be one of the happiest places on the planet. What could go wrong?

I open the back seat and pull out Evelyn's disguise.

'What, in the name of all things magic, is that?' Evelyn leans over my shoulder, her nose wrinkling.

'This—' in my hand is a curly brown ball '—is your wig!'

'Over my dead body am I wearing that! Can't I just glamour myself a costume?' She snaps her fingers and her hair is now as pink as her earmuffs.

'Nuh-uh,' I say. Evie pouts and her hair returns to its natural colour. 'We're heading into the Wilds now and who knows *what* that will do to your glamour.' I've heard stories of the Wilds – protected areas of nature that amplify and distort all human magic – distorting a glamour so badly, the wearer became permanently disfigured. Since Princess Evelyn is one of the world's most powerful magic users, I hate to think what might happen to her. I have no ability to use magic at all, so I don't have to worry.

'Come on,' I say. I give the wig a little shake so that it falls into a more hair-like shape. It still looks like the fur of a shaggy dog. 'You can't be spotted out here.' This is the busiest season for Sventown and even though we're only going to be passing through, I can't risk her being photographed. Her face would be *all over* social media, and the secret service would be here quicker than you can say *Midwinter* to whisk her home. Not only is she at risk of attack (there are always threats to Evelyn's security, even if she plays them down), if the royal family knew I was helping her sneak out, they might not let me see her again. And, selfishly, it would suck for me. I would still be left empty-handed on the gift front.

Evie throws her hands up in the air, then takes the wig. 'Okay, okay, you win! You owe me after this.' She ties her long blonde hair into a low bun, then slips on the furry hairball. After a bit of tucking and adjusting, the wig falls smoothly over her head. She leans down and makes a few final adjustments in the wing mirror of the car.

'Wow! Only you could pull off that wig!' I exclaim. 'Here are some funky glasses to complete the outfit . . .'

She wrinkles her nose again, but dutifully puts on the glasses. I tilt my head to one side and squint. I *think* she looks different enough not to be recognized at first glance. Anyone paying too much attention might guess – it's hard to disguise her distinctive Novaen features: the bright blue eyes, aquiline nose and sculpted cheekbones. I'll just have to drive quickly through the town and pray no one takes a closer look.

We hop in the car and I plug the co-ordinates of the elves' home into the GPS on the dash. Excitement tingles through my veins. Although plenty of tourists visit the elvish headquarters every year, the *true* magic behind Midwinter presents – like how the elves deliver them around the world in just one night, or how they know the perfect gift for just about everyone – remains a mystery.

Evelyn blasts the radio and we end up singing the newest hit by mega popstar Damien at the top of our lungs. As we drive, the snow becomes heavier, coating the road in front of us with a dusting of sugar. The trees glisten in the low light, their spindly, leafless branches nestled in gloves of ice. It's a pristine winter wonderland.

'I can't wait to see the Sventown decorations. Maybe we can get a few tips for next year's Kingstown Midwinter Spectacular.'

I nod eagerly. The Midwinter Spectacular is my favourite time of year. Kingstown undergoes a transformation overnight. Thousands of fairybugs descend on the Royal Lane, covering it with a canopy of twinkling lights. The big department stores update their window displays, competing for the most extravagant dressing. Pop-up stalls swap costume jewellery and knick-knacks for hot chocolates, roasted nuts and wood-carved Midwinter ornaments. The city even smells different: like cinnamon and oranges, pine cones and mulled wine. Sventown is like the Midwinter Spectacular – but all year around.

'Apparently, in Sventown, they have so many fairy lights, they outshine the Northern Lights!' I say.

Evie shivers with anticipation. 'Should be amazing.'

'Well, we'll be there any moment now. Keep your eyes peeled for a glow.' Even though it's the middle of the day, there's a dark, dusky tint to the sky – the result of being so far north that the sun only rises for an hour or two. I look down at the GPS and back at the road ahead. According to the map, Sventown is just around the next bend.

And when we turn the corner, we almost need to shield our eyes from the multitude of fairy lights, baubles and neon signs that confront us. Sventown is everything that I imagined and more. The streets are filled with tourists, wrapped up in their winter warmest, milling in and out of the shops selling stuffed-toy versions of the Svenland elves, bags of fake, glittery elvish dust and elaborate wreaths of holly, pine cones and dried oranges. There are burly men offering rides in horse-drawn carriages – or dog sleds for the more adventurous.

My jaw hangs open as we drive through. My younger sister Molly and I used to beg our parents to bring us here, to wrap up in furs and ride in sleds pulled by huskies, to stroke the reindeer and maybe, just maybe, to ask for the absolute perfect present from a Svenland elf. But Mum and Dad couldn't afford a trip like that – not back then. They just told us to continue writing letters to the elves, with a list of the things we wanted, in the hope of a reply. The replies never came, but somehow we always managed to get *something* off our wish lists on Midwinter morning – as well as gifts we never even knew we wanted.

'Oh, please can we stop for a while?' Evie asks, her nose plastered against the car window. She looks as excited as the children outside.

I realize I've slowed the car down almost to a crawl,

despite my resolution to drive quickly. I shrug my shoulders, trying to shake the hypnotizing effect of all the bright lights and music. I almost wonder if the town's been glamoured to make people feel happy. 'We can't,' I say reluctantly. 'You might be spotted. And besides . . . we don't have much time.'

Evelyn pouts, but nods. She turns away as a girl on her dad's shoulders does a double take at Evie's face. She lifts a finger to point.

'Okay, we have to get out of here,' I say, putting my foot on the accelerator. We zoom out of the one-road town, leaving the bright lights behind us. A few moments later, we pass a guard building with a sign that reads: WELCOME TO THE NORTH SVENLAND WILDS. The Wilds keeper checks our passes, lifting the barrier up.

'You're visiting the elves?' the keeper asks, surprise in his voice.

'Yes, we have an invitation,' I reply.

The guard wipes his brow. 'Phew! No one's been up there this year. Normally, we get a steady stream of tour groups in from Sventown, but the elves cancelled them all this year – no explanation given. Maybe they're working extra hard this Midwinter. Or maybe they've made it VIPs only . . .' He leans down to peer closer through our car window.

'Uh, best be off! Can't be late!' I say, trying to distract him.

Thankfully, he steps back. 'Just be careful. We had reports of wild animals roaming close to the elvish gates – a tour group who chanced a visit without an invitation were chased away. But if the elves are expecting you, you shouldn't have a problem. Wish them a Merry Midwinter from Hans – tell them not to forget my children!'

'We will!' says Evie brightly. When we've driven out of earshot, she turns to me. 'I wonder why they stopped doing the tours . . .'

'No idea,' I say.

A creeping finger of doubt works its way along the bottom of my spine. But the elves wanted us to come. The invitation in my backpack is proof. I'm sure it's all fine.

The GPS tells me to turn into a side road that looks like it hasn't been ploughed all winter. We make it a short distance before even the winter-ready tyres begin to spin in the deep snow. The moment we fishtail towards the forest, the steering no longer under my control, I slam on the brakes. 'So I think we're going to have to walk from here.'

'No problem,' says Evie, jumping out of the car with a lot more enthusiasm than I have. The glow from Sventown seems to have attached itself to her, and she grins widely. 'We're not far, right?'

'No, it's just up ahead.'

'Great.'

My fingers tingle, half from cold and half from nerves. If all goes well, I could be about to get Evie the perfect gift. *If* all goes well.

Out of the car, I'm grateful for my thick, fake-fur-lined winter boots, waterproofed against the snow. I wrap a scarf around my neck and pull on a pair of knitted mittens. Across from me, Evie is doing the same. 'Ready?' I ask.

'Absolutely,' she replies. 'You came for a present, and we're going to get one.'

I swing the backpack out of the back seat and lock the car. With the warnings about the wild animals ringing in our ears, we walk close to each other, our breath steaming in front of us.

Out of the drifting snow, we see our first sign of the elves' dwelling: an outline of a tall gate. But the gates are closed. Locked. We reach them and I tug at the deadbolt wrapped around the iron bars. It doesn't budge.

I sift through the backpack to find the invitation the elves sent me. The paper is a little crumpled, but according to the address, this is definitely the place. There's even a little embossed image of it at the top of the card. Except in that image, the gates are open. I frown, my stomach churning. I don't like to ignore my instincts, and right now they're screaming at me that something isn't right.

'Uh . . . Sam?'

'Hang on a sec.' I crane my neck to inspect the fence, trying to see if there's another entrance or maybe a buzzer to let the elves know we've arrived.

Evelyn tugs on the sleeve of my jacket. 'No, Sam . . . you need to turn around.' Her voice is quivering, and I spin around to look at her. Her face has drained of colour.

Then I hear it. A low growl. I hold my breath as I turn my

head in the direction we've just walked. Only a few paces behind us, a dark grey shape materializes out of the falling snow. I grip Evelyn's hand tightly in mine.

A wolf.

Evie and I both take a step backwards towards the gate, the cold iron pressing against our backs. The wolf takes a step forward, head low and swinging from side to side. Its amber eyes are fixed on us, and I don't dare to break eye contact.

I still have the backpack on the ground from when I searched for the invitation. Slowly, trying not to make any sudden movements, I take out a metal thermos carrying hot chocolate I'd made for the road.

The wolf takes another step, stalking us. There's another growl from a second wolf, this time from our left. Further away than the other, but getting closer.

The first wolf leans back like he's about to pounce, and I know we can't wait any longer. I launch into a sprint along the gate, pulling Evelyn with me. At the same time, I rattle the metal thermos along the rails, attempting to make as much noise as possible – both to scare away the wolves and to wake up the elves to rescue us.

Beside me, I feel Evelyn's hand heat up with magical power. 'Evie, no!' I cry out. The last thing we need is for Evie's magic to go crazy in the Wilds and blow us up – even before the wolves can eat us.

'Argh, I forgot!' Her hand goes ice-cold, but grips mine

even tighter, her nails digging into my skin. Without magic, she's just as powerless against the wolves as me.

Now there's no mistaking that there are other wolves chasing us along the edge of the gate. When I whip my head around, I count at least four shapes, slippery as shadows, tracking us through the forest. My mind whirls, trying to think of a plan, the fear of the wolves on our tail and the jangle of the metal-on-metal jarring my nerves ...

'Miss Kemi! This way, quickly!'

The raspy voice is an answer to all my prayers. A metre or so ahead, there's a small hole in the ground beneath the gate, and a little face – not much bigger than my fist – peeks its head from beneath the bars.

'There!' I shout at Evelyn.

'We'll never fit!' she screams.

But I don't give us the opportunity to debate. The wolves sense they're about to miss out on their dinner, and they change direction. I can smell them now more than see them, the metallic tang of stale blood on their breath and the strong musk of their fur ...

Evelyn's right. The hole does look too small for us. Still, I drop down into a slide, heading feet first. We slip through the hole – which is deeper than it looks – and I crane my neck back, just in time to see the bars lower on the snapping jaws of the wolves.

We crash-land on a pile of soft snow.

'Are you okay?' I ask between pants of breath, laying my

hand on her own heaving back. Her white puffy jacket is torn down one side, her wig askew and half covering her eyes.

Too late, I realize an unoriginal gift from a department store would *probably* beat getting mauled by wolves. Oops.

To my relief, she smiles. 'Are you kidding? I've never felt more alive! I really thought we weren't going to make it! And without the need for any magic at all. Now where's that elf who saved us?'

'Good point.' I stand up and take stock. We're inside a tunnel, the walls gleaming with compacted snow. It's just big enough for me to stand, although the bobble on top of my hat brushes the ceiling.

I shout, 'Hello!', only to be greeted with an echo. I wonder what's happened to the cheery, welcoming elves I've seen in the movies. They definitely weren't supposed to be this mysterious. The elf that saved us also looked suspiciously young. I hope this isn't one big practical joke to get the princess here, for some reason. 'I think the only thing we can do is keep going. Maybe he's gone to let the others know we've arrived?'

'Absolutely,' she says, and I grin at her optimism. She stands up, too, brushes herself down and pulls off the wig. 'I don't need this any more?' I shake my head. 'Then I'm ready.'

Our footsteps are the only sounds – strange, again, in a place that's supposed to be in its busiest season. I expected to see toy-makers at work, or at least some sign of industry.

We pass a cut-out in the snow, filled with the most incredible ice-sculpture of a reindeer. Or, at least, once it might have been incredible. Now the reindeer's antlers are half-melted stumps, its face a lump of ice. This must be where the tours pass through. If they were running.

'Do you think this is . . . normal?' Evie asks.

'Most definitely not.'

'Oh, good, me neither.' She edges closer to me, and a knot forms at the base of my throat.

This present had better be worth it. *If you even get one,* an annoying voice says in my brain. Nothing about this feels right, but I can't think that way. I can't have dragged Evie into all this danger for nothing.

'Maybe when we reach the end of this tunnel, we can get some answers. That elf must be here somewhere.'

I nod, hoping she's right. *He's gone to alert the others,* I tell myself. The thought distracts me from watching my step, and I slip on an icy patch. My legs splay in separate directions, my arms windmilling, and I collapse onto the ground.

'Are you okay?' Evelyn gasps.

'Fine, I think. But it might be time for these.' When I'm sure of my footing again, I open the backpack and pull out two sets of crampons – spiky soles that we can strap to our shoes to prevent us from slipping.

'My boots have never been so undignified,' Evie says, stomping into the ground to test the strength of the spikes.

'At least you're not going to make an undignified fall on the ice, like me!'

'True.'

'Oof, no wonder my bag was so heavy,' I say, pulling out a pair of small ice picks as well. If I'd searched the bag thoroughly beforehand, maybe I could have used them against the wolves. Serves me right for not thinking I'd need to be prepared.

Wrapped around the ice picks is a note from Kirsty: *IN CASE OF A FALL ON ICE: Do *not* try to stop yourself with your crampons – you will only break an ankle! Use the ice pick to slow your fall. Then help each other!*

Evelyn grimaces. 'Come on – this is the home of the Svenland elves, not some kind of perilous mountain climb.'

No, not a perilous mountain climb. But maybe ... I remove my glove and touch the tunnel walls, snatching my hand away at the bite of cold. I remember something I read about Svenland, and how it is dominated by great oceans of ice. 'I think we're inside a glacier? That means there might be cracks or crevasses we could fall into. Watch your step.' As if in response, the tunnel groans, the ice shaking beneath our feet. I don't like this one bit; no matter how much Evelyn is enjoying herself. The situation is too unpredictable, too out of my control for me to be comfortable. 'Okay, let's not mess around. We need to find that elf – and if we can't, then we need to get out of here.'

Crampons on, we pick up the pace. It takes a few steps

to get used to the extra grip, but we walk with a lot more confidence now. Within only a few minutes, we reach the end of the tunnel.

I stop dead, and Evelyn almost collides with my back. I look up, struck still with awe. Hanging above us are constellations of snowflakes, each at least as big as the palm of my hand, forming a snow-white web across the ceiling of the huge cavern. The walls have changed from bright white to azure blue, so blue I wouldn't be surprised if we'd walked into a cave of sapphires instead of ice.

'Look, there's a door over there,' says Evelyn, pointing to a spot on the far side of the cave. 'It's opening!' she says with glee.

A head pops around the door and we get a good glimpse of a real Svenland elf – the same young one as before. He's got a small, sharp face, every part of him angled to a point – from his nose to his chin to his diamond eyes – but his broad smile makes him at least seem friendly. He beckons us with a gloved hand, then disappears behind the door again.

'Wait!' I cry out across the cavern, but he's gone. 'Argh, are the elves really this annoying?'

'At least we're getting somewhere,' says Evelyn. She squeezes my arm. 'The wolves were just a little setback, right?'

'Right,' I say. I try to match her smile, but it doesn't quite reach my eyes. My first footstep into the cavern produces an echo that in turn makes the ceiling of snowflakes shake and tinkle, like a wind chime in the breeze.

I exchange a glance with Evelyn, trying to ignore the ominous sounds from above us. Evie talks to break the tension. 'So have you thought *at all* about a present for Zain? I mean, it's not exactly like Midwinter is a surprise . . .'

'I know, but with all that's happened this year, it kind of slipped my mind. Plus,' I glance sideways at her, 'some people are *really* hard to buy for.'

Before Evie can reply, a snowflake the size of a dinner plate lands a few steps away from us. It doesn't land softly, drifting to the ground like normal snow. It lands like a ninja weapon, one sharp point slicing into the ground.

'Oh, dragons,' I say. Then we run.

The snowflakes slice the air around us, whistling past like multi-pointed throwing knives. One whizzes close to my jacket, ripping my sleeve before I can dodge it. Adrenaline and fear pump through my veins, my legs careening towards the door. Evelyn's right behind me, but the crampons make it difficult to move with any real speed, as they dig stubbornly into the ice.

Just ahead, there's a dip in the snow. I leap over it, crashing against the door. I tug it open, then turn to help Evelyn through. 'Watch the snow!' I shout, but I'm not clear enough. Evelyn thinks I mean the snowflakes, and she looks up.

'Jump!' I cry, but it's too late. Her foot sinks into the

dip. In a split second, my worst nightmare comes true: the ground opens beneath her feet – a hole hidden by the snow – and Princess Evelyn of Nova disappears into a crevasse. I jump forward, but the ceiling of snowflakes comes crashing down and I'm forced to retreat into the safety of the next tunnel. There's a sound like the slam of a wooden door from where Evelyn disappeared.

'Evie!' I scream.

But the princess is gone.

There's a sharp cough from behind.

I turn slowly from the wall of ice, wiping tears from my cheeks before they can freeze in place. If Evelyn's hurt or worse …

Six elves are in front of me. There's no sign of the friendly elf from before and they look different from the elves in the reference books and movies I've seen. Their eyes are hard and sharp, glinting like black diamonds in the flickering torchlight – the only colour an unusual ring of bright blue around the edges of their irises.

'Please, please help me!' I choke out. 'My friend might be hurt …' My words die in my throat as I register that four of the elves are pointing icicle spears at my middle.

An elf steps forward, swathed in an elegant reindeer fur coat. His head only comes up to my waist and he wears a circlet of holly and rich crimson berries on his thick head of dark hair. His paper-white skin is wrinkled with lines, but – as he comes closer – I can see that the lines aren't like normal human wrinkles. It looks instead like his skin has been touched by Jack Frost – delicate spindles of ice making patterns on his skin like a windowpane.

'Who are you?' the elf says, his voice like gravel. 'What are you doing here? This place is closed to humans.'

I shake my head. 'I came with my friend, and she's fallen down a crevasse. I have to find her! Now!'

'Your friend is safe,' says the elf with a sneer. 'How *you* managed to get so far is another story. Explain yourself!'

'She's ... safe?' I almost fall to my knees in relief – I'm only held up by the thought of not impaling myself on those pointy spears. Then I explode. 'Where is she? Take me to her! She's ...' *She's the Princess of Nova* is what I want to say, but I hold my tongue. I don't know what these elves want from me – they don't appear to have been expecting us. I hold my head high. 'You *invited* us! Here, look – I have a letter, signed by a Snorri Elf.'

The elf frowns. 'That is not possible ... I am Snorri Elf and I have invited no one to North Svenland all winter. It is strictly forbidden.'

My mouth opens, but no sound comes out. I have no answer to that, because if he didn't invite me, then who did?

There's a commotion from behind Snorri, and a high-pitched voice says, 'Wait, wait!' The four scary ice-spear-pointing elves grumble as they're pushed apart by the young elf who saved us from the wolves and waved to us from the doorway. 'I invited her,' he says, between gulps of breath. He's leaning on his knees, panting hard. He's dressed much more like the traditional images of a Svenland elf – with a red pointed hat, red scarf, green vest and tights, and little red booties. His irises are only tinged with a pale blue. I ball my hands into a fist, barely keeping myself from exploding with rage. He's the one who led us into this.

I'm not the only one who's angry. Snorri looks ready to turn the spears on the young elf, too. 'Uyuni, explain yourself.'

'Grandpa, I'm sorry. When I saw her letter, I had to respond. This is *Samantha Kemi*.'

The emphasis on my name makes me blush, but the old elf remains unmoved.

'Samantha Kemi, you know, the great alchemist who won the Wilde Hunt?' the young elf rambles on. 'She can help us; I know she can!'

The white rage on Snorri's face fades and more frost lines spread across his face. He faces me again, his eyes wide. He looks . . . relieved.

'She wrote to us?' he asks.

'*Yes*, Grandpa, that's what I've been trying to tell you.'

'Then maybe it's not too late . . .'

'Excuse me!' I shout out, unable to keep it in any longer. 'If my friend is safe, I need to see her RIGHT AWAY.'

All the elves turn to look at me, and Uyuni shrinks into his scarf. 'Oh, you can't,' he says.

'What? Why?' I cross my arms over my chest.

'I need you to help us first, and then I will return your friend to you,' says Uyuni.

'Help you with what?' I ask, my mind racing at a hundred miles an hour.

They want Samantha the alchemist, I remind myself, and I look closer at my captors. The Jack-Frost lines spreading across their skin. The blue rings around their eyes.

As if on cue, Snorri lets out a huge sneeze that covers the guard-elves in front of him with a layer of snow. They don't flinch, but one of them lowers his ice spear to let out a sneeze of his own.

They're all symptoms, I realize.

'Oh, dragons,' I say, far from the first time today. 'You all have sneasles!'

Sneasles – or snow measles – a highly contagious and debilitating disease that is most at home in sub-zero temperatures. Thought to have been eradicated by the start of the twentieth century through vaccination.

I make a mental note to change my research file: *not* eradicated. I clamp my hands over my mouth, but I already know it's too late. I must have it, too.

Uyuni steps forward, his gloved hands spread in front of him. 'Another reason I can't bring you to the princess. Quarantine.'

'Oh, that's just great,' I say, my arms folded across my chest. 'So you trick me into bringing the princess with me so you can use her as a hostage and then infect me with a disease, and you expect me to help you?'

Uyuni shrugs. 'Yes. Will you?'

I swallow and then nod. 'Do I have a choice?'

I'm taken to a room equally as big as the one with the snowflakes, where hundreds of cots are lined up in a row, each one only big enough to fit a small child. In every cot, an elf lies prone. It looks as if the entire Svenland elf colony has come down with sneasles – and the sound of sneezing and coughing is almost deafening.

I spot a female elf in a bed near me, her hair brittle and her skin covered in flaky white patches. As I approach, she lets out a low moan. I take one of her hands and feel her pulse. It's extremely fast – she's in the grip of the worst of the illness.

Sneasles – an old cure is needed. Mix one part dried chilli flakes, two parts yak's milk, with a phoenix feather, and make sure to administer hot – the steam is part of the cure.

I could mix it, if I was at home.

'She was one of our head present-makers,' Uyuni says, from behind me. 'One of the first to become ill. The disease spread through our colony too rapidly for us to contain it – we only managed to quarantine the very youngest. In the meantime, all present production has come to a halt.'

'But sneasles isn't a *deadly* disease,' I say, scouring my mind for everything I know about the unpleasant sickness. 'She should recover eventually – maybe a week or two?'

Uyuni stares me straight in the eye – difficult when he's shorter than four feet and I'm almost six. 'But for us, you see, it is *worse* than deadly.' He takes a deep breath. 'What I'm about to reveal to you is a prized Svenland elf secret.'

I bite my lip. 'I have to know, so I can help you,' I prod, when he doesn't say anything further.

His eyes dart to Snorri, who gives him the nod of approval. Only then does he continue. 'The gifts we give at Midwinter spread joy to children around the world, everyone knows that. But there is a second purpose. The act of giving renews our elf-magic, and if we do a good job, the goodwill lasts us all year. If we aren't healthy by Midwinter, we cannot make any presents. Without presents, we cannot spread joy. Without joy, there's no elf-magic ... and there might never be Midwinter gifts again.'

'Ever?' I gulp.

'Ever.' The finality in his voice is deafening.

It takes a few seconds for me to register the gravity of the situation. 'And you waited until *Midwinter's EVE* to ask for help? I don't understand – don't you have your own healers?'

He shakes his head. 'Our healers have fallen sick as well.'

'But there must be specialist alchemists in North Svenland who could help you,' I splutter. 'Any alchemist on the planet would have helped, if you'd asked!'

The little elf's hand flutters to his chest. 'Us? Ask for help from humans?' He blinks several times, processing my question. 'You don't understand ... we never write to the outside world without receiving a letter first. It is our Midwinter Law. That's why it was a stroke of fortune that you wrote.'

'Fortune?' I blink, unable to comprehend how close the world has come to disaster. *You're the only alchemist who would have written to them,* I realize. Letters to the Svenland elves are written by children. *Or by teenagers in a bind.* I shake the fear away and slip into alchemist-mode. 'Okay. Do you have any alchemical ingredients here at all? Phoenix feathers? Yak's milk?'

Uyuni shakes his head.

'Then I need to get back to my lab, at home. Do you have a Transport panel?' I scan the room, looking for a large, mirrored surface that could send me back home in an instant. Transporting would definitely be the fastest way for me to get back to the lab so I can start mixing.

To my horror, he shakes his head again. 'No, we don't deal with any of that kind of human technology.'

'Then how am I going to mix the cure?'

'Well ...' He squints at me. 'You humans are too big for the traditional chimney method I *would* have suggested.'

'There's *no way* I'm fitting through our fireplace at home! It's half blocked up!'

'Hush, hush.' After a few moments, he snaps his fingers. 'Aha! Have you met our friendly neighbourhood reindeer?'

'Reindeer?'

'Why, yes! They're how we get around in Midwinter – I know just the one that will be perfect for our cause.'

'Fine,' I say. Then I scream. One of the wolves from outside the compound has followed us inside. His vicious teeth are bared, his hackles raised ... until Uyuni reaches inside his pocket and pulls out a treat. Then the 'wolf' turns as friendly as a teddy bear, rolling on the floor with his paws up. I blink and see that it's not a wolf at all, but a huskie ...

Uyuni sees the look on my face and has the decency to look sheepish. 'The "wolf chase" was one of the precautions set in place by Snorri in case anyone from Sventown tried to enter the compound. As were the snowflakes, and the holes in the snow. We don't want the infection spreading to the outside world. Not in this highly contagious form.'

No, not with all the children around, I think. Sneasles might be nasty in adults, but in the young and vulnerable it really can be deadly. Then I frown. 'But *you* knew I was coming? Why didn't you clear the "precautions"?'

Uyuni's pointed face twists into a sly grin. 'Don't think I've forgotten why you came here.'

I hold my breath. *Evelyn's perfect present*.

'It is all part of the plan – if you can save us.'

I swallow hard. 'If you say so.'

Cure the elves. Save the princess. Get the gift. Simple, right? Oh, but first ... *ride a reindeer*.

No problem. Gulp.

The reindeer takes the bright orange carrot from my hand, his slobber covering my mittens. I make a special effort not to grimace. We're about to share a long journey together and I don't want to offend him.

'You two should get along,' says Uyuni. 'Your name is Sam, and his is Sami. There aren't any special tricks to riding our reindeer,' he continues, stroking the white fur underneath the reindeer's chin. 'I'll tell him the destination – you just hold on tight.'

I bite my lip and catch one of the reindeer's deep brown eyes. He munches away on the carrot, not appearing too bothered that he's about to fly me to Nova. 'Are you sure there's no other way?' I ask.

'There's no time for anything else.'

I nod, but it's more to give myself encouragement than to accept Uyuni's words. I grip the front and back of the saddle and launch my legs over the reindeer's shoulders. I lean forward and whisper in his ear. 'Okay, Sami ... it's just you and me.'

My legs snuggle into his thick white fur, and already it feels different from the very small amount of horse-riding I've done in the past. I'm much higher on the reindeer's shoulders than I would be on a horse, and there are no stirrups for me to put my feet into. 'Uyuni, what should I do with my—'

There's no time for questions. Uyuni takes a handful of elvish dust from a pouch at his side and throws it over me, then slaps poor Sami on the haunches with the flat of his palm. Sami takes two steps forward and then a flying leap into the air. I have no choice but to fall forward onto Sami's neck and grip his fur as tightly as I can.

Only sheer alchemist's curiosity forces me to keep my eyes open. The experience is similar to Transporting, except that Sami does actually appear to be doing some work. With every step he takes, the miles disappear, and although I can tell there is wind rushing by at terrifying speeds, I don't feel any cold. Still, I nuzzle deeper into Sami's neck, willing him not to make any sudden movements. I'm only holding on by the strength of my thighs and the grip of his fur in my mittened fingers.

Within minutes, the bright lights of Kingstown come into view. So *that's* how the elves manage to get presents to the special children all over the world on Midwinter. Despite the chill in the air, warmth spreads through my toes, and I can't help but grin widely. The elf-magic is pure joy, and it's the feeling that Svenland elves spread to children around the world. I need to cure them to make sure it stays that way. It can't be gone for ever.

Lost in my thoughts, I cry out in shock as Sami's hooves hit our rooftop. It must have snowed here, too, as there's a dusting of white powder on the tiles. 'Uh ... Sami, do you think you could land on the ground, rather than the roof?'

The only reply I get is a *whuff* from his nose, and he lowers his head to lick the snow. He doesn't budge, and when I attempt to use my legs to guide him towards the edge of the roof, he gives me a stubborn shake.

Sliding from the saddle, I whisper silent curses to elves and reindeer and all things Midwinter. I've never set foot on our roof before – it's just not something that I would ever do in my ordinary life. But since becoming one of the most famous alchemists in Nova, nothing about my life is ordinary any more.

At least Sami won't be noticed. Somewhere in the back of my mind, I remember that Svenland reindeer (and their riders) under the influence of elvish dust are invisible – hence why there have never been any sightings on Midwinter night. I hope that's true. I'll have a hard time explaining myself otherwise.

The magic only works while I'm touching Sami, and I let go very reluctantly. I drop to my knees and creep to the edge of the roof on the street-side, but there's absolutely no way to get down. Towards our back garden, there's a drainpipe that leads to our kitchen extension. It's going to have to do.

Taking a deep breath, I lower myself slowly off the roof, grateful for the crumbly brickwork on the back of our house that enables me to dig my toes in to get some grip. I slide down the drainpipe inch by inch, my face pressed so close to the metal that it stings my cheek. Higher than I would like, my foot slips and I have to let go. I land on the ceiling of our kitchen with a thump.

From there, I clamber down our rose-bush fence and into our garden, grateful that there are no sharp thorns in the wintertime. When my feet touch solid ground, I could almost kiss it. Instead, I look up to make sure that Sami is still waiting for me. He seems patient enough. I'm not looking forward to the climb back.

My watch tells me that it's just gone noon – it's barely been two hours since I met the princess. Did that really happen so quickly? Thankfully, it's Sunday, so our store is closed and my family have gone out for last-minute Midwinter shopping – I won't infect them. I still have no time to lose, as they could return at any moment. I creep into the kitchen.

There's no sign of anyone. Thank the dragons for that.

I run as fast as I can through the kitchen and into our laboratory, heading straight to a drawer in the lab that is painted bright red. Inside, I pull out a paper mask that I secure over my mouth to prevent me from breathing the disease on any more surfaces. *Lab containment rules: in case of infectious disease.* There's also a pair of gloves, which I put on, and a jar of specially mixed anti-magical-disease spray, which I use to wipe down every surface I might have touched since I opened the door in the kitchen. Lastly, I go around and secure every lock in the house. No one is going to be allowed in until I've finished the cure.

I hope Grandad's game takes a nice long time, and the rest of my family doesn't return from their Midwinter shopping until I'm outta here again. Otherwise, they're going to be very confused when they try to enter.

Once everything is sanitized and locked up, I get to work.

My first stop is the bookshelf in the lab. I search under 'W' for 'Winter cures' and find what I'm looking for – a recipe book for *Winter Ailments and Distresses (including, but not limited to, frostbite and ice blindness)*. I flip through the book like a madwoman until I find it: *Sneasles – a cure*. Just as I had suspected. Phoenix feather, chilli flakes and yak's milk, mixed together until steaming hot. Ah, but there's something else, too, that I hadn't thought about. The yak's milk can't be reheated by flame once the potion is made. If I need to make sure it's still steaming when it reaches the elves, I'm going to need lava pebbles, which I can heat up and drop into the mix right before giving the cure.

Next I have to go into our store itself to collect the ingredients. The Kemi Potions Shop storage system is a series of shelves that extends almost three storeys high, accessible by ladders and pulleys. I clamber up the first ladder with practised speed, heading straight for the ingredients that we need and praying that we have everything in stock.

Jars labelled 'phoenix feathers' and 'lava rocks' tucked under my arm – I can get the chilli flakes from our kitchen, and the yak's milk from the huge fridge in our laboratory – I slide down the rungs of the ladder back to ground level. This is exactly what I live for, and I'm thrilled to be mixing such an interesting potion – rather than the decorative ones I've been trying out for Evelyn, or the innumerable cures for the common cold I've been mixing for customers ever since winter started.

As I walk through the threshold from the store and back into the lab, I let out a huge sneeze and almost drop the jars. On the ground in front of me, spikes of frost coat the hardwood flooring like a scattering of icy-white pine needles.

Highly contagious. Yeah. They weren't kidding. *And spreading fast.* If I didn't have enough incentive to make the cure as quickly as possible, I sure do now. My first job is to bring the yak's milk and chilli flakes to a boil. I place a stout, black, cast-iron pot onto an open flame, pour in the ingredients and set a timer on my phone. Next up, the phoenix feathers.

The jar is tightly sealed, and I have to twist with all my strength to get it open. When it finally comes free, I gasp. I rarely get to work with such a beautiful ingredient. Despite the years in storage, the feathers haven't lost any of their natural lustre. The sharp quill ends are such dark red they might even be black, but the colour progressively lightens to crimson, then burnished orange, finishing in beautiful, bright, golden-yellow tips. These are the feathers that a phoenix sheds naturally, the ones they *reject,* so I can only imagine how beautiful the real thing must be.

Out of habit, I consult the recipe book one more time. Next to the image of a phoenix feather, there's a warning printed in thick bold font: **PREPARE FEATHER WITH EXTREME CAUTION.** *Phoenix feathers have a tendency to combust and dissolve into ash when introduced to the air. Work speedily to avoid this.*

'Oh, no!' I cry out. I quickly spin the lid back on the jar, only now realizing why it was done up so tightly to begin with. In our lab, we have an airless glass box for reactive ingredients, and I curse myself for not thinking about it sooner.

I rush towards, it, placing the jar inside. Once I press a button, the air is sucked out, making it safe for the feathers. Using special handholds ending in gloves, I remove them from the jar again. All I need to do is strip the fine strands from the central spine of one feather, then mix them into the potion when it's come up to the boil.

Don't combust, don't combust, don't combust, I beg as I slowly begin to tear off the delicate strands. They fall onto the base of the box like hair on a salon floor.

My phone beeps, and I spin around to check on the yak's milk. It's just about boiling and there's plenty of steam rising. I pull on some thick oven mitts and bring the steaming cauldron over to the sealed glass box where the phoenix feathers are.

Unfortunately, some of them are already turning to ash. 'No, no, no!' I say, frustrated at my bad alchemy. Working at double speed, I rescue the strands that haven't yet turned and bring them out of the box, chucking them into the boiling milk with only half the care I might normally take.

There should *just* be enough. I now need to leave it to dissolve for half an hour. I take off my gloves and collapse onto the bench, my head dropping into my hands.

My palms feel scratchy and strangely cold. I lift my head to see white flaky patches covering my palms, and leading up into the sleeves of my hoodie. Not good. Not good at all. My sneasles is spreading at an alarming rate. No wonder the elves were overcome so quickly, with such a virulent strain of the disease at work. Their healers didn't stand a chance.

Uncontrollable shivers wrack my body, so I set another timer and curl up on the bench.

When my phone buzzes again, I'm jolted awake. I've slept almost the entire time, the sneasles overcoming my immune system and making me drowsy. I rush over to the potion, which has turned a vibrant red. I lean forward and inhale the steam, a soothing sensation spreading down my throat. I sip a tablespoon of the mix, and my head clears, the white patches on my hands fading and the urge to sneeze lessening . . . I've made the cure after all.

I pour the mixture into a heat-retaining flask, then throw some lava rocks in my pocket. I can use the fire there to heat the rocks – and therefore the potion.

When I look down at my hands again, the symptoms of the disease have disappeared completely. I put the flask into my backpack and set about unlocking all the doors. How I'm going to get back on the roof, I have no idea. Thankfully, when I step into the backyard, I see that Sami has decided to be nice after all, and has come down to ground level.

'Come on, then,' I say, giving him a tentative pat on the flank. 'Let's do this one more time.'

Uyuni is waiting for me as soon as I arrive back in North Svenland, and together we administer the cure to the elf colony with lightning speed. The lava rocks make the potion bubble and boil, the steam rising into the air and enabling all the elves to breathe a little easier.

The first to recover is the head present-maker, who introduces herself to me as Layla. I kneel so that she can give me two big kisses on the cheek, before she rushes off to start the production on the presents. North Svenland is instantly transformed. Newly healthy elves scurry on the ice, like ants in a colony, stringing lights and decorating trees. Even Snorri has tears in his eyes when he sees it. 'I thought this would be the first time Midwinter wouldn't come to North Svenland – and I don't think our spirits could have survived that. Is there anything we can do for you?'

'The princess?' I ask, still nervous that I haven't seen her this entire time.

'Of course!' says Uyuni, jumping up and grabbing my hand before Snorri can answer. He drags me through the ice tunnels – and back through the snowflake cavern. I look up in terror, the ninja-like snowflakes back in place, but Uyuni just giggles. 'Don't worry any more. Now, I promise, the giant snowflakes are perfectly safe. In fact, they are unique to North Svenland. You won't see them anywhere else in the world.'

I look up again, swallowing my fear. He's right – they are beautiful when I can admire them without worrying they're going to crash on my head. Combined with fairy lights that another group of elves are setting up, they twinkle and shine like the world's most perfect chandelier.

We descend a snowy staircase into a small room, lined with furs. Princess Evelyn is sitting in the centre, a picture book open on her lap, surrounded by tiny elf-babies who are crawling over her and cuddling under her arms. Her brown wig is being used as a pillow for one sleeping baby, and her long blonde hair is curled over her shoulders. She looks up at me when we enter, her bright blue eyes sparkling. 'Sam, where have you been? Aren't they so cute?'

I can't help but grin. 'They're adorable.' One elf-baby tugs at my trouser leg, and I pick her up. Her cheeks are chubby like she's carrying two little snow globes in her mouth, with none of the sharpness of the grown-up elves. I laugh as she pulls my bobble hat. 'Are you okay?' I return my attention to Evie. 'It looked like you fell a long way. Are you hurt?'

'You mean you didn't get down here using the awesome ice slide? I had the time of my life! I'm thinking about installing one at the palace . . .'

My jaw drops and I turn to Uyuni. 'An ice slide?' So it wasn't a dangerous glacier crevasse after all.

He winks at me.

'So, Sam,' continues Evelyn. 'Did you find out what to get Zain for Midwinter?'

A flush of heat rises in my cheeks and I wonder if I should just tell her the truth. But Uyuni gives me a warning look and I make up a lie on the spot. 'I'm not allowed to say – it's a secret.'

'Well, let's be getting back so that we can be ready for the Gathering!' She smiles broadly. 'This has been a *really* long yoga session – but it was worth it.'

'We'll show you the way,' squeaks the elf-child in my arms, and I lower her to the floor. Evie is led away by an army of young elves, giggling and squealing as they pull her arms.

When it's just me and Uyuni left, I turn to him. 'I helped you with your cure ... can you help me with my original request? What did all this have to do with finding the perfect present to get the princess?'

My heart drops as he shakes his head. 'I'm sorry, Samantha. I thought by bringing her here, I would be able to determine the perfect present for her. But I'm afraid I have no idea what it is. Maybe the sneasles took the magic out of me.' His voice is sad, but there's a strange twinkle in his eye.

My shoulders slump. 'That's okay,' I say. 'I'll just be the first person in the history of Palace Gatherings to show up without a Secret Solstice. I'll never be invited back again. I'm a terrible friend.'

'I'm sorry that I couldn't help you,' says Uyuni, with a small shrug.

I nod, and let him lead me back through the ice tunnels

to the entrance of the elvish home. It's like a different place already – the ice sculptures are back to their original magnificence, bright, colourful lights shine all around the entrance and there's a smell of rich cinnamon and apples in the air. The perfect Midwinter palace.

'Wow, someone turned on the Midwinter magic!' Evie exclaims.

I give her a small smile. 'I guess I'm not the only one who's last-minute when it comes to Midwinter presents.' I look down at Uyuni. 'Goodbye and ... stay well.'

'Thank you,' he says, taking both my hands in his and giving them a kiss.

Evie glances at her watch and lets out a gasp. 'Oh, dragons! We're only just going to get back in time to get ready for the Midwinter Gathering! At least you have a gift for Zain – I hope it was worth it.'

I look into Evelyn's bright blue eyes, and I know I have to tell her the truth. 'I'm sorry, Evie. This whole trip was supposed to help me find *you* the perfect Secret Solstice gift. Not Zain. I couldn't think of anything to get you. But not even the elves can help me. You're not going to have anything for the Solstice. I'm the worst friend ever.'

The pause that follows seems to last an eternity. She's been chased by wolves, nearly killed by snowflakes and fallen through a glacier. I've almost killed the princess several times, and if this was 400 years ago, I bet she'd have my head for treason.

But instead, she throws her arms around me and gives me an enormous hug. 'Are you kidding me? I haven't had this much fun in years. This day out is the best Secret Solstice present anyone could have given me.'

I think back to the twinkle in Uyuni's eye. How he invited me to bring the princess in the first place. To all the precautions he 'left' in place to ramp up our adventure. And how there wasn't really any danger to her – at least apart from a bad case of sneasles.

Maybe there *is* something to the elf-magic, after all.

Later that evening, I show up at the entrance to Castle Nova in a festive maroon dress, made from the softest crushed velvet, the palace's invitation clasped between my gloved fingers. I pause outside and take a deep breath. Even though I know she will treasure the memory of our day for ever, I still feel bad that I haven't got an *actual* present for Evie.

A drop of cold lands on my cheek, and I look up to the sky to see snow falling, a cascade of tiny white drops lit by the glow of twinkling fairy lights. *Was it only earlier today that we saw those giant snowflakes?* I think. This day feels like it's lasted a lifetime. *Dear Svenland elves . . . if only I could bottle a snowflake for Evelyn. That would be something.* I send the thought out into the snow, and steel myself to head inside.

There's a puff of wind, and my coat pocket bulges with a hidden weight. I frown. I slip my fingers inside the pocket and my heart stops as they touch smooth glass. I pull out the mystery object. It's a snowflake the size of my palm, encased in a special elvish glass so it won't melt.

It's special. Unique.

It's the perfect present for Evelyn. A memory of our day together.

'Thank you, Uyuni,' I whisper.

Then I race towards the warm glow of the castle doors, where the princess is waiting.

the Voice in the Snow
MICHELLE HARRISON

'The Voice in the Snow' is a short story from the
world of *The Other Alice*, a novel also written by
Michelle Harrison.

I

The girl moved silently through the darkened corridors. With her companion behind her, she crept from door to door, listening. The few rooms which still had occupants were silent, except for the occasional snore or mutter. Most of the rooms, however, were empty.

The house smelled of smoke. Though years had passed since the place had almost been destroyed, in certain areas the scent lingered like the ghosts of those who had lost their lives that night. The girl shivered, drawing her hood up further. It was winter now, but since the blaze, fires were not permitted. She soon found the door she was looking for. She crept closer and pressed her ear to the wood, hearing shuffling feet and whispering. Her stomach became a hard knot of dread. These were the sounds of someone who never slept. Of someone not right in the head.

Gathering her courage, she tried the handle, pushing the door the tiniest amount. Just enough to make sure it was unlocked. Then she kicked it open with such force that it hit the wall on the inside of the room with a crack.

For a moment, she thought she had made a mistake. The stooped man who had stopped dead in the centre of the room stared at her with hollow, blank eyes. He seemed incapable of anger, or fear, or any kind of emotion. These she needed, for how else could she get what she wanted from him?

She took a step inside. The look in his eyes changed. The mad, staring quality remained but there was hostility now, too.

'Who are you? Why are you trespassing in my house?' he hissed.

The girl stepped aside, allowing him to see past her, where another girl struggled in her companion's arms. A glinting sliver of metal was pressed to the other girl's throat.

The mad eyes widened. 'My daughter ... if you've harmed her—'

'We haven't.' The accomplice's voice was cold. 'Yet.'

'You *dare* threaten me?'

'Give us what we want or it won't be just a threat.' The hold on the girl tightened. A tear ran down her cheek.

'One for sorrow, two for mirth, three for a wedding ...' the man muttered.

'What you talking about, old man?'

'I was counting magpies,' he said slowly. 'There were three.'

'Forget magpies. You'll be counting down the last moments of your daughter's life if you don't open that door.'

'Door?'

'You know which door. The locked one in the North Wing.'

The man's face twitched, but he continued muttering. 'Four for a birth. Five for heaven, six for hell—'

'Move, old man, if you want your daughter to see tomorrow. And when you've given us what's inside that room, you can tell us exactly how you got it.'

'—seven you'll meet the devil himself,' the man whispered. Then he started to walk.

II

Some years earlier, a daughter was born to a rich man and his wife. She was perfect in every way – except one: she had been born without a voice. Her father and mother visited doctors and wise men to try to find a cure, but the years passed and the girl never made a sound. Though she was happy enough, her father could not let it rest. His daughter *would* have a voice, he vowed, no matter what it took.

In secret, he visited a witch, his last hope. She led him to a concealed room full of cages. Inside the cages were birds; some commonplace and other kinds he had never seen before. Some of the birds sang, but others huddled together and spoke in whispering voices.

'Are they ...?' the man began, eyeing the creatures in wonder.

'Talking?' the witch replied. 'Yes.' Her eyes swept over him greedily, taking in his expensive clothes, the fatness of his pockets. 'This one?' She clucked to it and the bird spoke in a plaintive voice: 'Choose me, choose me, this voice is not fit for a bird! Choose me, for here I am seen, but never heard!'

The man thought of his daughter's sweet face and rosy lips, shaking his head. 'Too plain.'

The witch beckoned him after her, stopping beside a golden cage containing a gleaming black bird with red feathers in its tail. She chirped to it and it cried out: 'Choose me, choose me, this voice is not fit for a bird! Choose me, for here I am seen, but never heard!'

The man closed his eyes, again picturing his daughter. This voice was better than the last, but was it him, or did it sound a little pinched? Nasal? He hesitated.

'There is one other,' the witch offered slyly. 'Only, the cost is considerably higher ...'

Sweat beaded on his upper lip. 'Cost is irrelevant. Show me.'

She turned away, grinning a grin he couldn't see, and led him to where another bird sat on a wooden perch, tethered by a silver chain. This one was a beauty, with silver eyes and teal feathers that appeared powdery to the touch, like a moth's wings. Already he sensed this one was a prize.

'Make it talk,' he whispered.

The witch chuckled. 'Oh, I can do better than that.' She whistled to the bird, and it sang in a clear, sweet voice:

> *'I will seek you, I will find you*
> *Wherever you may go*
> *Come with me now, hide away now*
> *Nobody will ever know.'*

'It's perfect.' Wide-eyed, he fumbled in his pockets. '*Perfect*. I have to have it.'

The witch smiled, handing him the silver chain and a long, gleaming pin. 'Have your daughter stick this through its heart, and then have the bird prepared into a meal for her by the finest cook you can find. When the last mouthful is eaten, the voice will be hers.'

His face blanched. 'My daughter has to be the one to kill it?'

The witch nodded. 'It will not work otherwise.'

He took the silver chain and the pin, slippery between his fingers. The bird was silent now, its silver eyes fixed on him. He settled the payment and, with no further words, left with his prize.

The witch watched him from her doorway, smiling at the weight of his money in her pockets. The smile vanished as a mountain cat slunk into view, creeping closer to her door having scented the feathered morsels within.

'Away!' she muttered, kicking a stone at it. It missed but she took pleasure in watching the cat flee, its fur on end. She'd always detested the creatures.

The witch closed her door and unloaded her pockets, stacking the coins in gleaming piles. The man hadn't asked, and she would never tell, how such magic was possible. How, for one person, the true cost was immeasurable.

III

Mrs Spindle had a pail of water
As well as a liking for slaughter
She was first scratched and bitten
As she drowned three white kittens
Before—

On a narrowboat leaving the town of Fiddler's Hollow, Gypsy Spindle stared at the words in the notebook in front of her. It was a rhyme used to taunt her through her childhood, sometimes jeered in the schoolyard, other times whispered slyly in the street as she passed. For a long while, she had never heard the end of the rhyme: whenever it was uttered, she'd turn, and the culprit would say no more, vanishing into a group of smirking children and Gypsy would be left furious, holding back tears.

She lifted her pen and completed the final sentence:

Before moving on to her daughter.

The rhyme was about Gypsy's mother.

It was six years since she had first heard that sentence. In ordinary circumstances, time might have dulled the horror she felt upon hearing it, or the ache in her heart. The sense of betrayal, upon learning that her own mother had tried to do away with her when she was just a baby. Tried, but not succeeded, thanks to Gypsy's papa.

Gypsy had been sitting at her kitchen table, but now she got up, walking to the steps that led out of the boat's cabin and up on deck. Johnny Piper stood at the tiller, his dark eyes fixed on the horizon. She crossed the wet deck to stand beside him. A cold wind stung her cheeks and whipped his long, black fringe across his eyes. She felt him watching her from behind it, and was almost glad she had an excuse not to speak, for she wouldn't have known what to say.

'It's been a long time,' Piper said eventually. 'Six years.'

She nodded, and stared into the dull green canal water, rippling as the boat cut through it.

'Didn't think I'd ever see you again,' he murmured.

She shot him a sharp look. *Now* she had words, angry ones, but no real way of communicating them – not for him at least. For everyone else she wrote things down in a notebook. But Piper couldn't read, although he had interpreted her expression easily enough.

'I know, I know,' he continued. 'It's my fault. I'm the one who ran away. But I came back.'

She gazed at him questioningly. That was news to her.

He swallowed. 'About a year ago, but your papa told me you were gone.'

She shook her head and shrugged, the unspoken word clear enough: *Why?*

''Cos we're not kids no more, and I . . .' He trailed off. 'I knew I needed to go back and find you. To face up to what I done . . .'

They had been children when it had happened. Just gangly-limbed, tangle-haired children. Having fun one minute and fighting the next. But at sixteen, almost seventeen, Gypsy wasn't really a girl any longer. Nor was Piper a boy. He towered above her. His face had lost its roundness to a strong jaw and high cheekbones. Only his eyes and hair had remained unchanged: those brown pools of bitter chocolate and the boyish hair cropped short at the back and sides but with its long fringe sweeping his eyes.

She wondered what he made of her now. Whether he looked past the scrape of make-up she used to make her lips a little pinker, her eyes a little greener. Whether he saw beyond the tough girl biker boots and leather jacket . . . past the scorpion inked on to her neck. Did Piper see through it all? Was it just a layer of dress-up to him, like when they had been younger?

'We're not kids now,' he repeated, interrupting her thoughts. 'I know I need to try to make it up to you, somehow.'

Their last words to each other – and Gypsy's last words at all – had been spoken in anger. She had held on to them, remembering all of it. She only had to close her eyes and she was back in Twisted Wood, following Piper through the grass as he played his flute, leading a trail of enchanted blue butterflies after him. Soon they had been alone, having wandered from the riverside and crossed into the edge of the wood. As it had so many times before when they were by themselves, conversation turned to their parents: Gypsy's mother, who had left soon after she was born, and Piper's pa, who had abandoned him alone and penniless, to be taken in by the Spindles.

Only, on this day, something had made Piper ask whether Gypsy would *want* to see her mother again. It was then he'd revealed to her the final line of the rhyme, sending her into a rage that saw her storming off, deep into the woods – but not before lashing out with harsh words of her own. Words that made Piper out to be a fool for hoping his pa might yet return for him.

Eventually she found a glade where she lay in the grass. It felt cool against her hot skin, but her anger still burned fiercely. How *dare* Piper say that about her mother! Even though she knew it had not come from Piper himself she was still furious with him for only telling her now – and for believing it. Her mother ... trying to *drown* her? Papa must have been mistaken. Perhaps Gypsy had slipped and her mother had been lifting her out.

If only she could hear her mother's version of events ... but she didn't know how to find her. After a while she had got up and brushed herself down, calmer now. She found herself humming the melody Piper had been playing earlier. As she often did, she couldn't help but put words to it. It wasn't that she was trying *not* to think about what Piper had said, but the tune was stuck in her head. She hummed some more, trying different words and sentences until the right ones fitted together. When she had them, she sang aloud in a clear voice, almost as a peace offering to Piper – if he had caught up and were listening.

> *'I will seek you, I will find you*
> *Wherever you may go*
> *Run away now, hide away now*
> *Nobody will ever know ...'*

There came the sound of wood snapping underfoot nearby. 'Piper?' she called. 'That you?'

There was no reply. Gypsy began to walk, half-humming, half-singing, unable to shake the feeling someone had been watching her. After a couple of minutes she started to relax a little, and so at first, did not pay much attention to the sound of wings in the air. Only when the sound of Piper's melody carried down to her did she look up to see an exotic-looking bird. It was teal-coloured, with silver eyes and a long tail, which swept down like a musical note.

'You heard my singing?' she asked in wonder.

The bird tilted its head, listening.

She whistled the tune again, and the bird copied her. Gypsy laughed, her anger all but forgotten. 'What a clever thing you are!' She stared at the bird. 'Wherever you're from, it's not round here. There's magic in you.'

The bird sang Piper's melody once more, and unthinkingly, Gypsy sang along.

She faltered as the bird opened its beak and mimicked her word for word . . . in Gypsy's own voice. She frowned and took a step back from it. Magic or not, there was something unnerving about such a perfect imitation.

'That's enough. Away with you,' Gypsy muttered – or tried to. No words came out. She cleared her throat and tried again. Her lips moved but there was not a sound, not even a whisper. The bird watched, silent and still. Gypsy had never experienced any kind of second sight before, but as she stared into the creature's bead-like eyes a terrible premonition came to her.

Seconds later the bird's beak opened and her words tumbled out: *'That's enough. Away with you!'*

A cold horror spread throughout Gypsy's body. Her mouth formed a single, soundless word: *Noooooo . . .*

When that same word emerged from the bird, the creature took off from its branch, startled, and flapping into the air. Gypsy ran after it, calling out. Her voice returned from above like a mocking echo, ringing through the woods.

'What's happening to me? Why can't I—'

She broke off as the sound of a flute caught her ears. She turned towards it, catching sight of the bird swooping down from the branches.

'Help!' Gypsy had cried. 'Somebody help me!' She arrived in a clearing, where Piper stood with his flute at his lips, ashen-faced. He stopped playing when he saw her, dropping the flute and running to her. For the smallest of moments she thought she saw a figure behind him, all frizzled hair and bones, silhouetted in a shaft of sunlight. Gypsy had stared at Piper in fear and confusion, his expression mirroring hers. He turned back and spoke over his shoulder.

'That's enough now. Let the bird go—' He cut off abruptly. 'Hey!' he yelled.

He turned back to Gypsy, his eyes wild. 'Did you see where she went?'

Who? She had tried to say. This time the woods stayed silent. The bird was gone, and so was her voice.

'Gypsy, I'm s-sorry . . . I never meant to,' Piper stuttered. His face was pale, waxy with shock. 'She said it was just a trick . . . to teach you a lesson. So I played the tune to the bird, and . . .'

He couldn't go on. He didn't need to, she understood now.

Her voice had been stolen because Piper had allowed it.

He spoke, stirring her from the memory.

'You don't believe me, do you? That I came back? I was still looking, you know.'

She shrugged. Six years was a long time. Piper could have changed. Back then she'd been able to tell if he was lying. Now, she had no idea.

He took something out of his coat pocket. She glimpsed a fold of cloth and a flutter of gold through his fingers. Piper took her hand and placed the object in it, then turned away, leaning over the side of the boat.

Gypsy looked down. In her hand was a small figure made of straw. It wore a white cotton dress and had golden embroidery thread sewn to its head for hair, and had two tiny green glass beads for eyes.

It was her.

Unexpectedly, she found a lump in her throat. So Piper *had* wanted to find her.

The town where they'd found each other, Fiddler's Hollow, held a custom called The Summoning every year. Likenesses were made – little dolls of straw and cloth – and burned on a bonfire in the town square. It was said that if the magic worked, the person whose Likeness had been created would appear to whoever had made it and answer one question. It was a way of finding the lost, the disappeared, the dead.

'Told you, didn't I?' Piper said quietly. 'Never thought it'd work, but I was willing to give it a go. Only, I didn't need to.' He turned to face her, taking the doll gently from her. 'I just played that tune . . . and there you were. Like I'd summoned you myself.'

Gypsy watched as Piper slid the Likeness back into his pocket. She remembered hearing that tune, drifting through the streets of that unfamiliar town. She'd followed it, heart racing, fists clenching, knowing she would find him at the end of it.

She gave a wry smile, shaking her head.

'What?' he asked. 'What's funny?'

She held a finger up, motioning for him to wait where he was. She went down into the cabin and took something from the little cupboard next to her bed, then went out on deck again. She placed the item in Piper's hand. He turned it over, combing the honey-coloured wool hair with his fingers; smoothing the blue dress. Gypsy had used sequins for the eyes, but they were the same shade of green as the beads Piper had used on the Likeness of her.

'Your mother,' he said.

He didn't ask why she hadn't gone through with it; why she hadn't burned the Likeness on the bonfire with the others. All her life she'd wanted to find her mother – or thought she had. But if what everyone said about her mother was true, then perhaps not knowing her was easier. At least that way she could pretend there was some misunderstanding, or that her mother would have had good reason to do what she did.

As if there could be any good reason for a mother wanting to kill her child.

She turned away so that Piper wouldn't see her eyes glistening.

'Gyps?' he said softly. 'It's time we went home.'

IV

Winter had arrived in Twisted Wood, and Gypsy and Piper followed it soon after. Gypsy turned her key in the front door, breathing in the scent of home. Woodsmoke, bread and her papa's tobacco all mingled into one and, after months of living on the water, the air felt so wonderfully *dry* and warm. She realized now how damp her clothes were, her hair was. Just being here made everything *lighter*.

She lifted her hand and tapped twice on the little shelf just inside the door. Almost immediately it was answered.

'Gypsy? Gypsy, is that really you?'

And then Papa was in front of her, sweeping her into his arms, almost crushing the breath out of her in the ferocity of his hug. She laughed and squeezed him back, ready for his usual scoldings that she was too thin, but they never came. The hug froze around her and too soon he pulled away, staring over her shoulder at Piper.

'You came back, then,' Papa said.

Gypsy held her breath. Piper said nothing but she knew he was squirming.

Papa hesitated, before pulling Piper to him, into his arms. 'Welcome home, both of you.'

They talked and talked as Papa made dinner, and Piper lit a fire, and Gypsy brought in armfuls of clothes from the boat, *Elsewhere*, to be washed. Then they sat and ate and talked some more until their eyes were heavy with sleep and their stomachs with food. Gypsy watched Papa's face, orange in the firelight. The lines around his mouth and eyes were deeper since she had last seen him, a reminder that he wasn't a young man any longer. Nor was she a little girl, but even so, she'd been careful to keep the tattoo on her neck hidden. Papa didn't know about that – yet.

She told him about the places she had seen, the people she had met. How she and Piper had come to find one another again. Papa listened, reading the words off her lips and speaking them aloud for Piper to hear, too. And still . . .

Still . . . none of them mentioned the reason Gypsy had gone off in the first place, the thing she had been searching for. None of them mentioned her voice. They all knew that the fact she had returned without it meant she had failed.

It was late when talk turned to her mother. 'There's nothing I can tell you that you don't already know,' Papa said, stoking the fire hard. 'Lydia was a Romany. There was a way about her that drew me in.' He stared into the flames.

'I've often wondered whether she enchanted me somehow. She was always dabbling, mixing cures and ointments; she'd learned it all from her folk. Old magic. She even bewitched most creatures. Birds would eat from her hand and she'd charm mice out of the kitchen just by singing.' He paused. 'Though she never liked cats or had control over them.'

'Is that why she drowned them?' Piper asked, with an apologetic glance at Gypsy.

Papa shrugged. 'The night Lydia was born, her mother's cat had kittens, but they died as there was no one to tend them. They were all too busy with the baby to notice. Lydia believed that was why she had no way with them, that it had left a mark on her. A curse.'

Do you think she'd have known how to undo my curse? Gypsy wrote.

Papa hesitated. 'I was hoping to ask her that myself—' He raised a hand for silence at their indignant interruptions. 'Yes, I went looking for her. I thought she might have returned to her people.'

And had she? Gypsy asked, wide awake now.

He nodded. 'She had tried. But they'd heard about what she did . . . to you. They cast her out. And I've never heard of her since.'

The night gave way to the early hours. Soon Papa could stay awake no longer.

'I'm happy you're home,' he murmured, rising from his chair and kissing Gypsy's forehead. 'You, too.' He patted

Piper's shoulder, pausing. 'There's no extra bed made up but the chair's comfortable enough.'

He left them alone, staring into the fire. She and Piper were sitting on the rug before the hearth. Before, when they were younger, there would have been a scramble for Papa's chair, but now, neither of them moved. 'You should go to bed, it's late,' Piper whispered.

Gypsy shook her head faintly. She wasn't sleepy. She stiffened as Piper's fingers brushed against her neck, pushing aside her hair.

'When you gonna tell him about that?' he asked, nodding to the scorpion tattoo.

She shrugged. Her face felt hot, but not from the flames. She hadn't sat this near to Piper for a long time. He felt familiar and like a stranger all at once. Slowly she turned to look at him, and found his eyes, dark and watchful.

She had loved him before, they both knew that. It wouldn't have been possible to hate him so deeply if she hadn't loved him first. Blood rushed through her body and pounded in her ears.

All she could think was, *He came back*.

He stared at her, almost for a beat too long, almost a hesitation where either one of them could have reconsidered. But then, they kissed. Of course they kissed.

Too soon he broke away. 'Gyps,' he whispered, stroking her hair. He leaned forward, touching his forehead to hers. 'Your papa . . .' He kissed her again, light and final.

106

She nodded, unable to look at him. In silence they laid down on the rug, both facing the fire, and he held her still.

Papa wouldn't be so shocked, surely? He'd seen their bond, growing up, and how devastated Gypsy had been when Piper had left. They weren't brother and sister, weren't related by blood.

It was an excuse, a lie. But she would go along with it.

The real reason was unsaid. Unsay-able, by her at least.

Eventually the flames died down. She waited until Piper had drifted to sleep, then eased out of his arms, creeping to her room. It didn't matter that Piper had come back. What mattered was that he should never have left her in the first place.

V

A week passed. Gypsy settled into life on dry land once more. Papa checked *Elsewhere* over, noting a few small repairs, but nothing that made the boat unusable. Once she went on to it, lighting the burner and trying to write in the snug, but it was too cold, and she found she wanted to be near Papa. Or at least, not to be alone.

She and Piper had not acknowledged what had happened. They had barely seen each other, for he hadn't taken up Papa's offer to stay, instead choosing to pay for a room in a local alehouse called *The Mermaid's Dagger*. There, he'd also taken up with a band of musicians to play live music in the evenings. She wondered why he chose to stay in Twisted Wood at all.

Papa noticed, too. 'You can't punish him for ever, my girl,' he'd said. 'Everyone makes mistakes. Piper wasn't to know that a childish prank in the woods would cost you so dear.'

Gypsy shook her head; Papa didn't understand. She had known from the moment she returned home that she wouldn't go searching for her voice again, nor her mother. It wasn't about that. So instead, she patted Papa's hand, and told him, *I know I'm not going to get my voice back, Papa. I don't want to keep searching for something that's gone. I want to be happy for what I* do *have. Bad things happen to people all the time, and they learn to live with it. I can live with this. I already am living with it.*

Papa kissed her forehead. 'Wise words,' he said. And Gypsy took comfort from that, because she knew he meant it. And oddly, she did not feel like she was giving up. She felt like she was letting go. Perhaps Papa was right and she *was* wise. He'd been wrong about one thing, though. She could punish Piper for as long as she wanted.

However, Gypsy was wrong, too. She was about to discover that lost things often reappear when they're no longer being looked for . . . and then, much closer than expected.

It was her ninth night back in Twisted Wood when Gypsy unexpectedly needed to buy some milk. There should have been plenty, but the bottle she'd opened was sour. She set out for the shop, shivering in her thick coat and letting her mind conjure stories of cross house fairies making the milk go off. It wasn't a long journey, but she hurried, not just because of the freezing wind, but because it took her past *The Mermaid's Dagger*. She couldn't help looking in the window as she passed, then wished she hadn't. Piper was leaning over a table in a corner with the landlord's daughter, Jess. She felt sick, sure then that something was going on between them. This was the third time she had peered in and seen them sitting so cosily together.

She stomped past, returning minutes later with a refusal to look again and thoughts more sour than the milk she'd replaced. Head down against the bracing wind, she didn't see the figure rushing out of the alehouse door in time to stop herself colliding with it.

The milk flew out of her hand and smashed, turning to slush as it ran over the icy cobbles. She stared up into the face of the person she'd bumped into, shocked to see it was Piper. She lowered her gaze and went to step round him, but his hand shot out and took her wrist.

'Just who I was coming to see.' His voice was low and urgent. 'Come with me.'

Warm air that smelled of stale beer hit Gypsy's cheeks. She followed Piper to an alcove next to the fire. They both took a seat at the small table, and Gypsy waited for him to take off his coat or offer her a drink, but he did neither. She stared at him, her heart racing. His dark eyes were moving quickly, studying her face in a way that was excited, yet nervous. Maybe she'd been wrong, the other night. Maybe he *did* love her enough, after all.

She pressed her hands between her knees: she wouldn't let him see them trembling.

'Gyps, something happened today.' Piper cleared his throat. 'I would've come to get you earlier, but I was working—'

'Hey, Piper!' a voice interrupted. Gypsy turned to see a large man drying glasses behind the bar, watching them with a sly smile. 'Time you stopped charming the ladies and gave us a tune, 'ent it?'

Gypsy's stare at Piper cooled a couple of degrees.

'I'm on a break,' Piper said evenly, without turning round. He shook his head almost imperceptibly. 'Acts like he's the one doing *me* a favour by letting me play here. Only favour he's doing me is giving me somewhere warm. I'm the one who keeps the money coming in. He used to say I was bad luck. Him and everyone else.'

Gypsy remembered, too. Piper was a foundling, something that always drew suspicion in Twisted Wood. She'd heard it muttered throughout their childhood: *If your own parents didn't want you, then why should anyone else?* Similar things had no doubt been said about her, after what her mother had done. But the difference with Gypsy was that she still had Papa.

110

'Anyway.' Piper blew out a long breath. 'There's this girl . . .'

Gypsy felt as though the fire had gone out, like a blast of icy air had snaked round her heart.

'Wait,' Piper muttered as a slight girl brushed past them carrying a basket of logs. 'Here she is.'

Gypsy turned to look at the girl who set the logs on the hearth. She was young, with a small, worried-looking face that reminded Gypsy of a scared rabbit.

'Maggie,' said Piper. 'Here a minute.'

The girl came closer, chewing at her thumbnail.

'Sit down,' Piper said. 'Tell her what you told me,'

The girl took a seat, fidgeting. Gypsy sat up straighter, sensing this wasn't what she had been expecting – dreading – after all.

'She works here, doing a bit of cleaning and cooking, that sort of thing,' Piper said. 'I never really spoke to her before today, but I was here when she came in to get her wages. And while she's waiting for him to bring them, she starts humming this tune . . .' He paused, his voice gentler now. 'Go on. You're not in no trouble – just sing that tune, the one from earlier.'

Maggie shuffled in her seat, then quietly, so that Gypsy was straining to hear, she began to sing.

'I will seek you, I will find you
Wherever you may go . . .'

Cold seeped throughout Gypsy's body. She raised her hand and the girl halted. She didn't need to hear any more. Did this girl know the old woman who had taken her voice? Had she been there, that day, watching and listening?

'I asked her where she'd heard it,' Piper continued. 'She said ... she said she'd only started working here a few weeks before we came back. Before that, she worked at Larkwood Hall.'

A chill ran over Gypsy's skin. She had never seen the place, but she'd heard of it; a once-beautiful mansion owned by the wealthy Lord Larkwood. The story went that the man had everything, more than his money could ever buy ... and yet he still hadn't been content. One night, a fire had burned the grand house to a shell, taking half its occupants with it. Larkwood survived but was half-mad from grief and now a recluse.

Quickly, Gypsy pulled out her little notebook and opened it, reaching for her pen.

Who sang this? she wrote.

'I – I never saw who it was.' Maggie's voice was little more than a whisper. 'I just heard it sometimes, coming from a room in the North Wing. A female voice.'

Did you ever go into that room? Gypsy scrawled, impatient. *How long did you work there for?*

'Five years,' Maggie replied. 'During that time I noticed the voice changing.'

'Changing?' Piper asked.

Maggie nodded. 'Growing older. When I first heard it, it sounded like a child. By the time I left it sounded like a young woman. I never went in – the room was always locked. Once or twice I tried speaking to it but it just stopped. I even asked Larkwood for a key once, but he flew into a rage.'

A tremor went through Gypsy's body. It was her voice; she knew it in her bones. *Her voice was in that house.*

'You're going to go there, aren't you?' said Maggie, wide-eyed.

Gypsy nodded, clenching her jaw.

'You shouldn't,' Maggie whispered. 'It's a terrible place. Even if you get in the house, he'll never let you into that room.'

We'll see.

Maggie stared at her. 'The only way you might get the key is by asking his daughter, Mitali, for help. She's different to him. Kind.'

'So what's the best way in?' Piper asked. 'Is there a spare key hidden, something like that?'

Maggie shook her head, and taking Gypsy's pen, began to sketch a little map. 'No. But there's a trapdoor at the back into the cellar. Once you're in, find the laundry room. There'll be aprons or something to put on there. Pretend you're staff.'

Won't they know I'm not?

'There's only one worker who was there longer than

me: Duncan. All the rest ... they come and go. No one stays long.'

Gypsy couldn't stop shaking. She jerked up, jogging the table. Piper grabbed her hand.

'Gypsy, wait.' He stood. 'I'm coming with you.'

VI

She never told Papa she was going.

Instead, she waited until he was in bed and wrote him a note before packing a bag, and then she and Piper slipped out into the night.

Elsewhere creaked under their weight as they clambered on, as though its short rest hadn't been quite enough. Shivering, Gypsy lit the stove and took out Papa's map while Piper unwound the rope mooring them. The boat cut through the water silently, with the frosty moon ahead of them and Twisted Wood behind.

It was a tense journey. Mealtimes were the only times spent in each other's company, for while Piper steered, Gypsy slept and vice versa. That evening as they huddled over steaming bowls of soup, Piper set his spoon down, not meeting her eyes.

'Gyps ... what happened the other night ...' He cleared his throat.

She lifted her hand, wanting him to stop – and succeeded, for she clumsily slopped her soup over her legs. She shook her head, red-faced, and went to the kitchen to get a rag, glad of the distraction. She didn't want to hear that it had been a mistake. In silence, he helped her and then they finished their meal. The kiss wasn't mentioned again.

They arrived in Castletown at dusk the following day. It was easy to find the house. It stood alone on a hill overlooking the rest of the town, built on the foundations of where an ancient castle had once stood. On a high stone arch above the gates, a statue of a stag was silhouetted against the moon. As they neared it, Gypsy eyed the battered gates uneasily. They hung open on loose hinges, choked with weeds. It was evident that no one had locked them in a long time.

Piper nudged her, pointing to the stag. 'Look,' he whispered, and she saw from his eyes that he, too, was disturbed by something. She glanced up, not seeing it straight away.

'Five legs,' Piper said, shaking his head. 'He's just as crazy as everyone says.'

Gypsy stared at the statue, frowning. Why on earth would it have five legs?

'Come on,' Piper muttered. 'This place gives me the creeps. Faster we get in, faster we get out.'

If we get out at all, Gypsy thought darkly. They crept through the gardens, following the instructions Maggie had given, eventually finding an ivy-wreathed trapdoor at the back. With a couple of angry pulls it shot up, releasing a shower of dirt with it.

They peered into the dark, silent space beyond.

'I'll go first.' Piper lowered himself into the gap. 'Careful, it's slippery.'

Gypsy followed, finding herself on a set of stone steps that were slick with moss. She pulled the trapdoor back in place letting her eyes adjust to the dark. Soon she made out a sliver of light ahead.

'That must be the door into the house,' Piper whispered. 'Leave our coats here, don't look like anyone comes down here.'

They shivered out of their coats and hid them among a bundle of mouldering furs. The place was piled with junk. They slipped out into a dim hallway, where Gypsy took out Maggie's diagram of the house and gestured for Piper to go to the right.

A short way along, they found the laundry room. There were piles of clean folded clothes and towels on a table, and hooks upon which several aprons hung. Gypsy threw one to Piper, sliding another over her head and tying the strings. They each took a pile of laundry and tiptoed out of the room. She checked the diagram again, locating Larkwood's daughter's room. If Maggie was right then perhaps the daughter could help them get the key. As they moved along the hall, Gypsy took in the blackened paintings and frayed wall hangings. There was nothing warm about this place; it was as though it no longer knew how to be a proper home. Soon they came to a vast staircase, but when Piper went to go up it Gypsy pulled him back.

'What?' Piper mouthed.

She tugged him away, pointing to a narrow corridor ahead. There they found a smaller staircase. *This* was for the servants' use. They climbed it, up and up, until Gypsy's legs burned. At the top, she heard Piper gasp as a weary-faced woman trudged past. 'Second bathroom needs a few towels,' she muttered, barely glancing their way.

They ducked their faces behind the piles they were carrying, and Piper muttered his thanks. Gypsy looked at the drawing again, then counted the doors until she found the one they wanted.

She knocked softly, but there was no reply. Instead she heard two faint knocks on wood from within. She tried the door, finding it unlocked. She and Piper entered the room.

A thin girl sat by the window, with a deck of cards laid out on the table before her. She wore a deep red dress, and her black hair hung in ringlets. Her dark skin was smooth and flawless, and she looked up at them with curious, intelligent eyes. She wrote something on a sheet of paper next to her and waved them forward to read it. Piper stayed where he was, so Gypsy moved to the girl's side.

I never asked for clean towels.

Gypsy threw the towels in a careless heap and took the pencil. *Mitali?* she wrote. The girl nodded. *We're not here to wait on you. There's something in this house we want.*

Mitali finished reading, then looked up at Gypsy with a knowing in her eyes. Gently, she took the pencil back.

If you can't speak then I can guess what you're here for.

The girl was calm, almost as if she had been expecting them, and the small movement of the tip of one finger caught Gypsy's attention. The girl was lightly tapping one of the cards on the table. They were not playing cards, as Gypsy had first thought. Each one was an image cut from paper, delicate and beautiful and strange. On the girl's hands were thin silk gloves.

'Fortune cards.'

Piper's voice at her side made Gypsy jump. He'd come to stand next to her so silently she'd almost forgotten he was there.

Mitali nodded.

'So maybe you knew we were coming, as well as what we're here for,' Piper said.

The girl shrugged, then spread her hand above the cards in a gesture of invitation.

Piper shook his head. 'No, thanks. I make my own fortune.'

But Gypsy took a seat opposite the girl, her eyes still fixed on the card beneath her fingers. It was a scorpion, its tail raised to strike. Almost identical to the one inked on Gypsy's neck.

'Gyps, we ain't got time for this—'

She held up her hand, silencing him, then wrote on the paper. *Read mine.*

The girl placed another pair of silk gloves in front of Gypsy, then swept the cards into one stack, offering them to her. Gypsy put the gloves on and shuffled the pack carefully, taking in a jumble of images: a black cat; a person walking under a ladder; a child throwing crumbs into a fireplace. *They're all superstitions*, she realized.

She handed them back.

Why paper? she wrote. *Why not painted pictures? These are so fragile.*

Isn't life itself? the girl wrote. *Isn't the future? They remind me to be careful.*

The girl took the top three cards from the pack and lay them before Gypsy.

Past, present, future, she wrote.

Gypsy stared at the first card. It showed the outline of a girl standing before a shattered mirror, fragments at her feet.

'Seven years bad luck,' Piper murmured.

The girl nodded. *A curse.*

Gypsy shifted in her seat. It was almost seven years now since her voice had been taken. The middle card, the present, was the one the girl had been touching when Gypsy entered the room: the scorpion. Only now, as she looked at it a second time, she saw that the creature was about to be crushed by a huge boot that loomed above it.

A powerful card, the girl wrote. *You have enemies, ones who could crush you. But you can still defeat them. Your weakness can also be your strength.*

'Gypsy, this is mumbo jumbo . . .' Piper began. 'We need to go!'

Once again she silenced him, this time with a look. Then she saw the third card, her heart sinking.

A single magpie had been carved out of the paper, its feathers mingling with the twiggy nest in which it sat.

One for sorrow.

This was to be her future?

Piper was right. She would make her own fortune. She swept the card away in disgust and went to get up, but Mitali caught her hand firmly, then placed the card in front of her once more.

Look again, she wrote.

Reluctantly, Gypsy did. This time she saw something else; a tiny outline of a second magpie in the distance, silhouetted against the sun. So there had been *two* magpies, and one was leaving? She glared at the card ... and then saw it.

An egg, nestled beneath the magpie's breast. A tiny crack zigzagged along its smooth surface. So the magpie was not alone, after all.

One for sorrow, two for mirth ...

Your future has hope, Mitali wrote. *But it's fragile, easily broken. You must take care, or the magpie will stay alone.* She pushed the card at Gypsy. *For luck. Take it.*

'Enough of this claptrap,' Piper muttered. 'The locked room. Where is it?'

I could take you there, but only my father has the key. Mitali looked regretful. *He'll never let you in.*

120

What's in that room? Gypsy wrote. *Who has the voice?*

An enchanted bird. My father bought it from a witch. From a box on the windowsill Mitali withdrew a golden pin and gave it to Gypsy. *She told him I was to kill it with this, then eat it, and the voice would be mine.*

'What's she saying?' Piper asked impatiently.

Quickly, Gypsy used her hands to mime a bird flying, then pointed the pin at her hand. She then mimed eating the bird, and a voice emerging.

He nodded. 'So why didn't you kill it?'

The girl stared at him for a long moment, her answer written in her eyes.

'You couldn't,' Piper said. 'Even though it's the thing you wanted most.'

She shook her head, grabbing the pencil. *It was what my* father *wanted most, not me. I was born this way. You don't miss what you never had. I was happy enough, but my father couldn't let it rest. For him, everything has to be perfect.* She paused, giving a bitter chuckle and nodding to the window. *You see that stag out there? It was put there by my grandfather and at first it had four legs. From my father's room only three could be seen. But he had another leg added, for his view alone.*

Why not just move the statue, or move rooms? Gypsy asked.

Why not? the girl replied. *Because you can't reason with madness.*

And Gypsy understood then. Even if the girl had been able to kill the bird, she still would have chosen not to, as an act of defiance. She had learned to live with herself. Now her father must.

'Gypsy?' Piper said questioningly. She shook her head. An explanation could wait until she had her voice back, and she was closer now than ever.

Take us to your father, she wrote.

He'll never open the door.

Gypsy lifted the golden pin, studying the girl's throat. *He will if he thinks we're going to kill you.*

VII

'Hurry up, old man,' Piper repeated through gritted teeth.

Gypsy glanced back at him and the girl in his arms. Mitali's face was a mask of fear, despite their reassurances that they were not going to hurt her, and Gypsy couldn't tell whether it was an act, or genuine. For all the girl knew, Piper really would pierce her throat with the pin ... he'd already nicked her accidentally a couple of times as they'd moved through the house, for her neckline was dotted with blood.

Every now and then, her father cast quick looks behind, muttering threats before shuffling on.

They arrived at the door and were met with silence. Immediately Gypsy wondered if this was not the room, whether Larkwood had plans to try and imprison them somehow ... but as she stepped closer she felt light crunching under her boots. She looked down. A scatter of birdseed had carried on draughts from the gap under the door into the passageway. Her heart began to thud, and she was glad Piper was the one doing the talking. Her mouth was as dry as if she had swallowed a mouthful of the seeds.

'Open it.' Piper's voice was soft but threatening.

The man shot him a look of hatred and pulled out a key on a chain from around his neck. He twisted it in the lock, then slowly pushed the door open. Gypsy cautiously followed him into the room, with a warning glance for Piper to stay outside. It would be too easy for the door to be slammed and locked with them on the wrong side of it.

It was dark and cool inside. As her eyes adjusted, Gypsy saw that the stone floor was covered in a layer of feathers and seed. A wooden perch stood at the centre of the room. For a moment, she almost wept.

The bird was pure white, not teal, like the one which had taken her voice. There must be some mistake . . .

But then it dawned on her. It was winter. She looked closer, remembering the silvery eyes and long tail. Yes, this was the same bird, in its wintry plumage.

Say something, she mouthed, willing it to speak.

It stared back at her, its silver eyes knowing.

'Say something,' it repeated.

She staggered back, steadying herself against the wall.

It was her voice. *Hers* . . . only six years older. No longer a little girl, but now a young woman.

123

My voice, my voice, she whispered soundlessly, and it came back at her like an echo.

'My voice, my voice . . .'

'Gypsy,' Piper hissed. 'Grab the bird and let's go.'

Snapping herself out of her daze, she pushed away from the wall, approaching the perch. The bird flitted to a higher branch, regarding her warily.

A low chuckle made her pause and turn. Larkwood was watching her, sneering. 'You expect to keep hold of that bird when it knows you want to kill it? You won't be cooking it or eating it in this house, make no mistake.' He laughed again. 'It's a wily thing. It'll escape you first chance it gets.'

Gypsy stared back at him. *I don't plan on killing it.*

The words emerged from the bird. It gazed at her, as though it understood what had been said. No one answered her; even Piper looked at a loss.

'I don't see why the bird should die for me to get something that's mine by rights. Tell me who you got it from and where.' Gypsy took a step closer to the bird. This time it stayed still, and when she held out her hand it hopped on to her outstretched fingers.

Larkwood's eyes narrowed. 'You won't make it. It's too cold now.'

'Tell us,' Gypsy snapped.

He smiled eerily. 'Fine. It'll give them a good run.'

Gypsy glanced at Piper, confused, but Larkwood continued. 'I got it from a witch up in the mountains.'

'How do we get there?' Piper asked.

'Why should I tell you? Find her yourselves.'

Piper lifted the golden pin away from Mitali's throat, instead pointing it at her eye. 'I think your daughter wants you to.'

The girl squeezed her eye shut, nodding vigorously.

'You'll pay for this,' Larkwood said through gritted teeth. There was a beat of silence, then he added: 'Follow the stag, until you can follow no more. Then follow the birds.' He paused. 'If you get that far. They're hungry . . .'

'Stop your muttering,' Gypsy said through the bird. 'And give me the key.'

'Give me my daughter!'

At his roar, Mitali jumped violently in Piper's arms. Larkwood growled, his eyes alive with anger and Gypsy saw that the sudden movement had jerked her against the long pin Piper held, scratching her cheek. A bead of fresh blood appeared instantly.

Seizing the distraction, Gypsy lunged for the key and snatched it from Larkwood's hand, then bolted for the door, slamming it and jamming the key in the lock.

Almost immediately he hit the other side with a grunt, shrieking and swearing, kicking and pushing.

'Help me!' Gypsy gasped, struggling against the door. Piper released Mitali and threw himself at it with all his weight, yet they were still losing. Larkwood's hand shot through the gap, reaching for her. He howled as a third weight lent itself to the door; Gypsy looked up in surprise to see Mitali between her and Piper, pushing with all her might. Larkwood's hand retreated back into the room with another yelp and finally Gypsy was able to turn the key.

They staggered away from the door, breathing hard.

'You helped us?' Piper said, looking at the girl in wonder.

Mitali nodded, her eyes full with dread. *Go*, she mouthed, urgently. *Go!*

Gypsy stared at her, her own fear mounting, trying to figure out what it was she knew that they didn't. Before she could, Piper grabbed her hand.

'Run,' he said breathlessly. 'Just run . . .'

Gypsy followed him, with a final glance back at Mitali. She saw her face for only a fraction of a second before Piper pulled her onwards, but the girl's expression struck terror into her.

Then she heard it, a furious bellowing from above, a single word repeated over and over, each time accompanied by a heavy thud. The sound of someone hurling themselves against wood, hard enough to break bones. And the word . . .

'Hounds! Hounds! Hounds . . .!'

She followed Piper blindly, one hand in his and the other cupping the bird nestled in her apron pocket as they zigzagged through the corridors, this way and that, down a swirling spiral staircase.

'Where is it?' Piper hissed. 'Where's the cellar door?'

She stumbled as they changed direction yet again, and then Piper pulled her through a doorway. She found herself in the cellar through which they had entered. She stood there uselessly as Piper shoved an old chest in front of the door.

'Gyps, snap out of it, will you?!' He rummaged through the piles of junk, retrieving their coats, then pushed up through the trapdoor. Freezing air blasted around them. She took off the apron and gently moved the bird to a pocket of her coat and slipped it on. Piper urged her out into the night, with Larkwood's bellows echoing round the grounds from the window above.

'The hounds! Release the hounds!' he screamed.

'Run,' Piper whispered.

The wind whipped her hair around her face as they raced away from the stag, away from the river, away from *Elsewhere*, for it could no longer carry them where they needed to go. Instead they followed the direction the stag was facing: to the north, where white tipped mountains crashed in the sky like waves. Below them, a dark mass of trees clustered as far as they could see. Around them, a chorus of howls and snarling struck up.

It'll give them a good run . . .

Gypsy understood now, replaying Larkwood's words in her head.

They're hungry . . .

'To the woods,' Piper panted. 'It's our best chance to hide ...'

'But the dogs ...' she gasped, her voice muffled from within the pocket. 'They'll be released any minute! They'll kill us!'

'They won't.' Piper seized her hand tight, pulling her along. 'I won't let them. But we can't outrun them.'

The barking began moments before they reached the border of the woods, growing louder with each thud of their feet. She ran harder, not daring to look back. Were they close enough to see yet? She could hear ragged snorts and snuffles, the thundering of paws over winter-frozen earth.

'Climb!' Piper gasped.

But there was nothing to climb; these were young, weak trees. They needed to go deeper. As they plunged further into the woods the moon vanished above the canopy of branches, and as the trees grew closer together Gypsy was forced to drop Piper's hand.

'This one!' he said frantically, already further ahead than she'd anticipated. She followed his voice, her breathing ragged above ever-growing howls of Larkwood's dogs.

'Quick!' Piper's voice was panicked. She felt his fumbling hands pushing her up into craggy branches. She twisted, reaching blindly, scraping her cheek on bark. She stopped on a thick branch, reaching for Piper's hand as he clambered after her. His fingers grazed hers then jerked backwards. He cried out but it was lost to a thick snarling below.

'Piper!' Gypsy lunged for his hand, finding it once more. Piper yelled as she pulled, his body jerking as something shook the other end. Wrapping her legs around the branch she grabbed him with both hands. She sensed rather than saw him fumbling with his other hand, wincing with each movement. Below him the dog growled, joined by another and another, jumping and snapping their jaws up the bark of the tree. A glimmer of silver caught her eye.

Piper's flute. His weapon.

He brought it to his lips and started to play; a haunting, lilting melody. Almost instantly she felt herself softening, her eyelids growing heavy. Her fingers relaxed in his, but he grabbed them tight. The snarling subsided into snuffles and grunts, and then little snores that were almost comforting. Gypsy wanted so much to join them, to simply lie down and sleep, but Piper's grip was too tight; painful. It kept the fog from taking hold. She felt another jolt as he was released from the creature's jaws, toppling forward.

'Are you hurt bad?' she whispered, but he continued to play, softer and softer until below them was nothing except snoring. Finally he stopped, sliding the flute back in its case.

'Is it bad?' she repeated. She slid her other hand into her pocket, checking on the bird. It was barely awake either, stirring only to sleepily murmur her words.

'I dunno.' It was a lie; his teeth were gritted. 'We can't stay here. We've gotta lose them.'

'But you're injured . . .'

'We got no choice.' He winced, sliding back down the trunk. Piper held a finger to his lips, then together they began wading slowly through the sea of dogs.

It was several minutes before they stood clear, and Gypsy was weak from supporting Piper as well as herself. 'How long will they sleep?' she whispered.

'Hard to say.' Piper's mouth was set in a grim line. 'Maybe an hour. Long enough for us to get away.'

They continued onward, Piper limping at Gypsy's side. They moved in silence, the woods growing colder every minute. Soon they could not keep up a good enough pace for warmth. Despite his discomfort, it was Piper who insisted they keep going. Eventually she heard what should have been a welcome sound, but which brought only dread.

A trickling stream up ahead, rushing downhill. This, she knew, was what Piper had been looking for. She glanced longingly at a fallen tree laid across it, but Piper nudged her away, his breath misting the air.

'We've gotta go through it. It's the only way they'll lose our scent.'

The water was below her knees, but its iciness made her bite her cheek as she waded through it. Thin ice on the surface bumped against her shins. She emerged staggering, the bones in her legs aching, her feet numb. She reached into her pocket, feeling warm against her fingers and a gentle, almost affectionate nibble from the bird's beak.

'We have to sleep,' she begged.

'Soon.' Piper limped on. 'We need shelter. We won't survive the night otherwise.'

They trudged forward, miserable and silent, damp clothes clinging to their legs. Once or twice, Gypsy was convinced she heard the howling of dogs, but when she paused to listen she heard only the wind. A snowflake rested on her cheek, blisteringly cold.

'There!' Piper said suddenly. He pointed to a dark shape ahead and they hurried towards it. 'It's an old hunting lodge,' he said as they drew level.

Gypsy stared dismally at the broken windows and sagging roof. 'It's a ruin.'

'Well, it's all we've got.' Piper pushed the door open. She followed him inside, feeling leaf mulch and rotten wood under her boots, then heard the hiss of a match as Piper lit the nub of a candle. Creatures skittered away into the shadows. There was a pile of old sacking and a stash of newspapers in the corner.

Gypsy pulled at the sacking. Surprisingly it was dry; the roof in this part intact. She arranged it as best she could, then lay back, hugging her knees to her chest while Piper used handfuls of newspaper to stuff the whistling gaps in the windows and roof. Once done, he hesitated for a moment, then lay down next to her.

'For warmth,' he muttered.

They lay there like that, shivering until some semblance of heat finally crept back into her and the trembling stopped.

'Piper?' she whispered eventually. Her voice drifted up from the folds of her pocket. 'Why didn't you play your flute before? When we got into the house, I mean. Maybe the dogs and everything could have been avoided, if . . .'

'If I'd played to Larkwood?' he finished.

She nodded.

'His madness could have stopped him responding the way he was meant to,' Piper continued. 'I've seen it before, in crowds. The one who doesn't react, or who looks at you a certain way. I couldn't risk it.'

She said nothing, instead leaning further into him. He put his arm round her, pulling her closer wordlessly, and his lips brushed her forehead. She felt his breath on her lips and waited for them to touch hers, too afraid to open her eyes. Eventually she drifted off to sleep, dreaming of a kiss that never came.

VIII

They woke still damp, but warmer, to a dazzling white light bouncing off everything. Gypsy sat up, checking her pocket. The bird looked at her, its silver eyes curious. She fed it a few crumbs of bread and icy water, then eased over the still-sleeping Piper to look out of the window.

At first she thought it had snowed in the night, but then saw that it was a thick frost covering the ground and nestling in the crooks of tree branches as far as she could see.

'Piper.' She nudged him. 'Wake up.'

He struggled into consciousness, rubbing his eyes. They ate a little of the food they had brought, then Piper removed his boot to examine his ankle.

It was swollen and red and, although the leather had taken the brunt of the bite, there were several red welts where the dog's teeth had punctured the skin. Gypsy helped him bathe it with icy water, collected from a dip in the roof.

They walked, rested and ate, speaking little and listening often, waiting for their pursuers to catch up with them. But their luck held, so much so that they even found an old upturned carriage abandoned on the border of the woods. While its wheels were smashed beyond repair, the cabin itself was practically intact, and warmer than expected.

Again, that night, they held each other for warmth. Once, Piper said her name, but when she answered him he didn't continue.

The next morning they woke, ate and said even less. Both knew that today the food would be gone and the journey even harder. Piper moved slightly faster now but he was still slow, and as they left the woods and found the mountains stretching before them they knew the hardest part was yet to come.

Piper shielded his eyes from the sun and gazed back over the diminishing woods. The stag stood proud upon the gate in the far distance. But as they headed up the mountain path, it vanished from sight.

'Now what?' Piper asked, his exhaustion evident. 'Can't see no birds, can you?'

The mountain appeared desolate; there was no sign of life at all except themselves and the little bird in her pocket and scrubby plant life jutting out from the rocks, half-killed by the frost. 'No,' she answered, kicking at a stone with a 'V' shaped scratch on it. Neither of them said it, though they both thought it: perhaps Larkwood had lied. There were no birds to follow. 'But we may as well keep going up.'

Up they clambered, over rock after rock after rock. Piper winced after losing his footing and jarring his weakened ankle. 'Let's rest a minute and eat,' he began, but broke off at the sight of Gypsy's face.

She was frowning, having crouched down to inspect another stone, bearing the same curling 'V' etched on its surface. 'Have you been noticing these?' she asked. 'This is the third one I've seen.' She picked the stone up, then dropped it as a high pitched shriek swept over them from above at the same time as a small, unmistakeable shadow. She looked up quickly but the sky was empty, and yet her eyes caught the shadow gliding away once more. She looked at the 'V' on the fallen stone, now seeing it for what it really was.

'A bird,' she whispered. 'Follow the birds . . .'

'Gyps, wait,' Piper began, but she was off, picking her way up the mountain, through the chill air, following the path, following the birds. She heard him hobbling behind her, struggling to keep up, but she found she couldn't slow down. She was close, so close.

The air turned colder still, turning to ice around them as snowflakes began to fall so fast that Gypsy could barely see her outstretched hand in front of her. She reached into her pocket, stroking the bird's head. It losing heat quickly. She ploughed onward, upwards, clasping Piper's hand. She lost track of time, not knowing whether they had been walking for minutes or hours. She couldn't tell how high they were, either. Once or twice shapes moved quickly out of the corner of her eyes, darting away between snow-covered rocks. Piper pointed to a track of prints, his voice muffled from under his hood, but she could hear it was low and fearful.

'Mountain cats. Probably waiting to scavenge what's left of us if we don't make it back.' He paused. 'Or attack if we show any sign of weakness.'

Gypsy glanced at another cat slinking past. More were circling, but they kept their distance. They were skinny – not at full strength – yet she knew better than to underestimate their hunger. Gritting her teeth she strode on, then stopped as something crunched under her boot.

'What is it?' Piper asked as she knelt to pick it up.

She brushed away the snow, her gloved fingers closing around the object. It was smooth – or had been before it had shattered under her heel. A bird's skull. An eerie stillness settled around them; the wind died and the snow eased to a light flutter.

'Look,' Piper whispered.

A shape was visible in the mountain, blocky at first but as they drew nearer Gypsy could make out something that looked like a window, and above it a sloping roof. Coming closer still, to round a jutting rock, a small door was tucked away. Above it the skeleton of a bird was pinned by its wings like a warning.

Gathering her courage, Gypsy crept to the door. She stopped a couple of paces short, feeling Piper's hand on her arm.

'You sure about this, Gyps?'

She nodded and took the final step, raising her hand to knock. The door swung open, startling her. She stared, her hand still raised as though in a salute. The woman before her was not what she had been expecting, not the hobbledy little crone with frizzled hair she'd caught a glimpse of all those years ago.

This woman was tall and slender, with braided flaxen hair and high cheekbones. Her nose was long and thin, adding a sharpness to her face that just prevented her from being truly beautiful. And though Gypsy did not remember this face, it was familiar, for more reasons than one. She reeled backwards, the blood draining from her cheeks.

'Hello, Gypsy Spindle,' the woman said.

Gypsy took the bird from her pocket and clutched it to her breast.

'Hello, Mother,' the bird replied for her.

'What?' Piper gasped. 'Your mother? No, it can't be. There's been a mistake ... this wasn't her!'

'Her?' The woman smiled. 'Oh, you mean ... *her*.' She undid her braid and combed her hair out with her fingers, and as she did so it lost its colour and spread, becoming wiry until it stood out from her head like a grey dandelion. At the same time, she shrank and became wizened and birdlike, all knobbly fingers and knees and cracked brown teeth.

Piper's face went white. 'You ... it *is* you! You're the one who took Gypsy's voice!'

'All this time it was you,' Gypsy finished. She paused, swallowing anger and tears. '*Why?*'

Her mother shook her hair, and the grizzled fuzz gave way to gold once more. Her face plumped out; white teeth grew back.

'Why? I needed a disguise. I couldn't set foot back in Twisted Wood as Lydia Spindle. I was known. *Hated*. Your little quarrel worked out well for me, but the truth is, I'd have taken your voice anyway.'

The words washed over Gypsy like iced water. She saw that Piper, too, was struggling to comprehend this news: all this time he had believed he was responsible.

'No.' Gypsy's voice emerged from the bird harsh and loud. '*Why?* Why did you take my voice? Why did you try to drown me? *What did I do to make you hate me so much?*' she screamed.

Lydia gave a pitying smile. 'I didn't hate you,' she said at last. 'I could probably have grown rather fond of you, had you been a boy.'

'*What?*' Gypsy whispered. 'You didn't love me . . . because I was a *girl*?'

'I couldn't allow myself to.' Lydia reached out, touching her hand to Gypsy's cheek. Though her face felt half frozen, her mother's hand felt colder. 'It was the foretelling, you see.'

Piper cut in. 'Foretelling?'

'When I was a child, I crossed a fortune teller,' Lydia replied. 'He'd come to our camp one day, lost, and my people gave him shelter. In return he told their fortunes. My friend Talia and I were too young to have ours read, but we weren't about to miss out. We hid behind a curtain and eavesdropped.

'When the last person had left, we waited for the traveller to settle down to sleep so we could leave unheard. Instead he called out to us, having known we were there all along. He said he would tell each of us one thing of our futures. One of us would not live out the year, he said. And the other would meet their end by the voice of their own daughter.'

With mounting horror, Gypsy listened. She had long thought about what she would do if she ever found her mother, played out a hundred different scenarios in her mind . . . but none of them had gone like this. This stranger with her face was her mother; someone Papa had loved once.

'We crept away unseen, our faces burning,' Lydia continued, her eyes faraway. 'The next day the traveller left and we never saw him again, but his foretellings haunted us. Which of us was which? Whose time would run out within the year and who would be killed by their own daughter's words? We were just twelve years old. We should have had our whole lives ahead of us, but now our futures held shadows and dread – and one future was worse than the other.

'Yet I knew I was at a disadvantage. I was a sickly child, while Talia was strong as an ox. Winter was approaching, and I knew that if sickness took hold the way it had the year before, I'd be the one to perish and Talia would live on.'

'But you were wrong,' Piper murmured.

Lydia shook her head. 'No. I knew I wasn't meant to outlive her.'

'But you did . . .' Gypsy trailed off, the pit of dread growing in her stomach.

'Because I chose to,' Lydia said softly. 'One night down by the river, I saw my chance. One quick push, that's all it was. She was a strong swimmer, but the current was stronger, and the water so cold it took her breath. I could have run for help, I almost did, seeing her bobbing there like an apple . . . but I only ran when I was sure she'd gone under for the final time.' She reached out again for Gypsy's face, but Gypsy slapped her hand away. 'It was her or me, don't you see? And I was right. I lived.'

'That still don't explain why you tried to kill Gypsy,' Piper spat.

'Yes, it does.' Gypsy recoiled in disgust. 'Because when you killed Talia, you took her future for your own. She had been destined to meet her end by her daughter. You killed to live once, and you tried to do it again to me.'

'Yes.' Lydia nodded. 'But you're a survivor, my girl.'

Tears spilled over Gypsy cheeks. 'I'm not *your* girl.' Her words emerged forcefully from the bird cradled to her chest.

'Why didn't you take her voice the first time?' Piper asked. 'Instead of trying to drown her?'

'I didn't possess the skill then. I knew that by the time I mastered such a spell it could be too late. I might have grown to care for you ...'

'That tends to happen,' Piper interjected.

' ... and you would have destroyed me.'

'That's the difference between us,' Gypsy said. 'I always loved you, even though I knew what you'd done! And I'd never have used my words to harm you, even if I knew how.' She gulped back tears, staring her mother in the eye. 'Now I'm here I still don't want to hurt you, but I won't waste any more love on you.'

Lydia nodded without a hint of remorse.

She reached out and took the bird from Gypsy's fingers, cradling it in her own, and for the first time since Gypsy had been standing there she realized how cold and numb her hands were. Half-frozen and useless. 'Bringing the bird back here was a mistake,' Lydia continued, almost kindly. 'If you'd stayed away, you'd have kept your voice for a time ...

however long is left of this bird's short life. But here, I'm the one in control. And the enchantment will last as long as I live. Which I intend to be a long time.'

'And when the bird dies?' Piper demanded. 'What happens to her voice then?'

Lydia shrugged. 'I'll hide the voice. Somewhere you'll never find it.'

You're poison, Gypsy tried to say. But no words came. Now, in her mother's grasp, the bird no longer spoke for her.

'Turn around, Gypsy,' Lydia said. 'Go home, and don't come back. Because if you do it'll be the last journey you ever make.'

A fierce rushing began in Gypsy's head. The wind was blowing up a gale around them, driving slivers of ice into her face, and the hatred she felt then made her question whether one of the shards had found its way into her heart. She rushed at her mother with a silent shriek that echoed only in her head, giving a mighty push that caught Lydia off guard and sent her away from the safety of her doorway and toppling into the snow. The bird fell from Lydia's clutches and fluttered to the doorstep, huddling pathetically for shelter. Gypsy threw herself on her mother, cursing, kicking, dragging her by the hair towards the edge of the mountain, and they fell heavily on to the frozen ground.

'Gypsy, no!' Piper cried, hurling himself at her. 'Don't do this, don't be like her! You're better than that!' He heaved her out of the snow and held her tight.

141

Gypsy paused, gasping, tears freezing on her face, and for a moment her whole body felt frozen with the shock and shame of what she had done. Clumps of her mother's golden hair came away in her fingers. Bright blood criss-crossed Gypsy's boots, trailing from Lydia's mouth as she crawled through the snow, dotting it red. At some point during the struggle, the magpie fortune card Mitali had given to Gypsy had escaped her pocket and caught on the wind. It danced along, pausing, then spinning out of sight.

Snow swirled around them, catching in Gypsy's eyelashes only to be replaced the moment she blinked it away. She could barely see Piper even though he was standing right next to her. The only trace of her mother was a crimson trail leading away from them.

'She's nothing,' Piper shouted above the howling wind. 'She'll die here alone, with her spells and charms. She's got no one! But you, you've got Papa, and you've got me, Gyps. You've *always* got me. But we've gotta get off this mountain before we die here!' He tugged her arm, but still she resisted. This time, however, it wasn't for the thing that was her mother.

The bird . . . the bird . . . where is it?

Gypsy shielded her face, trying to see where the cottage was, stumbling against hidden snow covered rocks. She did not notice the quick shapes moving straight away; circling them against the snow. Only when she heard a muttered curse from Piper did she realize they had been hunted, stalked. Yellow eyes flashed, hungry with the scent on the air; her mother's blood. And Gypsy was covered in it, too.

'The mountain cats,' Piper hissed in her ear, drawing her close. 'They're gonna attack!'

The bird, she mouthed, and at the same time she heard her mother calling out.

'Where is it? *Sing*, curse you!'

It was so cold now, cold and blind. Gypsy could see nothing, and could barely even feel Piper she was so numb. His lips were pressed against her ear, murmuring. 'Keep still, keep quiet . . . they're circling. They can smell the blood but the wind is throwing them off . . .'

Then through the snow they heard it, a faint little voice singing as the witch had commanded.

'I will seek you, I will find you, wherever you may go . . .'

Gypsy's voice, ringing out from the snow.

And just for a moment, the wind lulled as though it, too, were enchanted by that little voice. And the mountain cats heard it, and were guided by the promise of blood at the end, finally locating their weakened quarry.

Gypsy saw her mother's blood-smeared hand reaching out, and white-furred winter starved limbs springing towards it.

No! she shouted soundlessly, but only the wind and the screams of her mother answered her. She scrabbled at Piper's coat, but he beat her to it, taking out his flute. 'Cover your ears,' he commanded, and so she did as he blew exhausted breaths into the flute, melding a tune that she never heard.

143

One by one the mountain cats were lured away from the silent heap on the snow, their yellow eyes blank and their mouths dripping red, and at a graceful run swept past Gypsy and Piper to soar through the air, vanishing over the side of the mountain as though carried by the snow.

Finally Piper stopped playing and Gypsy lowered her hands. Together, they edged towards the cottage, fighting through the blizzard.

Lydia Spindle lay dead in the snow, a tangle of rags and hair, blood and bone. One pale hand was strangely untouched, reaching out towards something, the forefinger extended as though it was pointing. Gypsy sank to her knees, searching for white feathers stained red. But the bird was gone, no trace of it or the voice that had betrayed her mother's whereabouts; her daughter's voice. Her daughter's words ... ones that had been put to a tune some years ago, and which had ultimately drawn the mountain cats to her.

Lydia Spindle had always detested cats.

Gypsy had begun to stand when she saw it, half-hidden in a snowdrift.

A speckled teal egg, perfect and smooth. She picked it up, breathing warm breath on to it. Had her mother conjured it in her dying moments, as a peace offering or salvation? Or was it simply all that remained of the bird now that the witch who had enchanted it was no more?

'Inside, quickly.' Piper heaved against the cottage door and they half-fell into the hazy warmth. Wordlessly, they huddled by the fire, heaping it with wood. Soon, smoke curled away from it and the flames grew. When her hands were warm enough, Gypsy removed her gloves and cupped the egg, fingers tingling as heat flowed into them.

Faintly, there came a tap-tapping from within, followed by a tiny crack in the shell as a little beak nudged its way out. A downy white head came after, with two silver-coloured eyes like jewels. Gypsy watched as the shell fell away and the bird stretched its wings. When its beak opened she held her breath, but all that emerged was a croak, then a chirrup. And she smiled, because then she knew.

'Gyps?' Piper said questioningly.

She nodded, her eyes shining. 'Snow,' she said, tasting her voice for the first time in almost seven years. 'I'll call her Snow.'

He pulled her into his arms, holding her so tight she could barely breathe.

'Careful!' she scolded, laughing. 'You nearly crushed us!'

He drew back just enough to let her catch her breath before kissing her, stealing it away again.

'What was that for?' she whispered.

'For you,' he said simply.

'But Jess ...' she began, confused. 'I thought ... you said ...'

'*Jess ...?*' He shook his head in confusion. 'There's never been no one else, Gypsy. Only you. *Always* you.'

'But all those times ...' she looked away, embarrassed. 'I

saw you with her, in *The Mermaid's Dagger*. You were sitting so close ...'

'Gyps, no.' His voice was soft.

She searched his face, failing to understand.

'She was teaching me to read.' He paused, stroking her cheek. 'Because I couldn't be with you without some way of ... without me knowing how you felt. Without you able to tell me.'

They stared at each other for a long moment.

'Surely you don't need words to know that,' she said.

Slowly, they lay down side by side, as they had that night in front of Papa's fire. Outside, the wind howled, but already it was weakening. It would soon pass.

On the mountainside, caught in a tiny snowdrift, a fortune card flapped like a magpie. If Gypsy had looked at it again, she would have seen it differently. For sometimes a silhouette of a bird flying can look as though it's moving away from you, when, in fact, it's coming your way.

the Cold-Hearted
GERALDINE McCAUGHREAN

'I need to go. Sorry,' said Fergal. His father appeared not to hear, but little by little, gingerly-gingerly, the car came to a halt. Dad was not a timid driver, but this was a car hired for the holidays and he did not know the terrain. He certainly had not been expecting snow. On the steep, narrow road which wound up and around, up and around Fuachd Munro, Dad had started to chew the collar of his pullover.

There had been no snow until they reached the mountain. There was none lying on the grassy landscape down below, but now the bristly trees on either side of the road were caked in the stuff. Slabs and walls and folds of whiteness all but hid the black mountain peak, and wrapped the bushes in Puffa jackets of snow.

'You pick your places,' said Fergal's older sister, Ella.

'Mind where you tread,' said Mum. 'It might be deep.'

'Can I go, too?' said his littler sister. 'We could do snowballs!'

'The snow would make your socks wet, Zizzi,' said Mum, always ready with a reason.

'Fergal doesn't want you watching him,' said Ella, always ready with the truth.

'You could take the dog, though,' said Dad. 'Now I'm stopped.'

Fergal and Summer picked their way over hard-packed snow that creaked underfoot. It was good to be out of the car: Scotland might be picturesque, and home to Grandma, but it seemed to take a fearful long time to get from anywhere to anywhere else. More motorways: that was what the place needed. More service stations with toilets. Each time Fergal looked back he could see four oval faces pointing his way. So, of course, he went out of sight of the car and behind a tree. His pee sank golden into the snow-crust and steamed. He did not object to the dog watching him. Or the cockerel.

The cockerel was spinning gently round and round with a shrill, grating sound. Painted metal. Its perch was an arrow which, in the raw wind, pointed in every direction. Despite the cold, Fergal was mesmerized by the *graunch-graunching* noise and the crooked arrow. What was a weathercock doing sticking up out of a snowdrift?

Summer, the family's golden retriever, breath turned to dragony smoke in the fierce cold, began digging in the snow so excitedly that she fell tail over nose onto her back. Daft dog.

Fergal's father blew three impatient blasts on the car horn.

A moment later, there was a crack – muffled, like something breaking underground – and then a rushing noise.

Then Fergal was smothered in snow.

It came down on him out of the tree, knocking him off his feet, splattering him with pats of cold, on and on, until the colour of his clothing was lost and he was pinned to the ground. When he opened his mouth to yell, it filled up with snow, right to the back of his throat. The rushing, creaking, splashing noise went on, until he thought he must be buried utterly under fathoms of snow.

But no.

Crawling his fingers upwards, he sent them to look for air. They found their way to his face and scooped away the white blindness from his eyes, the suffocation out of his nose.

He started to give himself orders: *sit up, get up, get out* – which he ignored. His parents would come. His sisters would have seen it happen. They must be coming, even now, teetering over the slippery snow to dig him out and tell him off and get him into the warm car. A pain slashed into his knee – Summer looking for him with clawed paws. Not his parents.

Sit up. Get up. Get out. This time he obeyed, emerging like clotted milk from a bottle ... into a world utterly changed.

Snow had not simply fallen from the tree, but from the mountain itself – an avalanche cascading off sheer rock carrying away trees, boulders, holly bushes ... Nothing was as it had been – even the tin weathercock, now lying on its side, bent and twitching in the wind. The road was nowhere to be seen. Fergal hesitated, turned this way and that, looking for something he recognized so as to get his bearings; looking for the car. A whimper of sheer terror scaled his windpipe and escaped his mouth. A scream threatened to follow, but he clamped his hands to his mouth for fear he might bring down more snow – enough to expunge all trace of the living ...

The car was nowhere, nowhere. Foothills of snow lay at the base of the blank black cliff and the air was awash with glittering particles of ice, swirling, settling, settling. There was not so much as a radio aerial to show him where the car lay, sunk, buried, silent.

Again the scream clogged his throat. '*Someone help!*' he shouted. The mountain only at jeered him with echoes of his scared little voice. *Someone help!*

Returning to the tree, he tried to work it out: how many steps had he taken? How far had he departed from a straight line? It was important. It was life and death important. But nothing looked the same! Everything had been rubbed out by the avalanche. His family had been erased. Somewhere, beneath the snow, his father, mother and two sisters were trapped inside a tin box ... He looked around, but he seemed to be the last person living – the very last person in the entire world – for the mountain was silent, except for the creak of snow and the sorrowful moaning of the wind.

Panic-stricken, Fergal began to dig – with his hands at first and then (when his hands went blue with cold) with a broken branch. The clods of snow fell straight back into place. The dog dug, too, but in utterly the wrong place, over by the tree. 'Summer! Come here!' She must think it all some kind of game. Useless dog. A retriever that did not retrieve. A guide dog puppy that had failed her exams on grounds of stupidity. Fergal went to drag her back.

But Summer had unearthed something, even if it wasn't the car. Her claws squealed on some smooth and hard surface – slate – overlapping slates. As Fergal reached for her collar, there was a crack and a bark and a whimper and she ... disappeared – fell into her own hole, and into the gaping space beneath it. The smell of charcoal filled Fergal's nose. It even seemed to get into his mouth: charcoal and mouldy mildew. Both snow and earth had fallen away into some subterranean space – been swallowed by a gaping hole the shape of a startled mouth.

Summer was caught, upside down, in a kind of wooden cradle, surrounded by candles, which mostly went out in the rush of snow, or fell from their holders at the impact of the dog. Three or four flames fell away through the darkness and revealed a circle of paper-pale faces looking up at this sudden delivery of dog-in-a-basket. People! He was not alone after all! The mountain had shown him pity and offered up people! (Even so, let them not drop his dog.)

'Play dead, Summer. Play dead,' Fergal urged. 'Don't wriggle. You'll fall.' Summer continued to wriggle the best she could but, being wedged into the wooden chandelier, was not actually able to fall out of it to her death ten metres below.

There was an argument going on as to whether the people below should lower the chandelier or not. Over by the wall, a girl about Fergal's age was unwinding the rope from a cleat with that very idea in mind. But the adults were barking at her, *'Wolf! Wolf! No, lassie! Stop!'*

'She's not a wolf, she's a retriever!' called Fergal. 'And she weighs a tonne! Help her-over-there! Help her! She'll never hold the weight!'

The girl with her hands on the rope hesitated.

At the sight of Fergal's head beyond the hole in their roof, the adults all but lost interest in the dog-dilemma. They gaped at him – elderly faces without a drop of colour, boggling and goggling; gnarled hands held to cricks in their necks. Snowflakes spilled, in slow motion, down into their colourless eyes.

''Tis a boy.'

'An angel, is he?'

'Nah. Just a *balach*.'

Summer gave a long, baleful howl.

From a next-door room, more people arrived. The hair on the tops of their heads was thicker, but though they seemed younger, that hair was still almost white, their eyes wrinkled and peering. They, too, came to stare blankly up at Fergal.

'Please come. I need help. The car . . .'

One or two joined the girl in lowering the dog-in-a-chandelier slowly from the roof space. As it reached the floor, Fergal, on a wild impulse, jumped aboard the rope and climbed down it to the stone slabs below. He must make them understand the urgency! They had to come and help, even if he had to drag them out of this ... what? This ... where?

The crowd of old folk scattered to a safe distance.

'We've no been dancin'!' said an elderly gentleman, pointing at Fergal with his walking stick. 'We've no. Ye canna say we have!'

Fergal knelt for a while, hugging his dog. He tried to explain – about the avalanche – about the car – but he was suddenly helpless with shuddering cold and fearful of these strange, colourless, underground, inexplicable people. They seemed only to part-believe in him and the feeling was mutual. They were all dressed in such dark, plain clothes, mittens, moccasins that, away from the sparse candlelight, they virtually disappeared, moving in and out of invisibility. As people do in dreams. Finally, the girl came and placed a hand on him. 'S'a bonnie hound,' she said.

The room he found himself in was a church. As his eyes became more accustomed to the gloom, Fergal could make out the altar at one end, the font at the other, the brasses set into the floor.

'You have to come. You have to help me.' He said it so many times – like the chorus between the verses of a song.

'There's Mum and Dad and Ella and Zizzi ... You have to come. You have to help me. Dad blew the horn three times, and next thing you know ... You have to come. You have to help me. If I had a shovel ... the air ... they won't be able to breathe! You have to come. You have to help me!'

There was no dash to fetch spades, no stampede for the door. Perhaps the church, too, had just been buried by the avalanche ... though they did not have the look of people newly hit by disaster.

'Fetch the Teller,' said one of the elderly men, his back as bent as a question mark demanding of an answer. 'She can tell the *balach* how we sinned and were punished for it.'

'No! I don't want to know ...' Fergal began, but they were either deaf or refusing to hear his pleas for help.

They brought in – literally carried in, by armpits and elbows – a prodigiously old, blind woman, and sat her on a sack of ancient wool. She seemed to be gearing up to tell a story. Fergal had no time for stories! Could they not see that precious moments were going to waste? He writhed at the slowness of their speech and movements. When the woman spoke, she laid down each word like a playing card in an unbelievably slow game of Patience.

''Twas Christ-mass. A Sunday Christ-mass, a thousand year past.' The eyes of the villagers glazed over. Their lips moved silently, speaking each familiar word in time with the Storyteller. They had heard it a thousand times. 'We were exceeding happy. Fowl were cooking. Our childer were clad in new clothes. New clothes at Christ-mass, new clothes at Easter: that was the old way. Old Popser was mulling ale for after the Mass. We had brought along our beasts for a blessing. There was a piper among us – and a wee drummer-boy, too: we had learned a new carol to sing. Our hearts were merry. The cold was rare. The stove sang with the heat in its belly. In our mouths was music. In our souls was jollity. We gave no thought to our badness. We gave no thought to our wickedness. The music of the pipes was so braw that one Mary of the Grange did begin to dance – here in the very midst o' the kirk.' And the blind Storyteller pointed at the pulpit. A dozen hands made the same gesture, pointing (more accurately) at the aisle. Fergal wanted to shake her – to yell that nothing – *nothing* – that had happened in their mildewed past mattered as much as the people suffocating in that car buried under the snow outside ... But it was as if he had been caught in a spider's web of words and even his mouth was sutured shut with gossamer.

'Others were roused to dance also. Then did the piper play more loud. Men and women laid hold on the bell ropes and pulled mightily till the bells swangeth to and fro and the skies were knocked with clamouring!'

A change came over the Storyteller at this point, and all the faces fell into a similar expression of sorrow.

'Then awoke the angels and spoke one to another. "Who wakes us with this unholy noise? Is it no' Sunday? Is it no' the day o' the Lord? Is it no' a day of silence? Who are these noddies and why do they not think upon their sins and wickedness, and kneel down and beg forgiveness?"'

'Because it was Christmas?' suggested Fergal.

The interruption was greeted with fifty shocked expressions. No one had ever interrupted the Storyteller while she retold the Legend of Fuachd Munro. She reeled in her seat. Someone tucked a blanket around her, pulling it up over her head so that only her huge, hooked nose was still visible.

'Then did the angels weep tears of red blood. "Let judgement fall on every head!" said the angels. "Let the mountain open and let Winter swallow them up. Yeah, and their childer after them, even unto the Final Day!" Then came down Judgement upon the souls of Fuachd Munro. Then came down snow and tree, rock and tears of blood. And we were sunk into darkness and the place of wailing and chattering of teeth.'

The Storyteller gave a phlegmy cough and glared in the vague direction of Fergal. She also gave a yelp of alarm as something licked the hand she had left dangling outside the blanket. Summer had got over her shock and was on the prowl for titbits. Obviously, the Storyteller had been fetched away from her lunch to recite, and still had traces of food on her fingers.

As the coughing subsided, she took up her story again. Even Summer sat down to listen as the words fell from that age-puckered mouth, like dizzying snow. She spoke of a

Christmas 800 – maybe 900 – years before, when snow had been falling past the thick, wrinkled window-glass of the kirk. All those years ago, the assembled villagers of Fuachd Munro had been trapped inside the church when, like the roar of a hundred canons, a torrent of rock and snow had fallen on the kirk. Inside his head, time stopped for Fergal, too, and he could vividly picture them desperately boarding up the windows with bench seats, to keep out the weight of frozen earth pressing against the glass.

'That was the Christ-mass Day of Judgement,' said the Storyteller. 'Though we are suffered to live on, generation by generation – being born, marrying, dying – still, for us, Time stopped that fearful day when we transgressed.'

The assembled crowd uttered a sorrowful sigh as the recital ended.

Fergal, though, was once again unable to breathe – buried under a freezing drift of words. His hand clawed at the air over his head. He must get out. He must get help. There was surely some door out of this subterranean tomb of a place! He ran to and fro in search of one.

Over the centuries, the villagers had made their prison bigger, digging tunnels into the mountain, replacing their houses-above-ground with underground warrens, like rabbits. Except that rabbits go outside. Rabbits graze grass, dig up carrots, catch the sound of the wind in their long ears, and flash their fluffy scuts in the bright sunlight. Fergal realized, with growing horror, that the people of

Fuachd Munro never saw sunlight. They did not try to escape. They had remained for ever where they thought they deserved to be: sealed into the past by a roof of slate, earth, ice and snow.

'Rubbish!' he spluttered, finally recovering the power of speech ...

Fifty throats drew in the damp and chilly air in sharp gasps.

'Well, it was an avalanche, wasn't it? Like the one just now. You have to come. You have to help me. Give me a spade at least! But someone *do* something! You can't just sit there! We have to be quick! *There's no time!*'

But nothing could hurry the people of Fuachd Munro. He saw it in their shineless, doubting eyes. No time? There was plenty of time. Time was the iron prison ball that had been chained to their ankles hundreds of years before. Time was the sentence that had been passed on them by the angels, and they must spend it underground, meekly, not rushing about at the bidding of this rowdy boy.

'Will I show you the angel tears?' offered the girl who had lowered the chandelier.

Her name was Mariah, and she alone seemed excited about Fergal dropping in. She dabbed him dry of snow with a scratchy piece of sacking. The others were unsettled by his sudden arrival, annoyed about the hole in the church roof, and positively scared by his noisy disrespect for the Storyteller. They told Mariah to keep away from him.

But Mariah led Fergal to the altar and, because she was

about his age, and because her hand was warm on his, he let himself be led. There, in a box carved from the root of a yew tree, lay a dozen shrivelled little balls the colour of beetroot. Mariah's colourless eyes shone with wonder at the sight of them rolling around in the box.

'They're holly berries,' said Fergal. 'They're dried-up holly berries.'

Already as pale as milk, Mariah's skin turned paler still. 'Angel tears.'

'Nope. Anyway, why does it matter? Mum and Dad matter. Ella and Zizzi matter. I just want a spade and a way out.'

'There is none.'

'There must be. You must go out to get food.'

'Mushrooms. Potatoes. Rabbits stray in upon us. Mice. Worm potage is wholesome fare.'

'I'll pass,' said Fergal. He had a feeling she was lying to him and not just about the worms. 'You must go out to get those candles. The makings. Bees? Something.'

'Tallow.' Which stopped the conversation, because neither of them knew what tallow was made of.

'You couldn't live like this. People can't live like this,' he insisted, at which Mariah shrugged and led him on a tour through a warren of tunnels where pale roots reached out of the soil to catch in his hair. Side chambers led off to animal pens with sheep in them – descendants of those beasts brought into the church for a Christmas blessing, Mariah told him. There were warming places with grates burning charcoal; and sleeping holes, and 'dripping places' where leaks of rain and snow melt were captured in bowls, for drinking. Like angel tears.

They must have spades, he thought, *to have dug these.* He looked for daylight – an escape route – but found none. 'I'll just have to go out the way I came in. You'll have to haul me up to the roof again. You have to.'

'I cannot. I dunna have the strength.'

Fergal looked at his watch: it had stopped when the snow fell on him. He pocketed charcoal from one of the grates, and when they got back to the church, he began to draw on the wall. The villagers of Fuachd Munro stared at him in outraged horror, but no one quite dared to wrestle the charcoal out of his hands. What did he care what they thought of him? They were old people – even the younger ones behaved like the old – slow-moving, out-of-date, timid and too stupid to see what was staring them in the face.

'This is a mountain,' said Fergal, and drew one. 'The snow falls on it – *fall-fall-fall*.' He dotted the granite wall with black snowflakes. 'It freezes to the mountain when it's winter and very cold – *freeze-freeze-freeze*. Then the sun shines on the mountain – *sun-sun-sun*. See?' He drew a sun – something the people of Fuachd Munro had never seen, but did believe in because there were carvings in the church of suns and moons decorating the beams. 'One day, there's much too much snow hanging about. The sun shines on it and, under the snow, the ice melts a bit. Not so sticky, you know?'

'*Sticky*,' repeated a voice here, a voice there. *Sticky*. It was not a word they knew. They pictured walking sticks and tree roots.

'Then if there's a big *BANG* or shout or something, it makes the air shake, and the snow shakes, and the ice can't hold on to the rock, and *whoosh* it all comes rushing down the mountain!'

As he said it, Fergal relived it, the sharp blasts of the car horn, the aching groan and the rumbling rush, the tumbling noise and confusion, and the cold and terrifying career of snow and trees and bushes down the mountainside engulfing everything in its path. He drew a car and, in it, four heads ... before his knees gave way and he sank into a crouch of fear and horror.

'Dad sounded the horn, and it made an avalanche come down. I have to get them out. You have to come. You have to help me.'

'So ... not the angels' doing?' said Mariah, and somebody punched her in the back.

'Science!' pleaded Fergal. 'We did it in Science at school! You know? Avalanches?'

But the very word was foreign to them. 'Avalanche.' It had no meaning. It was not Scottish, not centuries old. It was not a word that had ever fallen from the lips of the

Storyteller. They must know, of course, how the mountain sometimes shivered, groaned and terrified them with its rumblings. Surely the upheaval overhead must have broken the tiles on the roof before and sprinkled them with snow. But clearly it had never brought them a boy before – or a lesson on avalanches.

'Dunna heed the beast. S'a demon,' said a man dressed all in black. He seemed to wield some kind of authority for the others cleared a path for him as he advanced on Fergal. ''Tis sent by the Devil to fill our minds with untruths. Mark me, 'twill tell us soon that dancing is lawful, also the making of music and the clapping of hands and the ringing of bells in merriment.'

'Course it is! It's just a bit noisy, that's all! It made that avalanche happen that fell on you.'

That word again. That mystical, meaningless word: *avalanche*.

Fergal appealed to Mariah. She seemed like a sensible girl. 'Nothing wrong with dancing, is there?'

Mariah took several steps backwards.

Now Fergal was not one for dancing. It was embarrassing. He never knew what to do with his arms and legs, and sometimes girls took it for an excuse to hold hands. His sisters danced a lot: it was embarrassing ... but not actually *wicked*. And he had to prove that. So, breaking the habit of a lifetime, Fergal pulled himself upright again and began to dance, lumbering about like a drunken bear. The only song he could call to mind was not the least bit churchy and, in his fright, he could not even remember the words.

To his huge relief – and aching embarrassment – Mariah took hold of one of his hands and joined in. He could see in her eyes the terrified surprise at her own daring. They danced idiotically, like frogs in a tumble-dryer, singing:

> *'It's time to dum-di-dum-dum,*
> *It's time to light the lights!*
> *It's time to get things started,*
> *Dah-di-da-di-da tonight.'*

Summer barked excitedly, unnerved. Her noise was huge in the big, hollow space of the church. What if the barking brought down a fresh avalanche?

But that was not what stopped the people dancing. They stopped because the man in black snatched the walking stick from the aged man and came at them. The stick's owner toppled over, and somehow that was Fergal's fault, too. A universal purple rage rose up like floodwater gushing into the church. It fetched everyone to their feet. It made them gasp and hop about. It made them raise their fists over their heads and wade towards the two young people cavorting in the gloom. They fell over the dog. They collided with each other. But they also congealed into a mob, with one thought and one thought only: Fergal was a disaster that must be averted before Heaven's rage came down on them again, as it had done centuries before.

'*S'a demon sent to tempt us with the forbidden things!*' wailed the man in black, slashing the air with the walking stick.

Fergal grabbed Mariah's hand again and fled. He fled towards the font and the church door which had not opened for 800 years: a door with fathoms of earth and snow behind it. He fled into a granite cul-de-sac with no way out. When Mariah made for a ladder rising towards the wooden loft, he followed her up it: there was nowhere else to go.

'I'm sorry,' gasped Fergal, but only to Mariah, not to the rabble pursuing him. It was rage against them, and the thought of his sisters and mother and father, that lent his bruised and shaking legs the strength to reach the ladder's top.

Once, sunlight had squeezed between the plank walls of the bell tower: now it was buried under hard-packed earth and all the two could make out in the darkness were two loopy bell ropes hanging down like dusty plaits. Their pursuers were already starting up the wooden ladder, shouting and shaking their fists. Though there was nowhere higher to climb to but the cobwebby ceiling, Mariah flung herself at one of the ropes, Fergal followed her example, and they climbed, jabbering with fright, like chimpanzees shinning up jungle greenery. The man in black struck at their legs and then at the wall beneath their disappeared legs, little pieces of wood breaking off the walking stick and flying about.

Now it just so happened that, high above them, the ancient bells had recently been laid bare by the latest avalanche. Earth, rocks, the pine cones and needles of generations of pine trees had been swept aside by the latest collapse of compacted snow. The bells had been left bulging out of the ground like giant, dirty helmets. Tugged on by the efforts of boy and girl to climb, the bells writhed now within the ruins of their rotten wooden bell turret, which fell to pieces around them. They writhed and they rolled – first with a dull clank and then, as they shook off soil, with a clanging splendour. The ropes were tugged out through the loft roof with such force that the lashing rope-tails tore a great hole through wood, earth and snow. Then the bells tumbled down the slopes of Fuachd Munro, noisy as twin fire engines racing to a fire in the valley.

It was a noise loud enough to shiver the snowcap off Everest. It was a noise alarming enough to make angels wake and jump overboard from their clouds in terror.

Everyone in the subterranean church held perfectly still as, second after second, the bells spilled their rusty ringing down the mountainside. Nobody breathed. Nobody moved. The man in black stood with the stump of the walking stick raised over his head. Fifty heads cocked sideways to listen for Judgement to awake and hurl its thunderbolts.

But the avalanche which had buried the car had rid Fuachd Munro of all the snow curtains, dead trees and loose earth that had built up over winter. No thunderous rumbling came; only a profound silence after the bouncing bells had come to rest in the River Fuachd.

'Sorry,' said Fergal. 'I didn't mean to break things. But I have to get out. And you have to come, too. All of you. You have to help me get them out. They'll die if you don't help. And that *would* be wicked.'

Like statues they still stood immobile, heads cocked, listening for punishment to fall on them from Heaven. Then their eyes flickered in the direction of the boy who had laid hands on the forbidden bells and broken every rule.

'Who?' said Mariah suddenly. 'Who is it in the coach?'

He looked across at her. It was more than just a question: he could read it in her face. But his thoughts were wading in treacle. Despair was getting the better of him. Already it was too late. It must be far too late. 'Mum. Dad. Zizzi . . .' Even as he answered, he knew they would not understand: 'Mum', 'Dad': those were twenty-first century words. Not known at all to ye olde, olde world. What he should have said . . .

'*Why* was the horn blown?' Mariah demanded. 'Was it to proclaim that *someone of rank and power comes this way*?'

It was a hint, a clue. Suddenly he saw the scene through her eyes, their eyes: not a Ford Fiesta but a medieval coach pulled by horses, a trumpeter blowing his horn: *Make way! Make way for . . .*'

'He's the king,' said Fergal. 'Didn't I say? My father is the King of Scotland!' It was a desperate lie – an absurd lie – a ridiculous lie. They would laugh at him. Then they would pitch him off the mountain. Wouldn't they?

'King Mum?'

'King Dad. My father is King Dad of Scotland. My mother – Mum – is the queen. Scotland needs them! You have to help! It's your duty as Scots!'

'But if he's dead, then ... are you no' the *new King of Scotland*?' Mariah blurted, lobbing down another reason for the mob not to kill them.

'No! Don't! I mean, I don't want to be king!' Because suddenly, into this hysterical whirlpool of lying had fallen the stone-cold word 'dead'. And it was no lie that his father might be ... Why could these people not just care that a family had been buried under snow, royalty or no royalty?

'Look ... Your rules are all "Don't". Don't you have any rules that say "Do"? *Do* help people? *Do* save people? *Do* lend your spade when someone needs it? *Do something!*'

The Storyteller under her blanket muttered something so muffled that no one could hear what it was, as they peered down from the bell-ringers' loft. Her head emerged, tortoise-beaked, from the blanket. 'Many a prince has wished his father dead, so that he might wear the crown the sooner.'

'No! I don't *want* to be king,' he burst out. 'I'd be a rubbish king! Kings don't cry! I just want my dad!'

It was so cold (what with the hole in the church roof and the new hole in the bell-ringers' loft) that Fergal's tears steamed as they rolled down the sides of his nose.

The man in black lowered his fist. He studied the damage he had done to the walking stick in his hand. He was not deaf to reason. He hoped people would never remember him as a man deaf to reason.

'This boy prizes his parents more than power. These are no the words of a demon,' he said, adding as an afterthought, 'in my feeble judgement.'

They pulled up the ladder into the loft and, from there, Fergal climbed towards the hole ripped in the ceiling by the ropes. It was large enough for him to reach both arms upwards and push at a knot of tree roots blocking his escape. Nothing fell in his face but sunlight. He ripped and tore at the snaking roots then used them to haul himself up through the gap he had made. Then he turned and pulled Mariah through as well.

And so for the very first time in 800 years, the villagers of Fuachd Munro wormed their way out of their buried home and into the forbidden daylight. Fergal led the way, and Mariah followed. It was from the hole in the church roof that she shouted down commands to the strongest men, to haul up Summer aboard the chandelier, and it was Mariah who set the dog back on all four paws on the mountainside.

The rest emerged unwillingly, in fear and trembling. After candlelight, the glare was like the open door of a furnace, and twice as fearful. Their eyelids closed over their pale eyes. So they crawled, half-blind, out of the earth, like moles in spring. Then, pulling themselves to their feet, they staggered uphill towards the road. The sunlight was an agonizing pain, and they did not *want* to see the terrible crime they were committing – escaping the imprisonment they had been sentenced to by the angels all those years ago. They could not help seeing that the Outside World had no walls – no safe, comforting, cradling walls holding them tight. The Outside World was open as far as the eye could see. They felt as if they might float off into the sky and never be found. And serve them right. Or did it?

They dug in silence, so anxious that they barely gave a thought to those trapped beneath the snow. Anyway, a carriage – even a king's carriage – was hardly likely to have saved the lives of the king, queen and two royal princesses (what with its open windows and fragile, gilded wood). So, as they dug – with slates and planks of wood ripped from the church roof – they thought instead about the waste.

What if it was true? That dancing and singing and bell-ringing were *not* to blame all those centuries ago; that Fuachd Munro had been buried by nature and not by angels weeping tears of blood? The waste! Many had had their doubts about those angel tears in the box, but had never dared speak out. They looked around them now at the way this latest thundering had smeared chaos down the mountainside … but saw that further off, lower down, the slopes were still blossoming into spring.

It was a sight of surpassing beauty – enough to make them stop their digging and shield their eyes against the fearful snow-brightness. At the bottom of the mountainside, the fallen bells had smashed the ice on the frozen river, and the sun-warmed water had swept the broken pieces aside. Inside their chests, the villagers felt something similar happening to their hearts. It was alarming.

What if the ancestors *had* been mistaken 800 years before? The waste! What if every generation since then had spent their entire lives needlessly paying for the sins of their dancing, singing, cheerful ancestors? The waste! What if, even now, their own horrible, underground existence was some terrible mistake? The cold. The dark. The waste! *No*, they told themselves: it could not be true. The story they had heard so often must be right. The boy was wrong!

But with the sun on their backs, the cold hearts within them refused to refreeze.

So taken up were they with such thoughts that it startled them when their digging struck metal, and the Ford Fiesta appeared. It did not *look* much like a royal coach. And there was no sign anywhere of the golden horn that had blown three times to announce the coming of a king. They knelt down (hands and hair as pale as the snow) and paid homage to King Dad of Scotland. When he did not stir from the steering wheel, they wrapped him, the queen and the two royal princesses in blankets from the boot, carried them to a green drift of pine needles. The dog Summer lay down beside the two girls, her warm bulk squeezed between them. All this Fergal witnessed like a film playing out in front of him, as he watched from a distance, standing stock still, too afraid to go closer and find out the truth.

'D'you no wish to be king? Truly?' asked Mariah, emptying snow out of her moccasins.

'No! Really! Truly! Not ever!'

She looked at him, disappointed, as if she might have married a prince if only he had had grander ambitions.

'... Anyway, it was *you* who started in with that "person of great importance" business,' he reminded her. 'I just went along with it. He's just my dad. My father. *You* should be Storyteller here, when the old one goes. You'd make up some great stories. Cheerful ones. Ones no one's going to be fool enough to believe.'

Mariah considered this, smiled and wandered off murmuring softly to herself:

'... *It's time to light the lights.*
It's time to get things started ...'

A truck came throbbing up the mountain road – a terrifying sight to people from a different age. They simply ran away – towards their burrow, their subterranean world. Lifting their knees high to negotiate the snow, they looked almost as if they were dancing.

'*I'll tell him you helped!*' Fergal called after them, full of frantic, belated gratitude at what they had done, for his sake. '*I'll tell the king you are good, loyal Scots!*' It was the thing, he thought, that would please them most. In future, let the Storyteller recount the Legend of the Rescue by the people of Fuachd Munro of . . . But Fergal's heart stopped short of completing the sentence.

The public-works truck, come to clear the landslip, pulled up at the sight of a half-buried car, its four doors open, its roof slightly crushed. Fergal led them to the row of blankets. When they looked around for signs of local rescuers, they saw no one.

'You got them out, lad? On your own?' All three men were already jabbing at their mobile phones. And Fergal was too tired to explain. Too tired. Too cold. Too afraid.

'Are they dead?' was all he wanted to know.

They were not.

Perhaps he had spent less time than it seemed inside the mountain. It had felt like centuries, but perhaps time passed differently here on Fuachd Munro where the biting easterly wind could turn beating raindrops into slow-floating snowflakes. Perhaps the wind had frozen the passing minutes, too, into seconds.

'You so are. You so are the King of Scotland,' Fergal informed his father, in the ambulance on the way to the hospital. Afterwards, Dad did not remember, and Fergal did not say it twice.

Perhaps he doubted what had happened on the mountain, thinking the snow had blown in at his eyes and clogged up his brain. Perhaps he thought people would call him a liar or a fool if he spoke of an underworld. Or perhaps it was just unbearable: to think of anybody living underground – without music or clapping or dancing or sunlight; so unbearable that he wanted none of it to have happened. From the avalanche eight centuries before, to the avalanche now blocking the road over Fuachd Munro, he wished it all the stuff of Legend.

Beneath his feet, Mariah, direct descendant of Mary of the Grange, studied the charcoal drawing on the church wall. Inside her, the legend crumbled like a stick of charcoal. Her toes tapped the shiny brass of an ancient memorial set into the floor. *Everyone makes mistakes*, she thought. *The great thing is to put the mistake right.* The men were already seeking out nails and wood to mend the holes in the roof and belltower. But somehow or other, Mariah would find a way to let the sunlight stream into the heart of Fuachd Munro.

Casse-Noisette
KATHERINE WOODFINE

Stana gazed out of the window at the softly falling snow. It was only two weeks until Christmas, and it had been snowing all day long: now the blue-and-green tiled roofs and gold domes of St Petersburg looked as though they had been spread with a thick white counterpane. Stana balanced on her toes, watching the snowflakes twirling. She watched the sleighs flying by on the street outside, jingling their bells, and the brightly lit windows that twinkled across the square. She thought to herself: *If it keeps on snowing, the ballet will go perfectly. If the ballet goes perfectly, if I dance every step just right, then Olga will get well.*

She had been making these promises to herself for weeks. If she did exactly 100 pliés; if she did not step on a single crack as they walked around the frozen garden, two by two; if she got out of bed at the very stroke of the rising bell, then Olga would get well again. At prayers each morning, she stared very hard at the icon beneath which a tiny lamp gleamed out like a red star, and repeated her promises to herself in her head, as if she was casting a spell. *If I do all these things, then Olga will get better. She must.*

'Come away from the window, Stana,' scolded Mademoiselle. 'The director will be furious if you catch cold! You are supposed to be resting before the performance!'

Stana turned away from the window. After two years at the Imperial Ballet School, she knew better than to disobey the governess, but just the same, she knew that it would be difficult to rest. It was impossible to sit still when your insides were dancing a tarantella. How could she rest when she knew that in little more than an hour, she would be up on the stage of the great Marinsky Theatre, with every important critic in St Petersburg watching her – not to mention the Tsar himself?

She had been in a fever of excitement when she had first been given the role of Clara, the young girl in the Marinsky's new ballet, *The Nutcracker.* Everyone at school had been talking about it, and all the girls in Stana's class had longed to be the lucky one chosen. It was certainly a rare and special role. Students at the ballet school did sometimes play tiny parts in the ballets at the Marinsky – Stana herself had been one of the crowd in *Coppelia*, and one of the six pages of the Lilac Fairy in *The Sleeping Beauty* – but for a pupil to play a leading role was unheard of.

'They're looking for a girl of twelve years old to play the

part of Clara – that's the same age as us!' her best friend Anna had whispered to her in the dormitory. Somehow, Anna always managed to find out everything first. 'And a boy to play her brother, Fritz. Everyone is saying that will be Vassily, of course. But there will be many other children's parts besides. They say they will need forty pupils to dance!'

'Forty pupils!' scoffed Lydia, the maid, as she combed out Stana's hair in sharp, swift strokes. 'It'll be a circus!'

Lydia was not the only one who was sceptical. 'I only hope the director knows what he is doing!' Stana heard the ballet mistress say to Mademoiselle, as the girls filed into the practice room and lined up along the barre. 'So many children on the stage! Who can imagine what the critics will make of it?'

'But this is Mr Pepita and Mr Tchaikovsky,' argued Mademoiselle primly. 'They are masters of the art! With the two of them in charge, how could it possibly fail?'

The ballet mistress shrugged and sighed. 'That's what you might think. But I've heard that Pepita is unwell – he's an old man now.' She lowered her voice to a confidential whisper. 'And you know they say that Tchaikovsky has not been the same since his sister died.'

But Mademoiselle would not be persuaded. 'Just look at the triumph of *The Sleeping Beauty*!' she protested. 'Whatever you may say, I'm sure this new ballet will be just as delightful.'

Most people agreed with Mademoiselle, of course.

181

The Sleeping Beauty had been a marvellous success; and now there would be another new ballet for the Marinsky Theatre based on a children's story. This time it would be a Christmas tale; the Marinsky's first ballet master, the great Pepita, would be responsible for the choreography; and Mr Tchaikovsky would compose a new score. The ballet was to be called *The Nutcracker*, although Stana liked the title better in French. In Russian, *The Nutcracker* sounded spiky and hard; in French, the words *Le Casse-Noisette* were as soft as snowflakes, sweet as a Christmas sugarplum melting on her tongue.

The words tinkled, like the notes of Mr Tchaikovsky's music. When Stana had first heard that music, she had known that she wanted to play Clara. The glistening notes of the piano had swept her far away from the Imperial Ballet School on Theatre Street: away from grey holland practice dresses and bread-and-butter breakfasts; away from lessons and walks around the garden two by two; away from lying awake in the dormitory at night, whispering with Anna about Olga or worrying about how Mama would be able to pay the doctor's bills.

Now she was stepping through a pine forest, glittering with frost in the moonlight, her footsteps crunching in the snow. She was gliding through St Petersburg's most elegant ballroom, twirling in a silk dress, her skirts spinning out as she danced beneath the twinkling chandeliers. Then she felt the warmth of the fire against her face, and smelled the scent of home; she saw the candles on the Christmas tree, decorated with Mama's homemade gingerbread angels; and she was kneeling on the rug with Olga, drinking tea with jam.

It was really because of the music that she had won the part at all. One day, word had flown around the school: Pepita himself was coming to watch them dance, and to choose who would play Clara. The girls were in a great flurry, rushing to the looking glass to check their hair was smoothly combed and that the ribbons of their shoes were tied just right, but Stana was distracted. A letter had come from Mama that morning: Olga was worse; they had taken her to the hospital.

'Whatever is the matter with you?' hissed Anna, as they took their places in the practice room, but there was no time to answer. Pepita had arrived.

It was strange to see the first ballet master here in the ordinary surroundings of the practice room, with its familiar stale smell of resin; the dust motes rising up and gleaming in the sunlight that striped the caramel-coloured wooden floor. As they each swept their most reverent curtsey, Pepita strutted before them, looking them carefully up and down in turn. He was an old man now, but his eyes were sharp, and he was still as dapper as ever in his smartly cut suit. Everyone called him 'Maître' and he called out his instructions to them in French: even though he had lived in St Petersburg for years now, he had always refused to learn Russian.

Following a little way behind him was the second ballet master, Mr Ivanov. He was a little younger than Pepita and a little less definite. He had an eyeglass and an elegantly twirled moustache: people called him Pepita's shadow.

To her surprise, Stana saw that with them, seating himself at the piano, was the composer, Mr Tchaikovsky. Pepita and Ivanov were familiar enough figures for the ballet students, but Mr Tchaikovsky was far less so. She knew about him, of course: he was one of the most famous composers in all Russia; he had been awarded medals by the Tsar; and he had travelled all the way to far-distant America to share his wonderful music. But here in the school practice room, sitting behind the piano, he looked surprisingly ordinary – just another old man with white hair and a tired face.

'Now, mademoiselles, let us begin!' announced Maître.

Excited and eager to prove themselves, the girls began to dance. They had been carefully drilled by the ballet mistress; their technique was faultless; their footwork was perfect – yet Pepita did not seem satisfied.

'You must *feel* the music,' he told them, looking from one to the other keenly. 'Do you not see the pictures that Mr Tchaikovsky has painted for you?' Suddenly, he pointed to Stana. 'You – little girl. Tell me what you think of when you dance to this music. What pictures do you see?'

Stana flushed scarlet. She felt tongue-tied; the other girls were staring at her; but she knew that this was her big chance. She thought of Tchaikovsky's music again, and she was able to give Maître an answer – a snowy pine forest, a grand, gilded ballroom, the warm fire and the Christmas tree, her sister safe at home.

After she had finished, there was a moment of echoing silence, then Maître nodded. '*Bon!*' he said approvingly. '*Très bon, mademoiselle.* You must all use your imaginations like this when you dance, *oui?*'

He waved a hand to Tchaikovsky at the piano, and they all began to dance again, Stana feeling at once lighter and more purposeful than she had before.

She knew that she must have danced well, because Anna would hardly speak to her after they had finished, and flounced out of the room without waiting for her. Anna always wanted to be the best at everything, and she could not bear anyone else to be the centre of attention – not even her best friend. Anna liked to be the star, and there was no doubt that she danced very gracefully, although the truth was she was not really the ideal build for a dancer, being small and slight. Nina and some of the other girls in their class made fun of her for it, calling her 'Anna the broom' because she was so skinny, and laughing at her when she could not achieve the proper 'turned out' position that was expected of all dancers. But Anna held her head high and ignored them. She worked hard, and even dosed herself with disgusting cod-liver oil to try and make herself stronger. Stana knew no one who was more fiercely determined to dance.

In that way, Anna often reminded her of Olga. Olga might be three years younger than Stana, but she had always been intent on keeping pace with her big sister. She wanted to do whatever Stana did: to walk as far, to jump as high, to read the same books, to play the same pieces on Mama's old piano, even if she did have to sit on two extra cushions so that she could reach the keys. And just like Anna, she was fierce as a tiger, flaring out into a fiery temper when she could not keep up. She had long been impatient to come to study at the Imperial Ballet School, like Stana. That had been before she was ill, of course. Students at the Imperial School were always expected to be in the most perfect health. Stana knew that there would be no ballet for Olga now.

That thought had only just crossed Stana's mind when she realized, rather to her astonishment, that Mr Tchaikovsky himself was standing before her, a sheaf of sheet music tucked under his arm. For a moment she felt alarmed by his sudden appearance. Was he going to criticize her – or scold? But when he spoke, his voice was hushed, unexpectedly gentle:

'You answered Pepita's question well,' he said. 'Tell me, are you fond of music?'

She stared up at him, too surprised to know quite how to answer. 'Very,' she said at last.

'You said the music made you think of Christmas and that you imagined your little sister safe at home,' he went on. 'Where is your sister now?'

'She is in the hospital. She is very ill,' Stana managed to reply.

He contemplated her for a moment. His eyes were large and sad, his expression quizzical, rather like an owl's. 'I am sorry to hear that,' he said, then he bowed and turned away, following Pepita and Ivanov out of the room.

No one said any more to her about *The Nutcracker* that day, but a week later, Stana was told that she had been given the part of Clara. The other girls made a tremendous fuss about how envious they were. They talked of her costume – a frilly white frock with a blue ribbon sash. 'And just think – you'll be able to wear your hair *curled*,' sighed Nina, who loathed the way they had to wear their hair at school, parted in the middle and combed tightly back. They chattered about how Stana would now be excused from dull mathematics lessons and dancing practice for rehearsals in the glorious surroundings of the Marinsky Theatre. She would get to know all the star dancers – like the beautiful Italian ballerina, Antoinetta Dell'Era, who would be dancing the part of the Sugar Plum Fairy. 'And you'll get to dance with Vassily!' exclaimed Nina. Anna stood a little to one side, her arms folded, saying nothing at all.

But Stana did not care so very much about her costume or her hair, or even Antoinetta Dell'Era. It was the music that filled her with delight – the music and the wonderful story of Clara, who is given a Nutcracker doll by her godfather,

Drosselmeyer, on Christmas Eve. After night falls, the doll comes to life, and whisks her away on a magical adventure. When Stana played Clara, dancing to Tchaikovsky's music, she became someone else – the heroine of a marvellous fairy tale. Her worries about Olga; Anna's sour face; it all faded away.

Instead, she found herself inhabiting a world of dancing sweets and flower-fairies. Spending day after day at the theatre, she looked on, entranced, as the spectacle came to life. She stood in the wings and watched as the men constructed the great Christmas tree, hung all over with stars and coloured candles. She saw them build the magical Kingdom of Sweets – a masterpiece of glittering electric light and gold paint and real working fountains. She saw them painting scenery with pine trees and snow for her favourite sequence of all – the Waltz of the Snowflakes, in which almost sixty ballet dancers would perform in snow-white tutus, decorated all over with tiny white pompoms. Dancing together under the soft shimmer of the lights, they looked like a snowstorm that had come to life. As Stana watched them from the side of the stage, it was not in the least difficult for her to conjure up Clara's sense of enchantment – and delight.

But rehearsals for *The Nutcracker* were not always easy. The days in the theatre were long and tiring. Pepita was ill, and after the first few rehearsals, the second ballet master had to take his place. Ivanov was so much more uncertain, always worrying about this dance or that one, changing a step here or a step there until Stana felt she did not know where she was to go or what she was to do.

She felt very small among the company of grown-up dancers, and often, she wished that Anna was there with her. Before, they had always done everything together: they walked together in the garden, in their matching coats with the fox-fur collars; they practised together at the barre; even their beds were side by side in the dormitory. Now she was by herself, and even back at school, Anna was giving her the cold shoulder. She would not walk with Stana in the garden; she no longer whispered to her after lights-out, but instead closed her eyes in offended silence. Stana lay awake in the dark, cold and alone.

It was Mr Tchaikovsky, at the piano, who was a reassuring constant. Day after day, wonderful music flowed from his fingers. He was far too busy to speak to Stana, but she liked to know he was there. Sometimes, he would nod to her from behind the piano, or give her a little bow; and once or twice he paused, as he hurried past in the echoing maze of passages, backstage at the Marinsky, to ask: 'And how is your little sister? Is she getting well?'

Stana would curtsey and say: 'She is still in the hospital, sir.' She found it difficult to say any more, even to the great composer himself. She hated even thinking of Olga, as she had seen her when she had gone to visit, so small in the little hospital bed. Her skin looked pale and waxy, like a doll's; she could not even smile. All of the fire seemed to have burned out of her; she was a stranger, someone else's sister. Mama had told Stana that she should not come to the hospital again, 'for fear of spreading infection', she said, but Stana knew that truthfully, Mama did not want her to know how sick Olga really was. Instead, Mama sent letters, full of happiness about Stana's success in *The Nutcracker*, though behind her soft words, Stana could see the truth as clearly as if it had been spelled out in plain black ink. Her sister was sicker than ever; hospital bills were terribly expensive; Olga needed good food and medicine that they could ill afford.

And there was nothing for Stana to do except dance. She practised harder than ever, grimly determined that she would be a success. There was a sort of logic to it at first: after all, if she was to be noticed as Clara, it was sure to help her dancing career. It would not be many years now before she could leave school and join the company, and then she would be a real dancer, earning money to help take care of Mama and Olga. But soon it became simpler, a vow she made to herself. She whispered promises in her head. *If I dance the first scene quite perfectly in the morning rehearsal, then Olga will be a little better. If Ivanov praises my dance with the Nutcracker doll tomorrow, that means that Olga will begin to get well.*

Before long, Olga and *The Nutcracker* had become tangled – twisted together like the satin ribbons on Stana's ballet shoes. Dancing as Clara was no longer an escape: it was a bargain, a promise, a trial like those that princes must perform in the fairy stories Mama used to read them at bedtime. The relentless rhythm of the piano twined with the drum of the dancers' feet on the boards of the stage. Stana worked hard, and then harder still. Her bones ached, and each night, she dreamed of dancing. She was more and more convinced that if she could only dance well, then Olga would be certain to get well, too – and they would all be able to have a happy Christmas.

Now, waiting for the curtain to rise on the first performance, Stana felt drawn tight, quivering like a violin string. Backstage at the Marinsky smelled of excitement, rouge and powder, the faintly metallic scent of silver tinsel: and around her, the other pupils were laughing and chattering, thrilled to be staying up so long after their usual bedtime, and to have the chance to dance on the great stage, where so many famous dancers had gone before them. Vassily, who played the role of Fritz, was noisy with pride; Nina and some of the other girls from her class were comparing their glittering fairy dresses in delight; a group of the children playing soldiers in the army of the Mouse King were shouting and waving their swords. Mademoiselle was ticking them off, telling them that they did not know the proper way to behave in a theatre. Stana envied them. She wished she could be loud and excited: instead, she felt only frightened and as cold as the snow that was falling outside.

191

More than ever, she wished that Anna was here. She knew that Anna would never sit by herself, her stomach twisting itself into complicated knots. Anna would have been quite certain that she would dance well. But Anna had not been chosen to dance in *The Nutcracker*, and that had made things worse than ever. She still would not speak to Stana at all, and Stana missed her with an ache like the bitter December air against her face.

Anna's strength made Stana strong, too; her fierceness made Stana feel cool and poised. Without her, Stana felt as though the edges of herself were being rubbed away. But most of all, Stana knew that Anna understood her. Unlike Nina with her expensive hats and pretty, lace-trimmed frocks, Anna was not well off. She had no papa, and her mama was only a washerwoman – not that she ever seemed to be ashamed of it. Stana knew that Anna could understand how she felt about Olga, and her worries over the hospital bills. But knowing that made Anna's aggrieved silence seem cruel. She already dreaded losing Olga – it felt as though she was losing Anna, too.

Almost, she wished that she had never been chosen for the role of Clara, and that she and Anna were both getting ready to perform quite ordinary roles in the ballet – dancing as dolls or flower-fairies, or sugar candies, like Nina and the rest. Almost, she wished that she had never heard the enchanted words *Le Casse-Noisette*, nor heard Tchaikovsky's haunting melodies. Almost, she wished that she could wave the Sugar Plum Fairy's glittering wand and magic herself far away from the Marinsky Theatre – and back home, sitting with Olga on the rug in front of the fire, toasting their cheeks and drinking tea with jam.

Almost, but not quite. She could hear the stirrings of the overture: the shimmering of the strings, the bright piping of the flutes rising above them, and all at once, her feet longed to dance.

'It's time to go,' said Mademoiselle.

Waiting in the wings beside Vassily, ready for their cue, Stana lost herself in the rise and fall of the music. Beyond the stage, she could see the haze of the footlights, and then little glimpses of the audience – elegant ladies in furs and jewels, smart gentlemen in uniforms, the gleam of chandeliers and brilliant gilding, and above them all, the Tsar himself in the grandly draped Imperial box. But as the music swelled, it seemed to lift her up, as though she was being carried on magic wings. She swept away, high above the gilt and velvet of the theatre, above the Imperial Ballet School on Theatre Street, above the frozen garden and Olga's hospital bed. She soared above snow-dusted trees, above churches and palaces, fountains and canals. She saw the golden spires and coloured rooftops of St Petersburg; she saw the twisting shape of the ice-blue river, running out to the sea; she saw mountains and pine forests, glittering with snow. And then she ran out onto the stage, into the bright glare of the lights. It was time to dance.

*

It was not until after midnight that the ballet finally drew to a close. As she took her curtain calls, she heard the clamour of the audience's applause, but all she could think was, *Have I done it?* Had she danced all right? Had her ankle trembled in that arabesque? Had she missed a step? Had she done enough to make Olga well again? Would it be a happy Christmas for them after all?

Backstage, the grown-up dancers were clapping each other on the back and shaking Ivanov by the hand; they would all go out to dinner at St Petersburg's finest restaurant to celebrate, but Stana and the other ballet school pupils must return to school, and go to bed. Mademoiselle's hand was already on her shoulder, though for a moment Stana lingered, frozen by the excitement of it all. Tchaikovsky hurried by, as usual clutching a sheaf of sheet music scribbled all over in his spiky black handwriting. Among the tumult, he alone paused to give her a quick nod and a smile. At least he thought she had done well, Stana realized, with relief.

'Come along now – it is long past your bedtime,' Mademoiselle was saying as she hurried her to the dressing room to change, and then into the carriage and back to school.

But once she was in the dormitory, Stana found she could not sleep. She lay awake, staring into the dark, hearing the soft, rustling breaths of the other girls sleeping around her. The notes of Tchaikovsky's music were still racing around in her head. She heard the clock downstairs strike two, before at last she fell into a restless sleep – and when she slept, she began to dream.

She found herself back in the Marinsky Theatre in her Clara costume. Now the audience had gone, and the Imperial box was empty. The ladies in their furs and jewels, the gentlemen in their uniforms – they had all quite vanished. Instead, the theatre looked just as it had during rehearsals: the gallery was dark and empty, the formerly bright chandeliers shrouded, and brown covers were spread over the plush of the seats.

Then the music began – and Stana danced. She twirled and leaped with a springy lightness she had never experienced before; she felt she could dance forever. Her frothy white skirts flew out, as she soared across the stage. This time Anna was there too, wearing the glittering costume of the Sugar Plum Fairy, dancing more beautifully than Stana had ever seen her. Ivanov performed the role of the Nutcracker Prince; and Mr Tchaikovsky was Drosselmeyer, his owl-face looking down at her from up in the clock.

She danced to the tune of the Waltz of the Flowers, but all at once the music seemed to fracture, like ice shattering. The clock was striking again. *Time is running out*, she heard Drosselmeyer say, and somehow she knew that he was talking about Olga. All at once, she knew she had to find her little sister; that she was here, somewhere, among the dancers. But Stana could not find her. She was not among the gingerbread soldiers, nor the rowdy army of mice-children.

The Mouse King tried to bar her way, but just as in the ballet, she hurled her satin shoe at him and he turned tail and vanished. Still she could not find Olga: she was not in the Palace of Sweets, nor among the dancers of chocolate and coffee and tea. She was not among the bonbons or the sugar candies, the hummingbirds or the flower-fairies.

At last, Stana thought she caught a glimpse of her, dancing with the snowflakes, wearing a white tutu and a crown decorated with white snowballs. She ran towards her, but even as she did so, the snowflakes seemed to whirl and blur before her eyes. At last, she stretched out her arms towards her sister, but her hands closed on nothing but air, as Olga fell away – not a dancer at all, but snowflakes, just the merest shape of a girl made of snow.

Stana woke up shivering and calling her sister's name, her heart pounding and the bedclothes tossed all about her like a stormy sea.

'What's the matter with you?' whispered Anna grumpily from the next bed.

'I had a nightmare,' Stana whispered, her heart beginning to slow as she realized she was back at school, in the darkness of the dormitory.

'There's no need to start getting so dramatic, just because you played the part of Clara,' said Anna sniffily. But she sounded more like her usual self as she rolled over and said: 'Shut up, Stana, for goodness' sake, and let me go back to sleep.'

*

Stana slept dreamlessly after that, and was still sound asleep when the rising bell rang, jolting her suddenly awake. The first performance was over, and it was another day just like any other: the bell tolling solemnly at eight o'clock, washing under the cold tap, dressing in their practice dresses and blue fringed shawls, having their hair combed by the maids.

'Stana had a nightmare last night,' Anna reported to Lydia, who was known to be something of an expert on dreams, being the possessor of a dog-eared dream-book.

'What was it about? Did you see a man in black? Were you running down a staircase?' asked Lydia.

But already, the dream was fading. 'No . . . I don't remember anything like that. I just remember that it was snowing . . .' said Stana uncertainly.

'Well, bad dreams do sometimes mean a change in the weather,' said Lydia with a shrug, as she pulled the comb through Stana's hair, making the Clara curls disappear.

'Hurry along now, girls, don't chatter,' scolded Mademoiselle, who was waiting by the door to check their teeth and hands and nails before she let them downstairs.

In every way, the morning was ordinary: the same stale smell of resin in the practice room, the jangle of the piano, the echo of footsteps on the stairs, the tap of the ballet mistress's cane hitting the floor, beating out the rhythm as they practised the same string of pliés and battements. It was as if the ballet itself had been only a dream, melting away to nothing at the sound of the rising bell. But by lunchtime, the first reviews of *The Nutcracker* had been published, and all at once everyone was talking about them:

'The *St Petersburg Gazette* said it was "tedious",' reported Nina, her eyes round. 'Nothing to compare to *The Sleeping Beauty*!'

'They said that Ivanov just copied Pepita's other ballets,' sniffed another girl.

'They said that Antoinetta wasn't a bit like any kind of a fairy,' added Anna. 'They said she was "podgy"!'

'But she got five curtain calls!' argued someone else.

Stana put down her fork. She felt sick and she could scarcely touch her lunch. The ballet had not been a success; and as the day drew on, the news grew worse and worse. Some critics said the ballet was confusing, others that it was all spectacle and no substance. Some said it was not even a proper ballet. Even Tchaikovsky's beautiful music was criticized. Ivanov was said to be inconsolable; Antoinetta to be in floods of tears.

Stana herself was not left out. '"The dance of student Stanislava Belinskaya with the injured nutcracker is quite unsuccessful both in composition and in execution,"' Nina read aloud from the newspaper.

'That's not fair,' said Anna indignantly. 'You danced it well!' Whether it was her nightmare or the bad reviews, Stana was not quite sure: but somehow in all this, Anna had forgiven her.

As for the ballet mistress, she just shrugged and shook

her head. 'I knew all those children on stage would never work,' she said.

'I suppose not every ballet can be a great success,' sighed Mademoiselle, sounding disappointed. 'Not even at the Marinsky.'

The fairy tale was over now; the sugarplum tasted bitter, not sweet. Stana's magic chance to shine had melted away. She felt dazed: she had danced as well as she knew how, and yet somehow it still had not been enough.

That afternoon, a letter arrived from Mama, and Stana ran up to the dormitory to open it. Anna followed behind her, not caring in the least that it was against the rules. Sitting on her bed, Stana tore open the envelope and shook out the note inside with trembling hands. It was only short – Mama wrote that she was sorry she had missed her performance, and that she was sure that Stana had danced beautifully. She could not leave Olga's bedside, but there was good news. Her sister had taken a turn for the better. There were still the bills to pay, of course, but the doctors said that with careful treatment, Olga would get well.

Stana stared at the words, a lump rising in her throat, and she seemed to hear the final triumphant chords and drumbeats of Tchaikovsky's music. *The Nutcracker* had failed; but it did not matter. They would have a happy Christmas after all.

'What does it say?' asked Anna, dropping down beside her on the bed.

'She says that Olga is getting better,' said Stana, trying to keep her voice from wobbling.

Nina, who was nosy, had run up behind them to see what the fuss was about. Now she pointed to something small, shining on Stana's pillow. 'Look – what's that? Someone has left you a Christmas present!'

Stana put out a hand in surprise, and picked up a little note, folded and tied with a red and gold ribbon like a Christmas bonbon. To her surprise, she saw that in black, spiky handwriting, the label read, *For Clara.*

'What can it be?' asked Anna, leaning forward, eager and curious.

'A note from an admirer!' suggested Nina excitedly. 'Maybe it's from Vassily!' she added with a giggle.

Stana unwrapped the crackling paper very slowly. Inside was a note, scribbled on a small slip of music manuscript paper. It was just four words, in the same spiky writing. *To help your sister.* Beside it was a hundred-rouble note.

'A hundred roubles!' exclaimed Anna, her eyes wide.

'What a Christmas present!' gasped Nina.

'But – who is it from? What does it mean?'

Stana's fingers traced the black, spidery writing. She thought she knew who it had come from – and exactly what it meant.

As the other two bent their heads over the note, speculating eagerly, she gazed out of the dormitory window. She could see the distant lights of Christmas trees in the houses across Theatre Street, and she realized that she would soon be sitting beside her own with Mama and with Olga, eating gingerbread angels, and drinking tea with jam. Fat, feathery snowflakes twirled and pirouetted past the window, and there came a faint jingling of bells outside – as light and dainty as the dance of the Sugar Plum Fairy – as the sleighs raced by, through the softly falling snow.

AUTHOR'S NOTE

While this story is fictional, it is based on the real history of Tchaikovsky's famous ballet, *The Nutcracker*, which was first performed at the Marinsky Theatre in St Petersburg in December 1892. Just as in this story, the ballet was not at first a success, receiving mixed reviews from critics. Now, of course, it is one of the best-known and best-loved ballets of all time, and is performed all over the world each year at Christmas.

Twelve-year-old Stanislava Belinskaya, a student at the Imperial Ballet School, really was the first person to play the famous role of Clara in this very first production. The real-life Stanislava also really did have a friend and classmate called Anna: if you know about the history of ballet, you might be able to guess what happened to Anna when she grew up ...

That first production of *The Nutcracker* had an open ending, leaving the audience wondering what would happen to Clara and the Nutcracker Prince. In later versions of the ballet, and in most productions you will see today, the ballet finishes with Clara waking up in her bedroom, and realizing that her wonderful adventures with the Nutcracker were only a dream after all.

Someone Like the
Snow Queen
BERLIE DOHERTY

I love the story of the Snow Queen more than anything. My dad used to read it to me when I was little. I used to curl up inside the curve of his arm, warm against the frostiness of the story. He would say things like 'Can you hear the snow whispering, Orla? Can you hear the ice?' We would listen for a moment to silence, and imagine the streaking snow and hear the creak of ice in it.

'Would you like to meet the Snow Queen?' Dad asked me.

I nodded and shivered. 'Maybe.'

'Maybe you will, one day.'

Dad died last year, and nothing has been the same since. Nothing.

I was always sure that the Snow Queen was a real person, and that I really would meet her one day. I would know her as soon as I saw her. She would be irresistibly beautiful. I imagined she would be tall, with long white hair and eyes as cold as ice. She would try to steal me just as she stole Kay in the story, but I would never go with her. I used to daydream the strange adventure that Kay's friend Gerda had when she was searching for him, the people she met on her journey: the Robber Girl and the old woman in the igloo, the crow and the reindeer, and there was a part of me that longed for the magic and mystery of it all.

The house was so quiet after Dad died. So cold and unfriendly.

But one Sunday in early December everything began to change. That was the day the magic and mystery started.

For once Mum was home. This was unusual. Usually, she was out, working, walking, doing things, anything not to be in the house that didn't have Dad in it any more. She left me to look after my little brother. I kept telling her it was against the law, I was only thirteen, but I don't think she cared. During the week I had to take Flynn to the Infants and collect him again on my way home. I was supposed to stay with him until she got back from work. I didn't, though. *Why should I?* I thought. I hated being in the house too. I hated that waiting, awful silence. And Flynn was always too tired by that time to go trailing round with me. Mum said that he mustn't be left in the house on his own, so I used to leave him standing at the front door, and I carried on walking round the block and through the shopping precinct with my friends, until they'd all dropped off at their houses, and then I would go home and let him in. If it was raining, he waited in the shed. He moaned at me for that, but he was all right. He couldn't come to any harm there.

But that Sunday, we were all home. It was one of those yellow days when the sky moves from dark to lightish to dark again without any real change of colour. We were almost a family that day. Mum was cooking in the kitchen. I was watching a film on my tablet. I had my earphones on because Flynn was making so much noise, scrabbling in his Lego box and talking to himself. At least he wasn't begging me to 'play' with him as he usually does. He never gives me any peace. So I was lost in my film when a sudden rapid sort of cackling sound made me look up. The room turned icy. Flynn stopped and looked up sharply, too, his face suddenly alert. I lowered my tablet and took out one of the earphones.

'What was that?' I whispered.

'No idea.' He bent down again to his building.

I stood up and went to the window. Maybe I hadn't heard anything, not really. How could I have done, over the noise of the film? But I had felt something, for sure. I'd felt such a coldness, a stillness. And so had Flynn. I knew he had. It was as if someone had passed by our house and cast a shiver over it. Gran used to say, 'Someone just walked over my grave.' She would shudder and pull her knitted cardigan tighter round her bony shoulders.

I went and opened the front door and peered down the

street. It was empty. No people, no cars, not even a cat on its loping prowl.

'Shut that door!' Mum yelled from the kitchen.

'I think it's going to snow,' I said. I love snow. It always brings a kind of magic with it.

'I hope not. There's no snow forecast anyway. Shut the door now. I work my fingers to the bone keeping this house heated, and you go and squander it in thirty seconds.'

'I wish you wouldn't,' I said, half to myself, but Mum heard me and came into the hall with a clutch of cutlery in her hand.

'Wouldn't what?'

'Work all the time,' I muttered.

'Oh, Orla. I have to. You know I do.'

I closed the door and went back to my film, but I couldn't settle. I was tense and uneasy. Flynn listlessly shovelled his Lego bits into their box and started to play with his Minecraft pieces. But he wasn't mumbling to himself and whooping and sighing any more. He was completely silent. After a bit, he stood up and gazed out of the window at the darkening street, as if he was listening and watching for something.

'What's going on?' I asked him, uneasy again.

'Nothing. Leave me alone!'

Mum came in and closed the curtains. 'Stop bickering, you two,' she said. 'This is Home Sweet Home, remember?'

*

Next morning Flynn and I walked to school together. At the corner of our street, I always meet up with Zania and Kirsty, my best friends, and he trails behind us, but at that moment we were still together. And just like the day before, I had a strange sensation that time had dawdled and strayed away for moment, making the traffic pause, as if there was nowhere for it to go. For a second all sound stopped, all colour faded, and I felt as cold as if I had been gripped in ice. I paused, and so did my brother, but a second later the sensation had passed. I turned to Flynn, and he looked away, lips tight.

'What happened?' I asked.

'Nothing.'

'Why are you looking like that, then?' He can be so annoying at times. He knew something strange had happened, so why was he pretending again that it hadn't?

A woman in a long pale blue coat was walking away from us. She must have walked right past us, yet I hadn't noticed her. She was very striking, with straight, shimmering hair that was almost white. As if she had felt me looking at her, she stopped and turned her head. Her eyes were icy blue. For a second she reminded me of someone, and I realized that she looked just like my childhood image of the Snow Queen. She smiled at me, a cold, hard, beautiful smile, and then her gaze lingered on Flynn. Again, I turned to look at him. His eyes were shining.

'Who is she?' I asked him. He shrugged and pulled away

from me. I glanced back. Children were piling off buses and out of cars, mingling and shouting and jostling. There was no sign of the woman in the pale blue coat.

I forgot about her until the end of the school day. I collected Flynn, left him outside our house, and wandered off with Zania and Kirsty. Kirsty asked us in to see her new dress, and we all tried it on and did each other's hair.

'Will Flynn be all right?' Zania asked. 'It's really dark outside.'

'He's fine,' I said, annoyed at being reminded about him when I was enjoying myself.

I suppose it was quite a bit later than usual when I arrived home. It didn't matter. I knew Mum wouldn't be back from work until after six, so she wouldn't know, but I was feeling guilty now about leaving Flynn on such a cold night. I saw immediately that there was no light on in the shed. Why wasn't he in there? I wondered.

'Flynn,' I called. 'Flynn, stop messing.'

I couldn't find him. I searched behind the bushes in the garden in case he was hiding. I went into the house and switched on the lights. I took off my coat, turned on the TV, tried to be normal. But my heart was beginning to thud. Where was he? Surely, if he was out there in the cold and dark, he'd come running in when he saw the door was open and the lights were on. I called again, searched again. He wasn't there. Flynn wasn't there.

For one panicky moment I remembered the strange

woman in the long coat. She knew Flynn. They had looked at each other. He had pretended not to see her, but he had. I remembered the ice moments, and her brittle smile, and how Flynn's eyes shone when he looked at her. What if she actually *was* the Snow Queen, and she had stolen my little brother, just like she had stolen Kay in the story? No, it was crazy to think like that. But then where was he?

Perhaps he'd followed me earlier; perhaps he'd gone to the shopping precinct for warmth. That would make sense, wouldn't it? I went racing down the road. I had forgotten to put my coat back on, and the air was beginning to spit, more sleet than rain, with grits of ice in it.

'Flynn!' I kept shouting. 'Flynn!' But my voice was swallowed in the roar of the rush-hour traffic. I ran along the whole of the shopping precinct and back again, and then I did it again, and at last I stopped for breath in the bright doorway of Tesco. I was shivering with cold and fright. A *Big Issue* seller was sheltering in the doorway, too, hopping from one foot to the other to keep himself warm. He was wearing frayed jeans and old trainers, and his feet must have been nearly frozen.

'Here,' he said. 'Here y'are.'

'No, thanks,' I muttered, and then I saw that he wasn't holding out a magazine for me to buy, but a two-pound coin. His hands were red and raw with cold.

'Take it,' he said. 'You look half starved. Go and get yourself a nice cup of hot chocolate from the cafe.'

I shook my head. 'I've lost my brother,' I whispered. 'Have you seen him?' I hesitated. 'He might have been with a woman in a long blue coat.'

The man narrowed his eyes. 'I know that woman.'

'Do you?' I was surprised, and quite relieved. Was she just an ordinary woman after all? But what did she have to do with my brother?

'I've seen her often enough, walking round the town. Yes, I saw her not long ago, and she had a little boy with her. About five, he was.'

'That's Flynn!'

'He looked quite happy.'

I remembered the rapt expression on Flynn's face when we had seen the woman this morning on the way to school. What on earth did he think he was doing, wandering off with her? He could be in terrible danger. 'Where did they go?'

The man blew on his fingers one by one, as if they were birthday candles that refused to go out. 'I think they went down Chapel Alley, just over there. But you watch out. That's where the Alley Gang hangs out. Not for your sort, that lot. Get yourself that hot drink instead.'

'I have to find him,' I said. 'But thanks.' I rolled the bottom of my school sweatshirt round my hands to try to keep them warm, and made my way through the traffic towards Chapel Alley. I knew about the gang that hung out there. I'd seen them loitering, swigging from cans, girls shrieking and boys loud as lions. Mum called them louts and tarts. 'And be thankful I've given you a decent upbringing. Never have anything to do with rough kids like that.'

I didn't *want* to have anything to do with them. I wanted to turn away and run back home, let myself into the warm house, make toast for me and Flynn. Flynn wasn't there, though. Flynn had been stolen, and it was all my fault. Why had that woman stolen him? The story of the Snow Queen came flooding back to me. I thought about the piece of ice in Kay's heart. I thought about him being trapped in her frozen palace. No, she isn't the Snow Queen, I tried to tell myself. But if she wasn't, who on earth was she? What would happen to him? I would never be able to go home until I'd found my brother, even if I had to walk around all night.

I calmed myself and walked into the black shadow of Chapel Alley, away from the bustle of shoppers and the cheerful Christmas lights of the High Street. I could hear the gang, the snap of their cigarette lighters, the twitter of their voices. I felt tiny and timid, as if I was a mouse venturing into a den of wild cats. A motorbike throbbed. Boys threw their voices against the walls like bouncing balls. Girls screamed with laughter. They all seemed to have to make a noise. I could see that one of the girls was straddling a pushbike, jabbing at the bell again and again in an angry, bored sort of way, and there was something about the way she did it that made me think she was their leader. She was wearing a red woollen scarf, and every so often she whipped the end of it round her neck and glared at everybody.

213

I shrank against the wall and tried to creep past, but one of the boys saw me and decided I was just right to make a game of.

He twisted his face into a snarl. 'Who said you could come down our alley?'

'Yeah, like no one comes down here without our permission,' another one growled.

They crowded round me, holding out their arms to stop me going any further. The girl with the red scarf just watched them, smirking. A scar-faced boy started tweaking my hair.

'Eh, it's Goldilocks!' he laughed. 'You won't find no bears here, kid.'

'Only you!' a girl giggled at him. 'Paddington, your mam should've called you.'

I was sick with fright, panicking because they were trapping me there. 'Let me get past,' I begged, desperate. 'I've got to find Flynn.'

'Ooh, Flynn! Is he your little teddy bear?'

'Leave her alone,' the scarf girl said suddenly. 'She's only a kid.' She walked her bike forward and parked it in front of me, like a shield. 'What are you doing here?' She didn't speak in the brutal way of the others.

'I'm looking for Flynn,' I said. 'He's my brother.'

'There's no Flynn in my gang,' she said.

'He's only five,' I told her.

'Five! He's a dwarf, then! She's not Goldilocks, she's Snow White!!' the hair-tweaker said.

214

The girl shoved him with her elbow. 'Think you're so clever, don't you? Shut up, the lot of you!' she snapped, and amazingly they did.

'I think he's been stolen by someone,' I said. I couldn't bring myself to mention the name of the Snow Queen in front of them, to be taunted again. And I had no idea who she was really. 'A woman with white hair and a long blue coat.'

The girl whistled slowly. 'Oh, yes. They came down here all right. Walked right through us as if we didn't exist. The little boy didn't look as if he'd been stolen, though. He was holding her hand and smiling up at her.'

'It's him, I know it is.' *Why, oh why, does that woman make him happy?* I thought angrily. He used to be happy with me; he used to hold my hand like that. I started to move away, but the girl put her hand on my arm.

'Here,' she said. 'Take my bike. Go on. You'll be much quicker. Go on, take it.' She helped me to get on it. 'You'll have to stand on the pedals, you're such a titch,' she told me. 'Go straight to the hovel at the end of Townhead Lane. You know where that is?'

I nodded. 'I think I do. I've never noticed a hovel there.'

'Take my word for it.' The girl was speaking urgently now, as if she knew exactly what I had to do. She suddenly made me think of the Robber Girl in the story. But how could she be? How could these people have come into my life? I had to trust her, though, because I had no idea what else to do.

215

'Leave my bike with the old lady there,' she went on. 'She's my grandma, and she's a strange person, I warn you. But she'll tell you where to go next. And here, have my scarf. You look freezing. Quick!' And she pushed me away.

When I reached the end of the alley, I stopped, not sure which way to go. I could hear the gang shouting, 'Go left! Go right! Go straight ahead! Turn round!' And then I saw a white cat staring at me with strange ice-blue eyes. It turned and darted across the road and disappeared into a farm track, and I recognized it as Townhead Lane. I had never noticed before how narrow and bumpy it was, how overgrown and snaggly the hedges were. I followed the cat, swivelling into the dark and silence, desperate to find my brother and take him home. I felt as if the real world was slipping away from me. Of course there was no Snow Queen, I kept trying to tell myself. Of course the girl with the red scarf was just an ordinary girl. And yet something made me carry on, as if I was in the grip of a nightmare and couldn't wake myself up from it. The old woman would tell me what to do, the girl had said. Hadn't Gerda been helped by an old woman who lived in an igloo?

It was sleeting now. Wet, sharp flakes were bumbling in the light of the bike lamp, making the farm track slithery, pitting into my eyes like wet darts. As I rode, I kept shouting, 'Flynn! Flynn!', hoping that any minute I would see a small boy darting towards me. But no boy came. I was alone. The track was getting steeper. The sleet had turned to snow, buzzing relentlessly towards me. There was no sign of the cat. When the track was too steep, the bike wobbled sideways and I fell off, and then I saw a small light that seemed to be set inside a pile of rubble.

I picked up the bike and wheeled it towards the light. I could see now that it came from an old barn of some sort, reeking of acrid woodsmoke. This must be the girl's grandmother's place. Not an igloo at all. How stupid I was to have thought that, or to have believed that she could help me. She wouldn't even know who I was.

A door opened, the pale light flickered and a voice called, 'You, girl! Here! Here you are!'

An old woman stood in the doorway, arms folded, smiling as if she had been expecting me. The white cat was winding round her boots. 'Come in, come in, you'll perish out there! Temperature's dropping like a stone. Eh, but it's no place for a child like you.'

I wasn't cold, though I was exhausted. I'd never cycled so far before. But I had to go on. 'I'm looking for my brother,' I said. I was so tired that I could hardly speak.

'Oh, yes, I know you are. The little boy,' the old woman said. 'Come in, come in,'

Thinking for the moment that she had Flynn safe in her cottage, I stepped inside. The heat was almost overwhelming, but the woman drew me closer to the spitting fire. A pot of stew was hanging over it, bubbling like a witch's brew, and it smelled wonderful.

'Is Flynn here?' I asked. I gazed round at the room. It was nearly bare except for a bed of some sort next to the fire, with a bundle of ragged blankets heaped on it.

'Oh, no, she'd never bring him here! A queen in my hovel?'

I started. So I was right. It *was* the Snow Queen who had stolen Flynn. The old woman touched my hand. 'Sit down on the bed and I'll give you a bowl of mutton stew. It's all I have, but it's good and hot and it'll keep you going. You've a long, hard journey ahead of you, if you intend to carry on.'

Once more I felt like crying. Would it never end? Would I never find Flynn? Was he locked in ice somewhere? What on earth could I do if he was? All I had wanted was to get him home. Mum must be in from work by now. She'd have found the house empty. She would be angry with me, and frantic with worry. 'I have to go on,' I said wearily. 'I've come all this way, and I don't know if I'll ever see him again.'

'He's all right,' she said. 'For the moment. Believe me. It's you I'm worried about. You need looking after, you do.' She stirred the cauldron and ladled out a helping. She sipped a little herself, and emptied the rest into a chipped bowl. 'Here.' She held it out towards me. 'It's good. I want you to eat before you go on.'

I was so tired. I would have given anything to lie down and cover myself with the stinking pile of rags.

'Please can you tell me where Flynn is?' I begged her.

'I do know, and I will tell you. Eat, go on.'

'Is he with the woman in the long blue coat? Is she the

218

Snow Queen?' There, I had said it. Nothing seemed real any more. If I had really slipped into that world of ice and story, what would become of me? What would become of Flynn?

'Ooh, she's a beauty, she is! Skin so pale, eyes that shimmer like ice, long white snowflake hair ... I've known her all my life!' the old woman crooned. 'If you're going to find her, you have to be strong. You're a fine, good girl to have come all this way, but I tell you, you have to be strong. Here. Eat.'

She held out the bowl again. Her eyes were so full of concern and kindness that I took it and ate the stew. It was delicious.

'Good girl. Now I'll tell you what I know. She lives up in the castle beyond this house. That's where she'll be. That's where the boy will be.'

I stood up quickly, but she held out her hand to stop me going yet. 'It's a good climb up there. You'll follow this track, but it'll be rough and stony soon. You'll lose sight of it, but take my torch and follow the cat. The higher you go, the colder it will be. The snow will soon turn to ice, and those flimsy shoes of yours will never get you there. Take them off, and wear these old boots of mine, and you'll be quite safe.'

'And Flynn will be there?'

'I promise you. Flynn will be there.'

I was afraid, but something even more powerful than fear had taken over. I had no name for it yet. I slipped off my school shoes and wriggled my damp feet into the leather boots the old woman had been wearing. The white cat stretched himself awake from his nest of rags in front of the fire and sauntered over to the door. He turned his blue-eyed stare towards me, and then scratched open the door with his paw. The blast of icy air nearly drove me back inside again. My only thoughts were that I must go on, whatever lay ahead. I had to find Flynn. There was no going home without him.

'Keep climbing, my dear. I wish you luck when you get there.' The old woman closed the door behind me, and there was no more light from her hovel, and no reek of smoke. I was alone again in the swirling snow. The cat had disappeared. I trudged on, thinking how helpful everyone had been to me – the *Big Issue* seller, the girl in the red scarf and the old woman. I wondered where Mum was now, what she was thinking, what she was doing to try to find us. And I thought about Flynn. He should never have gone off with a stranger. But I should never have left him on his own. I was the only one who could rescue him, and he was somewhere up there in the icy, terrifying darkness.

I tucked the scarf inside my sweatshirt and marched on, head down, following the tiny dance of light from the torch. If there had ever been a track, it was covered now, but what I could see were paw marks, and sometimes they doubled back, as if the cat had run back to make sure I was still coming. I couldn't see him at all, but then what use was a white cat in a snowstorm? And then suddenly he was there, stopped still right in front of my feet so I nearly tripped over him. He turned his face towards me, and then crouched and let out a low moan. Was he afraid, too? I wondered. Or was he telling me to go on alone? I looked up, and there was the castle looming ahead of me, and slowly, one by one, lights began to flicker in all the narrow window slits.

I bent down and stroked the cat's wet back. 'You don't have to come any further,' I told him. 'Not if you're afraid.' And instantly, he gave a small mew and scuttled away into the darkness.

I walked slowly and steadily towards the castle, trying to control the pounding of my heart. 'Keep going, keep going, Orla', I kept muttering to myself. The steps up to the castle were so slippery that even in the old woman's sturdy boots I was skidding. My fingers found a railing and clung to it, burning cold though it was, and I hauled myself to the huge oak door and pushed it. It was bolted. I banged on it weakly until my fist hurt, and then I heard laughing, cackling voices behind me and around me. Blue, darting flickers of light danced like small phosphorescent imps.

'She won't let you in yet!' the voices screeched. 'Not until you give us things!'

'Give you things?' I felt like crying with frustration. I was almost too exhausted to speak. 'But I don't have anything to give.'

'Give us your scarf!' they said, and the red scarf was whisked away from my neck before I could save it. 'And your torch. Ooh, give us that!' Again, the torch was snatched out of my hand. 'What else? What else?'

'I didn't give you anything! You just took them!' I shouted. 'And they weren't mine to give.'

'Oh, that doesn't matter! What's theirs is yours is hers is ours! And back again. Ooh, look at her boots!'

Now they were fiddling with my bootlaces, lifting my legs one at a time and tugging off the old grandmother's boots, and away they went, snickering, and I was left standing in my thin school socks. Desperately, I banged on the door again. It opened immediately.

I walked into a great, lofty hall lit by candles. Their flames flattened like the cowering cat until the great door closed silently behind me. How warm and welcoming it felt now in all that dancing light! This was not at all what I had expected, not a bit like the story of the palace of ice. I tiptoed forward. From behind one of the other doors, I could hear music, and the high laughter of little children, as if a party had suddenly been switched on. Eagerly, I ran to the door and opened it.

I saw Flynn straight away. He was not pushing cubes of ice around like Kay in the story, not wrapped in frozen chains. He was sitting on the floor by a big open fire, playing some sort of building game with other children. They were all laughing. I couldn't remember when I had last seen Flynn looking happy. The beautiful queen woman was standing near them, smiling, but as soon as I moved from the doorway, she turned, very slowly, and looked at me. The music stopped. The laughter stopped. All the other children stood up quietly and drifted away. Flynn was left, sifting the Lego bricks just as he did at home. He looked up for a moment in my direction, frowned, and lowered his head again. It was as if he hadn't even seen me. Or hadn't wanted to.

'Flynn, Flynn!' I whispered urgently. 'Come on! We've got to go home!'

'Home!' the children moaned. They were walking slowly round the room now, not together but separate and lonely and in different, aimless directions as if they didn't know each other, didn't see each other; heads down, hands behind their backs.

'Home!' the queen repeated. 'Home! Do you call that home, when you leave a little child all on his own outside his house?' She stood in front of me, so I couldn't see my brother.

'Who are you, and who are all these children?' I asked, trying to hide my deep shame at her accusation, trying to be bold and not intimidated by her.

'These are the lonely children, the doorstep children, the home-alone children. And I am their protector, their queen. I bring them here to be warm and safe. I bring them here to be happy.'

'They don't look happy,' I muttered.

'Oh, they were until you came, my dear. You have made them unhappy.'

'But will you never let them go?'

'Of course. When they have proper homes to go to.'

I tried to get past her. 'Flynn,' I called. 'Come to me. I'm going to take you home.'

'How dare you?' the queen shouted, and drew herself up tall and terrifying, eyes hard and cruel. 'How dare you try to take him away from me?'

I thought of the moment I had walked into the room. I remembered the sound of fun and laughter, the sense of happiness in there. Could I take Flynn away from that? But he didn't belong there! She couldn't keep him! 'You must let me,' I begged. 'I've come all this way, in all this weather, with no coat on my back! I didn't take the money for a hot drink, I didn't run away from the Alley Gang. I went all the way in the snow to the grandmother's house, and then I climbed up here, and it was bitterly cold and icy, and I let the cat go even though he was my only company. And now I haven't even got a torch, or a scarf, or boots, and I want to go home. But not without Flynn. Not after all that. You must let him come with me.' I turned away, not bold any longer. I didn't want her to see my tears, which were coursing freely down my cheeks. I didn't want her to see that I was afraid of her. Maybe I could have pushed her aside and grabbed Flynn and made him come with me, but I was too frightened to do that. Besides, what might she do to me if I tried? Turn me to ice?

As if she knew what I was thinking, the queen stepped

away so I could see my brother again. 'Flynn,' I called weakly, but still he didn't look up. He just kept playing with the coloured bricks as if he hadn't seen me, or didn't know me, or didn't care that I had come for him.

The queen smiled. 'Everything you say is true, Orla. Oh, yes, I know your name. And I know everything you have been through to get here. I know you've done all these things. But have you learned nothing on your journey, child?' Her voice was sweet and gentle.

So, it had been a kind of test, I realized. Had she made all those things happen to me? Was it a kind of game to her? And why, and what was I supposed to do, what was I expected to say? I felt small and alone, and far more frightened by her gentle, smiling manner than I had been of her anger.

This time she didn't stop me when I stepped towards Flynn. I sank down helplessly on the floor next to him, knowing now that I was completely in the queen's power. Flynn shoved some of the little bricks towards me, and I saw that they weren't building bricks or Lego, but something like jigsaw pieces made up of fragments of letters. He had stuck several pieces together to form his name. He sat with his arms looped round his knees, looking at the letters, frowning. I was aware of the queen watching me. I was aware that the lonely children had stopped their restless wandering and formed a silent circle round us all.

I gazed helplessly at the pieces. I had a puzzle to

solve, and I would never get home until I had solved it. I concentrated on what I had just told the queen. It was all true, she had said, but what had I learned?

I pictured the *Big Issue* seller, his raw red hands, his frayed jeans. He was poor, yet instead of asking me for money he had given me some of his own. I thought about the Alley Gang. Instead of attacking me, their leader had given me her scarf and lent me her bike to help me on my way. The grandmother lived in a tumbledown shack and yet she had invited me in. She had hardly anything in her cooking pot, yet she had fed me. Even the cat had brought me as far as he dared towards the castle.

I picked up the jigsaw letters and fitted some of them together. KINDNESS, I wrote.

The queen didn't even look. I could hear her tapping her foot on the ground. 'Not enough!' she snapped. 'Not enough!'

I felt myself beginning to shiver. I glanced at Flynn. His face was pale. I could see his breath hazing. I could hear, very faintly, the crackly laughter of the imps.

I shifted the jigsaw pieces round again. What was greater than kindness? What more had those strangers given me?

'I know, I know!' I shouted suddenly. I fitted the letters together. CHARITY.

The queen laughed. 'Charity!' she repeated. 'Is that what a home needs? Charity? Is that all you've learned on the way here?'

My tears were burning on my cheeks, turning themselves into tiny, frozen drops.

'Look into your heart, Orla, before it turns to ice,' the queen said. She sat down by Flynn and put her arm round him. He rested his head on her shoulder. His eyes were shining, he was smiling again, but he was pale, paler than ever, he was almost transparent now, a ghostly, still figure.

I remembered how he used to smile at me like that, how we used to play together, draw pictures, make up stories and songs and silly jokes. How I used to read to him at bedtime, cuddle him when he fell over. It wasn't his fault that Dad had died. It wasn't his fault that the world had changed, and that Mum was always out, and that I had to take her place and look after him. He was only five years old – how could any of it be his fault? *I'm going to lose him.* The thought that he was drifting away from me, that he was choosing to stay with the queen, that I would never see him again, was more than I could bear. It was breaking my heart.

Suddenly, I knew the word the queen wanted. I knew the word that meant more than the kindness and the charity that the *Big Issue* man and the girl with the red scarf and the old woman with the hot stew had shown me. I knew the word that had been even more powerful than fear, and that had driven me on to find my brother. I reached out for the jigsaw pieces. I only had to make four letters. With shaking hands, I fitted them together. LOVE.

The queen clapped her hands with delight. Flynn jumped out of her arms and ran to me. He put his arms round me and hugged me just like he always used to, and I hugged him tight, tight.

'I'll always look after you,' I told him.

There was a distant sound like bells peeling, and I realized that it was made up of many voices, many names, over and over again. The children around us were laughing excitedly, hearing their own names called. Then I heard someone calling Flynn's name, and then my own. 'Flynn! Orla!' over and over again. And the voice was Mum's.

'It's Mummy!' Flynn shouted. 'Can we go home now?'

The other children were shouting, too, dancing up and down, clamouring to be allowed to go back home because their mothers and fathers were calling out for them.

'Of course you can go!' The queen laughed. 'Everyone's ready for you now!' She ran round them all, kissing and hugging them, waving them goodbye as they all ran to a far door and disappeared down a brightly lit corridor.

She turned to me. 'You've learned the most important word of all,' she told me. 'Love. Never forget it, Orla.'

'I won't,' I promised.

'Off you go, then. Follow the children. And don't come back, ever.'

I took Flynn's hand and walked along the corridor to a line of many doors. I knew which one to open, because my school shoes were in front of it. I slipped them on. 'It's going to be cold outside, Flynn,' I told him. 'And we have a long way to go. Are you ready?'

He nodded, too full of happiness to worry about that. He clutched my hand again and we went through the door . . .

. . . and it opened straight into our house. Mum was standing with her back to us, clutching the phone. She swung round when she heard us, dropped the phone, ran forward and knelt on the floor, hugging us both at the same time. Her cheeks were wet with tears.

'I've been so worried about you!' she said. 'The door was open, I didn't know where you'd gone! I searched everywhere, up and down the street, the school, everywhere. I was just phoning the police!'

'Orla came and found me,' Flynn said. 'A lady was looking after me. She was a bit like—' he looked at me helplessly '—a lady in a story.'

'A bit like the Snow Queen,' I added. 'But kinder.'

Mum laughed. 'The Snow Queen! I'm sure! You're home, you're safe. That's all that matters. Hot baths, supper, bed and a story.'

We sat together when we were ready for bed. 'This won't ever happen again, I promise,' Mum said. 'I'm going to change my work hours so I can spend more time with you both. Now who's going to read?' She put one arm over my shoulder. Flynn snuggled into the crook of my arm. We didn't need a book, because I knew the story off by heart.

And as I told it, I could hear Dad's voice, from all that time ago.

Would you like to meet the Snow Queen? Maybe you will, one day.

The Room with the Mountain View
LAUREN ST JOHN

When Lexie broke her leg in two places – in the first hour of the first day of the school skiing trip to France – she was overjoyed.

Ironically, the accident did not happen on a black run or even a nursery one. She simply tripped over a ski pole in her clunky new hire boots and fell down the sports-shop stairs.

A great deal of drama followed. A mountain-rescue helicopter airlifted her to the nearest big town to have the fracture properly set. Along the way the distraught teachers accompanying her argued over who was responsible and whether or not they could have foreseen that Lexie would pole-vault onto a concrete walkway, snapping her fibula (a fancy name for calf bone).

Through a haze of painkillers, Lexie heard them marvelling at her bravery.

'Any child who can still smile after being traumatized and

having their holiday ruined before it has even begun is a hero in my book. *Incroyable!* cried Miss Hannah, who wasn't French, but employed French words at every opportunity because she found them romantic.

'She's an absolute trooper,' enthused Mrs Woodward, keen to keep Lexie sweet in case her banker parents withdrew their generous financial support for the new school gymnasium. 'We must do everything in our power to make it up to her.'

Unbeknown to the teachers, Lexie had good reason to smile. She hated sports, especially vigorous, death-defying ones like skiing. The mere thought of spending hours trudging up slopes in freezing gales or swinging above an abyss in a flimsy chairlift, for the dubious reward of racing head first down a mountain, was enough to bring her out in a rash.

She'd begged her parents to take her with them to Barbados, but they'd already booked their flights.

'Sorry, hon, our hands are tied,' her father said, lifting those same hands to the heavens. 'It's an adults-only resort. We would far rather have had you with us, but we assumed you'd want to go on the school trip with your friends.'

'Besides, it's so much nicer for you to be with children your own age,' added her mum. 'Just think how much fun you'll have learning to ski. If you master the basics, we might think about buying a chalet at a resort. That way, we could hit the slopes several times a year.'

Faced with yet another reason to avoid skiing at all costs, Lexie had in the weeks leading up to the school trip prayed fervently for a volcano or similar disaster that would give her the excuse she needed to get out of it. Relatively speaking, she'd got off lightly with a broken leg. With any luck, she'd now have hours and hours to read mystery novels.

Prone in the hospital bed, she beamed up at Miss Hannah. Mrs Woodward was in conversation with the doctor.

'*Mon dieu!*' The teacher clasped her chest in sympathy. 'We will salvage this situation if it's the last thing we do. Don't worry, Lexie, I'll call your mum and dad as soon as we get to the resort. I'm sure they'll want to rush back from the Caribbean to be with you.'

'NO!'

Lexie's smile vanished. Her parents were lovely, but they'd forgotten what it was like to be eleven and have a head full of crazy dreams and whole months when you couldn't stop obsessing about a character from a novel who seemed to be the only person on the planet who understood you. Their primary concern was her far-distant future. They were already squabbling about which university was better, Oxford or Cambridge.

Lexie's home life was an Excel spreadsheet of post-school activities such as Mandarin, violin and extra maths. Even sleep was scheduled. If they turned up in France, they'd hire a local tutor and have her studying round the clock until her leg healed.

235

'Please don't bother them, Miss Hannah. They need a holiday.'

'Yes, but this is so much more important. They would want to be with you.'

'What I mean,' said Lexie a little desperately, 'is don't you remember what it's like to lose yourself in a book?'

A spark fired in Miss Hannah's green eyes. A former librarian whose library had been shut by the local council, she understood better than anyone the magic of losing oneself in a story.

'*Mais oui, ma chérie.* Indeed I do. I have a duty to inform your mum and dad that there's been an accident, but Wi-Fi can be so unreliable, don't you find? When an email does reach them, it'll say that all is well now and you're keen to stay on with your friends and use this week to brush up on your French and do some studying. Would that make you happy?'

Lexie almost cried for the first time that day. She'd known the teacher for less than twenty-four hours, but already she was warming to her. 'Thanks, Miss Hannah. Yes, it would.'

Lexie and the teachers arrived back at the Beau Montagne Resort in a taxi to find a gigantic silver tour bus blocking the driveway. Their driver wasn't pleased. Just as he was adding some colourful new phrases to Miss Hannah's French vocabulary, the bus door hissed open. Out swaggered a woman wearing a motorbike jacket and a scowl that matched her snarling tiger tattoos.

Next came five nimble dancers in fake furs, feather boas and shiny tights. They were laughing and joking and shoving each other playfully. A muscular black man did a handspring on the icy tarmac just because he could.

'No prizes for guessing that this is the circus we were told about,' said Mrs Woodward in annoyance just as Lexie was thinking how thrilling it would be to share the hotel with such exotic performers. 'Trust them to arrive at the very time we needed to get our patient as close to the front door as possible. They'll be ages, no doubt. Nothing for it except to push her there.'

Lexie had been given crutches, but wasn't allowed to use them until she'd practised in the safety of her hotel room. She felt self-conscious being helped into a wheelchair in front of the finely honed acrobats and dancers.

'Don't worry, Lexie, you'll be fit and tearing down the slopes in no time,' said Mrs Woodward, wrongly reading her thoughts. Lexie shuddered and thanked her lucky stars again that her leg was in plaster, even though it was starting to throb. She was glad when Mrs Woodward went on ahead to reception to organize a new room. Another benefit of the catastrophe was that Lexie would no longer have to share a dormitory with seven other girls. Six of them were skiing and fashion fanatics, with whom Lexie had absolutely nothing in common. The seventh was one of those boisterous, permanently chipper types. Whenever Lexie saw her, she felt an overpowering urge to hide under the duvet and devour an entire packet of chocolate digestives.

The tour bus was still disgorging fascinating characters. Out came a woman in a red Stetson and fringed tan chaps. She was followed by a man with shoulders as wide as barn doors and another who was pale, fair-haired and gangly. The latter was carrying a bucket.

Lexie gasped. A snow queen was stepping out of the bus. That was the only way she could think to describe the woman. She had long blonde hair that reached almost to her ankles and shone like white gold in the light. As she moved, her cream coat fell open to reveal a blue silk dress.

The most handsome man Lexie had ever seen outside of Hollywood joined the snow queen on the step. Miss Hannah's mouth fell open and she involuntarily squeezed Lexie's hand.

'I believe that's Sofia Fontaine and Ricardo Rossi. They're like the Brad and Angelina of the circus. I recognize them from the poster I saw at the hospital. Ricardo is a world-famous Italian acrobat and Sofia is his partner. Sofia's French. She's a gold medal-winning Olympic gymnast who became fed up with the discipline of training and literally ran away with the circus.'

Ricardo flashed a startlingly white grin and waved to the fast-gathering crowd. A cheer went up. He swept a hand through his lustrous black hair and helped the snow queen down the bus stairs, like a prince assisting his bride. There was a collective sigh from every woman watching, including Miss Hannah.

Lexie couldn't understand his appeal. The man seemed more in love with himself than he did with Sofia. He was a show-off, too, and not in the fun way of the dancers. Perhaps that's why Sofia's smile faded as soon as she turned away from the crowd.

'Move along,' grumbled the car park security guard, shooing the loiterers as if they were geese. '*Allez, allez.*'

Miss Hannah opened the boot of the taxi and took out a magnificent bear that was nearly as big as Lexie, two boxes of chocolates and an enormous candy-striped bag of old-fashioned sweets. The sweets were from Lexie's classmates and teachers. The bear was a gift from the owner of the sports shop, who was hoping her parents wouldn't sue.

'I do hope these help cheer you up,' said Miss Hannah with a smile. 'Mind holding them while I pay the taxi driver?'

She piled them onto Lexie's lap, adding a fresh layer of embarrassment. Quite apart from the fact that Lexie could hardly see over the top of the bear, she didn't want to appear childish in front of such confident artistes. Fortunately, they were too busy playing to the crowd to notice her. She watched between the bear's ears as the young man with the bucket dipped a loop of rope into it and began to blow bubbles. These were no ordinary bubbles. They were enormous ones shaped like moose and polar bears. They sailed across the car park, each a shimmering miracle with its own rainbow.

Lexie was entranced until Red Stetson lady bounded over with a whip and started popping them.

To Lexie's surprise, it was Ricardo Rossi who rounded on the woman. 'Oh, why do you always have to ruin everything, Bianca?'

'Please don't worry, Ricardo,' interrupted the bubble-blowing man, attempting to head him off with a smile. 'It really doesn't matter. I was just having a bit of fun.'

The circus ringmaster barrelled past him. He confronted Ricardo and Bianca. 'Why are the two of you always at each other's throats like a cobra and a mongoose?' he demanded. It was a peculiar thing to say, but then, Lexie supposed, a great many peculiar things went on in circuses.

'You're driving me insane,' the ringmaster barked. 'Go into the hotel before someone videos you on their iPhone and puts it on social media.'

Miss Hannah came hurrying up. 'Lexie, I'm so sorry, but I'm going to have to run into the hotel to get more money for the taxi driver. The wretched man is asking for an outrageous sum. I'll park you over here by the hedge. Don't move. I'll be right back.'

The circus crowd had dissipated. Lexie was able for the first time to take in the scenery. The main hotel was a grand wooden chalet, with pale blue shutters and alpine flowers in tubs at the entrance. Behind it were two modern blocks that were less appealing, but had big glass windows so that the guests would be distracted by the view.

To be fair, the view was stunning. A pristine fall of snow had blanketed the valley. Beyond the resort and village were mountains so perfectly creased, and of such pretty hues of slate-blue, mauve and dove-grey, it was hard to believe they were real. Each fir and spruce tree looked as if it was auditioning for a part as the world's best Christmas tree.

But the afternoon was more than a little chilly. Lexie was willing her teacher to reappear when a disembodied young voice said: 'These artistic types are all the same, aren't they? So temperamental.'

Lexie's range of vision was limited by the bear, but she was quite sure that the voice was coming from the hedge.

It was. The hedge shook violently, creating a miniature snowstorm, and a boy of about her own age stood up. At least Lexie thought it was a boy. Only after she moved the bear aside did she realize it was a girl. One with short, tousled dark hair and the flushed, nut-brown complexion of someone who spends every waking moment outdoors. Her jacket and trousers were much-mended but practical.

'Don't you agree?' the girl demanded. She had a French accent, but spoke perfect English. 'What a prima donna that Ricardo is. Bet he spends half the day in front of the mirror.'

Lexie laughed. The girl had echoed her thoughts exactly. 'Probably.'

'Nice plaster cast, by the way. I saw you break your leg. It was pretty spectacular. You soared down the stairs like an eagle.'

'If I had been an eagle, I wouldn't have ended up in A&E. I was more like a blind octopus. It was my own fault. I tripped over something. I'm a bit clumsy.'

'Well, anyway, I thought you were very brave. You must have been in agony and now you won't be able to ski, yet you didn't shed a tear.'

Lexie was astounded. Her own classmates would never have noticed something like that, let alone praised her for it. In fact, she'd heard some of them laughing at her misfortune even as she was being stretchered away to the waiting air ambulance.

Often shy and awkward around new people, she found herself saying easily: 'Thanks. To be honest, I'm not that sorry about it. I can't ski and I wasn't looking forward to learning. I'd rather read.'

It felt good to confide in someone, particularly this girl who was nodding as if she completely understood. 'I love reading too, but it's fun to have the occasional real-life adventure.'

'Are you on a skiing holiday?' asked Lexie.

'*Non*, we couldn't afford one of those. I live here. My dad's recently become the groundskeeper at the resort. Before this, he spent years working for an English family who have a chateau in Bordeaux. That's why we speak English as often as we speak French. My mum died when I was three so now it's just him and me and our dogs – Siberian huskies. There are eight of them so that's plenty. I'm Natasha, but everyone calls me Nat.'

'I'm Alexis, but most people call me Lexie. You're really lucky to have so many dogs. I love animals, but my mum is allergic.'

'Is that why you have the bear, Lexie? He's the best bear I've ever seen. I used to have one quite similar. He was a present from my mama. Then the removal men went and lost him.'

On the spur of the moment, Lexie said: 'Would you like him? Have him.'

Nat's eyes widened. 'But he's yours and he's amazing.'

Lexie thrust him into her arms in response. 'Now he's yours. Enjoy. I also have enough chocolate and sweets here to feed an army. You can have it all. I eat far too many chocolates as it is.'

'Are you sure?' Nat was invisible behind her load. Her voice was muffled. 'Wow! Thank you so much. I'd better go – I have to feed the dogs. Nice meeting you.'

'And you too.'

After the girl had gone, crunching through the snow with the treats and big bear, Lexie couldn't stop smiling. She'd made a new friend. The hotel doors opened and Miss Hannah emerged. Lexie felt quite cheerful. Soon she'd be delivered to a warm room.

To speed up proceedings, she decided to wheel herself over to the taxi to meet her teacher. As she attempted to manoeuvre the wheelchair away from the hedge, there was a clicking noise. The brake had released.

That's when it happened. The wheelchair skidded on the icy path, spun round and began to pick up speed. Faster and faster it flew. But that wasn't the terrifying part. No, the really scary thing was that the car park ended in a sheer drop. Beyond it was a ravine from which issued the roar of a rushing river.

'Help!' yelled Lexie. 'Help me!'

Miss Hannah was sprinting like an Olympian in her direction, but not even Usain Bolt could have reached Lexie in time. The wheelchair was going so fast that it took flight on every small bump. Lexie had a sinking feeling that a broken leg would soon be the very least of her troubles.

She closed her eyes as the precipice approached. The wind whipped her face and burned her ears.

Then, like something out of a dream, the wheelchair stopped dead.

Lexie opened her eyes cautiously, unable to believe that she was still alive and not dashed into a million pieces at the bottom of the ravine.

A man was bending over her, his strong, sinewy hands gripping the arms of the wheelchair. He straightened and said sternly: *'Mademoiselle*, I'm afraid the ski jump is closed for the season.'

'I w-wasn't—' Lexie stammered, before it dawned on

her that he was joking. 'Thank you. Omigod, thank you so much. You saved me.'

'*Pas de problème.* But in future exercise caution on the steep slopes, young lady. I might not always be around fixing fences.'

Miss Hannah flew up to them, panting. 'Oh, Lexie, thank goodness you're safe. I thought we'd lost you. I've just aged ten years.'

Lexie felt as if she'd lost a few years herself. She couldn't stop trembling.

The man grinned. He had the same wide, easy smile and wavy dark hair as Nat. Lexie guessed he was her dad, the groundskeeper.

'It certainly doesn't show, *madame.*'

Miss Hannah became quite flustered. 'Uh, *merci, monsieur.* You're too kind and I am already in your debt. Thank you for rescuing Lexie. I'm Rachel Hannah, the irresponsible teacher who left a girl in a wheelchair on an icy slope.'

He bowed. '*Enchanté, madame.* Luc Chevalier at your service. Do not distress yourself. These things happen to the best of us. Now if you are both quite well, I must return to my work. *Au r'voir.*'

'*Au r'voir,*' they chorused.

As Miss Hannah wheeled a shaken Lexie up the path, she mimicked: '*Enchanté.* And I look such a fright.'

But Lexie, glancing behind, saw that her cheeks were pink and she was trying to hide a smile.

*

'Mrs Woodward wanted to do something special for you to make up for this awful business with your leg, and because you'll be missing out on skiing and all the other fun,' Miss Hannah said as she pushed Lexie's chair along the third-floor corridor. 'We decided to book you into the best room in the hotel. We had to pull some strings, but we did it. You're in what they call the "Room with the Mountain View". There are others, but this one, apparently, is quite sensational.'

She inserted the keycard into the lock of room fifteen. As Lexie entered, the air seemed to shift, breathe and close around her in a hug.

She wheeled herself over to the window and was unable to restrain a squeal of delight. The room itself was exquisite, the four-poster bed a vision of crisp white sheets and a red-and-gold embroidered duvet cover. But it was the view that blew her away. The snow-bedecked mountains seemed so close that Lexie felt she could almost reach out and touch them. And directly below was a frozen lake. The bridge that arched over it was like something out of a fairy tale.

'I trust this will suit,' her teacher said with a smile.

Lexie could only nod. She was afraid that if she spoke, the spell would break and she'd be ordered back to the dormitory with the 'Valley View' that really looked over the bins.

Miss Hannah helped her onto the bed. 'I know you've had a dreadful start, but I so hope you can relax and enjoy your stay. I'll check on you whenever I can, though I'm sure you'll want some young company, too. Which of your friends shall I send to visit you?'

'None of them,' Lexie said at once. She didn't want to admit that she had no friends – not close ones at any rate. Only the children of her parents' friends who she was made to hang out with on 'play' or study 'dates'. She thought wistfully of Nat, the groundskeeper's daughter. It was rare for her to instantly feel so at ease with someone. With Lexie confined to her room, it was unlikely that their paths would cross again.

She smiled at her teacher. 'I have all the company I need in my books. If I get lonely, I'll let you know.'

Miss Hannah stared at her for a moment. 'As you wish. I'll have meals sent up three times a day until you're feeling well enough to eat in the dining room. If you need more books or anything else, let me know. In the meantime, I hope you'll be content. You know the rules. Don't open the door to anyone apart from me, the room-service waitress or the chambermaid. Happy reading!'

It had been a big day and Lexie fell asleep as soon as she slumped against the stack of downy pillows. She was woken at 7p.m. by the room-service waitress. It was dark outside and her leg hurt as she hopped to the door. The girl set the tray on the table by the window. When she lifted the lid on the meal, a divine aroma wafted up. Lexie was starving. The ratatouille and bread rolls were gone in a flash.

It was while she was tucking into a crème caramel that a movement caught her eye. She'd been so busy eating that she hadn't noticed that the building behind – the hotel's modern section, where she'd been told that the circus people were staying – was near enough for her to see into the rooms if they were illuminated.

On the second floor, the man with the barn-door shoulders was clearly visible as he lifted weights. The ringmaster ranted into his phone in a larger room on the third floor, And two doors along, Bianca was sitting on her bed with her head in her hands. Earlier, brandishing a whip in her red Stetson and chaps, she'd seemed quite fierce. Now she looked dejected. Perhaps she felt guilty for bursting the young man's bubbles.

Ricardo Rossi was in a suite with its own living room. Ugh, he really was preening in front of the mirror.

Abruptly, Lexie turned from the window. Looking at people who didn't know they were being watched made her feel uncomfortable, as if she was spying on them. But then it occurred to her that the situation was not dissimilar to that of *Rear Window*, one of her mum's favourite films. It was a Hitchcock thriller about a photographer. Confined to a wheelchair after an accident, he'd become convinced he'd witnessed a murder in the building behind his apartment.

Wouldn't it be funny if she witnessed a murder from her hotel window? Not for the victim, obviously, but the thought was funny because there was no way it would ever happen.

So Lexie stayed where she was. A light flicked on in another suite. In swept the snow queen, Sofia Fontaine. She sat at the dressing table and put on her make-up. Next came a feverish hunt through the wardrobe for the right outfit. More and more clothes were strewn on the bed. She disappeared into the bathroom and emerged some while later in a long black dress with sparkly bits on it. Lexie was mesmerized. Even from a distance, Sofia was stunning.

She was perched on her bed, filing her nails, when she jumped as if she'd been shot. Someone was at the door. She hesitated before answering it as if reluctant to open it.

Ricardo Rossi entered. There were lots of smiles. Their gleaming dental work was visible even from fifty metres away. Lexie hoped that the circus world's most perfect couple wouldn't start kissing or something ghastly.

Then she noticed something odd. In the room Ricardo had just vacated, a dark shadow was moving around. Before she could decide whether or not it was a thief, something extraordinary happened. Ricardo Rossi dropped down on one knee.

The Italian acrobat was proposing! He had a ring in his hand! Lexie was witnessing a historic celebrity moment!

Ricardo lifted a strand of Sofia's long golden hair and pressed it to his face lovingly. Unfortunately, it had the opposite effect. Sofia tugged it from his grasp and flew into a rage. Lexie couldn't hear what she was saying, but there was no doubt at all that he was getting a roasting.

Ricardo stalked out of the room and slammed the door behind him. Sofia appeared momentarily at the window, a haunted expression on her face. Lexie ducked down. When she risked another glance, the curtains were closed.

There was a lot of toing and froing after that. Ricardo left the building and stormed off into the night. The bubble man appeared in the room of the tiger tattoo woman and was also given some sort of telling-off. Bianca had stopped moping and was practising backflips. Only the muscle man remained serene, bench-pressing ever more weight.

Lexie abandoned her post in order to brush her teeth. When she returned, a man with a woolly hat pulled low over his eyes was leaving the building with a rucksack over his shoulder. Lexie couldn't tell which of the performers it was. He set off in the opposite direction and was swallowed by the darkness.

The light flickered on in the lounge. The dancers swept in with glasses and bottles and a party started.

Lexie's eyes were drooping. Picking up her new crutches, she tested them out on the way to the bed. Crawling into the sheets, she fell sound asleep.

The tinkling of stones against her window woke Lexie. She forgot that she had a broken leg and was painfully reminded of it when she tried to spring out of bed. Leaning on a crutch, she hopped to the window. A freezing draught blew in as she opened it.

Eight wolves peered up at her from the snow below. Then she saw Nat and realized that they were not wolves but a team of Siberian huskies harnessed to a sled. Lexie felt a rush of delight at seeing both the dogs and her new friend. Nat wore a head torch. She grinned up at Lexie and said in a stage whisper: 'Your sleigh awaits, *mon amie.*'

'Are you out of your mind? It's pitch-dark and I have a broken leg. I don't want a broken neck as well, thank you very much.'

'It's more fun than trying to ramp a wheelchair into the ravine. Papa told me about that. I was upset to have missed it.'

'Okay, I'm going back to bed now,' said Lexie, wondering if she'd misjudged the girl. 'You're barking mad.'

'I get told that a lot. Sorry, sorry, sorry. Seriously, come for a ride with us. It'll be an experience you won't forget. If you can get yourself to the trade lift at the end of your corridor, I'll meet you at the bottom. Come on. You know you want to.'

To her amazement, Lexie found she did. For some reason a sleigh ride with a broken leg seemed so much more appealing than skiing had done when she was fit and healthy. She pulled on her skiing clothes and managed to manoeuvre herself to the door and down the lift quite easily on the crutches.

When the huskies surged forward to meet her, examining her with their eerily beautiful blue eyes and wet noses, she knew she'd made the right decision. She didn't care what happened next. She was prepared to follow these other-worldly creatures wherever they led.

For all her teasing Nat was responsible and caring. She helped Lexie onto the sled, strapped her in securely and wrapped her in a sheepskin rug. She also lent her windproof gloves, goggles and earmuffs. By the time she'd finished, Lexie felt ready to tackle Antarctica.

In another minute, they were off. Lexie couldn't get over how fast the dogs went and how much they relished pulling. They sped past the frozen lake. Nat's powerful headlamp made crystal sheep of the reflected shrubs and bushes.

Urged on by Nat, the huskies crossed the valley at racing speed and began to climb. Churning snow and mist swirled in clouds around the dogs. Sometimes all that was visible were their ears and tails. Lexie breathed in the minty freshness of the forest. Her normal world – the scrubbed, ordered, conservative world of school and her parents – fell away. For the first time in her life Lexie felt truly alive.

They were close to the top of the mountain when Nat shouted a command. The dogs slowed, breathing steam. They rounded a corner, where the track ended. Nat braked and hopped out to give the dogs treats. They were on the edge of a precipice, but Lexie felt no fear. The ground was solid and there was plenty of room for the dogs and sled. A line of rocks had created a low barrier along the edge.

'What do you think of my mountain home?' asked Nat.

Lexie gazed out at the black mountains, their ancient crags outlined against the deep purple sky. The lights of the resort and village sparkled like stars far below. It was all so still and silent. And just when she thought it couldn't get any more magical, a snowy owl swept by on silver-tipped wings.

'It's bliss,' was all she could say.

They were on their way down at a more sedate pace when Nat spotted tracks. She halted the dogs.

'Snowmobile,' she whispered. 'Did you notice these when we came by earlier? I didn't. There's no way that anyone would be here at this time of night unless they were up to no good.'

'*We're* here,' Lexie pointed out.

'Yes, but that's different. We're just kids having an adventure. Whoever it is can't be far away. The track ends at a clearing just beyond the trees.'

Adrenaline made Lexie feel bold and daring. 'Maybe we should take a look.'

Nat was impressed. 'I'm game if you think you can manage.' She nodded to Lexie's crutches. 'We'll leave the dogs here in case they start growling.'

They stole through the forest. Lexie, struggling on her crutches, was already getting cold feet in more ways than one, but she refused to admit it. Very soon they came across the snowmobile.

'It's a hire one from the resort,' said Nat. 'There are only three and they've all been rented by the circus people this week.'

'The circus people? What would they be doing up here in the dead of night?'

'Who knows. Burying a body?'

Lexie was horrified. She was starting to wish that she'd never left her hotel room. The forest seemed alive with spooky noises. She'd heard that wolves and bears were once more roaming the Alps. What if they decided to attack? Nat could run but Lexie couldn't. They hardly knew each other. Who was to say that Nat wouldn't abandon her if disaster struck? Sharp twigs scratched at Lexie's face like claws and she bit back a scream.

Sensing her fear, Nat gripped her hand. 'Don't worry, Lexie, I'll take care of you. I know these mountains better than I know my own backyard. Hey, did you hear that? Someone's moving just ahead. Let's get nearer. Lean on me if you need to. We have to be as quiet as owls.'

There was a slithering noise. Screened by snowy pine branches, they hardly dared breathe. In the yellow glow of a torch, a dark figure was dragging a large holdall across the snow.

'Told you,' Nat whispered. 'A body.'

'Don't be ridiculous,' snapped Lexie, but only because it was a human-sized bag and she was trying to convince herself that children out for a sleigh ride didn't usually happen across actual murderers. 'It'll only be a corpse if he or she takes out a spade and starts digging a grave.'

'I think he's already dug one.'

As Nat spoke, the man – or extremely strong woman – hauled the bag to the edge of a hole and tipped it in. It landed with a sickening crunch. He picked up a spade. It clinked against the rocks as he shovelled in snow and dirt.

Nat's chilled-out, wise-girl-of-the-mountains air was gone in an instant. The moonlight caught her face and she looked as terrified as Lexie felt. 'We'd better get out of here. I'm not hanging about if there's a psychopath on the loose.'

She grabbed Lexie's hand and practically dragged her through the forest. Lexie battled to stay upright, her crutches skidding and slipping.

'We don't know for sure that it is a body. It could be . . . buried treasure.'

'Yeah, right,' said Nat. 'And I'm Father Christmas. Imagine the scandal if a circus star has killed a rival in cold blood.' She shuddered. 'Hurry. We have to get away.'

When they reached the sled, Nat bundled Lexie in. She snatched up the reins.

'Hike!' she ordered the huskies. 'Hike!' And the dogs lunged forward.

Next morning the room phone rang as Lexie was working through a late breakfast of crêpes and strawberries. In the cold light of day, the events of the previous night seemed utterly surreal. If it wasn't for the tiny scratch on her cheek and a couple of muddy leaves on the floor, she'd have wondered if she'd dreamed the whole thing.

In the block opposite, Sofia's curtains were still closed. Ricardo's were open but his room was empty, the bed neatly made. The muscle man was doing bicep curls and watching cartoons. The bubble man was practising his bubble blowing. Neither of them looked as if they were axe murderers in their spare time.

Lexie swallowed a bite of crêpe and picked up the hotel phone. Nat was on the line, breathy with excitement. 'Are you sitting down? Breaking news. Sofia Fontaine has vanished. Foul play not ruled out.'

'But where are the police?' asked Lexie. She hopped over to the window again, nearly pulling the phone out of its socket as she strained to see the car park. 'There are none at the hotel. None that I can see anyway.'

'They're on their way. They want to question the other performers. Papa heard it from a friend who conducts investigations for the local *police judiciare*. They're like your Scotland Yard in London, only smaller. Sofia was reported missing first thing this morning when she failed to show up for a rehearsal in the town square. Maybe you should tell them what you saw – about the argument with Ricardo. But wait till I come to your room. Let's discuss our own investigat—'

A siren drowned out the rest of her words.

*

The situation rapidly escalated. Having counted on a peaceful week of reading, Lexie soon found that she barely had time to open a book. She'd always loved mysteries, but it was far more exciting participating in one of her own.

The media besieged the hotel. She watched from her window as the security guard repeatedly dragged photographers out of bushes. The police came and went, interrogating dancers, acrobats and superstars alike. Only Ricardo Rossi, Sofia's heartbroken boyfriend, seemed to be above suspicion. He'd been the first to report her missing and had a diamond ring to prove that he was planning to ask her to marry him. Nobody knew that he'd already asked and been passionately rebuffed.

Lexie and Nat had been unable to identify the person they'd seen burying something in the forest, and could not mention their suspicions to the police without also having to reveal that they'd been out on an illicit midnight adventure. They were forced to watch their prime suspect giving emotional press conferences and appealing for Sofia to 'come home' like a lovelorn prince.

'There's no such thing as a perfect murder,' said Lexie, repeating something she'd heard her mum say. 'If Ricardo has killed her, chances are he'll trip himself up in the next few days. If he doesn't, we need to go to the police and tell them everything we witnessed up in the forest. They can dig up whatever or—' she grimaced '—whoever was in that hole and do forensic tests.'

Nat had told her dad that Lexie had witnessed the golden couple have an argument on the night that Sofia was last seen. She also mentioned the shadowy figure that had prowled around Ricardo's room. Monsieur Chevalier passed on the information to his friend in the *police judiciare*, but it was impossible to know if it was ever followed up.

He did reveal something interesting. The police had discovered that Sofia had recently inherited a fortune. Her father had been one of France's top winemakers and his vineyard, now owned by Sofia, was worth millions.

According to Luc Chevalier, the police were considering the possibility that she'd been kidnapped. So far there'd been no ransom demand, but they weren't ruling anything out.

During the long days, Lexie kept a close eye on the rooms opposite. Other than dodgy Ricardo, her main suspects were the shadowy figure she'd seen in Ricardo's room and the new juggler, Pierre. Thrown into disarray by Sofia's disappearance, the circus had hired the only person they could find at short notice: a mediocre juggler who looked as if he'd cut his hair with blunt nail clippers. He had a terrible, unkempt moustache, but would not, by all accounts, be parted from it.

One afternoon, Lexie had seen him dart into Sofia's room, which was supposedly under guard, snatch something and dart out again. She'd reported it to Miss Hannah, who told a visiting policeman, but nothing had come of it.

'What would your parents say if they saw you now?' Nat

asked her later, as they pored over their list of suspects for the umpteenth time.

'They'd be proud that I wanted to see justice done,' said Lexie, more in hope than expectation. She suspected that her mother would think she was wasting her time when she could have been studying. And both of her parents would have a fit if they knew she'd withheld information from the police.

'I wish *I* had a mum,' Nat said longingly.

'It's not always all it's cracked up to be, especially when they're banging on about algebra and SAT tests and wanting you to sign up to yet another after-school activity, when all you really want to do is be left alone to read books.'

Her friend looked doubtful. 'But what about when you're sick or injured, like now? Isn't it nice to have a mum to bring you chicken soup . . . or minestrone,' she added hastily, remembering that Lexie was a vegetarian.

'I suppose so,' murmured Lexie, recalling Simona, the Romanian au pair who'd nursed her through a bout of chicken pox, and Charlene, the South African au pair who'd helped her survive food poisoning, and Pavlina, the Bulgarian au pair who'd been charged with taking care of her during a particularly nasty dose of flu, but had spent most of the time on her phone, yelling at her boyfriend.

But then she thought of the thousand occasions when her mum *had* been there: cuddling her as she taught Lexie to read, cooking Sunday roasts, helping her choose hundreds of books in dozens of bookshops over the years, and always, always wanting the best for her, even if they disagreed about what the best should look like.

'Fact is, I wouldn't exist without her,' said Lexie. 'I wouldn't be here with you. I wouldn't be having the time of my life.'

The breakthrough in their case came when they least expected it – on the evening before Lexie was due to return to the UK. She and Nat had been feeling down because they'd failed to crack the mystery.

'It's my fault,' said Lexie. 'If I hadn't been so clumsy and broken my leg, we could have done a lot more investigating. We could have tailed Ricardo Rossi to see what he was up to, or hung around when the circus people were rehearsing and watched to see if anyone was acting strangely. Grown-ups never believe that children are capable of solving mysteries so half the time they don't notice us.'

'If you hadn't broken your leg, you wouldn't have been in the wheelchair and we'd never have met and become friends,' Nat told her. 'You'd never have been given the Room with the Mountain View or seen Sofia and Ricardo argue. We'd never have witnessed the burial up on the mountain. Don't forget that we've agreed to tell the police everything we know first thing in the morning. It could still turn out that we have the key that solves everything.'

She leaned forward and stared out of the window. 'Speak of the devil.'

Ricardo Rossi had appeared in the room of Bianca, the depressed red Stetson lady. A moment earlier, Bianca had been sitting on the bed with her head in her hands yet again. Now she leaped up and flung her arms around him. They kissed.

'Gross!' exclaimed Nat.

'So much for the cobra and mongoose,' said Lexie. 'That's what the ringmaster called them. He said he was sick and tired of them forever attacking each other. It must have all been an act.'

Nat covered her eyes. 'What on earth does Bianca see in him? He's a cheat on top of everything else.'

'It doesn't matter what she sees in him, we've hit the jackpot.'

'*Pourquoi?* Why is that?'

'What we're looking at,' Lexie said grandly, 'is motive. If Ricardo was secretly in love with Bianca, he had a reason to murder Sofia, especially if he knew that she was planning to leave him her estate in her will. If he gets away with it, he'll inherit all of her money.'

'Even so, we still have to consider that she might have been kidnapped rather than killed,' added Nat. 'Ricardo or someone we haven't even thought of – the thief or whoever it was you saw in Ricardo's room, say – might be hiding her in a mountain hut somewhere. They might still be planning to demand a huge ransom.'

Moments later, the plot thickened further. Ricardo and

Bianca came hurrying out of their hotel block and jumped onto a snowmobile. Five minutes after that, the bubble man emerged, talking animatedly to the ringmaster. They, too, hurtled away on a snowmobile.

'Gosh,' said Lexie. 'Maybe they're all in on it.'

'As soon as Papa is asleep, I'll come with the dogsled and collect you,' cried Nat. 'We'll go after them.'

'Are you sure? I mean, they might be dangerous.'

Lexie heard herself being sensible and cautious out of habit. At the same time, she was buzzing with excitement. Her adventures with Nat made her feel so alive and happy that she found it impossible to imagine returning to dull suburban life.

'Yeah, but we have the huskies,' said Nat. 'If they try anything, the dogs will make mincemeat of them. We're going after them and we'll bring them to justice. Just think, Lexie. We could be heroes.'

'What shall we call ourselves?' asked Nat as she helped Lexie into the sled later. 'The Snow Squad? The Mountain Detectives?'

'How about the Two Foolhardy Children who are in a Whole Heap of Trouble?' growled her father, stepping out of the shadows. 'Back to bed, both of you, before you're grounded for the rest of your lives.'

'Papa, wait! This is an emergency.'

As speedily as she could, Nat brought her dad up to date

with the latest shocking developments in the case. Lexie listened gloomily. She had a feeling that her holiday was about to end in tears. Monsieur Chevalier would tell her teachers who'd tell her mum and dad. She really would be grounded for the rest of her days. And she wouldn't even have a solved murder or kidnap case to make herself feel better.

She was startled when Luc Chevalier stopped looking stern and became quite animated. 'Murderers, you say? Well, that changes everything. Let's go in pursuit.' And with that, he took the reins of the huskies from his daughter.

'You'll do nothing of the kind,' said Miss Hannah, emerging from behind a pillar. She'd been on her way to her room and had overheard everything. 'This is an outrage. Monsieur Chevalier, you should be ashamed of yourself, encouraging these children – one of whom has a broken leg – to go haring around snow-plastered mountains in the dead of night in pursuit of criminals. Quite apart from the danger, the lawsuit could bankrupt the school.'

Nat's father shrugged. 'I cannot deny that you are right, *madame*. I am a bad example. But will you join us?'

Miss Hannah hesitated for a full five seconds before jumping into the dogsled and sliding under the sheepskin between Lexie and Nat. Monsieur Chevalier shouted to the huskies and they were away.

On their journey across the valley, the sled skimmed so fast that at times it felt to Lexie as if they were flying.

She wondered if Nat had noticed that her father and Miss Hannah were holding hands. Halfway up the mountain, they saw a curious sight. The forest was aglow, lit by fairy lights.

'That's the same clearing where the body is buried,' Nat told Lexie. 'What's going on? Are they conducting some gruesome sacrifice?'

As they neared, they saw that an outdoor circus performance was in progress. They parked the sled under the trees. One of the dancers recognized them and invited them to join a small audience seated on bales of hay.

'It's a special performance for friends and colleagues of our beloved Sofia Fontaine, who has now been missing for six days,' explained the dancer. 'Jamie, who does the bubble routine, organized it in secret. He's been carrying stuff up here under cover of darkness all week. He wanted to do something to honour her.'

Scowling blackly at Rossi, who was putting gel in his hair off-stage in preparation for his performance, he added: 'Jamie's a whole lot more upset than Ricardo seems to be.'

'No surprise there,' Lexie whispered to Nat. 'What a beast that man is. I hope the police put him in jail and throw away the key.'

'It's important to remember that people are innocent until proven guilty,' commented Miss Hannah, overhearing her.

'Nothing we can do until this is all over,' said Monsieur Chevalier, who was quite extraordinarily relaxed, given that Sofia's life was at stake. Lexie wondered if he should be under suspicion, too. However, he had such a likeable way about him that she dismissed that thought as soon as it was born. He grinned at her as if he'd read her mind. 'Might as well enjoy the show, *non?*'

And what a show it was. They were just in time for a strength display involving a pyramid of twelve people. That was followed by Jamie's spellbinding bubble routine, and a trapeze act by the woman with the tiger tattoos, involving two trees and a Harley-Davidson motorbike. Ricardo Rossi and Bianca's dance and acrobatics show was brilliant, except that they seemed to forget that poor Sofia had only recently gone missing.

'Talk about dancing on her grave,' Nat remarked furiously.

Last and definitely least was the juggler with the bad moustache and choppy hair. He performed a knife-throwing routine that would have given a health and safety official heart palpitations. There was only muted applause when he finished. He was about to leave the makeshift stage when Jamie stopped him. He held up a hand for silence.

'As you all know, Sofia Fontaine, the brightest star in our circus, has been gone for almost a week. I asked everyone to come here tonight so we could celebrate her extraordinary life and career. Thank you for giving your best this evening in this unconventional but, I think, quite glorious setting.

'However, I asked you to come tonight for a selfish reason, too. I wanted you, my friends and colleagues, to support me as I asked for the hand of the person I love most in the world.'

And with that, he went down on one knee before the astonished juggler.

'Sofia Fontaine,' he said. 'Will you marry me?'

The juggler gave a cry of delight. He ripped off his moustache and Lexie saw at once that he wasn't a man at all, but the ravishing Sofia – bare of make-up and wig.

'Yes, Jamie darling. Of course I'll marry you.'

Ricardo ran onto the stage. 'What's going on? Sofia *bella*, have you lost your mind? I've been grieving for you for almost a week. I've been devastated and heartbroken. I haven't slept. I was imagining you in the hands of the Mafia, of filthy kidnappers. And all the time you have been right under my nose, playing a buffoon, a useless juggler. *Mamma mia*, what is the world coming to?'

He touched her spiky hair. '*Bella*, tell me who did this to your beautiful locks? You look as if you've been savaged by wild beasts.'

'*You* happened to my hair, you vain little man,' Sofia replied calmly. 'When you proposed, you seemed more in love with my beauty and my money than you were with me so I decided to test you. I removed my wig and make-up and returned to the circus as me – the real me. As you can see, I'm quite plain.'

'I disagree,' objected Jamie. 'You'll always be beautiful to me, both inside and out. You're the smartest, kindest, funniest woman I know.'

'I know that now, my love,' Sofia assured him. 'You've

always seen beyond the snow queen costume to the person I am underneath. Unfortunately, it took me a while to come to my senses. I became caught up in the whirl of fame and media attention. So many people told me that Ricardo and I were the perfect couple that I found myself believing it. He was very charming and convincing, too. Perhaps most importantly, the ringmaster put pressure on us to marry. We're the star attraction. He told me that the success of the circus depended on it.

'But I saw a text message Ricardo had sent to Bianca and I started to suspect that he had feelings for her and was only planning to marry me for my money. It was only when I took off my wig and became someone else for a week that I realized that the person I cared for most had been in front of me all along. Jamie is the best, most wonderful man I know.'

She turned to her new fiancé. 'That's why I want to spend my life with you, *chéri*. As for Ricardo, you're welcome to him, Bianca – when you can tear him away from the mirror.'

Nat could hardly take in what was happening. 'So no one was murdered?' she asked Miss Hannah. 'There was no decomposing body or crazed serial killer?'

'No, it seems that the police were in on Sofia's plan from early on and only pretending to investigate.'

'It's a proper happy ending,' added Lexie. 'Which is just as well because I'm starting to get the feeling that we're not cut out to be detectives.'

*

Lexie was awoken by hammering. She'd been dreaming about her parents. They'd survived a plane crash and decided to give up their jobs and make cheese and ceramics on a farm in Somerset. For a moment she couldn't remember where she was. Then she saw the snowy peaks peeping through the curtains and a slow smile spread across her face. She was in paradise, that's where she was.

Whoever was at the door was extremely impatient. Lexie was concerned that they might break it down before she managed to stumble out of bed, pull on her Beau Montagne robe and swing across the room on crutches.

'Hang on, hang on,' she called. Wary of stranger danger, she checked the spyhole. The magnified face of Nat grinned back at her.

'I thought you were dead,' said Nat, barging in when Lexie opened the door. 'I've been banging on the door for ages.'

'Sorry, I'm not used to late nights. What time is it anyway?'

'Late.'

'Late by your standards, as in 4a.m., or late by normal people's standards?'

'Who are these normal people anyway?' cried Nat. 'I've never met one. It's ten past nine. Papa and I have brought the dogs. We're taking you for one last ride.'

'But I can't. The coach leaves for Geneva airport at ten and I have to be on it. I still have to wash, eat breakfast and pack.'

Lexie slumped on the bed, a tsunami of depression

washing over her. She felt as if she was being sent back to prison. She missed her mum and dad, but she didn't miss the gilded cage that was her old life. It was all very well living in a big house and going on fancy holidays, but without friendship, huskies and the freedom to have adventures, none of those things really mattered.

'Please come,' begged Nat. 'We'll be quick. I can pack for you while you clean up and we'll grab a couple of croissants as we pass the breakfast room. The dogs want to say goodbye to you.'

Lexie's smile was sad. 'Okay, let's do it. You only live once, right?'

In her case, she feared it was all too true.

The sky was what her mum would have called 'happy blue'. The mountains cut into it, sharp and toothpaste white.

To the delight of the other guests and irritation of the hotel manager, two dogsleds were parked in front of reception. In the car park beyond, the school coach was being loaded up. Children were milling around. Mrs Woodward, who was supervizing, spotted Lexie and called to her, but fortunately someone distracted her.

The circus performers were leaving, too. They filed past with their eccentric luggage: chains, rolls of silk and a Harley-Davidson. Sofia and Jamie strolled by hand in hand. Ricardo and Bianca had already left. Rumour had it that they'd been offered mega millions to take their act to Las Vegas.

Lexie was leaning on a crutch, kissing the nose of the lead husky, when she heard a scream. She dropped her crutch in fright.

Her mum was running towards her. Only it wasn't the mother she remembered, but a bronzed stranger wearing a flowing purple-and-orange kaftan, a headband and a great many silver bracelets. Bringing up the rear was her father with an even darker tan. Weirdly, he was wearing ripped jeans, an orange T-shirt and a battered leather jacket.

'Lexie, angel!' cried her mother. 'Oh, my poor, poor darling. Will you ever forgive us?'

She skidded towards Lexie and threw her arms around her, almost knocking her over in her excitement.

Lexie smiled shyly. 'Careful, Mum, my leg.'

'Hi, honey,' said her dad, coming to her rescue and giving her a more restrained bear hug. 'I can't believe you broke your leg before ever setting foot on the slopes. That seems too cruel. Cool blue cast, though. But why aren't you tucked up in bed?'

'That's what I'll be asking Mrs Woodward,' his wife said crossly. 'If I'm not satisfied with how you've been treated, I'll be writing to the school authorities to complain and demand answers. And I think you should stop petting those dogs, Lexie. They look dangerous.'

Lexie was indignant. This was so typical of her parents. They'd been at the resort approximately two minutes and already they were laying down rules and trying to stop her having fun. 'These huskies are the kindest dogs in the whole world. At least they are if they know you. And you're not complaining about anyone. I've had a better time with a broken leg than I ever had without one, thanks to Miss Hannah and the Chevaliers.'

She retrieved her crutches and turned round. 'Mum, Dad, I'd like you to meet Nat, my best friend.' As she said it, she realized it was true. In less than a week, Nat had come to mean the world to her. 'Umm, and this is Nat's father, Luc Chevalier. They're the owners of these beautiful huskies.'

After hands had been shaken all round, Lexie frowned. 'Mum, Dad, what are you doing here? I'd have been home by tonight. And why do you look so ... ethnic?'

Her parents exchanged glances. 'It's a long story.'

'Try me.'

On second thoughts, she waved a crutch to include Nat and Monsieur Chevalier. 'Us, I mean.'

'Our plane had engine trouble on the way to the Bahamas,' her father began.

'You were in a plane crash after all?' burst out Lexie, thinking of her dream. She was in shock. The whole time she'd been thinking that life was so much more fun without her mum and dad and their rules and schedules, they were nearly dying in a blazing aeroplane. She'd almost been *orphaned*.

'After all?' Her father was surprised. 'No, it didn't come

close to crashing. It was a misplaced bolt or something. At any rate, we were diverted to Western Sahara.'

'The desert,' her mum supplied helpfully.

'Our plane was out of commission while they tracked down the special bolt and flight options were limited. We chose Goa.'

'Only our luggage got lost on the way,' continued her mum. 'Our phones died because the charger was in the suitcase. Then the bank cancelled our credit cards because we'd told them we were going to the Caribbean and we ended up in India. We had to stay in a beach hut and eat street food with the cash we'd had on us when everything went wrong.

'We never received the email about you breaking your leg until late last night when got to Heathrow and were finally reunited with our luggage. Naturally, we were devastated. We felt we'd let you down. We slept at the airport, caught a 6 a.m. flight to Geneva and here we are.'

Lexie's mum looked down at her baggy orange-and-purple kaftan and smiled sheepishly. 'Hence the funny clothes.'

'I like them,' said Nat.

'While we were in India, we had an epiphany,' said Lexie's father. 'A sort of revelation.'

'What revelation? Don't tell me, you want to buy a farm in Somerset and make cheese and ceramic pots.'

'What? No. That would be crazy. But we realized that we'd lost our way a bit, got too caught up in the rat race. We had become obsessed with making millions in order to buy things we don't need or want. That wasn't who we were when we met and that's not who we want to be.'

'We want to simplify things,' said her mum. 'Go for long walks on deserted beaches in Cornwall and Devon. Stop pressurizing you to take subjects that don't interest you and encourage you to spend more time lying in hammocks with good books. Eat dinner as a family. Unplug from the internet. Get a cat or a dog. I'm beginning to wonder if my allergies are all in my head. If the worst comes to the worst, I can take some homeopathic tissue salts. I tried them in Goa and they worked a treat.'

Lexie felt quite light-headed. 'A dog?' she said faintly. 'I'd love a dog.'

'But don't get a husky,' put in Nat. 'Huskies need epic amounts of exercise and they pull like trains. They're only really happy if they're flying through snow, pulling a sled.'

'In that case,' Lexie asked shyly, 'can I share in yours occasionally?'

Nat's smile was so wide it practically touched the Alps on either side. 'You can come to stay whenever you like, for ever and ever.'

Monsieur Chevalier, who'd watched the family reunion with amusement, cleared his throat and addressed Lexie's parents.

'*Monsieur, madame,* would you like to join your daughter for some dog sledding? I have a friend who will lend us an extra team of huskies.'

Lexie's mum was aghast. 'I'm not having my child going dog sledding with a shattered fibula. That's the worst idea I've ever heard.'

Lexie was grateful that the groundskeeper did not feel the need to enlighten her mum about the children's midnight husky safaris.

'*Au contraire*,' he said. 'Taking the air has been recommended by the best physicians for centuries. You might benefit from it yourself, *madame* – if you don't mind my saying so.'

Lexie saw something stir in her mum. Perhaps it was a forgotten memory of nights under the duvet with a torch, reading *White Fang* or pursuing smugglers across the moors with the Famous Five.

'Perhaps you're right, *monsieur*. We could all do with taking the air, especially in this ravishingly lovely place. I've never tried dog sledding and today seems as good as any to start.'

She hugged Lexie to her. 'I'm sorry, darling, In the midst of trying to prepare you for life, we forgot to schedule in the most important thing of all: adventure.'

Lexie rolled her eyes. Her dad grinned and interjected on her behalf: 'Love, you might want to take the word schedule out of the equation.'

It was only then that Lexie recalled that one of her father's favourite books was a true story about Alaska's legendary Iditarod race. The thought of tearing across the mountains behind a team of huskies probably thrilled him to the core.

'We'd be delighted to join you, sir,' he said to Luc Chevalier. 'Now that we're here, we're thinking of staying on for another few days so we can enjoy a holiday with Lexie.'

'Excellent,' said the Frenchman. 'Well then, I invite you and your wife to climb aboard with Nat. I'll drive the second team of huskies, accompanied by Lexie and—'

An unfamiliar frown darkened his brow. 'Nat, where is the wonderful Madame Hannah? Did you pass on my invitation?'

'Sorry, Papa, I forgot. I was knocking at Lexie's door for ages before she answered and then she didn't want to come at first and then Lexie's mum and dad arrived and—'

'There she is!' cried Lexie, spotting her teacher wheeling her suitcase out of the lobby. The fire and fun that had shone from Rachel Hannah as the huskies and Monsieur Chevalier swept her across the mountains the previous night had drained away. Her shoulders were hunched and she appeared completely dejected.

At that very moment, Mrs Woodward shouted from the car park: 'Where have you been hiding, Miss Hannah? You really are impossible. You're about to cause an entire planeload of children to miss their flight.'

Lexie rushed over to Miss Hannah and grabbed her arm. 'Don't go. Stay another day and come dog sledding with us.'

Her teacher paused. She looked longingly at the huskies, straining at their harnesses.

'I'm counting to ten, Rachel Hannah,' yelled Mrs Woodward, 'then the coach is leaving without you! ONE, TWO, THREE ...'

'Stay,' said Luc Chevalier, appearing at Miss Hannah's side. He took her hand. 'One word from you and my daughter and I will be happy to open up our hearts and home ...'

'FOUR, FIVE, SIX, SEVEN ...'

'... and spend a lifetime showing you our mountain paradise. And, it goes without saying, Lexie and her parents will always be invited.'

'EIGHT, NINE, TEN!' shouted Mrs Woodward. 'You're fired, Rachel Hannah!'

Miss Hannah waved goodbye as the coach rumbled out of the car park and picked up speed. As it went by, Lexie caught a glimpse of her dumbstruck classmates, faces pressed to the steamy windows.

Rachel Hannah smiled at Luc Chevalier. 'One word is all you require?'

'Just one word.'

'*Oui.*'

Then she and Lexie took up their places in the sled and were whirled away on another husky adventure.

Snow
MICHELLE MAGORIAN

Look, Old Teddy, see the snow
Falling on the window sill,
See it gliding to the ground,
Covering the road and hill.

Feel, Old Teddy, with your paw
The coldness of the window pane,
Watch me blow onto the glass
And draw a picture of a train.

See, Old Teddy, how the trees
Are bending under all the snow,
Even footsteps sound much softer,
Look how all the cars go slow.

Now, Old Teddy, here's your coat,
Your stripy mitts and bobble hat,
I'll wrap you up to keep you warm
And then we'll both be snug and fat.

Old Teddy, if you hold your face up
And let the cold flakes touch your nose,
You can feel them melt away,
That's what I like, when it snows.

Into the Mountain
JAMILA GAVIN

It had been the coldest winter ever when, one morning, Luke was throwing out the remains of foodstuffs to the pigs and glimpsed a figure within a swirling white mist. There was a small child, motionless in the falling snow, covered in white from head to toe, its hair standing on end, stiff with frost.

Luke was startled, not just by the child, but by the tune; the tune which had been churning round and round in his head suddenly stopped. There was silence, like the silence of falling snow. For a moment, it was as though he'd gone deaf – deaf even to the sounds inside his brain. He poked a finger in his ear, and shook his head as if trying to shake out the silence.

The figure raised an arm in greeting.

Luke called, 'Who are you?'

The figure replied, 'I am Everychild.'

The snow fell harder, and the child began to fade into the whiteness, and the tune in Luke's head returned. When he backed into the kitchen, it was churning and churning on and on, just as it had done ever since the Piper came to town; a tune which blotted out all other desires except the desire to get into the mountain.

It was hard to believe that the previous summer had been blisteringly hot, and the town had been plagued with rats that had overrun every room in every house, and every dwelling. Not only crawling into babies' cots and nipping them; not only swarming into the larders and eating all the food; not only getting into the barns and ruining the grain stores, but bringing disease. People were dying and everyone was desperate.

And then a piper came: a pied sort of fellow, dressed from his feathered cap, down to his pointed toes, in an outfit of every colour of the rainbow, who had said he could rid the town of its plague of rats.

'And how will you do that?' asked the mayor, dabbing his perspiring brow, looking distastefully at this dancing, prancing fellow.

'With my pipe,' the piper replied.

'Well, go ahead and try,' said the mayor, 'though why you think you can succeed where we have failed is beyond me.'

'And what will you pay me?' the piper had asked. 'I have to earn a living.'

'Pay you?' the mayor sneered. '*Pay you?* For playing your pipe – and you weren't even asked?'

'It's up to you,' the piper said, and began to skip and dance away from the town gates.

'What if he *can* make the rats go away,' someone murmured. After all – these were desperate times and nothing so far had worked.

'Oh, all right, I'll pay you. Will three bags of gold do?' laughed the mayor sarcastically.

'Is that a promise?' asked the piper, whirling round and fixing him with a glittering eye.

'It's a promise,' declared the mayor, winking at his town councillors.

But the mayor hadn't kept his promise; he didn't give him his three bags of gold even though the piper had done exactly what he had said he would do; he had rid the town of rats by luring them down to the river where they drowned – every single one of them. The mayor just shrugged. 'It's a coincidence,' he sneered. 'You're not telling me your silly, piddly piping was responsible for the rats leaving? Here's a shilling for your trouble,' and he tossed the piper a silver coin.

In every corner of the world, a promise is a promise. The piper gave a howl of rage. 'Give me my three bags of gold as promised or you will pay dearly for your treachery.'

'Get out of my town,' ordered the mayor, 'before I have you thrown out.' He turned on his heel and went back into the town hall.

And so the piper had begun to play his pipe again. It was a different tune from the rat tune; this was a tune full of the joys of youth and play and expectation; full of magic and merriment. It was a tune which wove its way into every room in every house; a tune which brought children leaping to their feet. This time, it wasn't rats that came streaming out of the houses, and barns, and woods, and fields; it was children.

It took a while for the mothers and fathers of the town to realize what was happening and, strange to say, they were paralysed; they could do nothing as their children – every single one of them – went pouring out of the city gates and down the road, following the Pied Piper.

Luke, too, had grabbed his crutches and tried to follow and, at first, he had kept up with his little sister, Susanna. For a short time she'd skipped beside him as he lolloped along, swinging his crutches as fast as he was able. Then she had slipped away, and danced ahead, crying, 'Keep up, Luke! Keep up, keep up!' But he couldn't. Though she was only four, she had left him behind, and had run hard enough to catch up with their older brother, Bruno. 'Keep up, keep up!' Bruno had called as he and Susanna rushed by. 'Keep up!' shouted his younger brother, Wolfgang.

'Wait for me!' wailed Luke. But neither Bruno, Susanna nor Wolfgang slowed down for him, and they never looked back. *They never looked back*, and that's what had hurt him most of all.

Still Luke kept going, even when the children of the town had streamed past him like a singing river, because the piper's tune was in his head. The music brought alive some kind of children's paradise, and the paradise was inside that mountain. 'Come on, come on!'

Luke was weeping now as he fell further and further behind until finally, he was alone; the others were far, far ahead, and the piper a mere speck at the front leading them inexorably towards the mountain.

At the foot of the mountain the piper stopped, the children stopped, Luke stopped, even though he should have kept going. But he couldn't take his eyes off the Pied Piper, who tipped back his head, lifting his pipe skywards, and played his magic tune. A vast door slid open in the side of the mountain and the piper led the joyful children inside.

Frantically, Luke had started moving again, swinging along on his crutches. He got there just in time to see the last child skip through.

'Wait for me!' he wailed. Too late, the great door in the mountain closed and he was left outside. There was nothing to show there had ever been a door. Bruno and Wolfgang and his little sister Susanna had gone; his friends, too – all gone – and Luke was left with the piper's tune revolving incessantly round his brain.

Now his mother joined him in their garden, leaning on their kitchen gate, staring down the road to the mountain beyond. She, too, was grieving, but she realized his grief was different.

He didn't weep for his brothers and sister to come home as she did, he wept because he had been left behind. She often heard him moaning in his sleep: 'Why didn't you wait for me? I went as fast as I could on my stupid crutches. Is it because I was cursed by heaven – born lame; imperfect; useless?'

'How can we get them back?' whispered his mother.

But he just turned a blank face to her, his eyes as dead as pebbles.

Every day, Luke set off again for the mountain, stumbling on the hard ground at its base, humming tunelessly, his exploring hands reddened and raw with cold, tearing through thorny shrubs, and pushing past boulders, searching for any clues which might reveal where the opening was.

There was one other child who had been left behind; another child who had tried to follow the piper. Elfie had been dying from the plague the summer the piper came. Her mother had already died, as had half the town. But her brother, Erik, had dashed out to follow the piping tune.

In a way, Elfie could say that the tune saved her life: it had entered her feverish mind and mingled with the blood flowing through her veins, bringing a kind of energy, which had got her tumbling from her sickbed. How desperately she had crawled towards the open door into the street, begging her young brother to wait for her. But he didn't, and she was too weak to get to her feet and follow.

By the time Elfie's fever had drained away, the town was

as silent as a graveyard. Nowhere were there the shouts and laughter and quarrels of children; only the feeble whimpering of infants in arms. It was as though all the town's happiness had followed the piper into the mountain.

People got to hear that Elfie and Luke had been left behind, and didn't know how to treat them. At first, they just stared as though they were freaks; they muttered and mumbled, distraught with suffering; their minds churning with questions: were these children of God, or agents of the devil? Were they precious to be guarded, or cursed and sent away? There seemed no one to ask; no one to make the judgement – as so many people had died – even the mayor. Some wanted to drive them away immediately; why should they be here when their own children had gone? More and more voices were raised in hostility.

A mob turned up at their houses and dragged them to the town square. 'What shall we do with them?' They stared at a platform which was usually used for executions, where ropes knotted into nooses were slung over the cross-beam. Luke's mother made a passionate speech. 'Don't judge my son. He tried to follow the Piper – but you can see he's lame, and couldn't keep up. Let him stay at home with me. I'll watch him and take responsibility,' she pleaded. And Elfie's father stammered with fear, 'She had been dying of the plague,' he told them, 'and was too weak to follow. My son is in that mountain. Have pity; spare me my last child.'

'For God's sake let them go,' rasped an old woman. 'Why

make scapegoats of these innocent children? It wasn't them who broke the bond with the piper.'

At that, the townsfolk dispersed, though, feeling cheated of some kind of retribution, most shunned the children as if they might somehow carry the plague.

Then one day, while Luke and Elfie scrambled over the frozen mountain and snow had started to fall once more, there it was again: Everychild; standing so still among the fluttering snowflakes, watching them in the grey light of another winter's day. And there was that same muffled silence; as if their ears had clogged up, and they didn't even hear the sharp *caw, caw* of the raven as it swirled in the leaden sky. The child spoke:

'You'll never find the door without a pipe which plays the piper's tune,' it said.

For the first time Elfie and Luke looked at each other properly.

'Where can we find a pipe?' called Elfie.

But the child was already fading away into the whiteness of the snow.

'I'm going home,' muttered Luke, chilled to the bone. Swinging his crutches, he set off down the road. Where could he find a pipe?

Elfie followed along a little behind. 'Have you got a pipe?'

'Nope,' said Luke. 'I can't play the pipe.'

'Me neither,' said Elfie. 'Why don't we ask old Heinrich the shepherd? He plays a pipe.'

'Hmmm,' grunted Luke, acknowledging that it was a good place to start. Elfie caught up with him, and they now walked side by side, heading towards the upper meadows where Heinrich had a hut. Here he kept watch over the town's flocks of sheep through the winter.

They hummed the tune to Heinrich. He turned pale and backed away. 'I'm not giving you a pipe to play *that* tune,' he muttered. 'Go away, you cursed children,' and he shook his fist at them.

They stumbled away back to the town and went to see Helga. She had been their teacher at school, and she was the village piper's wife. Surely she would help? After her husband died a few years ago, she had taken up the pipe, and piped for village occasions. 'Can you teach us to play this tune?' they asked, humming it for her.

'What a horrible tune you sing me!' she cried. 'I hate it, I hate it. Of course I won't teach it to you.' And she pushed them out of the door.

Almost every house had a pipe of some sort, but though Luke and Elfie traipsed from door to door, most wouldn't open to them, and others shooed them away. 'Don't you ever sing that devilish tune here!' they shouted. Once again, voices were raised against the children. Once again, the town, gripped with grief and loss, wondered what they could do to break the curse.

How cold it was that winter. Nothing shifted the terrible chill. Birds fell dead from the trees, and the elderly and babies began to die of cold. It seemed that the spring would never come, and nothing would ever grow again. There was a dread of famine. 'This is an omen,' declared some bitter voices. 'These children must die if our land is ever to recover.'

Once again, a mob gathered and went in search of Elfie and Luke. This time the crowd was bigger. As they marched down the road, they saw the children returning from the mountain. They began to charge towards them. Luke and Elfie stopped dead, horrified. These were their own townspeople, their own kith and kin; their friends and neighbours whom they had known all their lives. As the citizens stomped closer and closer, they saw faces distorted with grief, and starvation, and a wild desire for revenge.

Then, from the mountain there came a great white snowstorm, swirling and whirling. In the middle of it was Everychild.

I am Everychild,
That ever lived and ever died,
And ever swam and ever drowned,
Was ever lost and never found.
I am Everychild,
That ever laughed and ever cried,
That ever searched to find a land,
That ever reached to hold a hand.
I am Everychild.

A blinding whiteness enveloped everyone on the road. When it had dispersed, the children had gone. The road to the mountain was empty, and the townsfolk turned and went home with a feeling of shame.

Luke found himself lying in a soft, cold bed of snow, gazing up at tall, gently creaking pine trees. The sky stared down at him like a chill blue eye between the finger-like tips of the evergreen branches. They reached for each other far, far above his head, and sent flurries of snow tumbling onto his face. He could hear a voice singing a little way off. It sang the piper's tune, and it wasn't coming from inside his head. He sat up and brushed away a coating of snow from his clothes.

Then he saw Elfie; she was kneeling beside an icy-cold stream gushing out of a rock in the mountain. On the banks of the stream were some reeds growing through the snow. Elfie had broken off one of the reeds and, whistling and humming through her clenched teeth, was hollowing out holes with a small knife.

He scrambled over to her. She looked so blue with cold, so white-sprinkled with snow.

'Elfie?' he muttered.

She held up her reed. 'I've made a pipe!' she cried triumphantly. 'I've never made one before.' Then she put it to her lips and blew across the open tip; a sound as pure as the song of a thrush broke through the air. Excitedly, she ran her fingers up and down and then – out came the first notes of the tune they both knew so well. She stopped, amazed.

'Play on, play, play!' urged Luke. 'You have the tune. That's it. Don't stop.'

She played. He helped her to her feet and, still playing, she moved round the base of the mountain. Behind them was the road along which the Pied Piper had brought the children from the town. She played and suddenly, with a tumble of pebbles, and a helter-skelter of snow, the whole side of the mountain juddered. First a crack appeared and then opened up, wider and wider like a giant yawn. They found themselves staring into the void beyond an open door. They stepped inside.

It was like stepping into the mouth of the Great Creator; into another universe: a universe with sky and stars and planets; with sun and moon, oceans, rivers and lakes. Everything that was in the world outside was here in the mountain: forests, jungles, deserts, hills and valleys.

Coming from deep inside the mountain, they heard a magical humming like a swarm of bees. 'Come, come!' it seemed to sing. 'It is always summer here.'

They felt a glorious warmth flooding through their limbs, and they went deeper into the mountain, following the humming.

'Come and find a world of mysterious forests teeming with every animal: not just cats and dogs and foxes and badgers, and squirrels and rabbits, but prowling tigers, roaring lions, slithering crocodiles, coiling snakes and towering bears – none of them dangerous – at least not to children in this magical land, but just there to amaze you, to give you the shiver of fear, but never terror; and birds – as you've never seen birds before, with amazing wings, and dazzling colours, and spell-binding songs. And there are playgrounds, my dears! Playgrounds of wonderful, scream-inducing helter-skelters, and swings which rise into the stars, and merry-go-rounds with golden horses which gallop round the entire earth, and roller coasters swooping up and down and whirling around. Come!'

Elfie stopped playing and began to run. 'Erik!' she cried. 'Erik!'

'Wait for me,' pleaded Luke as she raced ahead. But she went on running into the sunshine, and she never looked back. Desperate to keep up, Luke swung along after her.

Elfie stopped. Her shadow stretched behind her long and thin, as she stood stock-still in a shaft of sunlight. Luke reached her side. And there before them was a playground.

They stared in bewilderment.

There was no sound: no children's voices.

There were swings and roundabouts, a merry-go-round, and a roller coaster; there were waltzers and helter-skelters and a pirate ship, too – everything to thrill a child; all piled with boys and girls; all in violent motion, yet still. There was no laughter; no screams of joy, and excitement; no shuddering giggles of terror; just silence.

But the joy they felt turned into a nightmare.

There were their friends from the town: Paul, Marta, Gunter, Jacob, Rachel, Peter, Heloise; but they showed no signs of recognition; they didn't move and they didn't make a sound.

Elfie ran among the children, calling for Erik, but he was nowhere to be seen. Luke suddenly saw his brother. He hobbled over to Bruno, bursting with joy. 'Bruno!' He clasped him, but Bruno's body was rigid; his eyes saw him, or did they? – for they were as blank as strangers. Were they begging him for help?

'Wolfgang?' He reached out to his other brother, but Wolfgang, too, though open-mouthed with excitement, made no sound; no movement. They were both as still as stone; and there was little Susanna, frozen in a game of hopscotch, standing on one foot, about to leap to the next square.

'Look at me, Suzi! I came after all! I managed to come into the mountain!' Luke hopped in front of her. But she didn't look up and, when he touched her, she was hard and cold.

Elfie came and stood next to him. Quietly, she took Luke's hand. Thank goodness; it was warm and pulsating.

'Are they dead?' she asked in a small, scared voice.

'Their eyes are alive,' murmured Luke.

They heard sounds coming nearer: horses neighing and trumpets blasting, and above it all came the sound of a piper. It was a leaping, dancing tune, yet full of menace. Luke didn't know why, but he was gripped by anxiety. Something made him hiss, 'Hide!' And he dragged Elfie behind the waltzer, pulling her to the ground. 'Whatever you do, don't move; don't say a word.'

They peered through the gaps, and saw a woman on a snowy white horse. Alongside her was a young boy riding on a black horse. When Elfie saw the boy, she gasped. It was Erik. She was about to yell his name, but Luke clapped a hand over her mouth. He held it there till her body slumped as she understood that she must not give them away.

Servants helped the woman and Erik off their horses and, while she was taken to be seated in a red velvet chair overlooking the playground, Erik ran among the stone children in the playground. 'Time to play!' he shouted.

'Where's the piper?' demanded the woman.

'I'm here, madam,' called an obliging voice. And the piper appeared: the same pied sort of fellow, dressed from his feathered cap, down to his pointed toes, in an outfit of every colour of the rainbow.

'Pipe, pipe, pipe! Make the children play,' ordered the woman. 'My boy wants to play.'

Obediently, the piper began to play his pipes. The leaping, dancing tune got faster. It was a whirling tune which unfroze the children and made them burst into activity. The rides went into motion, and a great sound of merriment filled the air as they all went spinning and twirling, and twisting and flipping and whooshing and swooshing.

Erik watched with delight, clapping his hands, and throwing back his head with laughter. Then he leaped among them, shouting, 'Play with me, play with me!'

Elfie wanted to rush forward and clasp her brother in her arms, but Luke grabbed her hand and tugged her away as if in play. 'Something's wrong. We must pretend to be like the others: play when they play, stop when they stop. Stay away from Erik till we know what to do.'

So they went on the slides and the swings, and swung about on the merry-go-round till they were dizzy; they threw balls at coconuts and fished for prizes; they helped themselves to great fluffy piles of pink candyfloss.

'All right, stop now,' said the woman after a while. 'It's time to go home.'

The piper stopped playing. The children stopped dead wherever they were: on the merry-go-round, on the pirate ship – frozen in full tilt, on the roundabouts and roller coasters, or just rough and tumbling on the grass. They stopped, as if they had been playing a game of statues.

'Stop,' hissed Luke. 'Don't move a muscle; don't move your eyes.' He and Elfie dropped to their knees as if playing marbles.

The boy clicked his fingers, and his servants came.

'We'll come again tomorrow, won't we?' asked Erik.

'Of course, my darling boy!' laughed the woman, and soon the horses turned and rode back through the forest with the piper following behind.

Luke and Elfie waited a long time before they finally moved. Taking up his crutches, Luke got to his feet and looked around anxiously, ready to freeze again. Then he nodded to Elfie that all was clear. Cautiously, they wandered among the stone-still children. Luke hugged and kissed his hard siblings, and thought he saw a small tear come into little Susanna's eyes. 'Wake up, please, Suzi,' he pleaded.

'What are we going to do, Luke?' wept Elfie. 'How can we wake them up? And what about Erik?'

Luke moaned in despair. 'I don't know.'

A strange flurry of snow whirled around them. They shivered and looked up. There, a little way off, was Everychild.

'Everychild!' Luke stumbled to his knees. 'What are you doing here?'

'Everychild is Everywhere,' a voice told him.

> *In tumbling house and rubbled street,*
> *In palace gardens cool and neat.*
> *In sinking boats, on foreign shore,*
> *Looking for an open door.*

> *Everychild is Everywhere.*

> *And where the deer and tiger stroll*
> *Where imams call, or church bells toll*
> *Where the children play in peace*

Where song and laughter never cease
Where people hate, or others care,

Everychild is Everywhere.

The child began to recede down the track on which the woman and Erik had ridden away.

'We've got to follow!' cried Elfie, pulling Luke to his feet. 'Let's go where they went.'

They hardly knew if they walked through a landscape, or if somehow, the landscape moved around them, but one moment they were in dark forests and jungles, where golden-eyed tigers prowled through the undergrowth, and monkeys leaped from branch to branch; then they were staring across an endless desert of shimmering sands, where black shadows sliced down the dunes, and camels moved along the thin horizon, and desert foxes prowled in the scrub. Then they were in a rich green countryside, of haystacks and leafy lanes, and suddenly in towns and cities and roaring traffic. But all the time, it was warm; it was summer: a perfect summer. It was as though winter had been banished from the mountain.

At first, Everychild was always in sight, though its body changed with the background: now it was no longer white as frost, but green and brown; golden, then dark. Dark became shadows of night, then shadows of day which sliced across bright sunshine.

They had just crossed a glistening desert, rolling like a

golden ocean, when there ahead of them was a great castle made of sand, with ramparts and towers and bridges. At first, it seemed to be a long way off, but in three strides, they stood before the castle gates.

The gates were closed – and there seemed to be no gatekeepers. They tried to knock – but a door of sand made no noise. Still, it opened silently.

Tentatively, they stepped upon a drawbridge, wondering if the sand could hold their weight. But it did, and they crossed into a courtyard, but there was no sign of anybody; not even guards. At the far end were some steps rising to a first floor where they could see beams of yellow light through the windows.

Side by side, Luke and Elfie walked to the steps and began to climb. They reached another door and opened it. They found themselves staring down a vast hall where, at the far end, sat the woman and, sitting at her feet, was Erik. Luke held Elfie's hand like a vice to stop her rushing over to her brother, and she pushed her hand into her mouth to stop her calling out his name.

The woman looked up. 'Who are you?' she asked.

Elfie answered. 'I am Erik's sister, Elfie. I've come to take my brother home.'

Erik didn't move. It was as if he was under a spell.

'Who are you?' Luke asked the woman.

'I am the Woman of the Mountain. I am Everymother,' she said.

Everymother whoever cried,
Whoever loved and ever sighed
Whoever lost a child that died
Whoever grieved and ever wept
Whoever paced and never slept
I am Everymother.

'Have you come to take away my boy?' The woman seemed afraid.

'He's not your boy. He's my brother,' said Elfie quietly. 'I want to take him home.'

'Piper!' she shrieked. 'Where are you? I paid you to bring me a boy who could be my son. You promised me. We made a bargain!' The woman began to wail.

A figure stepped out into a shaft of sunlight. It was the piper.

He spoke to Luke and Elfie. 'I am a Bargain Maker. I made a bargain with the Woman of the Mountain to bring her a child.'

'And the other children?' cried Luke. 'My brothers and sister, and all the children of the town? Were they part of the bargain? Why do you keep them too?'

'The children are mine,' insisted the piper adamantly. 'They became mine when the mayor of your town broke his word, and the boy I brought to the Woman of the Mountain needs playmates, doesn't he?' His voice became as flowing as honey. 'But let us make a bargain together. Bargain with me and all will be well.'

'We don't want to bargain with you!' shouted Luke. 'We can't make bargains. We want to go home, and take all the other children home too. You're nothing but a thief.'

'Me, a thief? Oh, no. It is you out there who are thieves; you and your mayor, and all your greedy counsellors – you are the thieves. You steal justice; you steal from the poor and ordinary, decent people. I make bargains, and I always keep my side of the bargain. I can make things happen. I can make deals with angels or devils. I fulfil wishes – but always at a price. If you break your side of the bargain, then you must pay the price. Come, let us bargain together. Listen to me. I have brought spring and summer into this mountain. Out there is nothing but winter and starvation. Here there is eternal youth and joy. Stay in the mountain.' His voice was soft and enticing. 'There is nothing for you outside. Stay with the Woman of the Mountain; she is Everymother. Stay here and be happy for ever.'

The piper put his hand into his jacket and drew out his pipe. He blew a soft note across its tip. Luke stared in horror, instantly feeling his blood quiver in his veins, and his brain blur as if a net of enchantment was being cast over him. If the piper played his pipe, and played *that tune*, they would be trapped in his power for ever, and would never leave.

Suddenly, the hall darkened to a leaden grey. It became deathly cold. The piper shivered. A flurry of snowflakes blew round the hall, and there, standing before them, all white with snow, and hair rigid with frost was Everychild.

A strange, starry light seemed to glow all over its body as it lifted an arm and waved at Elfie to play her pipe.

Elfie thrust the pipe to her mouth and blew. It was a gentle tune which floated out; a melody she and Erik used to sing with their mother.

The tune soared free into the air. It brought Erik to his feet.

'No, no!' The Woman of the Mountain clasped Erik in her arms as if she would never let him go. 'I can't lose my boy. He's not anybody's child but mine. He's no one's son, no one's brother. Not any more. I made a bargain with the piper. I paid him three bags of gold to bring me a child.'

Elfie ran round the hall, piping away: she played all the nursery tunes and folk tunes that they had ever heard. She thrust her head through a window and played so that her notes floated over the deserts and forests, all the way to the playground of everlasting childhood. And all around them, the castle of sand began to crumble away.

From far in the distance, they heard the sound of laughter and joyful clamouring. The stone children had reawakened. They came nearer and nearer, and though the piper tried to play, his tune was drowned out by their voices and Elfie's piping.

Erik pulled his hand away from the woman and rushed to his sister's side.

'Don't leave me, boy!' begged the Woman of the Mountain. 'Didn't I give you everything a child desires?'

'I want to go home!' cried Erik.

'All any child really wants is to go home,' said Everychild.

Everychild walked over to the woman and took her hand. 'I'll bargain with you,' it said. 'I will be your child if you will let the other children go home.'

'That sounds like a good deal to me,' said the piper. 'A good deal, madam,' he nodded. 'And, as you don't need me any more, I'll be on my way.' With a wave, he skipped into the swirl of sand and snow and vanished.

Then from every side of the mountain – from the north, south, east and west – great doors began to slide open and howling winter winds swept inside. Now the sandcastle walls were tumbling down. Sunshine and sand whirled about and mixed with snow brought in by winds from Russia, winds from the ice caps, winds from the Alps and Himalayas, whirling winds of icy snow which swept round the children and tossed them about. Now the mountain itself was open, and the children were flowing outside, and the animals, too: the lions and tigers, monkeys, bears and flights of glorious birds, all heading for their own homes.

Elfie stopped playing. They listened to the winter wind moaning and sprinkling snow on the sand dunes, and the distant sounds of children's voices as they ran for home in every direction.

Luke, Elfie and Erik stepped out of the mountain. The world glistened like a wonderland, and a pale sun set the crystals of snow on fire. Erik turned round to look back inside and wave farewell, but Everychild and Everymother had gone, and the door into the mountain had closed up again. They were free.

Before them, the children of the town streamed towards home, skipping and laughing. And there among them were Bruno, Wolfgang and Susanna. 'Wait for us!' shouted Elfie and Erik, running and laughing to catch up with them. 'Wait for me!' Luke called out. So they stopped, and turned round to wait for him.

As they waited, they heard a sound coming from the frozen river; a sound they always listened for at the end of every winter: the crick … crack … crick. The ice was cracking. The thaw had begun, and spring was on its way.

> *Somewhere, along another road,*
> *The piper skipped his merry way,*
> *Wondering what other lucrative deal*
> *He could make this day.*

the Wishing Book
PIERS TORDAY

Let me tell you a story about this thing which happened when I was a little girl, and you can decide if I am lying or not.

I was just ten years old when my grandmother gave me a present for Christmas that would change my life for ever.

At the time, I had two grannies: Granny Bike and Granny Car.

Granny Car was my stepmother Christine's mummy, and she was super rich, because she had invented Skinny Pop – the amazing fizzy drink, which made you thinner and thinner. I didn't like Skinny Pop, because I didn't think I needed to be any thinner, and also, it tasted of nail polish.

Christine always told me to be on my best behaviour when Granny Car came to visit.

Granny Car liked to arrive in her chauffeur-driven Bentley, and her driver Godfrey would take off his coat and put it down on the front path so her feet didn't have to touch the ground we lived on.

'Frightfully common!' sniffed Granny Car, as she trampled his jacket into the mud.

Granny Car thought that about lots of things. Like my name, Ethel. 'Frightfully common!' she said. Or my dad, because he worked for the local council and hadn't invented a global soft-drink sensation. 'Frightfully common!' My school, because we didn't wear the same hats and skirts she used to wear when she was little. And my pet goldfish, Silver – because he wasn't a poodle dog. 'Frightfully, awfully, vulgarly, obscenely, hopelessly COMMON!' she squawked.

The only person in our entire family Granny Car didn't think was common was her daughter, Christine.

'My princess,' she used to purr. 'My golden duchess, my peach, my prize,' she cooed. 'Why did you have to marry into such an embarrassingly common family?'

(That is another story, but it has quite a lot to do with my real mum dying when I was little, my dad being quite lonely and something called a holiday romance.)

And every Christmas, Granny Car always brought us lots of presents.

Lots and lots.

They were always wrapped in glittering gold paper, tied up with silk ribbon in frilly bows. There were always loads of boxes, which Godfrey struggled to carry from the car. The pile always made Silver's eyes pop out of his head when he saw it stashed under the tree.

And the presents were always, always, never anything we wanted.

Like last year – Lycra jogging bottoms for Dad, who hated running or exercise of any kind other than walking in the park and whistling, which he did a lot. 'Frightfully slimming!' said Granny Car.

The latest mobile phone for Christine, covered in so many diamonds that she had to keep it in a safe. 'Frightfully smart!' said Granny Car.

And a designer dress for me. WHEN SHE KNEW I HATED DRESSES. 'Frightfully pretty!' said Granny Car.

Silver always hid in his toy plastic cave whenever Granny Car visited. But he reappeared as soon as he heard a certain noise coming up our path.

Squeak! Squeak!

That was the noise Granny Bike's ancient bicycle made as she wheeled it along. It was an old-fashioned cycle with wonky handlebars and a basket tied on with string.

Dad told me that it had been his granny's bike before it had been his mum's and before that, it had been her mum's bike, and before that . . . well, that didn't matter, it was such a long time ago. But Granny Bike looked like she might have been around even longer than that.

She was tiny and wrinkled. Her pale skin looked like it was made of paper, or the material wasps built their nests out of. And she had a crooked nose, with whiskers on her crooked chin.

She also never spoke.

Granny Bike had got seriously ill once and the doctors had to take out her tongue. This was before I was born. I had never heard her speak.

I didn't mind.

She always had a nice, big, lopsided smile for me, and a twinkle in her ancient eyes.

Granny Bike wasn't super rich. She hadn't invented Skinny Pop. I never was quite sure what Granny Bike did. She didn't live in a big mansion like Granny Car. She lived in a little tumbledown cottage on the outskirts of town, and was either always cooking something that bubbled in a pot or growing strange-smelling herbs in her garden.

When I asked Dad what she did, he would mutter, 'It doesn't matter, and anyway, she's retired now.'

Christine always shuddered when Granny Bike visited. She said she smelled of dishcloths and old cheese, which wasn't true, she didn't. If anything, she smelled of bonfires and autumn leaves, which were two of my favourite smells.

Now on this Christmas Day, Christine decided to be meaner to her than ever before.

'I don't want her dragging that filthy old bike in and stinking up the place,' she said between gulps of a special seasonal Skinny Pop, which tasted of Christmas pudding and grown-up chocolates. 'If you want to go and see her, why don't you visit her on Boxing Day? Or the day after? You can take her my present.'

Christine held up the tiniest bottle of perfume you'd ever seen. 'Mummy's latest,' she said admiringly. 'Eau d'Skinny Pop. You spray it on anything – your skin, furniture, old ladies – and they smell like a sticky, fizzy drink for a whole week.'

'That's kind, dear,' said my dad, from his favourite chair, where he was busy reading his favourite book, *The Birds of Britain.* 'We'll do that.'

I knew Dad loved Granny Bike as much as me. But I wished he would stand up for her once in a while.

The snow had been falling all morning, and I wanted to go outside and play in the park with the other children in our street. A few of my friends were pressing their faces against our window, wrapped up in woolly hats and gloves, making funny expressions, until Christine shooed them away.

'You'll catch your death, or worse, if you go out and play in that filthy park!' she said. 'Just imagine how much dog mess there is out there under the snow.'

I said there were plenty of other things I would prefer to imagine.

Then Christine went red and grabbed the golden necklace around her throat, which she always did when she was upset, and called for my dad. 'Stewart!' she yelled. 'Your daughter seems to have forgotten what day it is.'

'Don't upset your mother,' said Dad, still looking at pictures of lesser spotted tits.

I hated it when he said that as well. I mean, Christine wasn't my mother. She was just pretending to be. Besides, how could I forget what day it was? There were endless Christmas songs burbling out of her state-of-the-art laptop in the kitchen. They all sounded cheesy to me. I was wearing the horrid Christmas jumper Granny Car had given me last year, which was decorated with a picture of a huge knitted bottle of Skinny Pop, covered in holly and snow. It made me feel stupid and I hated it.

Before either of us could say another word, there was a loud honking outside.

'Mummy!' said Christine, and she ran to the door, to let Godfrey in, who was struggling under a heap of golden gifts. I may have been imagining things, but I thought I heard Dad let out a long sigh as he stood up to help him. Silver blew some bubbles to the top of his bowl and dived back into his cave.

I don't mean to sound ungrateful. It was kind of Granny Car to get me the jumper the year before. And this time, as I opened the layers of thick, expensive paper, to discover a huge, professional make-up set, I did smile and say thank you.

I knew there were lots of other children who might have wanted the glossy box, with photos of glamourous models on the front, and all the different weird-smelling pots and creams inside. But I wasn't one of those children, and I was sad that Granny Car never seemed to notice that.

I was sad that Granny Car, Christine and even Dad never seemed to notice lots of things. Perhaps sad isn't even the right expression. Boiling mad might be better.

Granny Car ran her bejewelled fingers through my hair. 'You're turning into a young woman, my gel. Don't keep it cut this short – frightfully common. Start with this kit to sort your face out, and then Mummy can make an appointment to see my hairdresser, Gustave de Florie – you'll love him.'

If I stared through the snow piling up against the glass, I could see other kids making a snowman in the park across the road. I wished more than anything I could join them.

In fact, this Christmas, I wished I was anywhere but here in our overheated front room, with Granny Car not only beaming down from her gold-framed portrait above the TV, but sitting at the end of the table, talking loudly over us. I wished my real mum was here instead of Christine, and I wished Dad was like he used to be.

The Dad who used to laugh a lot and put me high on his shoulders, and run around the park till we could both hardly breathe for having so much fun.

I wished Dad would smile at things rather than sigh.

I wished many, many things.

I suddenly didn't like my life, and I wished it not to be my life. I wished it so much that I nearly snapped the pencil I was holding. (I was a bit of a doodler, always getting told off at school for drawing pictures of our teachers in my exercise book. I always kept a pencil and pad to hand because sometimes losing myself in drawing and colouring in a picture was the only way I could stay calm.)

But before I could do any drawing, or go and join my friends outside, we had to have Christine's special microwaved Christmas dinner. 'Just pop it in and *voilà*!' she said.

She popped it into the microwave, and it popped out moments later. I had just popped a forkful of the rubbery goo into my mouth – and can assure you there was nothing *voilà* about it – when I glanced out of the window to see how my friends were getting on with their snowman.

It was beginning to snow harder and harder, and I couldn't see them clearly any more. I hoped that they hadn't been turned into snowmen themselves.

But what I saw instead, dimly appearing through the white swirls, was a familiar bent figure wheeling something along.

Squeak! Squeak!

'Granny Bike!' I said.

'Oh, how frightfully dreary,' sighed Granny Car, trying to spear some rubbery peas with her fork.

'I thought we agreed she wasn't coming,' said my stepmother, looking at Dad.

Dad shrugged. 'You know how she is.'

Silver was at least pleased, swimming up from his cave

and blowing bubbles along the surface of the water. I pushed my chair back and ran to the door.

'I don't remember saying anything about getting down,' said Christine.

'Frightfully rude,' muttered Granny Car.

I didn't care. It was Christmas Day after all.

I opened the door, and a gust of snow blew in, stinging my face. There was Granny Bike, wrapped in a raggedy bundle of scarves and shawls, her crooked nose poking out like a beak. With great care, she leaned her bike against the wall.

'Happy Christmas, Granny Bike!' I said. 'We've just sat down to dinner. Do you want to come in?'

She shook her head, showering snow over the doormat.

'Are you sure?' I said. 'Don't you want to get out of the snow?'

Granny Bike gave me one of her biggest, warmest, most lopsided smiles, and a large snowflake fell off her nose onto her whiskery chin.

Suddenly, I wanted to tell her everything. How unhappy I was, how no one understood me, how horrid Christine was, how snobby Granny Car was. 'Granny Bike,' I started to say.

But she put a mittened finger to her lips to quieten me, and, turning around, began to rummage in the basket on top of her bike. It was full of yellowing newspaper scraps, a ball of wool and some twigs. Eventually, she found something at the bottom, which she handed to me, beaming.

It was a parcel, wrapped in brown paper and tied with string.

'For me?' I said.

Granny Bike nodded, her whiskery chin bobbing up and down, and then she enfolded me in a hug. She was cold and damp from the snow, and she was as skinny as a skeleton, but I can promise you, it was the warmest and cosiest hug I had that Christmas.

Then she patted me on the head, and slowly began to wheel her bike back into the swirling flakes.

'Goodbye, Granny Bike,' I called after her. 'Happy Christmas!'

I dimly saw a frail hand waved in reply, then she was gone.

'What did she want?' called Christine, as I closed the door.

'Nothing,' I said. 'I told her we were eating.'

I hid the present under a pile of winter coats, because I knew that if Granny Car or my stepmother saw it, it would probably be deemed too common and put in the recycling.

'Oh, good,' said Christine. Then when she saw Dad's crestfallen face, she added. 'Come on, Stewart! You know she doesn't even like Christmas anyway. We'll see her on Boxing Day. Maybe.'

She patted his hand, and we carried on spooning special microwaved gloop into our mouths, listening to cheesy Christmas music from the computer, while the snow fell outside and the day darkened.

Later that night, when everyone had gone to bed, I crept

downstairs and took my present out from its hiding place in the coat pile.

Back in my room, hiding under my duvet with a torch, I carefully untied the string and unwrapped the paper.

And there was ... a book. It had a plain, rough black cover, maybe leather, I couldn't quite tell, and about a hundred pages.

Every single one of them was blank.

I turned the book over. There weren't any words. Only a long silver pencil, taped in place.

That was it. Nothing else.

Then, as I gathered up the wrapping paper, a tiny card fell out. I opened it and read:

To my darling granddaughter Ethel,
Happy Christmas!

This is no ordinary sketchbook. This is a wishing book. It has great power. Use it wisely and well, and may all your wishes come true. But always, always, be careful what you wish for.

Granny Bike

A wishing book? I picked up the sketchbook and examined it carefully. It was covered in a thick layer of dust, which I blew and rubbed off, but no genie appeared. There was no ancient spell written anywhere, no secret compartment and certainly no fairy dust. It seemed plain and ordinary to me. Apart from the fact that both the pencil and the book looked as old as Granny Bike herself, it couldn't have been less magical.

The pencil wasn't even that sharp.

I reread her message. The last line was a bit odd. *Be careful what you wish for.* Still, it gave me an idea.

As an experiment, I would draw something I had never wished for, ever.

The next morning, when I came down for breakfast, I knew straightaway that things were not right. Christine sat at the kitchen table, her head in her hands, sobbing, while Dad patted her on the back, and tried to offer her a mug of tea. Silver was swimming in circles quickly, which he always does when he's stressed.

I knew it had to be bad.

'What's happened?' I said.

'We've been burgled,' said Dad, and Christine started to scream.

I looked around. The front door was in one piece. No one had smashed any of the windows, and everything seemed to be still there. Anything a burglar might want to steal, that is – the TV, microwave, laptop, the expensive exercise machine Christine bought off the internet and never used, and Silver, of course. (Well, if I was a burglar, I would want to steal him.)

Except, not quite.

Because next to the Christmas tree and its twinkling lights, where there should have been the huge pile of presents from Granny Car, was an empty space. There was no make-up styling kit. No Wi-Fi slippers for Dad (that could be heated up remotely by a phone app). And no piles and piles of jewellery for Christine – all gone.

Not a single bow or ribbon remained. Just a flattened patch of carpet.

Christine wiped her eyes and stared at me. 'Who would do a thing like that to us!' she bawled. 'I'm a good person! I signed fifty online petitions to save donkeys last year!'

'There, there,' said Dad. 'We all know you're a wonderful person, love; perhaps they got the wrong flat.'

'How did they get in?' she demanded. 'Down the chimney! Like Father Thingummy?'

'Er, no,' said Dad. 'No one could get down that chimney. You do know the fire's not real, don't you?'

And she started screaming again. As usual, neither of them was paying any attention to me or what I was doing. I flopped down onto the sofa and opened the wishing book. Making sure no one, not even Silver, was looking, I turned to the first page.

The drawing I did last night.

Of the presents under the tree.

They were no longer under the tree, but they were in my book. I was quite good at drawing, yet this sketch surprised even me. The boxes, surrounded by wrapping paper, looked so real, I could almost reach out and grab them.

Like they were in the book.

I wondered.

Sucking on the silver pencil for a moment, I looked around the flat for something else that I hadn't wished for. There was quite a lot to choose from – and then I spotted it.

Sitting on the kitchen windowsill, a huge cactus.

Not only was it massively ugly, like a great big green monster's thumb, but every time I brushed past, I got stung by its prickles.

I started to sketch, first drawing a rough outline of the plant in the pot, and then shading it in, and adding the spikes last.

And the strangest thing happened.

The plant began to disappear, into thin air.

The more I drew it onto the page, the less it was there.

A tall shadow fell over my drawing. I looked up. It was Christine.

'Wot you doing?' she shrieked. Her eyes were red and raw from crying, layers of her make-up streaming down her face.

I closed the sketchbook, just in case she saw the picture of the presents. 'I'm drawing.'

'Drawing!' she bawled. 'A fine way to help your mother at a time like this . . .'

'You're not my mother,' I said quietly.

'. . . when you could be on your hands and knees, looking for clues! Or calling the police, or doing something useful to earn your keep around here. Is drawing going to get me my presents back? Is drawing going to pay our mortgage or our fuel bills? Is drawing going to mend the gaping wound in Granny Car's heart when we see her this afternoon and tell her this terrible news?'

I looked up at her. 'I thought we were going to see Granny Bike today?' I was looking forward to showing her my drawings and finding out more about this amazing present she had given me.

Christine dismissed the idea with a flick of her hand. 'I've cancelled it. Who wants to go and see that stinking old bat anyway; she never has much to say for herself, does she, Stewart?' And she elbowed Dad sharply in the ribs.

He looked wounded, but didn't say anything.

'No, we're going to go to Granny Car and you're going to get down on your knees and grovel as you tell her that your hundred-pound make-up kit has been stolen! How do you think that news will make her feel?'

'I didn't want it anyway.'

'Tough! I could have sold it on eeeeeBay!' she screeched, so loudly that Silver's bowl nearly cracked in half.

I absolutely didn't want to see Granny Car. I wanted to see Granny Bike. But there was no way out, unless ... Studying the gold-framed portrait which hung proudly above the TV, I began to draw ...

We didn't go to see Granny Car after all. She mysteriously disappeared that Boxing Day, right in the middle of taking a luxurious bubble bath (Christmas Cake and Sherry fragrance), in her specially custom-made gold bathtub. Godfrey came in with the king-size bath towel of finest Egyptian cotton, which he had spent the last half-hour specially fluffing on his mistress's orders – only to find that his mistress was no longer there.

He thought she might be hidden by the bubbles and the steam.

She wasn't. She had quite gone.

Almost as if she had been sucked down the plughole, even though she would never have fitted. After he had got over the shock, Godfrey was delighted to discover that not only would he never have to put his jacket down in the mud for her to walk on again, but that he had inherited her BMW.

The police used my 'incredibly lifelike' sketch to issue a missing person's report.

'Uncanny, isn't it?' said the desk sergeant, beaming with admiration as he studied my drawing. 'Almost like she was 'ere.'

Then Christine started demanding to see his superior officer and I quickly took my book away. I was beginning to get tired of Christine and all her yelling at everyone the whole time.

While she and the sergeant tore chunks out of each other, I sat back on my chair and, licking my pencil, began to sketch.

If I said so myself, I was getting pretty good at drawing now.

This time, the police came to our house to ask about my stepmother's sudden disappearance. The sergeant wasn't smiling any more.

Although it didn't matter. I shut the door in his face, and while he shouted and hammered on the door, I got out my pad. It wasn't the best sketch, a bit cartoony, but the hammering soon stopped.

That was the moment things started to go wrong.

I couldn't stop drawing. Anyone who annoyed me, anyone who stepped out of line, anyone I didn't like the look of, ended up wished away in the sketchbook. The kid on the bike who wasn't looking where he was going and nearly ran me over. A fox who looked at me funny from the end of an alleyway. Even the snowman my friends had made in the park, because I didn't like watching it melt from our window.

Then I wished our view could be improved. There were three tall blocks of flats right in the middle of it, and very ugly they were, too. Stained concrete, smashed windows, I didn't even know whether people lived in them or not. I thought maybe learning to draw buildings instead of people would make a change.

Soon the horizon was improved, and the buildings lived only in the pages of my book. It was uncanny how real they looked, almost as if the sketchbook made them look better than I could actually draw. Sometimes, if I held the sketchbook to my ear, I could almost hear thousands of tiny voices all chattering and screaming.

After the tower blocks came the big factory in the town, that did nothing but belch out oily smoke and toxic chemicals into the sky. I think some people worked there, but surely they would be better off working somewhere nicer and less smelly?

Then the church, because I went to a service once and found it boring. And the school, so I wouldn't have to go back next term. I drew the hospital, because it scared me, and thought at least all the ill people inside wouldn't be in pain any more.

Soon, there wasn't much left of our town, but just a kind of white space, like things had been rubbed out.

People began to go crazy.

There were riots, with people throwing things at policemen in riot gear, yelling that all the disappearances were a government conspiracy, while helicopters with searchlights buzzed overhead.

I had my nose pressed to the window, even though Dad wanted me to stay away.

I had never drawn an action scene before, now was my chance!

After the police disappeared, the government sent in tanks.

I wasn't wildly keen on drawing those, but sometimes you need to get out of your comfort zone, don't you?

Then the countryside began to look a bit patchy. All the gaps made it seem messier than before. I started to draw and draw and draw. Soon the messy, ragged world outside was all safely contained within the pages of my book.

The only thing that remained was our house and garden, Dad, Silver and me.

Dad had gone mad, though. He didn't understand what was going on. He looked wild-eyed and confused and started to babble, not making any sense. I gave him the biggest hug I could and asked if I could draw his portrait to cheer him up.

That was when Silver started to act funny around me. He wouldn't come out of his underwater shipwreck to play. Only the occasional bubble appeared.

He needn't have worried. I would never draw Silver.

Although, what was to stop me drawing his bowl?

The next morning, I woke up, stretched with a big yawn, got out of bed and went to open the curtains and see if the Christmas snow was still there.

Only I didn't. Because my bed wasn't there. Then I remembered. It had felt cold and uncomfortable, so I had drawn it and put it in my pad. There were no curtains to pull either, because they hadn't closed properly.

There was nothing to see at all.

It was all in the dark book clutched in my hand, which, along with the silver pencil, was everything I now owned. They were the only two objects which seemed to exist in the world.

All around was whiteness, wherever I looked. But it wasn't snow. Just blank space. Above, below and around me. I could have been in a film studio or on a screen, except I wasn't, I wasn't . . . anywhere.

I was utterly, completely alone. With Granny Bike's present, I had made everything disappear. I hadn't been careful what I wished for at all.

I sat down in the middle of the white space and opened my wishing book, turning right to the first page. There were all our other Christmas presents. My make-up kit. Christine's piles of jewellery. And Dad's Wi-Fi slippers. There on the page, almost as real as life. I never knew how good I was at drawing until I picked up that pencil.

If I held the book to my ear and shook it, it was almost possible to hear the jewellery rattling inside and the Wi-Fi self-heating slippers beeping as they searched for a connection.

What a stupid, dumb idea, I thought. Wi-Fi slippers that self-heated via a mobile phone app, so that they were warm, ready and waiting when you got home from work. Why would anyone give that to someone as a present? Or even buy it in a shop? It was so ridiculous and completely bonkers that I began to smile.

But I wasn't meant to like the things in this book. I had wished them away. I turned the page.

The prickly cactus, looking as sharp and deadly as ever. I remembered Dad once pricked himself on it while carrying a jug of hot custard, and he did a dance of pain and splashing custard, which gave rise to the family nickname, 'Custard-Cactus Dance', given to anyone either dancing badly or reacting to a stubbed toe.

No, that wasn't funny, I decided. Definitely not.

Then there was Granny Car, frozen in time. She was only wearing a shower cap, surrounded by a cloud of extra foamy bubbles. It might have been my imagination, but I thought I could hear – faintly, like a fly trapped between glass – her exclaiming, 'A dirty old sketchbook! How frightfully common!'

Granny Car, I thought to myself, looking at the picture. She was bossy and a snob, and not always nice to everybody. And I had started hating her for that. Now here she was, preserved for all time, stark naked apart from a handful of soapy bubbles.

Once upon a time, such a thought would have made me laugh.

Now, though, I felt a tug inside. A tug of sadness.

She was my stepgranny after all. She did come to visit us all the time, even if she was overcritical. All those presents, over the page, she bought those for us all the time. They were about the worst, waste-of-money presents to be found on earth.

But they were presents. I tried to remember what I had got Granny Car for Christmas this year.

Then I remembered. I had bought her a little wind-up

toy version of the Queen. If you wound it up, her jaw went up and down and her white-gloved arm waved. It was only a jokey thing from a toy shop, and I thought Granny Car would hate it, because she thought anyone who didn't stand up when the Queen was mentioned was frightfully common.

Actually, she thought it was the funniest thing ever and kept playing with it over Christmas dinner, until even Christine – her own daughter, who never laughed at anything – started to laugh.

I felt a smile begin to tug at the corner of my mouth.

I turned the page. The policemen, who were trying to help look after us. Christine, my stepmum, who wanted to know what had happened to her mum.

My school and my friends.

The town where we lived, tower blocks, factory and all.

Dad. Silver.

I looked up. I didn't know how long I had been absorbed in the drawings. As there was no sun (too hot, in the book) or clocks (too anxious-making, on the page), the sketchbook was absolutely bursting full of people, animals, places and things. It sounds strange, but it even felt heavier. And from every sheet of paper, in between the cracks and spine of the book, I could hear noise. Chatter, whispers, shouts, cars, rain, cats and dogs, all the noise of everyday life was seeping out, as if from the faintest radio signal in a distant galaxy.

Not everything in the book made me laugh. Some of it still made me furious. Like the cyclist who nearly ran me over at the zebra crossing. But all the same, I clutched the book tight to my chest.

There was a whole world in there. I didn't want to let it go. I wanted it back.

Then, to my surprise, I heard a noise not coming from the book.

Squeak! Squeak!

I looked up.

Far away, on the horizon of the huge blankness I found myself in, I could spy a tiny, dark, bent figure, wheeling her bicycle towards me.

Granny Bike!

As she got closer and closer, the noise of her bike got louder and louder, and the noise of the world in my sketchbook got fainter and fainter. Until she was standing over me. The one person I hadn't put in my sketchbook.

She didn't say anything, of course.

But she looked at me. Her whiskery chin was firm and her eyes were not twinkling with mischief like they often were. I believe it was physically impossible for Granny Bike ever to be cross, but this was perhaps the nearest she would ever come to it.

I hugged the book to my chest. 'Am I in trouble, Granny Bike?' I said.

Granny Bike didn't reply.

'I shouldn't have drawn all those people and things, should I?' I said. 'You told me to be careful what I wished for,

331

and I ended up drawing everything. I thought it was because I didn't want them, but actually ... I do. Now I don't have them, I can even love a pair of Wi-Fi-controlled self-heating slippers. Or a cactus. Even Granny Car.'

Granny Bike smiled a little at that.

'How did it work, though, Granny Bike?'

She shrugged.

'Are you a ...' Somehow, I couldn't quite say the word. Even though she had a crooked nose and greasy hair and a wart on her whiskery chin, I couldn't say that word about Granny Bike, or any granny, for that matter.

Granny Bike cocked her head at me, as if to say, *Go on.*

'I don't know,' I said. 'It doesn't matter. I just want to put things right now. Can you help me?'

Granny Bike nodded. She offered a wrinkly, papery hand, and pulled me up so I was facing her. I put the wishing book down on the floor of white nothing and gave her a hug.

She patted me on the back and took the pencil out of my hand. Then, creaking low on her ancient knees, she picked up the book, turned to the last blank page and began to draw.

'Granny Bike,' I said. 'What are you doing?'

And she started to draw, faster and faster, scribbling and shading in, till it seemed that sparks were flying off the page.

I began to feel a funny, tingling feeling in my feet. I looked down and they were beginning to disappear, vanishing into thin air.

'Granny Bike!' I screamed. 'No! That's not fair!'

I lunged, trying to grab the pencil out of her hands, but I couldn't, because my arms had disappeared.

The last I saw of her was her pen scribbling and scribbling away, until she dwindled to a circle of a grinning, cackling mouth and then—

I was inside the wishing book.

I felt flatter and squashed, at first, but then I shook my hands and feet around a bit and the blood began to return. Gasping for air, I looked around and was surprised to find that the pages weren't white-and-black, as I had imagined.

They were full of colour and life. The trees of the park across the street from us were there, still laden down with their winter snow. A snowman with a shiny top hat and a carrot for a nose. Tower blocks twinkling with light in the distance, clouds of smoke puffing into the sky from a factory chimney – a helicopter buzzing in between them.

A bell made me swerve sharply, as a cyclist sped past.

Then I felt a pair of hands on my shoulders, and I twisted around. 'Where did you get to?' said Dad. His face was flushed and he was out of breath. Then I looked down, and saw the snowball rolled up in his gloved palm. 'You don't think Christine's going to let you get away with it that easily, do you?'

Christine? I thought. *That doesn't make any sense. Christine would never—*

Then a snowball caught me square in the back, and I

333

whipped round, to see Christine doubled up with laughter. She was in a fur coat – which meant it was definitely my stepmum and not an impostor – but she was covered in snow and leaves and having a laugh. As was the older woman next to her, bright red in the face, as she tried to roll the biggest snowball I'd ever seen . . .

'Frightfully common!' said Granny Car. 'And frightfully funny! Come on, Ethel, chase me!'

And she tried to waddle off through the drifts.

It was like the world I knew, only changed a bit to the left. Only better.

There was just one thing. 'Dad?' I said, tugging at his sleeve, before he ran off to pull his mother-in-law out of the hedge she had fallen into. 'Is Granny Bike here?'

He looked at me weirdly for a moment, then mussed my hair, and gave me the biggest Dad-hug I'd ever had from him. 'Oh, love, I wish she was, I really do. But I know what you mean. And I like to think she still is, somehow, looking down on us all.'

Dad turned his head up to the night sky and I followed his gaze up above the snowy trees, over the tops of the tower blocks, through the cloud of factory smoke, and far, far away into the endless starry sky.

There, hanging in the middle of space, like a porthole shining down from another world, was a huge moon. And do you know the strangest thing? If you angled your head and looked at the moon in a certain way, it looked exactly like the white face of a crooked old lady, with her bent nose and warty chin.

With just perhaps the trace of a smile.

So, go on, then. Tell me if I'm lying or not.

the Snow Dragon
ABI ELPHINSTONE

There was nothing unusual or especially exciting about Whistlethrop. It was an ordinary English town. A string of shops and restaurants lined the High Street and behind them back roads filtered out into rows of red-brick houses, semi-detached gardens and a park with swings and a slide. The town had a church, too, with a steeple that towered above the slated roofs and a graveyard ringed with yew trees. And to most people who lived there, this was all that Whistlethrop was.

But to Phoebe, who peered at things more closely, the town was a very different place. She knew that there was a badger sett in the woods beyond the park; she knew that when almost everyone was asleep and the street lamps glowed bright, an old lady hobbled out of her house and then sat on a bench in her garden to watch the moon; she knew that if you listened hard enough you could hear the weathervane creaking on top of the church spire. She also knew, though she wished she didn't, that the vicar practised yoga without his robes (or indeed his trousers, shirt, socks or pants) in his bathroom on Wednesday nights. And Phoebe knew all of this because she watched, every evening, from the skylight window of an attic in *Griselda Bone's Home for Strays*.

She leaned forward onto the balls of her feet, and the tower of books below her wobbled. Then she clung tighter to the skylight and nudged it open, because she knew that although it was dangerous to stand on top of forty-three encyclopedias, it was also extremely important. She pushed her elbows through the gap in the window, rested her chin on her hands and let her blue eyes grow large and round.

It was Christmas Eve, and from her perch on the outskirts of town, Phoebe could see that Whistlethrop was covered in a thick layer of snow. It was the first snow of the winter and it had come silently in the night – the way magic often does – but unlike the shadows and the moonbeams and the stars, this magic had stayed until morning. It had covered her ordinary world and transformed it into a glittering white kingdom, and as Phoebe looked upon it, her body tingled. The snow felt like a promise somehow, a pledge that today might be different from all the other days and that possibly, *just possibly*, there might be even more magic waiting for her.

She ran her eyes along the rooftops. They were coated white and pricked here and there by the feet of tiny birds – the redwings, jays and fieldfares Phoebe often left titbits of food for. Pavements glistened in the early morning sun, unspoiled by trampling feet, and the countryside beyond the town – fields, hedgerows and copses of woodland – spread out like ripples of milk beneath the clear blue sky.

A holly wreath had been fixed to the door of the church across the street and just as Phoebe was craning her neck to look at the tinsel strewn along the windowsills of the house beside it, two boys clutching sledges hurtled out of the front door in hats and scarves. Phoebe watched as they scooped up handfuls of snow and flung them at each other, then she sighed.

She wanted to rush out and join them, but *Griselda Bone's Home for Strays* wasn't the kind of place you could easily leave. A high stone wall encircled the grounds, locking in the patch of gravel in front of the house, the kennels to the sides and the neglected garden at the back, and tall iron gates barred the way in and out. Once you were in, you were very firmly in. Until Miracle Day, that was ... Because at *Griselda Bone's Home for Strays* the strays weren't actually dogs – they were children – and the home was, in fact, an orphanage.

Once a month, Griselda opened the gates of the orphanage to parents hoping to adopt a child and they spent the day helping the orphans in lessons and talking to them over meals. For some reason Griselda dished out muffins instead of punishments on those days, and she even remembered to turn on the central heating so that Phoebe didn't have to wear three vests under her shirt. And at the end of the day, after the parents had left and Griselda had turned the central heating off, the orphans were summoned to the hall and told whether a family wanted to adopt them. A few weeks later, once the paperwork was complete, the child could leave the orphanage with their new family and *that* day – that marvellous day filled with longing – was Miracle Day. Only it never seemed to happen to Phoebe.

Griselda had a habit of forgetting to introduce her to the visiting parents and the only times she really seemed to acknowledge Phoebe was when she tripped over her in the corridor – and even then she seemed confused as to who on earth Phoebe was. And it was events like these that made Phoebe wonder whether she might in fact be invisible to Griselda, a thought that was both tremendously exciting and deeply troubling. But after thinking long and hard about the situation, Phoebe had come to the lamentable conclusion that she was not invisible. She was merely forgettable. Like an umbrella on a bus, or house keys when you're in a rush. And while many of Phoebe's friends had been adopted, Phoebe herself had almost given up hope of her Miracle Day ever arriving. After all, what would be the point of adopting someone you were likely to forget about before breakfast?

The pile of books beneath Phoebe swayed suddenly and she clung to the roof. Then there was a scratching sound followed by a yap.

'Stop distracting me, Herbert,' Phoebe hissed.

There was another yap and the encyclopedias swerved to the left. Phoebe peered down into the cramped attic. Objects had been piled up against the sloping eaves and dusty walls: boxes containing hand-drawn maps, trunks full of fir cones, feathers and owl pellets, and glass bottles stuffed with marbles and ancient coins that Phoebe had dug up in the garden. But a space had been made in the middle of the clutter for a wicker basket plumped with cushions. And inside that was a chestnut sausage dog wagging its tail.

Phoebe rolled her eyes. 'Up you come, then. It's a good morning for looking.'

The sausage dog clambered up the tower of encyclopedias – one paw on Einstein's ear, another smack in the middle of Alaska – until he reached the top and nuzzled against Phoebe's jeans. She lifted Herbert up, squeezed him through the skylight and set him between her arms.

'Snow, Herb. Isn't it brilliant?'

Herbert eyed the slanting roof then shivered. He was only really interested in two things: cuddles from Phoebe and, despite his little legs, dancing.

'Jack's Miracle Day today,' Phoebe said, trying her best to smile.

She thought back to the beginning of the month, when Griselda had told Jack somebody wanted to take him home. Phoebe remembered how happy she had been for him, how she had hugged him even though there was a strange little lump in her throat. And then later that same evening, when she was alone in her cold, empty dormitory, the lump had grown bigger and she had burrowed beneath her sheets and cried. Because with Jack gone, she knew that she would be the only child left in the orphanage.

Phoebe looked at the orphanage gates wistfully. 'In a few hours, Jack'll be part of a real family, Herb – with a mum and a dad and maybe brothers and sisters, too.'

Herbert snuggled into Phoebe's hair, which was long and blonde and a mixture of very big curls and even bigger knots, but Phoebe liked it that way because she could store small, useful objects inside the tangles. Today, there was a paperclip, a pencil, a reel of thread and four cranberries she'd pinched from the kitchen.

Phoebe stroked Herbert's velvet ears. 'It's just you and me now.'

There was a crash from somewhere further down the orphanage, then a woman's voice, low and gravelly, shouting something fierce.

'And *them*,' Phoebe muttered.

She twisted her head round to the gates in front of the house to see a car had pulled up on the road outside. A man and a woman were talking and laughing on the pavement with a young boy and though Phoebe smiled, she couldn't help wishing that Miracle Days might start happening *to* her rather than around her.

'I know it's against the rules,' Phoebe whispered after a while, 'and I know we're planning on staying out of Griselda's way so that we can spend the day together tomorrow and not get dragged into the Christmas Hunt . . .'

Herbert shuddered at the mention of the Christmas Hunt, an annual event that saw Griselda and her pit bull terrier, Slobber, chasing the children through the orphanage until Slobber found the juicy bones they were forced to clutch.

'. . . but if we're quick, we'll have time to wave Jack off *and* hurry back up here before Griselda finds us.'

Herbert gazed down into the attic until his eyes rested on the branch he and Phoebe had dragged up from the garden and decorated with tinfoil stars. It wasn't much of a Christmas tree, both of them knew that, but it was a start. And it was their secret. Phoebe scrambled out onto the slated roof with Herbert in her arms and the sausage dog let out a feeble little moan.

Whistlethrop was awake now: a man was shuffling along the pavement towards the newsagent's, a woman was hanging a string of fairy lights above her door and a whole family were making snow angels in their garden. Crouched low to the slates, Phoebe set Herbert down, slipped a hand into her hair and pulled out the cranberries she'd smuggled from the kitchen the night before. She laid them in the snow.

'Important to feed the waxwings, even if we're in a rush.'

Phoebe smoothed her duffle coat beneath her bottom then sat on it, and after scooping up Herbert and clasping him to her chest, she pushed off and slid down the roof towards the fire escape.

They skidded along, snow spurting around them and loose tiles shaking free, before coming to an abrupt halt as Phoebe's trainers hit the gutter. Herbert shook the snow from his fur and cocked one ear. Car doors were closing; Jack was almost off. Phoebe swung her body onto the metal rungs of the ladder that scaled the side of the orphanage, then with Herbert tucked under one arm, she hurried on down.

'Try to see this as an adventure, Herb.'

Herbert's head clanged against a rung and he groaned then Phoebe jumped off the ladder and they raced past the row of dog kennels, ducking low to avoid being seen from Griselda's study, before swinging round to the front of the orphanage. The car was pulling away now but Jack was looking over his shoulder, his brown hair flicked across his eyes, as if he was searching for something or someone. Phoebe waved through the gates and her friend's eyes lit up as he wound down his window.

'I'll miss you!' he shouted. 'And I'll write!'

Then the car slipped off down the street and Phoebe was left standing beside Herbert before the tall dark gates. She'd never received a letter before, but the thought of an envelope with her name on, and words inside it that were meant just for her, made her smile.

She glanced at the orphanage motto engraved into the wall next to the gates – *He Who Bites Hardest Usually Wins* – and then there was a low and very long growl, as if it was trying to make a point. Phoebe's skin crawled with dread as

346

Herbert scurried behind her legs, and with a sinking heart, she turned around.

A black pit bull terrier stood on the gravel before the front door. Its squat legs and hunched shoulders framed a big square head, two narrow eyes and a spiked dog collar while ropes of saliva hung from its muzzle.

There was another growl, but it came from behind the pit bull terrier and this time there were words attached to it. 'Slobber! Where have you got to?'

A woman appeared in the doorway suddenly: short and stocky, with shoulders that almost gobbled up her neck, hands that curled into large fists and dark hair pulled so tightly into a bun that it flattened her ears to her head. Had she not been squeezed into a pinstripe trouser suit she might have passed for a pit bull terrier herself. She held a briefcase to her chest, like some sort of protective shield, and at the sight of it Phoebe shuddered.

Griselda flicked the briefcase open and drew out a clipboard. 'I thought we had disposed of the last of the orphans, Slobber, but it appears there is still somebody left on the register.' She began to read: '*Girl with hair as white as snowdrops and eyes as large and round as puddles*. What an absolutely ridiculous description. Who is this?'

Phoebe was used to reintroducing herself to Griselda whenever they crossed paths – and realizing there was no getting out of this situation, she took a small step forward. 'Me, miss.'

Griselda peered over her clipboard, a barrel of indignant pinstripe, then her nose twitched. '*You?* I thought we got rid of you last year?'

Phoebe scuffed the gravel with her trainer. 'No. I'm still here.'

Griselda raised a whistle to her mouth and as she blew it, the fat on her cheeks jostled up and down. Eyes glued to the ground, Phoebe and Herbert walked towards the orphanage. They stopped in front of Slobber, who snarled, and then Griselda raised one of her shoes and glared at Herbert, who hastily scurried beneath it. Phoebe winced. She had often wondered whether the sausage dog's love for dance stemmed from being forced to lie completely still every day, as a footrest for Griselda.

The woman raised one greasy eyebrow. 'You're the one who's always daydreaming through lessons, aren't you?'

Phoebe picked at the cuff of her duffle coat.

'The one who looks under stones for beetles and peers at nothing through every window?'

Phoebe shook her head. 'Oh, it's never nothing, Miss Bone. There's always *something* to see, even when it's cloudy. In fact, it's often better when it's cloudy because the sky puffs out shapes: goblins, imps.' She thought for a moment. 'Even dragons, on really good days.'

Griselda pressed down with her shoe and Herbert gave a little squeak. 'Goblins, imps and dragons,' Griselda spat, 'are stupid and childish and absolutely not allowed.'

Phoebe tried to nod.

'You should know already that at this institution, daydreaming is banned, skipping is forbidden, doodling is frowned upon and—'

'—hide-and-seek is out of the question,' Phoebe finished.

She had heard the mantra for as long as she could remember – ever since the day she had arrived at the orphanage as a baby, after her parents had been killed in a car crash – and she knew the story behind it. Griselda had inherited the house, once a place of laughter and warmth, from her father many years ago on Christmas Day, but on that very day an unfortunate episode had occurred. During a game of hide-and-seek, an orphan had hidden inside a tumble dryer with Griselda's first dog, a Rottweiler called Drool, and regrettably, the machine had been switched on while the two were inside it. The orphan had survived the ordeal. Drool, however, had not, and incensed by the event, Griselda had vowed to wage war on 'childishness'. She dedicated every spare moment she had to working for the government, drawing up new and complicated policies to reform the education system where she believed the roots of childish behaviour lay. And while Phoebe was all for change, the kind of change that involved more exams, trickier tests, large filing cabinets and hundreds of reports wasn't really the sort she liked.

'So, do you have a name?' Griselda asked, smothering Herbert's face with the toe of her shoe.

'It's Phoebe.'

Griselda thought about it. 'Yuck. What a horrid little name. Who came up with that?'

Phoebe shrugged. 'I think I did, Miss Bone – when I was five. I saw on your register that you'd crossed out my name and put *Girl* so I thought that I'd make up another name and add a little description of myself in case you ever,' her voice shrank, 'forgot me. I chose *Phoebe* because silent letters are always exciting and I mentioned snowdrops in the description because they're my favourite flowers.' She paused because Griselda's jaw had gone very stiff and Phoebe wasn't sure whether this was because Griselda had forgotten her again, mid-conversation, or whether it was because she had said something ridiculous. She decided to offer up one more sentence, so that became clearer. 'I also added puddles because they're good for stomping in.'

Slobber let out a long, disgusted burp.

'Silent letters? Snowdrops? Puddles?!'

Griselda took her foot off Herbert, who promptly flopped over, then she rolled her shoulders back. 'You are the runt of my litter, but what I cannot understand is how someone as forgettable as you can be so absolutely infuriating. It is an extremely dangerous combination—' she paused as she searched for an appropriate metaphor '—like a banana skin left on a supermarket floor, a forgettable piece of waste that can cause a surprising amount of bother.'

Phoebe gulped.

Griselda pressed on. 'Your senses are unravelling, Runt. Your thoughts are spiralling into madness … And it is my job – no, my *duty* – to set things right.' She thrust her clipboard back inside her briefcase. 'This is a *war* and I will not rest until I have blasted daydreams, skipping, doodling and hide-and-seek from our country!'

Phoebe wondered where on earth all the daydreams and skipping would be banished to. Norway, perhaps? She'd seen photos of people skipping around statues of trolls in her encyclopedias. But she knew the contents of Griselda's briefcase – leg irons to prevent children from skipping, a neck brace to straighten necks that daydreamed towards windows, and duct tape to seal up nooks and crannies used in hide-and-seek – so she knew better than to question her.

Griselda blew her whistle sharply. 'I have decided to cancel the Christmas holidays and continue with lessons to prevent the collapse of your mind into absolute childishness.'

'But—' Phoebe started, as she thought of the secret Christmas she and Herb had planned in the attic.

Griselda blew her whistle again. 'No buts, Runt – embrace this change. Look nobly to your future. There is algebra there – and fractions, grammar and spelling.'

Shoulders sagging, Phoebe bent to pick up Herbert.

'Leave the footrest!' Griselda barked. 'It has legs of its own and will catch us up.'

Then Griselda was off, dragging Phoebe into the orphanage by the scruff of her neck, and as Phoebe's trainers skidded over the floorboards, she thought that as Christmas Eves went, this was by far one of the very worst.

They hurried through the hall, past the sculpture of Drool on a large round table, the portraits of Slobber hanging from the walls and the old grandfather clock in the corner of the room. Griselda flung open a door which had once led into a sitting room with sofas, patterned curtains and a beautiful grand piano. All that was now gone and in its place was a classroom: a blackboard at the front, four bare walls, windows blocked by blind-slats and row upon row of empty desks. Griselda hurled Phoebe forward as if she was tossing a stick for a dog.

'Sit!' she barked.

Phoebe wove her way between the desks to one beside the window. The blinds were down, closing off the view into the garden, but one slat had caught in the string and through the gap Phoebe could just make out the snow sparkling on the lawn and a robin perched on the wall. She shook off her coat and then swallowed as she realized she was wearing a jumper rather than a suit jacket. Griselda, standing so solidly and so squarely at the front of the room that she looked like a fridge encased in pinstripe, had very strict rules about uniform.

'A jumper?' Griselda roared as she looked Phoebe up and

down. 'Have I not made it absolutely clear that orphans are to wear suit jackets at all times? Even in bed!'

Phoebe shrank into her seat and tried to muster up a believable excuse. 'I thought that since it was cold and there was snow out maybe—'

Griselda punched her knuckles into the desk. 'It does not matter if you are cold, Runt! Suit jackets mean business. They speak of purpose and policies and power. I sleep in a business suit, I shower in a business suit, I exercise in a business suit.' She was swelling inside her jacket as she reached her full crescendo. 'I was *born* in a business suit, Runt!'

Phoebe tried to imagine a baby in pinstripe then gave up and nodded meekly.

'We will start with grammar,' Griselda spat. 'With some good, clean sentences to stamp this childishness out.'

She raised the whistle to her lips, blew hard, and seconds later Slobber burst into the room, thrashing his head from side to side before leaping up onto Griselda's desk.

Griselda wedged a piece of paper into Slobber's mouth. 'Go on, then, boy. Give it to the Runt.'

The pit bull terrier hurtled across the room like a runaway cannonball. Phoebe clutched at the edges of her seat as Slobber thumped the paper down in front of her, took a quick nip at the back of her ankle then tore back to his mistress.

Griselda settled herself in the chair behind her desk,

whistled for Herbert to resume his role as her footrest, and then pulled out a bone from her briefcase and chucked it to Slobber.

'Complete the sentences, Runt. I do not want to see a single mention of silent letters, snowdrops or puddles and if you so much as *mention* a dragon,' Slobber looked up from slathering over his bone and shot Phoebe a warning look, 'it will be the kennels for you tonight.'

Phoebe tugged the pencil from her hair. The urge to doodle a dragon in the corner of her page was almost unbearable, but she bit down on her lip and read the first sentence:

1. Snow falls ....
2. Rain feels ....
3. Food is ....
4. Children are ....
5. Dogs like ....

There were so many things Phoebe could put at the end of each sentence, but which words would please Griselda most? She took a deep breath, twizzled her pencil and then started writing:

1. Snow falls quietly, but if you listen hard there is a bit of noise. Sort of whispery.
2. Rain feels very nice to splash in.

3. Food is mostly good, but Brussels sprouts are terrible. Jelly is sometimes funny.
4. Children are a bit small, but they are often fierce and very brave.
5. Dogs like dancing.

'Excuse me, Miss Bone,' Phoebe said. 'I've done the sentences.'

Griselda leaned forward, her boots sliding further into poor Herbert's back, and for a second she looked almost startled to see Phoebe there at all. She shook her head.

'What a forgettable child you are, Runt. I turn my head for a moment and it's as if you never existed. And yet there you are with your blinking eyes and ridiculous hair. So,' Griselda stood up and Herbert gave a little gasp before scurrying into the corner, 'you have written the answers.'

'I've written *some* answers,' Phoebe replied nervously.

Griselda took a stride out from behind her desk, her clipboard in her hands. 'There was only *one* suitable response to each sentence so I very much hope you have answered correctly, Runt.' She scanned Phoebe's sheet of paper. '*Snow falls quietly, but if you listen hard there is a bit of noise. Sort of whispery.*' Griselda made a strange retching sound and Phoebe suddenly wondered whether she was going to be sick. '*Whispery* isn't even a word!' She carried on down the list. '*Rain feels very nice to splash in*?! *Food is mostly good, but Brussels sprouts are terrible. Jelly is sometimes funny*?! *Children are a bit small, but they are often fierce and very brave*?!' She shook her head. '*Dogs like dancing*?! DANCING?! Have you ever, in your life, seen a dog dance, Runt?'

Herbert made a sharp exit from the classroom then Slobber surged towards Phoebe, jumped onto her desk and wrestled the exercise sheet to the ground. He crunched it into a ball and then swallowed it – whole.

'There are no such things as dancing dogs and whispering snow!' Griselda boomed.

Phoebe's eyes slipped to the doorway, where she could just make out Herbert doing a quiet waltz in the hall, but no amount of dancing could cheer her up now.

Griselda rapped her clipboard. 'Snow falls down. Rain feels wet. Food is necessary. Children are annoying. And dogs like bones. *That* is how the sentences go, Runt!'

Phoebe hung her head.

'I was going to try you with some mathematics,' Griselda muttered, 'but I can see this is a slippery slope. Perhaps some time in the kennels will sort you out?'

Phoebe shivered as she remembered the time Griselda had caught her doing a cartwheel in the corridor and had sentenced her to an overnight stay in the kennels. There had been thunder and lightning that night, and while Phoebe found watching storms from the attic skylight extremely exciting, it hadn't been quite the same as sitting one out in a kennel.

She shook her head. 'Please don't send me to the kennels, Miss Bone. What if I promise to do better?'

Griselda licked her fingers then ran the saliva back through her hair. 'You find jelly funny. You think children are brave. You believe in *dragons*! And the only thing I have to say about that is KENNEL TIME.'

'But – but it's almost Christmas,' Phoebe pleaded.

Griselda cracked her knuckles. 'A horrid time of year – too much smiling and not nearly enough biting.'

'But – but . . .' Phoebe thought of her branch in the attic with its tinfoil stars. 'What if I made some decorations for us, and we got some tinsel – it might make Christmas feel a little less horrid?'

Griselda shuddered. 'Tinsel is disgraceful.' Tucking her clipboard under her arm, she pulled a dog lead from her pocket, widened the loop and forced it down over Phoebe's neck and shoulders until it was snug around her stomach. She yanked hard and Phoebe squealed. 'To heel again, Runt!'

Phoebe ran to keep up as Griselda tore from the classroom and paced across the hall. Slobber paused to lick a portrait of himself mauling a pug in the park and Phoebe glimpsed Herbert scuttling behind Griselda's study door, on which a gold plaque read:

JOIN THE WAR AGAINST CHILDISHNESS – YOUR COUNTRY NEEDS YOU!

Griselda quickened her stride. 'Chop, chop, Runt! I've got an appointment with my photocopier and I haven't got all day.'

'If – if I carried out some extra chores,' Phoebe panted as she skidded over the floorboards, 'perhaps I could spend the rest of the day in the attic, in Herbert's dog basket? I'd be completely out of your way.'

Griselda stopped for a moment. 'I might not notice you – you are an extremely unnoticeable person after all – but I would know that somewhere in my house there was a stupid little girl thinking that jelly is sometimes funny. And the horror of *that* would cause both Slobber and me unnecessary irritation.'

And though Herbert was doing a desperate body shake beyond the study door, Phoebe couldn't help the little tear that trickled down her cheek.

Griselda dragged Phoebe round the side of the orphanage, swerving to miss a clump of snow that toppled down from the roof. She paused beneath the fire-escape ladder and Phoebe swallowed as Griselda drew herself up, grey and bulging like an angry cloud. Had she spotted Phoebe and Herbert's footprints on the rungs?

But Griselda was eying the heap of snow that had fallen from the roof. 'If you can complete the sentence about snow correctly,' she muttered, 'I shall allow you back into the orphanage tomorrow. But if you fail, it will be the kennels for the rest of the holidays.' She consulted her clipboard. 'So, Runt: snow falls—'

Phoebe tried hard to focus her mind on an answer filled with suits and systems, but when she looked at the snow sparkling around them, she couldn't stop the words tumbling out: 'Snow falls with a *flumping* noise as it slides off the tiles and hits the ground.'

There was a stony silence.

'*Flumping*?!' Griselda snapped her clipboard in two over a pinstriped leg. 'I was braced for more dragons and puddles but tearing down the English language and replacing it with made-up words?!'

Slobber lowered his head to the ground then charged into Phoebe who staggered back against the orphanage wall.

Griselda took a step forward so that her nose was only centimetres away from Phoebe's. 'I tried to ignore "whispery" back in the classroom, but hearing you sabotage our language for the second time today has confirmed my worst thoughts.' A vein that Phoebe had never noticed before began to throb in Griselda's forehead. 'You are a Word Murderer, Runt, and *that* is the reason nobody wants to adopt you! They might just about get by with you being so forgettable, but no amount of earplugs would be able to drown out the poison that drips from your mouth! You bring sensible verbs crashing to their knees and heaven only knows what wicked plans you have for our nouns and adjectives … Only a long stint in the kennels will smash this childishness out of you!'

Phoebe tried to protest, but Griselda was already marching her over the gravel towards the row of kennels – each one small and wooden with a slanted roof – that lined the wall encircling the orphanage. Griselda tugged the lead off, flung Phoebe inside and fastened a metal cuff around her ankle. Phoebe's mouth widened as she realized that the cuff was attached to a chain, which in turn was fixed to the inside of the kennel. Whatever plans she had been making to sneak up the fire escape into the attic that evening had been ruined. She was trapped inside the kennel and her and Herbert's secret Christmas was no more.

'Close your mouth, Runt; it looks like an open toilet bowl.' Slobber sniggered as he and Griselda turned to leave. 'Now where's that wretched footrest gone?'

Phoebe huddled inside the kennel and sniffed as a tear smudged down her nose. Then, as Griselda and Slobber disappeared into the orphanage, there was a rustling from a rhododendron bush in the garden and a chestnut sausage dog scampered towards the kennel.

'Oh, Herb,' Phoebe sobbed as he climbed inside the kennel and snuggled into her chest. 'I used to think that at some point my Miracle Day would come – that I wouldn't be forgotten by absolutely everybody in the world – but no one's going to want me if I'm a Word Murderer.'

Herbert licked Phoebe's cheek then he scrambled off her lap and, on top of the rags behind her, he did the most joyful can can he could muster.

Phoebe blinked through her tears. 'I'm so glad I have you, Herb.'

She reached for a blanket and wrapped it around her then she sat with the sausage dog at the entrance of the kennel, and while families laughed and sang and played beyond the orphanage wall, Phoebe and Herb watched their Christmas Eve drain away.

Phoebe nibbled on the chunk of dry bread Slobber had tossed her for supper. 'The world looks almost blue now the sunlight's gone,' she whispered.

Herbert looked on in silence and Phoebe closed her eyes and listened sadly to the tawny owl calling from the graveyard. When she opened them again, though, she smiled – because tiny white flecks were now drifting down from the sky.

'It's snowing, Herb! Jack and I always used to say that fresh snow on Christmas Eve means magic is on its way.' She felt an unexpected tingle as the word 'magic' tiptoed out of her mouth.

They watched the darkening sky grow speckled as more and more snowflakes tumbled down. Phoebe stuck out a hand and let them fall into her palm, each jewelled pattern more beautiful than the one before, then she glanced at the cuff around her ankle.

'There'll be enough snow to build a snowman, Herb – and I reckon this chain's long enough for me to climb outside ...'

Herbert tiptoed out of the kennel first, then Phoebe

followed, bundled up in the old dog rags. They rolled a ball of snow back and forth until it was large enough for a body and though Phoebe's hands were numbed through they kept on building, pushing great handfuls of snow together to build the snowman's head.

After a while, Phoebe stood back and beamed. 'He's the most splendid snowman I've ever seen!'

The sausage dog did a quick flamenco dance to show that he agreed.

'But he needs a face,' Phoebe added. 'To make him even more splendid.'

She looked at the buttons on her blazer, chewed hard on her lip as she thought about what Griselda might say, then yanked them off anyway and pressed them into a smile on the snowman's head. She tugged the pencil out of her hair and slotted it in for a nose, then arranged the reel of thread in one eye and the paperclip in the other. She climbed back into the kennel with Herbert and they watched their snowman standing proud among the falling flakes.

'He's like a guardian, Herb – someone to watch out for us this Christmas. He's not going to make us complete sentences or wage a war on doodling; he's just going to be still and silent and,' Phoebe struggled for the right words, 'possibly a little bit magical, too.'

And as both the girl and the sausage dog looked, they had the strangest feeling that maybe there *was* something more to their guardian than first met the eye.

Phoebe shook her head and blew into her hands to warm her fingers. 'I'm almost certain that if our snowman could speak, he'd use words like *flumping*.'

Herbert wagged his tail to show that he agreed then his eyes grew large as a dark shape swaggered through the snow towards the kennels.

Phoebe tensed. 'Not Slobber. *Please* not Slobber.'

There was a growl and the pit bull terrier paused before the entrance to the kennel, his narrow eyes flicking between Phoebe (Herbert was now sensibly cowering beneath the rags) and the snowman. He prowled around their creation and for a moment Phoebe thought that perhaps that was all he was going to do – that he just wanted to snoop – but then he lowered his jaw to the ground, let the drool slop out, and headbutted the snowman. Phoebe's guardian wobbled and his pencil nose dropped out then Slobber reversed a few strides before charging full pelt and knocking the snowman's head clean off his body.

'No!' Phoebe cried, straining against her chain. 'Please don't!'

Slobber trampled on the head, sending snow and buttons and reels of thread flying, then he stood very still and growled into the kennel again.

'We just wanted *one* moment of magic on Christmas Eve!' Phoebe cried.

Slobber narrowed his eyes then he stamped through the scattered remains of the snowman before disappearing into the orphanage – and inside the kennel, Phoebe curled into a little ball beneath the rags.

Hours passed and still Phoebe lay, shivering, in the kennel. Her eyes were blotched from crying and she could no longer feel her toes, but she held the sausage dog tight. It had stopped snowing now and the sky belonged to the owls and the moon. A shooting star cast a path of gold through the dark and Phoebe pointed to a fox slinking through the shadows. Then all was still for a while.

Phoebe was about to suggest to Herbert that they should try to sleep, when a movement caught her eye. It was nothing dramatic – just the feeling of an image half glimpsed and the need to look again. But when Phoebe did look again, she saw that something extraordinary was happening outside the kennel.

The trampled snow – where the snowman had been – was *moving*. Phoebe blinked. Perhaps it was a trick of the light? Or a sudden gust of wind? Or maybe it was Griselda and Slobber coming back to deal out a midnight punishment? And yet Phoebe had seen the light in their bedroom turn off, and there was no wind rustling through the trees ... She peered closer. The snow in front of the kennel was indeed shifting, the snowflakes twisting and spinning until they rose before Phoebe in a swirl of glittering silver.

Phoebe crouched in the entrance of her kennel. 'It – it can't be ...' she whispered.

The snow was hardening into a shape Phoebe recognized: a long, swishing tail that finished in a cluster of icicles, a huge body sprouting jagged wings and a large, kind face with two shining black eyes and a pair of enormous ears. This, right here in the grounds of the orphanage, was a *dragon* – and its snow-carved body glinted silvery blue in the moonlight.

Phoebe craned her neck to get a better view and the chain attached to her ankle clanked. She froze, her heart thumping against her ribs as the dragon's mighty head swung towards the kennel. It paused, just a few steps away from Phoebe and Herbert, and Phoebe noticed there were white hairs as fine as spider-silk arched over the dragon's eyes – eyebrows, perhaps – and more wisps dangling beneath its chin and fringing its ears. The girl and the sausage dog stayed where they were, breathing in the dragon's smell, of pine trees and wild winds.

And then the dragon spoke – not a roar or a telling-off. His voice was soft and feathery and he simply said: 'Hello.'

Phoebe let the word rumble inside her. It felt wise and good and somehow she didn't feel afraid.

'Hello,' she found herself saying. 'I'm – I'm Phoebe.' Herbert nudged her side with his paw and Phoebe lifted the sausage dog into her lap. 'And this is Herbert, but you can call him Herb.' She glanced at the dragon's enormous limbs and his hooked talons splayed across the ground. 'If you want. Only if you want.'

The dragon smiled through icicled teeth. 'I've never met

a Phoebe or a Herb before.' Phoebe beamed and the dragon chuckled, a warm laugh that reminded Phoebe of a fire crackling. '*B* is one of my favourite letters so I'll enjoy saying both your names out loud.'

Phoebe was about to say that *B* was also one of *her* favourite letters – especially in the words '*goblin*' and '*bubble*' – but then she remembered she was a Word Murderer and she kept her mouth buttoned up.

The dragon frowned. 'Oh, I don't think the suit jacket will do.'

Phoebe glanced at the broken thread where the buttons had been. 'I'm sorry that it's all scrappy. I removed the buttons to make my snowman's mouth.'

The dragon nodded. 'But of course. Quite a sensible place for buttons, I would have thought. What I meant, though,' and Phoebe noticed that his eyes were shining, 'is that I have never known anyone set off on an adventure in a suit jacket. A conference or a meeting perhaps,' he shuddered, 'but not an adventure.'

Phoebe's chest swelled. 'We're – we're going on an adventure?'

The dragon nodded. 'All over the world, on Christmas Eve, dragons stir.'

Phoebe's eyes grew large because that was quite simply the best sentence anyone had ever said to her. She glanced at the ridge of spikes on the dragon's back. 'Are all dragons like you?'

The creature drew his vast body beneath him so that he

was sitting before the kennel. 'All dragons are a part of the landscape around them,' he said, and Phoebe noticed that as he spoke his breath puffed out into a mist of snowflakes. 'I am a Snow Dragon, but there are Cloud Dragons, Tree Dragons, Rock Dragons, Sea Dragons and even Fire Dragons out there.' His nostrils twitched. 'If you ask me, Fire Dragons are somewhat hot-tempered.'

Phoebe giggled and Herbert couldn't resist a quick moonwalk inside the kennel to show his delight at the conversation.

'I'm glad that we got to meet a Snow Dragon,' Phoebe said. 'I can't imagine Fire Dragons would have ears as glorious as yours.'

The dragon wiggled his ears and as the strands of hair rippled, a trail of snowflakes scattered into the night. 'Fire Dragons do have rather pokey ears.' He smiled and then he looked at Phoebe thoughtfully. 'Dragons only appear to those who need them, Phoebe. They stay for one adventure and then they melt back into the landscape.'

Phoebe thought of the ruined snowman and of how she had shouted to Slobber that she had only wanted *one moment of magic on Christmas Eve*. Then the dragon had appeared, as if he had listened to it all, as if he had heard the sadness rocking in her heart.

The dragon drew himself up. 'So, Phoebe and Herb, I suggest we get going. You can be late for many things in life, but you should *never* keep an adventure waiting.'

As he spoke, the cuff around Phoebe's ankle clicked open and her suit jacket vanished. For a second Phoebe shivered and then her mouth fell open as folds of thick white fur materialized around her body and up over her head. Phoebe snuggled into the mysterious fur coat, then she gathered Herbert up and crawled outside the kennel.

The dragon lowered his body to the ground and then nodded towards his shoulder. 'Always board a dragon from the front legs,' he said. 'I had one boy try to climb up my tail and he ended up with a bruised armpit.' He shook his head. 'I did try to warn him that icicles are stubborn little blighters . . .'

Phoebe glanced at the dragon's spiked tail and climbed carefully up his leg, before settling herself and Herbert into the bend of his neck, just below his giant ears. She glanced at the orphanage and sniffed as she thought of what Griselda had said just hours before: that she was forgettable, a stupid little runt whom no one wanted to adopt. But it was as if the dragon could sense Phoebe's sadness and in response, he flapped his ragged ears.

'Do you know why my ears are so large?' Phoebe shook her head and the dragon's weight shifted as he stood. 'So that I can listen to all of the wonderful things that you have to say, Phoebe.'

And on hearing those words, Phoebe's little heart glowed. There might be a woman in pinstripe who wanted to tear her down, but here, on Christmas Eve out by the kennels, there was a dragon determined to build her up.

The creature flexed its wings either side of Phoebe and Herbert, which sent the leaves on the holly tree rustling, and then the dragon lumbered forward. One stride and he was over the gravel, another and he was past the flowerbeds, and just as Phoebe thought they would career into the trees, he surged into the sky, his silver-blue wings beating around her.

Up and up they went, over the orphanage wall, before crossing the road and spiralling high above the church steeple. Phoebe laughed. Riding a running dragon had been bumpy, even bumpier than sliding down the orphanage roof, but riding a flying dragon – now *that* was like riding the wind.

They glided over the yews and Phoebe opened her mouth and drank in the wideness of the night. There were no walls to box in the world now and as the dragon wheeled above Whistlethrop, Phoebe threw back her head and laughed again.

'Look, Herb!' she cried, pointing to the streets below. 'They look like gingerbread houses! And there, on the bench in that garden, it's the old lady who watches the moon!'

Herbert wagged his tail in delight, and Phoebe's eyes widened as she realized they were flying over the vicar's house. He was in the bathroom – it was a Wednesday after all – and his naked yoga was in full swing . . . Phoebe cringed into her coat, but the dragon simply chortled, and seconds later, Phoebe found herself chortling, too, because magic with a sense of humour had to be a good thing.

She smiled at the Christmas trees winking beyond sitting-room windows and at the stockings hooked above fireplaces and as the dragon reached the end of the High Street, Phoebe noticed a gap in somebody's bedroom curtains. Two children were sitting up late on a bed and in between them there was an unopened present.

Phoebe thought of the letter Jack had promised to write her. Perhaps he'd send a Christmas present, too... And how exciting it would be to unwrap a gift that held an object somebody had picked out especially for her! But when Phoebe peered at the children more closely, she saw that they were snatching the present back and forth. She frowned. There was a lot more grabbing and wrenching at Christmas time than she had expected.

Phoebe pulled off her hood and leaned towards one of the dragon's ears. 'Why are they fighting?'

The dragon nodded. 'They do not realize how lucky they are, Phoebe.'

Phoebe stroked the sausage dog in her lap. 'How can they not realize?'

The dragon wheeled away from Whistlethrop and began soaring out over the countryside. 'Because they are always wanting more. They don't stop and look around, but if they did, they would know, like the old lady who watches the moon, that everything they could ever want is right here already.'

Phoebe looked down at the fields blanketed in snow and tried to imagine what it might feel like to have a family of her own, to sit around a kitchen table with people who didn't think she was forgettable or infuriating. And as they flew through the starry night, Phoebe made a promise to herself that if she was ever lucky enough to become part of a family, she would be happy just to know that she was loved.

The dragon raced on over country lanes dusted with snow and lakes locked in the cold, hard gleam of ice. The world was asleep now – curtains were drawn and lights had been turned off – but the landscape around Phoebe had never felt more alive. Sounds that she had missed before – the near silent footfall of a rabbit, the ruffling of a blackbird's feathers and the crack and groan of ice – were stirring all around her. A wisp of cloud drifted across the moon and the landscape changed again: new shadows shifted, hidden snowflakes sparkled, and the wildness of it all made Phoebe shiver.

She pulled her fur hood up around her face. 'Where are we going, Snow Dragon?'

The dragon's wings beat on. 'What do you like best in the world, Phoebe?'

Herbert gave a little bark from her lap. 'Other than Herb,' Phoebe said, 'I love trees. And mountains, though I've only really seen them in books.' She paused. 'And I think the sea looks very promising, too.'

The dragon chuckled. 'We'll go north a while, then, where the forests are bigger, the mountains are higher and the seas are deeper.'

And north they went, the dragon's wings shredding the pearly night. They passed villages and farms and marshes and rivers until they came, at last, to a very large forest. It spread below them, a rise and fall of fir, pine and spruce trees, every branch shelved with snow. The dragon dived, breaking just before the canopy, and Phoebe whooped as he let his tail sweep the snow from the treetops. She stuck out her arm and grabbed a fistful for herself then she held it before Herbert with large, round eyes.

'No one, except us, has touched this snow, Herb.'

The sausage dog gave it a little lick and Phoebe smiled to think that Griselda had insisted the idea of magic was ridiculous, and yet here she was, on the back of a dragon, exploring an untouched kingdom of snow and ice.

'Only the buzzards and the kestrels and the falcons get up here,' Phoebe whispered then she hurled her snowball out across the trees. 'We're like birds, Herb! As free and as fast as birds!'

The dragon sailed over the forest to where the trees parted and a railway line ran through the middle. Phoebe watched as a deer stepped over the tracks and melted into the forest then her ears filled with a new sound: the chugging of wheels against steel.

'The night train from London,' the dragon said,

'rushing the last load of people to their families in time for Christmas Day.'

'What if we're seen?' Phoebe gasped.

The dragon slowed and the chugging behind them grew louder then the train burst into sight, tearing through the forest as it made its way north.

The dragon followed its course. 'Oh, they won't see us, Phoebe. The passengers will be far too busy looking at their phones and their laptops to notice what is happening outside.'

'But—' Phoebe shook her head.

'Don't believe me?' the dragon asked, and before Phoebe could reply, he swooped down to the train and then darted alongside it, his great wings brushing snow from the tips of the branches on their left.

Phoebe looked through the carriage windows. There were shopping bags full of presents on the tables and all around them, men and women, their heads bent low over glaring screens.

The wind rippled through Phoebe's hair as they sped between the trees and the carriages and then she noticed something that made her jump. 'Those two people – they've seen us!'

An old man and a little boy had their noses pressed up against the window. Their eyes and mouths were wide, but they did not reach for their cameras or their phones at the sight of the dragon and the girl with the sausage dog on her lap. They didn't even turn to the other people in the carriage.

They just watched, in silent awe, because the magic of what they were seeing held them that way. The dragon winked suddenly and Phoebe gave a small wave then the man and the boy blinked and smiled as the dragon pulled back from the train and climbed into the sky.

Phoebe stroked one of the dragon's ears. 'Why those two? Why do you think they saw us when no one else did?'

The dragon's voice came soft and low. 'We all have the gift of wonder, Phoebe. It burns bright in children if they keep their eyes and ears open – and often in old age it shines, too – but it can get a bit lost in the time between. We become busy and knowing and we forget how to take a good, long look at the miracles all around us.'

'I won't ever be too busy,' Phoebe replied. 'Or forgetful.'

And the dragon shook his head. 'No. Because you are a fierce watcher, Phoebe – a peerer into corners, a looker behind doors. You see imps in clouds and castles in constellations' – Phoebe reddened in case that was a bad thing, as Griselda had said, but the dragon went on – 'and that is a rare and wonderful thing. It is a *gift*, Phoebe – one that you must never lose sight of.'

Phoebe cuddled Herbert to her chest. 'I won't ever stop watching, Snow Dragon,' she said. 'Never.'

She looked down to see that the landscape was growing rugged and that pages of the encyclopedias she had sneaked into the attic were opening up beneath her: valleys shrouded in mist, rolling moors and lochs crusted with ice. The dragon glided over it all and Phoebe realized where he was taking her – to the mountains in the Scottish Highlands where the peaks reached up and touched the sky. She had seen them in her encyclopedia, and they were the mountains she loved the most.

The ridges started small and gentle, but as they soared on, the land sharpened into peaks with plunging sides and crags so icy they could have been sculpted from marble. For as far as they could see there were mountains – dappled blue and silver and purple in the cold, hard starlight – and Phoebe watched them all, fiercely.

The dragon circled the highest peak and then sank lower, until his talons crunched onto the mountaintop. He folded his great wings in and they sat, Phoebe and Herbert tucked into the bend of the Snow Dragon's neck, with the whole world spread out below them. The mountains were home to golden eagles, wildcats and stags, but, for this moment, they belonged to Phoebe and Herbert, too.

The dragon didn't speak and neither did Phoebe. There weren't words big enough to hold in all that lay before them. But into the silence, the sky began to change. Ribbons of green shimmered between stars and then swathes of purple coiled through, sending new shades twirling across the sky.

Phoebe swallowed in disbelief. 'It's the Northern Lights, isn't it? I recognize them from the photos in my books!'

The dragon smiled and as the sky rolled with colour, Phoebe found herself struggling to her feet in an attempt to take it all in. She stood tall on the dragon's neck with Herbert nuzzled into her ankles.

'Would – would you mind if I howled?' she asked quietly. 'It's just all so – so – wonderflible.'

The dragon's wings twitched and Phoebe winced into her coat. She hadn't meant to blurt out one of her made-up words – she had been trying so hard not to accidentally murder the English language during her adventure – but the dragon was smiling, his snaggled teeth aglitter in the moonlight.

'I was thinking just the same thing, Phoebe.'

And Phoebe's heart danced.

'Howling on three, then?' the dragon asked.

Phoebe nodded then the dragon counted them in and at 'three' Phoebe cupped her hands either side of her mouth and emptied her lungs into the mountains and the sky. The dragon howled, too, and Herbert barked, and for a few minutes it was just the three of them sending their voices out into the wilderness as if they were a part of the ice and the rock and the swirl of colours around them.

Phoebe panted as her echo trailed through the peaks and was lost.

'That felt like – like what I imagine Miracle Day might feel like,' she said. 'Only with less shouting.'

The dragon rubbed his head gently against Phoebe as she settled herself back on his neck and though she tried to stifle her yawn, it squeaked out. He dipped down to gather strength in his legs, then pushed off from the crag and they skimmed over the mountains – south this time – but Phoebe noticed they were not following the route they had taken before.

'I prefer to fly in loops,' the dragon said, 'because sometimes the best route home isn't always the straightest one.'

They curved over glens and moorland and castles perched on lochs until they reached the coast and were whizzing just centimetres above the silver sea. The dragon's talons tore through the surface and Phoebe swung a hand down to touch the water so that she would know and remember, days later when she was trapped behind the orphanage wall, that she had ridden a mighty dragon over the North Sea. The chill bit her fingers and she gasped, then the dragon rose up, and from the distant waves Phoebe watched a porpoise arch out of the water and disappear into the depths.

'Happy Christmas, dear Phoebe,' the dragon whispered.

And Phoebe ruffled his ragged ears. 'Happy Christmas, Snow Dragon. It's been the best one of my life!'

Herbert did a little jig on her lap and then they sat watchfully as the dragon glided back over the countryside towards *Griselda Bone's Home for Strays*. The stars were still shining when they flew over the orphanage wall and as they touched down in front of her kennel, Phoebe suddenly wondered whether any time had passed at all.

'Thank you,' she said as she slid down the dragon's leg, 'for the adventure and the talking and all the other bits in between.'

The dragon dipped his head and Phoebe took a step forward. She stroked his jaw and felt the tiny wisps of hair slip through her fingers then she wrapped her arms around his neck and the dragon closed his wings around her. Phoebe could have stayed like that for ever, safe inside the wings of the Snow Dragon, but after a while, he drew back and as he did, he spoke his truth in a low, rumbling whisper.

'Some day your life will open up, Phoebe – far beyond the walls of this orphanage – and when it does, I want you to remember our adventure. Be content. Be watchful. Be brave.' He glanced towards her kennel and the snow around his big, dark eyes gathered into wrinkles. 'And never stop believing in miracles.'

The snow before Phoebe began to shift and swirl and as she blinked into the flurry of snowflakes, the dragon faded until all that was left was a patch of gravel scattered with snow. Phoebe's fur coat had vanished, too, and she could feel the metal cuff clasped around her ankle again. She turned to Herbert, whose tail hung limp between his legs, and together they traipsed back towards the kennel.

As they stepped inside, though, Phoebe saw that the dragon had left them one last reminder of his magic. There were no longer dirty rags spread across the kennel floor. Instead, there were furs, great drapes as white as swan feathers and as beautiful as untouched snow. Phoebe crawled between the folds with Herbert, then they burrowed deep and lay their heads down to dream of skies that danced with colour and mountains cast in ice.

*

Phoebe woke to the sound of footsteps. The furs were all gone, the remains of her snowman lay strewn outside the kennel and she and Herb were now shivering beneath a bundle of rags. The footsteps crunched through the snow and Griselda came into view, a rigid block of pinstripe as she walked Slobber down the side of the orphanage.

Phoebe backed further into the kennel, but the movement had been enough to rouse Slobber's interest and as he barked in Phoebe's direction, Griselda jumped.

'Runt! I had completely forgotten you were here,' she tutted as she marched towards the kennel. 'Tomorrow, I shall stick a Post-it note on my office door to remind me that you and your unforgivable brain do, in fact, exist.'

Phoebe tried to conjure up the Snow Dragon in her thoughts, tried to imagine herself soaring through the night sky on the dragon's back instead of huddled on a cold kennel floor. The dragon's magic had made her feel important, but as Griselda and Slobber advanced, a horrible emptiness spread out inside her. It was as if the night before had only been a dream.

Griselda stood in front of the kennel and raised her clipboard. 'Slobber and I were just mulling over our latest policy for the War Against Childishness, weren't we, boy?' Slobber gnashed his teeth and the rolls of fat on his neck juddered. 'It's entitled: *How To Stamp Out Word Murdering –* Fighting The War From All Sides.' She glanced at Phoebe whose teeth were chattering. 'And as you're sitting so comfortably, I'll let you have a sneak preview.' She cleared her throat and Slobber did a completely unnecessary howl. *'Method One: ban any books containing references to mythical creatures. Method Two: force child to complete multiple tests – without breaks. Method Three: only feed child if they can recite ALL modal verbs, subordinating conjunctions and prepositions – without mistakes. Method Four: apply neck brace to child who daydreams. Method Five: set pit bull terrier on child if words like "flumping" are used.'* She looked up and beamed, her face almost sweaty with excitement. 'Well, what do you think?'

Phoebe blinked and in that moment of not seeing she tried again to bring the dragon up in her mind, to remember the last words he had said to her. *Be content. Be watchful. Be brave. And never stop believing in miracles.* Phoebe glanced at Herbert shivering in the corner then at the snow sparkling on the trees outside and took a deep breath.

'Happy Christmas, Miss Bone.'

Griselda gripped her clipboard with sausaged fingers. *'Christmas?!'*

She ground the word between her teeth as if chewing on a lump of fat and Phoebe suddenly wondered whether Griselda was going to bend down and eat her for breakfast. But then, quite unexpectedly, the woman smiled, a dark smile that festered in the corner of her mouth as she spoke.

'I had forgotten all about our Christmas Hunt – the only thing that makes this miserable day even slightly bearable.'

Phoebe tensed. She had managed to avoid mentioning

dragons and *flumping*, but in trying to be polite, she had only reminded Griselda of the Christmas Hunt. She edged backwards because the hunt was a truly terrifying event (last year a five-year-old boy had been chased up a chimney and hadn't been seen since) and this year it would be unendurable – because Phoebe was alone.

Griselda did a couple of pinstriped lunges to prepare herself. 'I had thought there wouldn't be a hunt this year with all the orphans gone.' She sniggered. 'But Miracle Day didn't come to everybody, did it, Runt?'

Phoebe looked down and shook her head.

Griselda performed several squats, and the pinstripe covering her bottom split with a great ripping sound. But she was too excited to notice. 'No point adopting someone as forgettable and ridiculous as you now, is there, Runt?'

'I suppose not,' Phoebe said in a small, cracked voice.

Griselda stuck her hand into the kennel, knocking Herbert aside, and wrenched the cuff from Phoebe's ankle.

'Onwards, Runt!' she boomed. 'I think we'll do the hunt before breakfast to sharpen that appetite of yours.'

Minutes later, Phoebe was crouching at the top of the stairs on the landing, a bone clasped tight in her shaking hand.

'That's right, Runt,' Griselda barked from behind her as she held the slathering pit bull terrier back. 'Bend down into a sprint-start position! With only one bone in the hunt this season, it's wise to set off at pace!'

Herbert peered round the banisters from the bottom of the

stairs and did a little shoulder roll to cheer Phoebe up. Phoebe watched and tried hard to believe in the Snow Dragon's words: *Be brave,* he had said, but as Griselda's whistle blared through the house, Phoebe's whole body trembled.

'Run, Runt!' Griselda yelled as Slobber thrashed about in her arms. 'We'll give you a few seconds' head start before we commence The Rampage!'

Phoebe tore down the stairs, three at a time, before skidding into the hall and racing towards the grandfather clock. Herbert followed at a frantic pace, his little legs whirring like hummingbird wings. Phoebe turned the key in the door of the clock, her heart pounding as Slobber thumped down the stairs. She gathered Herbert into her arms, clambered inside and then pulled the clock door closed behind them.

Outside, paintings crashed to the floor, chairs splintered and doors were wrenched off their hinges. Phoebe hunkered down beside the pendulum bob of the grandfather and thought hard about dragons that appeared in the night and Miracle Days that came to forgettable children. She squeezed her eyes shut as she remembered the Snow Dragon's words: *Some day your life will open up.* Phoebe willed that day on. *Now,* she said inside herself. *Let that day be now. Let me be carried far away from the orphanage to a place where forgettable children aren't left behind and Word Murderers don't get punished.*

'To the attic!' Griselda yelled suddenly. 'Runt must be cowering up there!'

They tore from the hall, smashing vases and tearing down lamps, and it was perhaps unsurprising that they didn't hear the doorbell ring. But Phoebe heard it and as she opened her eyes, a flicker of hope stirred inside her. Quietly, carefully, she placed the bone by her feet, pushed the grandfather clock open and tiptoed towards the door. She glanced down at Herbert and then hoping so hard that her toes curled up inside her trainers, she turned the handle.

A man and a woman stood before her and Phoebe was extremely relieved to see that they weren't wearing pinstripe. The woman had long red hair beneath her bobble hat and a smile so full of warmth and kindness that Phoebe felt her knees wobble. She turned to the man beside her whose hair was dark, like midnight, but whose eyes were as bright and blue as his scarf. Phoebe glanced at the orphanage gates behind them – locked still – and yet this couple had come in . . .

The hunt raged on inside the orphanage as Griselda and Slobber crashed and clattered along the corridors, but the couple didn't seem interested in any of that.

'We received some paperwork this morning,' the woman said, holding up a file.

For a moment Phoebe wondered whether the man and woman were the latest recruits to Griselda's army fighting the War Against Childishness, but she noticed the woman's voice was soft and thoughtful, unlike Griselda's.

The woman went on. 'These are the legal documents for the adoption of a ten-year-old girl with hair as white as snowdrops and eyes as large and round as puddles.' She looked up and Phoebe's heart fluttered. 'It's you – isn't it? The child we've always been hoping for?'

Phoebe stayed very still and very silent. She didn't want to ruin the most exciting conversation she had ever had.

The man put an arm around his wife. 'The documents are signed by a lawyer from a firm called Snowdon Dragonis. And,' he glanced behind him, 'although the orphanage was locked and we didn't exactly get invited in by Miss Bone, we climbed over the gates anyway because we knew – because we *hoped* – that you might be inside.'

There was a series of frenzied barks from somewhere high up in the orphanage, but Phoebe hardly registered them. Because standing in front of her was her miracle, a miracle that had climbed over a gate to find her and take her home.

Phoebe shut her eyes for a few seconds and then opened them again, half expecting the couple to have disappeared from the orphanage steps. But they were still there and the paperwork was still there and the possibility that she might be wanted and loved – that was still there, too. Phoebe felt her body sway and then her toes began to unfurl inside her shoes as she realized: her Miracle Day had come and it was more wonderful and more magical than anything she could have dared to hope for.

'I'm Phoebe,' she said quietly. 'And this is Herbert.'

The man smiled and then, almost shyly, the woman held a hand out towards Phoebe. Phoebe blinked at the gesture – at the magic unfolding before her – then she slotted her own hand inside the woman's and giggled. And while Griselda and Slobber stormed through the orphanage, the man, the woman, the sausage dog and the ten-year-old girl with hair as white as snowdrops and eyes as large and round as puddles climbed over the padlocked gates and walked out into the world.

Magical Contributors

Amy Alward

Amy Alward is a Canadian author and freelance editor who divides her time between the UK and Canada. In 2013, she was listed as one of *The Bookseller*'s Rising Stars. Her debut fantasy adventure novel, *The Oathbreaker's Shadow*, was published in 2013 under the name Amy McCulloch and was longlisted for the 2014 Branford Boase Award for best UK debut children's book. Her first book written as Amy Alward, *The Potion Diaries*, was an international success and the second novel in the series, *The Potion Diaries: Royal Tour* published in August 2016. She is currently travelling the world, researching more extraordinary settings and intriguing potions for the third book in the series. She lives life in a continual search for adventure, coffee, and really great books. Visit her at AmyAlward.co.uk or on Twitter: @Amy_Alward.

Emma Carroll

Emma Carroll has worked as an English teacher, a news reporter, an avocado picker and the person who punches holes into filofax paper. She now writes full-time, which is a lifelong dream come true. Emma's books are usually historical, often mysterious, and full of strong female characters. They include ghost story, *Frost Hollow Hall*, the circus adventure, *The Girl Who Walked On Air*, and *In Darkling Wood*, which is based on the true mystery of the Cottingley Fairies.

Her next novel, *Strange Star*, is set on Lake Geneva in the summer of 1816, and takes inspiration from Mary Shelley's *Frankenstein*.

Emma lives in the Somerset hills with her husband and two terriers. Follow her on Twitter: @emmac2603.

Berlie Doherty

Berlie Doherty was born in Knotty Ash, Liverpool, the youngest of three children. She always wanted to be a writer, but when she was little there were many things she wanted to be – a singer, ballet dancer, air hostess, librarian... Her serious writing started at university, where she trained to be a teacher. Now she lives in an isolated cottage in the country and writes in a barn overlooking the Pennines. Visit her at berliedoherty.com.

Abi Elphinstone

Abi Elphinstone grew up in Scotland where she spent most of her childhood building dens, hiding in tree houses and running wild across highland glens. After being coaxed out of her tree house, she studied English at Bristol University and then worked as a teacher in Africa, Berkshire and London. *The Shadow Keeper* is her second book (*The Dreamsnatcher* was her first) and a third book will complete the Tribe's adventures in 2017.

When she's not writing about Moll and Gryff, Abi volunteers for Beanstalk charity, teaches creative writing workshops in schools and travels the world looking for her next story. Her latest adventure involved living with the Kazakh Eagle Hunters in Mongolia . . .

You can find more about Abi at www.abielphinstone.com or follw her on social media: Facebook: www.facebook.com/abi.elphinstone; Twitter: @moontrug; Instagram: @moontrugger.

Jamila Gavin

Jamila Gavin was born in Mussoorie, India, in the foothills of the Himalayas. With an Indian father and an English mother, she inherited two rich cultures which ran side by side throughout her life, and which always made her feel she belonged to both countries.

The family finally settled in England

where Jamila completed her schooling, was a music student, worked for the BBC and became a mother of two children. It was then that she began writing children's books, and felt a need to reflect the multi-cultural world in which she and her children now lived. Visit her at jamilagavin.co.uk.

Michelle Harrison

Michelle Harrison is a full-time author who lives in Essex. Her first novel, *The Thirteen Treasures*, won the Waterstones Children's Book Prize and is published in sixteen countries, including the UK. It was followed by *The Thirteen Curses* and *The Thirteen Secrets*. Michelle has since written *Unrest*, a ghost story for older readers and *One Wish*, a prequel to the *Thirteen Treasures* books. *The Other Alice* is her sixth novel.

For more information visit Michelle's website: www.michelleharrisonbooks.co.uk or find her on Twitter: @MHarrison13.

Michelle Magorian

Michelle Magorian began writing fiction between acting in plays and musicals. She is the author of *Goodnight Mister Tom* and the books it has led to, *Back Home*, *A Little Love Song*, *Cuckoo in the Nest*, *A Spoonful of Jam*, *Just Henry* and *Impossible!*

She has written two poetry collections, *Waiting for my Shorts to Dry* and *Orange Paw Marks*, and the lyrics for four adult musicals.

Currently wearing two writing hats, she is working on a musical called *Sea Change* with the composer Stephen Keeling, and carrying out research for a new children's book. Visit her at michellemagorian.com.

© Ailsa Joy, 2014

Geraldine McCaughrean

Geraldine McCaughrean has written about 170 books and had far too much fun ever to call writing a job. She has been published in forty-one languages, writes for every age level, and her awards include the Carnegie Medal and Whitbread Prizes.

As well as twenty or so novels, she has done many retellings of myths and legends, and hard-to-read classics. She has also written plays for schools, theatre and radio.

Born in 1951 in North London, she worked in magazine publishing for ten years before becoming a full-time writer. She now lives in Berkshire with her husband. Visit her at geraldinemccaughrean.co.uk.

© Dave Strathmore

Lauren St John

Lauren St John grew up on a farm and game reserve in Zimbabwe, where she had a pet giraffe, two warthogs, six cats, eight dogs and eight horses, the inspiration for her memoir, *Rainbow's End*, and bestselling *White Giraffe* and *One Dollar Horse* books.

When she isn't helping the Born Free Foundation save leopards and dolphins, she loves travelling, boxing and dreaming up mysteries. *The Secret of Supernatural Creek*, the fifth in her Blue Peter award-winning Laura Marlin Mystery series, will be out in September 2017. Visit her at laurenstjohn.com or follow her on Twitter: @laurenstjohn.

Piers Torday

Piers Torday's bestselling first book, *The Last Wild*, was shortlisted for the Waterstones Children's Book Award and nominated for the CILIP Carnegie Medal, as well as numerous other awards. His second book, *The Dark Wild*, won the Guardian Children's Fiction Prize 2014. The third book in the trilogy, *The Wild Beyond*, was published to critical acclaim in 2015. He recently completed his later father Paul Torday's final book, *The Death of an Owl*. His next book for children, *There May Be A Castle*, published in October 2016. Visit him at pierstorday.co.uk or follow him on Twitter: @PiersTorday.

Katherine Woodfine

Katherine Woodfine was born in Lancashire, and grew up reading a lot of books and writing endless stories. Until 2015 she worked for literature charity Book Trust as a children's books specialist and project manager of the Children's Laureate, working with leading children's authors such as Malorie Blackman, Julia Donaldson and Chris Riddell. She is also part of the founding team behind Down the Rabbit Hole, a monthly show on arts radio station Resonance 104.4FM about children's literature.

Her debut novel *The Mystery of the Clockwork Sparrow* (Egmont) was shortlisted for the Waterstones Children's Book Prize, and she is busy writing further adventures in the series. Visit her at katherinewoodfine.co.uk or follow her on Twitter: @followtheyellow.